THE FREEDOM OF THE VILLAINOUS

Also by William Rose

The Strange Case of Madeleine Seguin
Camille and the Raising of Eros

THE FREEDOM OF THE VILLAINOUS

By William Rose

First published in 2022 by
Sphinx Books
London

British Library Cataloguing in Publication Data

A C.I.P. for this book is available from the British Library

ISBN-13: 978-1-91257-382-0

Cover art by Lynn Paula Russell
Typeset by Medlar Publishing Solutions Pvt Ltd, India

www.aeonbooks.co.uk/sphinx

CONTENTS

CHAPTER ONE

The arrival

Marguerite Mercier, who would later, through marriage, ascend to Marguerite Comtesse de Bolvoir, landed at Whitby harbour in the early winter of 1864. She had sailed from France and had added the extra nautical miles to her journey so as to reach our North Yorkshire town directly, without need for further travelling by land.

She was 22 years old and was already a collector. Later to become a champion of art nouveau and the owner of many objects of great beauty, she was, at this early stage, simply a collector of events. For one so young, she had already formed a remarkable collection. Travelling through Europe, she savoured the cultures of great cities and, ever alert and eager, drew into her being those elements that marked each from the other, tasting and delighting in their contrasts. Each day was marked for adventure, and though the intensity could vary, some degree was required lest boredom set in. Marguerite did not find pleasure in the slow movement and rhythm of life that can appeal to the more contemplative soul. Stillness tended to alarm her and even to refer to "the soul" might here be an error. The excitements of life were her requirement and the portal offered by stillness beckoned to thoughts and feelings that she had decided to designate as alien. She already had considerable willpower and the early formations of a philosophy that served her well, though later it would come to rule rather than to serve.

An adventure could be born from a chance encounter. There were many fellow travellers, who, being of enquiring minds and of sufficient wealth, moved through the cities of Europe and beyond, even to Asia, Africa, and the Americas, and Marguerite, with a discernment uncommon for one so young, found ways of engaging the more interesting of these in conversation and even friendship, as far as the constant movement of the traveller would allow. Her presence in a hotel lounge, the foyer of a theatre, or the halls of an art gallery, would be noticed as if through an invisible force, one that is sometimes called charisma, though that term may not be sufficient. The powers that cause attraction are not always subject to definition.

Though such forces were at work, there were, as well, the more formal requirements when arriving in a strange city, and Marguerite would bring with her letters of introduction provided by her well-connected family. That her father was a high-ranking French diplomat added status to any request that his daughter might visit and perhaps stay for a period of time. Such requests would be couched within the understanding that his daughter was eager to learn more of the cultures and even the languages of the countries of Europe, and in this he was correct, though her manner of learning might not always have been as he intended. But, in truth, his disapprovals would go no further than an initial confrontation, which would soon lose its strength before the face that returned his gaze with not the slightest sign of yielding. Indeed, he feared his daughter.

For Marguerite, the traveller, each small encounter might offer something outside of the ordinary and a fresh stimulation. If it were of the intellect, she would converse, internalise, and retain the benefits of fresh knowledge, storing away the content of long and full conversations. Any suggestion of the amorous was happily added to the benefits. She took pleasure in her own charms and had realised, even as a child, their power of attraction; attributes that she soon came to utilise on becoming a woman.

And Marguerite was not to be frustrated. Her hunger for stimulation could be voracious, and those in her family who had observed her as an infant and watched the hungry baby grow into a demanding child and then a domineering adolescent had little difficulty in seeing an element in her development which had begun with the literal draining of three

2

wet nurses, each of whom was unable to maintain the necessary supply for the infant girl, and who left the family service with not only a sense of failure, but exhaustion and defeat.

For Marguerite, the grown woman, each new day contained supplies, manifest or hidden, to be found and tasted and, if not worthy of consumption, to be spat out. Ridding herself of what she disliked came as easily as possessing what she desired.

It is indicative that I have begun with a detailed account of Marguerite and have yet to mention her sister, for she did not disembark at the port of Whitby alone. She was accompanied by Mariana. It can perhaps be already imagined that one such as Marguerite could have little room for the inclusion of another in the daily pursuit of her desires, and if such another should be a sibling the resistance would be far greater. But when we are to consider that Mariana was no ordinary sister, but an identical twin, the matter becomes more complex.

It was a complexity into which I was drawn, as it was my father who was to meet the sisters after their long journey and indeed to be their host for several weeks. Such is the tradition of old friendships between families, even when the friendship was forged long ago. My father had never met these sisters and had hardly known of them until the introductory letter from their own father arrived.

I should now introduce myself, or rather, introduce the youth who witnessed the arrival at Whitby of these remarkable twins, though I do so with concern, as I have yet to give a description of Mariana. But, given the nature of the sisters and their relationship, this is predictable, as one so dominated the other.

Such a difference in personality can hardly be imagined. To the observer, each movement, utterance, and expression of the one bore no resemblance to the other, and all this was weirdly incongruous since their facial and bodily features were as identical as nature could allow.

I write now with the impressions of the 17-year-old who first set eyes on them, tempered by the considered thinking and experience that has taken place in the 40 years that have followed. We had lived in Whitby for four years. My father was an artist who had achieved great success in the painting of portraits. There were landscapes too, but without doubt his skill at expressively depicting the human face above an extravagantly dressed figure was the key to his reputation and wealth. He was also adept at financial affairs so that the spectre of insolvency that often stalks the professional artist was seen off before his middle age. Indeed, our move to Whitby was an early retirement from his busy London life, though it was in keeping with his usual good fortune, that he then found a rich stream of commissions from the Northern industrialists whose new wealth and status deemed the portrait of themselves and their families a social requirement. He happily acquiesced to this new visitation from success.

That portrait painting was his main occupation can suggest frustration with his creative vision. Not at all. He was an immensely fulfilled and contented man with a personality so calm, yet open to pleasure, that he seemed blessed by complete mental health.

A health that was ruined by that winter of 1864 and the events that followed. I know that no man is immune, even one as steadfast as my father, and his sensitivity to that indefinable concoction that drives the creative spirit and that had graced and elevated his portraits was also his undoing. Sadly, it left him beguiled and cast into failure.

CHAPTER TWO

The portrait

In my current profession as a doctor of the mind, I try to recognise and define the components and parameters of a human life, yet I know that such aims cannot reach to the essence of the self, something as unknowable and wondrous as the origin of our universe and its countless stars. Like the stars, some selves burn brighter, or bend and ripple the space around them, and this can be a cause for joy, though sometimes despair, and even ruin. We know that there are stars that are twinned and that, endlessly, they will circle each other, captured by gravity, nature's irresistible force. The two sisters who came to Whitby were also subject to the powers of nature, forever coupled through their sharing of a womb and the overlap of physicality into which they were born. Twin stars and twin sisters, with lives so deeply interlinked, but with souls so dissimilar, that it was as if one had been torn from the other leaving each with the qualities that the other sorely lacked. And my father welcomed this strange dynamic into our home.

And then, he wished to paint it, not as a commission, but because it excited him, and when completed, it remained in his studio, whilst the bravura of its execution gradually degraded into a baleful reminder that destructiveness can hide within beauty and that fascination can be a deadly chimera.

The painting hung upon a wall of the great studio, in a corner that I always felt was its most intimate space. The light was softer there and shaded from the plain, white brightness of the north-facing windows. It was in that corner that my father had placed an ancient, worn, armchair, covered in rough material of fading reds and golds, as if wrapped in tapestry, and here he would sit to smoke his white, clay pipes and contemplate the current work that rested waiting upon an easel, and those others, half or nearly finished, that hung upon the walls. The portrait of the twins seemed to be floating there in the soft light, unattached to anything, and its gentle luminescence was a product of the great skill and vision of my father, who had set the scene beside a calm lake and the time of day was early evening with just the beginnings of twilight.

And so, I can let the portrait and my father's vision now serve me as I describe the two sisters. They are, indeed, identical, but that would be to greatly devalue my father's work. It was as if his whole considerable effort in creating the painting had been to diversify, to search for, and to find the very essence of each and to celebrate the difference. He sought fulfilment in this need to observe and enquire, and such enquiry is so well served by the many hours spent gazing at a subject who must remain completely still.

And the movement of the brush upon the canvas, the mixing of the colours, all the formal rhythmic process, allowing the mind to roam freely and to be surprised and then rest upon the unexpected, even sometimes the extraordinary. And so, in this, my father was an adventurer, an explorer searching for clarity, but not averse to finding the uncanny in the strange phenomena of the two twins. For how can we who are singletons imagine a life lived with one who was there from conception, who shared our time of birth, laid simultaneous claims upon our mother's breasts, and whose existence might predetermine our very destiny. How close the word identical is to identity and how ironic that it should be so! Does identical allow for identity, which we see as such a singular thing?

All of this was surely a fascination for my father; reason enough for the many hours of work he spent upon this painting, though surely it was an unworthy object of his great endeavour since the complexity of his subjects was almost his undoing.

With his personal interest in the sisters, there was to be an element of theatre in the studio, as, with them, he freely and spontaneously voiced any imaginative ideas that came into his mind, accompanied by the most expressive of gestures and bodily movements.

It was Marguerite who could respond in a kindred fashion, so that, between them, a dance of words might ensue, sometimes warmly embracing, at others challengingly intertwined, and on occasions they would declare their distance with cut, thrust, and parry. He knew that there could never be a small encounter with this formidable young woman.

There was, though, a softly muted counterpoint provided by Mariana, which, through her presence rather than her few words, strangely added a lustre to the proceedings, as if an ethereal melody could just be heard, almost imperceptible, but tantalisingly there.

And so, he placed Marguerite at the front of the canvas, full and imposing, and defiantly meeting the eyes of any viewer who should deign to show interest. She looked magnificent, though to my mind, and maybe later events have affected my memory, with a hint of brutality. I think now of those later paintings of women by my father's friend Rossetti: magnificent, voluptuous, and absorbing orchids. I do believe that the feminine was eating Mr Rossetti up, though he loved it so. For my father, this was not a trend, but occurred in this one instance. And he clothed Marguerite in black silk, trimmed with lace as if a funeral had become confused with a grand ball. She wore black gloves that covered her forearms, and her light brown hair was free of any hat and was splendidly coiffured with generous curls that gently kissed her cheeks. He showed her height, which was true to life, though she would have been impressive without it. Her face was broad, her eyes wide apart, the mouth large with generous lips, and there were freckles which could only add irony to such an imposing vision.

My father portrayed her in a black dress as it suited his idea, but it was also in keeping with the scheme of the painting. The setting was a lakeside and the time of day, with its mood and subtle lighting, was the early evening with a hint of the softness of twilight. On looking at the painting, one could almost hear the occasional sounds that might drift across a lake or open countryside; strange, rare, and clear against a background of silence. The tones were of the dark grey and almost black of the water, rising gently up into lighter blue-grey, and then higher into a sky that still retained the palest of blue strips between clouds of white and grey. Somewhere, there would have been a streak of setting sun above the horizon, but this was not within the plain of the picture.

And behind the figure of Marguerite, by several yards and right at the edge of the lake with her feet just hidden by water, was Mariana, not dressed in black but in the colours of twilight, soft greys, with a little highlighting of white and the garment was more of a smock, or the plainest mediaeval robe that a lady of grace, but simplicity, might wear. Marguerite looked resoundingly of her time, and Mariana was of the era of King Arthur. In fact, the lake she stood before could have been the one whose waters parted to allow the hand to rise and receive the thrown sword of the dying king. Her body was shaped as by the brush of an artist of Japan, as if it were the product of one sensual and uninterrupted stroke as she gracefully leant to one side, an arm descending to the water and reaching into it for something she seemed to desire or need. Unlike Marguerite, her hair hung loosely, tied lightly by a bow, so that it rested upon one shoulder and could still descend to her waist.

In the distance, one lone bird, a sea gull, was airborne in the sky. And that was the painting in its fullness; it needed no more.

CHAPTER THREE

The meeting in the square

A chance and strange meeting took place in a square in Almeria in South East Spain. It was in one of those many plazas that offer relief from the main thoroughfares or that provide pleasant interludes as one strolls through narrow streets in the antique parts of such cities.

It was an evening in June and 18 months before the twins' visit to us in Whitby. The two young women had travelled to Almeria in May, and now the summer heat was urging them to retreat to the north of the country, and perhaps even to return to Paris. But, just then, as they walked in the square, the sun had dropped below the roofs of the buildings, and they were softly wrapped by the warm air of the evening. All was very still and they were alone apart from a black dog that sniffed its way across the plaza before disappearing within the shadows at its edge.

The young women did not dress in identical clothes. That habit had belonged more to the vision of their family and had long since been abandoned. It would, anyway, have been incongruous for such different personalities. Marguerite was ever the extrovert, and quite ready to bare her arms and neck in such a warm climate. The dress she wore now though rested upon the tips of her shoulders but covered her arms, expanding out at the wrists where it was fringed with lace. All was in black patterned silk, held tightly at the waist before flowing freely and generously downwards to just brush the ground. She was bare headed and in her light brown hair she had fastened a red rose. All was completely inappropriate for a French girl on an evening stroll, but Marguerite could accomplish such looks with panache, and anyway she was enjoying herself as "Dona Marguerita."

All about Mariana was its opposite: a simple white dress of cotton, her forearms just showing the golden tan acquired during their stay. Her face was shaded by a white hat with a large brim, and on her feet were cream leather sandals.

The sisters knew much of each other but spoke little. It was generally accepted that Marguerite would lead the way, but it was Mariana who had brought them to the square that evening and who had been the first to sit upon a wooden bench that was still warm from being heated through the day, the sun peeling its paint and exacting a musty perfume of seasoned wood.

It was, in fact, Mariana who related this incident to me, much later on, and who supplied the considerable detail as well as the atmosphere and its effect upon the senses.

It was very quiet as the sisters sat and the daylight was beginning to fade. The dog had returned once, but now, perhaps its dinner expected, had left for home. The large clock on the fascia of the most imposing building had shown 9 hours and 30 minutes when the sisters entered, and the hands had now moved to a quarter to ten.

As Mariana turned away from the clock, she saw that there was a person who had entered the square. He had emerged from out of the perimeter shadows and was slowly moving towards them.

Mariana knew that Marguerite had also seen the figure and sensed the familiar response of her sister—an anticipation and alertness which nearly always had the quality of meeting, and often rising to, a challenge. Her own feeling was of unease, as some response would be required of this man, who, in the fading light, continued on his course directly towards them.

He was now close enough for her to take in his features. They were impressive. He was slight of build but was handsome and moved with elegance and was immaculately dressed, though rather overly so for the climate. His suit was white as befitted the season, but of a heavy cloth, with a waistcoat of mustard yellow, and his hat, which was also white, was now removed in order to make a theatrical gesture of greeting.

10

He spoke to them in French. It was only later that the sisters wondered at his instant knowledge that they were from France. They could not identify his accent, though his French was fluent.

"Two such graceful Demoiselles in one of my cities. What a find! And such pleasure for me. I am Angel Fernando y Reyes, the Marques de Mansura—such a lot to remember, I know, and Don Angel will suffice— and I welcome you to Almeria."

His use of "one of my cities" was another topic for the girls to later discuss.

Mariana thought him perhaps 50 years old, though his age defied precision. She found it disconcerting that there could be ten years to easily add on or subtract. There were steaks of grey in his hair that was otherwise jet black, which also appeared to be the colour of his eyes, though not so dark as to dispel a brightness that seemed to light them from behind.

"You will view me as a furtive man—I know—and I regret it so much! But yes, I have spied on you. Well, such words are so dramatic. Really, as I took my stroll around this beautiful square, staying close to the stone walls whose coolness I love, I looked out and saw two Demoiselles, and then, despite the remarkable difference in their dress," and here he gave a little bow to Marguerite that may well have been slight mockery disguised as admiration, "I see two figures and faces that are so alike. My interest grows, so that I, in all indecency, walk towards you, and the closer I become, the greater my interest, growing to excitement, and I arrive and see—yes—you are identical!"

I can imagine how two pairs of grey eyes, each with a touch of blue, stared at him. How often they had been approached thus, to hear the interest and sometimes wonder expressed at their twinship.

Mariana was beginning to have an emotion, one that was familiar to her from instances that had grown since the girls passed puberty, and the desires of young adulthood had usurped the play of the child. She felt her sister's interest divert to this man, and with this the corresponding loss of a closeness that she had long depended on as a foundation for her life. Its removal left her, at best, incomplete and, at worst, empty and despairing.

She sat quietly as the Spanish gentleman spoke to them, his interest politely directed towards them both, though it was only Marguerite who was quick of reply and fully engaged.

"I love this city! Some claim that others are more beautiful, but I say Pha! Almeria has the history—it has known such times—it has been rocked by earthquakes, torn apart by invasions—the Muslims—the Christians—the Muslims—back to the Christians! They build their cathedral in the mosque, just like in Cordoba. Always here they rebuild. This city has been a centre for the trade in wonderful silks with a wonderful harbour, and looking over us for nearly a thousand years—the great fortress!"

For a moment, the Marques stood like an opera singer, head raised, chin aloft, with one arm swinging high as if reaching the peak of an aria: the tenor, singing magnificently of the great Moorish castle of the Alcazaba and, no doubt, turning towards its location.

"And then we have the desert. In Almeria we have mountains around us and also the great arid places where one can wonder and truly be alone to be ..." For a moment he searched for the word, and then in a fashion that was almost coy—"Oneself."

And here he looked directly at the sisters.

To Marguerite, "For you Mademoiselle, it must be the city, and in cities we will meet again." And to Mariana, his voice now softening and seeming tinged with sadness, "For you Mademoiselle—it is the desert."

The Marques, or Don Angel, as he insisted he should be called, prepared to take his leave, but before his final farewell he invited the sisters to be his dinner guests the following evening. "No, he could not possibly take a refusal." With the familiar sense of dread, Mariana felt Marguerite's pleasure in accepting on their behalf.

It was though, Mariana who received the last, dark penetration of his gaze as he parted with, "Adieu until tomorrow—Mademoiselle Marguerite, the lady of adventure, and Mademoiselle Mariana, the poet."

At that time of her life, Mariana, who was indeed to become a poet, had not written a single verse and never thought to do so.

Darkness was descending as the Marques strolled casually and elegantly towards the sole exit to the square until the whiteness of his suit was subsumed by the night; though before disappearing, he turned and gave a final flourish with his hat. Then he was gone and so too was Mariana's sense of reality. The Marques had affected the two young women in very different ways, but for both there was the knowledge that this was no ordinary Spanish gentleman.

As they made their own way towards the exit, Mariana looked again at the clock. The moon and a few soft lights from the surrounding buildings gave it ample illumination and she saw that the time was exactly as when she had last looked, prior to the arrival of the Marques. Was it the clock, or had time itself stopped?

"It must be the clock," she thought, yet knew that in her deeply troubled consciousness, this assertion was based mainly upon a wish.

CHAPTER FOUR

The visitor

The portrait by my father took many hours to paint and the project extended for almost a month. No doubt, the patience required of the sisters was facilitated by the hospitality that they received in our home. It was of a warmth and acceptance that can come so readily from the mother of the house, though in our case it could not be that, as my mother had passed away five years before. I was fortunate that my father could readily provide much of that maternal love that makes a home a place of containment and safety. And this was matched by our beloved Jane Crawford. I was still young when my mother died, and Crawfy, as I came to call her, permanently joined our household two years later. And behind this lies a story in itself.

It was before my parents' move to Whitby and they were living in Chelsea in a house shared with two other artists. It was the early 1850s and my father's career already looked promising, though he had yet to receive the portrait commissions that were to put his star firmly in its ascendency. And though he was already settling into portraiture, he easily mixed with a group of young artists whose aims were somewhat different. They were greatly influenced by John Ruskin and according to his creed, were painting nature in precise detail with bright colours.

They were also enjoying the subject matter that came from the poets and the ancient myths. It was all revolutionary. Many of them were grouped around that Chelsea area and my father was accepted amongst them, not for his aims of art, but for his easy going and entertaining personality. Like some of those artists, Gabriel Rossetti in particular, he had a huge reservoir of charisma.

These young male artists were riding on the excitement of their hopes for fame and the arrogance of their youth. The young women whom they recruited as models, were generally referred to as "stunners" and most had red hair, as if it was a definitive quality, but Jane Crawford was as blonde as could be, and with her dark brown eyes and the palest of skin she was definitely a "stunner" in her own right. So, she modelled for my father, who became very possessive of her, not lending her services to other artists, though some of them implored him to do so. I should say that I have no indication that there was any sexual impropriety between them, as my mother was still alive and I believe my parents, though they married young, had made a sound and happy match.

With my father's growing success, and the demands made upon him to fulfil prestigious portrait commissions, his dalliance in more decorative renditions of the female figure could no longer be maintained and his favourite model became a less frequent visitor to his studio. However, the resonance the two shared in those early days, is easily seen in the canvases that remain, one of which, an outstandingly beautiful, nude study, remained always in his studio.

It was when Jane Crawford became part of our household that she herself insisted that it should no longer lean with its face against the wall, but be proudly displayed, so that it became a prominent feature in the entrance hall of our Whitby house. My father, after my mother's death, had written to Jane and on the strength of their earlier friendship as artist and model, had invited her to become our housekeeper and so to live with us. She was still single and she accepted the offer.

In time, as well as giving me the love of a mother, she became the lover of my father, and though both were content that her official position remain as housekeeper, the "mistress of the home" would be more exact.

I also speak of Jane Crawford now as she was most definitely present in her position when the twins came for their sojourn at Whitby, and she had no small part to play in the ensuing events.

* * * * * *

16

The twins had been with us for several weeks when we received a visit of a most unusual kind. My dear Crawfy, responding to a short, sharp knock at the front door, found a man there who, strangely, remained with his back towards her, looking out at the street. An elegant coach, not one of the usual cabs for hire, was just disappearing as it turned the corner. The visitor, a gentleman and one of affluence, judging from the quality of his overcoat, was not watching his departing carriage, but instead was surveying nowhere in particular and certainly not the expectant Crawfy. She afterwards described her response as interest mixed with anxiety. She knew not why the latter, and to this was added a peculiar effect of time. It seemed to be completely stilled, or perhaps, she said, she just lost count of it. This may have been the case for several minutes and all was silent until he slowly turned to face her.

"Good morning, Señora. Please forgive my intrusion. You have had no notice of my visit. Please hear my excuse." And without pausing for her reply, "I suffer from such irresistible urges to see my friends. Many miles and even oceans are no obstacle and I can travel so fast that my arrival is speedier than any message of my intentions. In short, Señora, I just arrive!"

And with this declaration he gestured widely with one arm as if to show the breadth of the terrain that his wishes could encompass and looked very pleased with himself.

Crawfy was not sure of his accent, though it was already apparent that his English was clear and precise, with a voice that was light and almost wistful. The gaze, though, was direct and the pupils of his eyes glittered like two black jewels. He was of medium height and slim, with strong facial features, a pronounced nose, a strong chin, wide mouth, and shining black hair that was dramatically streaked with grey and swept back clear of his high forehead. She placed his age at around 50 years, but could in no way be sure of this. His gestures and manner were youthful, yet she had a sense of someone far older.

"I am Angel Fernando y Reyes the Marques de Mansura and I come to visit my friends, the young sisters Mercier, Marguerite and Mariana. They have no knowledge of my visit, but fear not, Señora, the girls are always ready to see me, at any time, and in any place."

Crawfy found the presence of the Marques so imposing that in a gesture of compliance she stood aside, and thus, allowed him to cross the threshold. He stood, expectantly, in the large entrance hall and Crawfy saw his gaze immediately directed towards my father's painting of her, followed by his unreserved smile of recognition. With a soft voice that was almost inaudible but that brought them into a sudden intimacy, "I am in the house of a great artist and one whom I see is open to the wonders of inspiration."

And Crawfy, who had already proudly insisted that the painting should no longer gather dust in the studio, felt not the slightest discomfort at her unclothed state and an extreme pleasure in his approval. It was a response that she never forgot and, in that moment, knew that they both shared a certain sensibility and that this was a man who took pleasure in engaging with the taboos of society.

She left the Marques to study the various artworks in the reception hall. His gaze had moved from his instant recognition and appreciation of the painting of her, to a small watercolour that my father had acquired on one of his many visits to Paris. It was by Gustave Moreau; very freely painted, and was of a scene from antiquity.

It was still the subject of his attention when she returned with my father. Despite the compelling nature of the Marques' introduction and the stated reason for his visit, she felt unable to bring the girls straight to him. Indeed, though there was as yet no evidence, such a course invoked for her a strange sense of danger.

My father had been working in his studio and hurriedly arrived, still wiping some vermillion from his fingers. Crawfy remembered, too, that there was a smudge of Prussian blue across his forehead. In fact, not an unusual sight.

The Marques continued his study of the Moreau. He registered the arrival of my father with a sidelong glance and then returned to the picture.

"Monsieur Moreau paints very nicely in watercolours, but we rarely see them. This is perhaps the sketch for a larger painting? And I know Moreau and was with him just some months ago."

And, continuing with an introduction that was decidedly mannered, he then turned to my father and looked him full in the face. The black eyes widened and shone in greeting.

"I see, Señor, that I have disturbed you in your work." The gaze moved to the blue smudge on the forehead and then back to my father's eyes. "An artist requires concentration. But, of course, this fine lady could not fetch your young guests without, first of all, receiving your approval. I would expect nothing else." And, just perceptibly, he inclined his head towards Crawfy.

18

Crawfy recorded that my father's response to the pomp of the Spaniard seemed very plain and English.

"Of course, you are welcome, sir, but please tell me more about your visit. Is it truly the case that you know the young ladies?"

"I know them—and they know me. We are fellow travellers. The sisters love to savour the moods of great cities and to have discourse with them in all their aspects. Mademoiselle Marguerite is an adventuress—this you will know, and Mademoiselle Mariana follows. They come to a new place and then—I pop up—so!" And one arm moved freely in an upward arc, as if to corroborate and emphasise this remarkable happening.

"And so, these young ladies will not be surprised to hear that now in England, and even in your small town of Whitby, Don Angel has called upon them!"

Though it required some effort in this new company, my father was adapting. He seemed to ease the current painting from his mind, and to be gathering his considerable powers of concentration. Crawfy was also in full attention, already knowing that she would want to record every detail in her diary. She was watching two men of powerful and possibly competing personalities.

"I should say too, Señor, that it is an honour—a rare delight, that a visit to my two young friends gives me the chance to meet an artist of great repute. The first one since I left Moreau, in fact."

My father was not one for such elaborate greetings, or for flattery. He politely nodded before turning to Crawfy and asking her to show the Marques into the drawing room. He needed first to discover whether the sisters truly knew this strange man and whether they would now wish to see him. Like Crawfy, he felt a strong sense of unease.

The sisters were sharing a room that had been my mother's favourite and her personal sitting room. It faced south, and from the first floor, looked over the rose beds of our garden.

He knocked and, speaking through the door, informed them of their visitor.

Inside there was immediate silence. Though it was clear that this was the response to his announcement, my father felt bound to knock again and repeat it.

The door opened and it was Marguerite. She looked flushed. Her hair was loose; it was still the morning and the girls had yet to apply the finishing touches to their appearance. This caused no inhibition to Marguerite who, ignoring my father, hurried past and descended the stairs.

This left him regarding Mariana, who looked as if the sunny room had been swept through by an icy wind. She half rose from her chair, sat down again, and then stood, perceptibly trembling. One hand still clasped the arm of the chair to prevent her from falling.

My father then followed an impulse that completely surprised him. He quickly crossed the floor to where she stood and he embraced her, holding her tightly until her body became still.

She buried her head in his shoulder and then raising it, stared at the window as if it offered the only means of escape.

"Who is this man?" whispered my father.

And with remarkable intuition, and without any evidence, "Do you belong to him?"

She now faced him. He still held her shoulders, but had moved slightly back. He could tell that his strange impulsive question had filled her with relief. The unmanageable had been put into words and could now be shared.

"Yes, we do," and then, "She wants it, so I am his creature too."

My father dropped his arms and moved away. He sat on the bed.

"I have to join her," she said. She took a deep breath and moved towards the door.

"Mariana, wait! You do not have to go. It is fine. I will say that you are not well. Dear girl, you are my guest, and I will protect you. Please, remain here and I will make the excuses."

Mariana looked at him. She now had a composure of sad resignation. Her voice was so soft, he could only just hear her.

"I have to go, you see. Please excuse me." And as one preparing for a great sacrifice, with the utmost attempt to suppress her fear, she gathered herself to leave.

"Mariana, later, we must speak of this."

"Perhaps."

When they entered the drawing room, the Marques, who had claimed the largest and most comfortable chair, rose up with an extravagant flourish of greeting.

"Ah, Mariana!" And to the room, "She is a poet you know. My dear Mariana, I disturb you on yet another of your lovely holidays. But I always find you! I am like a bird that migrates to the most exotic lands— all my instincts bring me to you and the distance means nothing. Pff! I spread my wings and I am here!"

20

This speech, that was delivered solely to the slight figure that still stood in the doorway, seemed to create some agitation in Marguerite, who forced herself into the metaphor with, "And like the migrating bird, Don Angel will fly night and day to his chosen place."

"We are that place," said Mariana, "We are the objects of an instinct that will never cease and that will defy the tempests of nature and the wildest storms at sea."

It was as if some other, unknown person was speaking, though the words most certainly came from Mariana.

"Ah you see!" interjected the Marques, "She is indeed a poet!"

My father and Crawfy could only wonder at the scene in silence, but the Marques seemed tremendously pleased at what he had just heard, though he then became more wary of the display of his effect upon the girls and his tone was more measured.

"Mademoiselle Mariana, you gather the elements of nature and gracefully bestow them upon the persons in your life. I, for one, am most grateful, and your friends here, must also be blessed."

Mariana walked from the doorway and sat beside her sister on the couch. My father and Crawfy sat in chairs that were close to each other but nearer to the wall and so were somewhat removed.

The Marques was eager now to show some context for his unannounced visit. For my father and Crawfy, this was certainly required.

And so, he spoke of cities; the miraculous way that he had first met the twins in a square in Almeria in Spain, his encounters with them in their native Paris, in Venice, and Vienna, and even on the twins' most extravagant journey, to Alexandria. And it was Alexandria that seemed to please him most, and that also caused Mariana, most visibly, the greatest distress. Whereas Marguerite, as if in an orientalist painting, was luxuriating amongst the silk cushions of the sofa, Mariana was shrinking back, as if she wished them to absorb her.

The Marques was deftly juggling two balls of possibility—the amazing, pure coincidence of the encounters, or the equally miraculous homing instinct that brought him to them or them to him.

My father was easily able to converse with the Marques on more superficial subjects. Such was necessary. The Marques, for an hour at least, had become a guest who should be attended to, if not enjoyed, and there was also the wariness at leaving him alone with the young women.

It was Marguerite who broke the impasse, speaking with a characteristic plainness.

"Edward," she was now on first name terms with my father, who was never one for undue formality, "I know that, in all your kindness, you wish to give us the protective care of your presence. But please, Edward, we know Don Angel so well, and you have no need to serve as our chaperone." And turning to Crawfy, "Nor you Jane."

"And Edward, we have kept you too long from your studio and you will surely tire as we selfishly enjoy with Don Angel the memories of our meetings. I also believe that he may bring news that he wishes to share with us." And with an intimate glance at the Marques, "He often does."

Of course, for the sake of etiquette, there needed to first be some more conversation. Both my father and the Marques knew of the rising star, Gustave Moreau, and they could share their appreciation of the major works of the artist, as well as his smaller and informal watercolours, one of which rested like a jewel upon the wall of our entrance hall.

"That one, never became an oil painting," said my father, "And remained just as a sketch in the mind of the artist."

"Indeed," replied the Marques, "Where it could remain free."

Later that evening, my father and Crawfy were to examine these events in great detail, but for now they retired, both still with unease, my father to his studio, and Crawfy to a nearby room. The door of the drawing room remained closed upon the three occupants, with no chance of sound escaping. An hour later, the Marques emerged. Crawfy, who had been listening for any sounds of distress, could now, with relief, fetch my father, and the two of them joined the Marques in the entrance hall. The sisters remained quietly in the drawing room. With farewells and due flourish, the Marques crossed the floor, giving a final glance, not to the Moreau watercolour, but to the painting of Crawfy.

CHAPTER FIVE

Alfred Tennyson

After the remarkable visit, I could even call it a visitation, from the Marques, our household entered an uneventful period, though life was certainly not dull as it was enhanced by the presence of our two guests. Marguerite would withdraw at times and remain in the sisters' room, but she was normally a great source of entertainment with her wit, intelligence, and energy.

Mariana brought pleasure to us too. She offered a sensibility that was finely tuned to those around her, so that from her very presence, one could feel cared for. Conversation was not essential to this, but when she did converse, it was clear that her intelligence was equal to her sister's, expected, I suppose, with identical twins, though there was no similarity in the subject matter and her delivery showed that each careful statement was the child of her thought and each thought would remain considered and nurtured. When it came to speaking of emotions, and of the arts and music that can be their source, she would become softly fluent, her lilting French accent lapping gently against the carefully chosen words. It was not known to us at first, but as the Marques had predicted in the deserted plaza in Almeria, she had begun to write poetry.

She was also kind to me. At 17-years-old, I was understandably taken with these two lovely young women, but when beset by the erotic impulse I could become speechless and, to my mind, idiotic. I know there were moments when I suffered the cruelty of the uncontrollable blush. In response, Mariana would feel no need to reduce her femininity, but would take my hand and calmly speak of ordinary things, yet, in her manner there was no denying her knowledge of my conflict.

Marguerite, could see into me as well, but would make no concessions, seeming to treat my discomfort as one of the more humorous factors in a boy's development.

One event that did occur in those weeks which added an extra beat to the rhythm of our daily lives was the annual visit of Alfred Tennyson. I say annual, as that is how it tended to be, though there was no fixed date in the calendar. I believe that it depended more on Tennyson's moods, which could be varied, as well as his particular location. He liked to move around.

Lord Tennyson is, of course, known to us as one of the greatest poets of his age, the Queen's Poet Laureate, and if such a thing can happen with a Queen—and with that Queen—her acquaintance and even friend. She certainly loved his poetry and, on several occasions, she offered her hospitality. If one should read the works that he dedicated to her, and his poem shortly after his elevation to Laureate comes to mind, one can see that she could hardly fail to favour one who offered her such lavish praise and in such beautiful language.

Tennyson had been introduced to my father by the sculptor, Thomas Woolmer, one of the founding members of that group of young artists known as the Pre-Raphaelites. For many of these, Tennyson was both an inspiration and a senior statesman. Over the years, his friendship with my father grew steadily, despite their age difference. They were both men of an independent nature, who had become embraced by the establishment, though my father preferred the phrase "entwined with," and I believe that Tennyson would have concurred. The two would meet at certain high societal events and share a twinkle of the eye at all the pomp and formality. In fact, in my youth, I often imagined Tennyson to have great circular earrings, like a gypsy, and on his visits would be surprised when my gaze searched into the mass of his hair and beard and found nothing there, just the glimpse of an ear. My impression, though, was not altered by the lack of such artefacts and to me he could always be, if not a Romany, at least a Spanish brigand. Actually, this tall and handsome man was none of those, but I am sure that the poet would not have wished to thwart an excited, youthful imagination.

I have to say, that on one of his visits, when he stayed for a week, he was so depressed that I hardly saw him, though he spent many hours at night, after my bedtime, talking with my father and smoking, the two of them creating such dense pipe smoke that the air was infected throughout next day.

On these occasions, Crawfy would soon be defeated by the tobacco and would withdraw to leave them to it, which is probably what they wanted, though I was mature enough to notice how the poet's eyes would often follow her around a room, the gaze sometimes lingering longer when she sat reading or sewing. Looking for inspiration perhaps.

His visit on this occasion was as unannounced as the arrival of the Marques two weeks before. A letter had been sent, but had never arrived. No matter, Tennyson was our friend, whereas the Marques was a disquieting stranger. And now we had the extra interest of his interplay with the sisters.

I was already aware that the inclusion of the twins in any social nexus was like the haphazard addition of ingredients to a meal that will produce the most startling effect, turning the mundane into the exotic, with flavours deliciously blending, or disturbingly bitter.

And the mix now was with the Queen's Poet Laureate who arrived resplendent in a Spaniard's hat, a long cloak, and, on this occasion, in an excellent mood.

I believe that there can be much of significance in a name. Firstly, there is the evocation from its sound: its rhythm, length, the emphasis upon the syllables, its natural tonality. And I find it easy to give any name a colour. I know that such response must surely vary between persons, but "Mariana" rolls rhythmically and gently off the tongue, and almost makes music, and if, with my later closeness to her, I imbue the name with romance, it was the case that Tennyson already had. The name graced the title of a poem of over 30 years before, and later he had returned to it to add mood and depth with three more words. It became "Mariana in the South," a work of love and great melancholy.

And then too, a name invokes the most personal memories, stirring recollections in thought and feeling of those who have born that name before, so that their qualities are passed along and bestowed upon the new subject.

And I do believe that this happened for Tennyson, for when he met "our" Mariana, he saw not a French girl who was the sister of Marguerite, but the Mariana of his poem, his creation of years before, and especially the deeply melancholic Mariana in the South.

I can extend this further by referring to that sense of knowing that flirts uneasily with reality, the tantalising phenomenon of synchronicity: the uncanny way in which chance events coincide and when the coincidence insists on having a meaning. Our Mariana conveyed all the attributes of singularity, quietude, and capacity for sadness that were expressed in Tennyson's poem. It was as if he had now met the creature of his imagination. He had written his Mariana poem before this one was born, and yet now here she was, with the same name and a perfect readiness for melancholy. Had his writing of the poem initiated their meeting, 30 years on?

I will pause for a moment, because I realise that a change has occurred. When I commenced writing this tale of the twins, partly as seen through my teenage eyes, partly from listening to my father's conversations with Crawfy, and latterly from the invaluable recordings in Crawfy's diaries, I wrote almost exclusively of Marguerite. I qualified this by stating that she was so much the dominant twin. Yet, as I look now at the progress of my account, I see Mariana increasingly coming to the foreground and that her qualities, so understated in comparison with her sister's, simply needed time; not just to emerge but also to be recognised. Hers were of a greater subtlety and, given time, a more profound source of attraction.

Mariana was becoming a poet and I have no doubt that Tennyson sensed this, and that in his short stay with us he became fascinated. Indeed, for Tennyson, time was not needed for his experience of Mariana to grow. I believe that he was attuned to her from their first meeting. And of course, there was also the name—the poem—and the synchronicity.

His "Idylls of the King," an epic poem on the Court of King Arthur, with its honours, loves, and betrayals, had gained great favour with the Queen through his dedication of the work to her late husband—a dedication that was a poem in itself and that placed Albert on top of the greatest pinnacles of statesmanship, culture and grace.

And Tennyson was chivalric with Mariana. As if still immersed in that age, he bestowed upon her the courtly grace of a knight to his fair lady. I think, as well, of his Mariana poem, as it was set in a similar time.

I cannot presume to know the man, but I do know that on this visit he showed no sign of the depression that could sometimes waylay him, and that if contact with the muse can lift and maintain the spirits she was doing so in our house in Whitby.

So, here now, I bring Mariana to the fore and Marguerite recedes, and so it was for Tennyson who showed no reserve in his preference for Mariana.

And her sister did not like it. There were times, after dinner, when we sat in the drawing room, the pipes of the men already filled and belching smoke, the brandy circulating freely—even to me—when I could observe the contest. A contest, though, of only one participant, as Mariana said little, stayed in the background, and seemed happy to simply listen. But Tennyson was directing so much of his conversation to her alone that Marguerite became increasingly agitated and forceful in her own remarks. Normally a person of wit and charm in conversation, her words now seemed forced and out of place. Though, in her life, she was to harpoon and sail away with many a male heart, Tennyson's was not to be such a prize. I can only assume that it was his stature as Poet Laureate that made his rejection of her and preference for Mariana unbearable. The final straw was when he recited aloud his verses of "Mariana in the South."

It was on the last evening of his stay, and was a gesture of affection to the young woman whom he had been so pleased to meet. Perhaps, though, it was a questionable choice, given the doom-laden narrative of that beautiful, but deeply sad, poem.

As he announced his reading and cleared his throat, Marguerite could no longer contain her jealousy and with apologies for feeling unwell, flew across the room, clutching her dress with clenched fists, and her cheeks burning red. As the door closed behind her, Tennyson mused, as if to himself, "Ah, la belle dame sans merci."

I do believe that the events of this evening cemented a change in Marguerite Mercier towards her sister that would grow darker and more malevolent over the following months. She formed a need for revenge that would feed on itself and never be assuaged.

The sudden exit of Marguerite gave Tennyson, and I should include my father, the opportunity to make a stupendous invitation. They actually asked Mariana to join them in my father's studio for their late-night session of tobacco, brandy, and conversation. And she accepted.

I remember, the next morning, at breakfast, the normal Mariana smell of soap and mild perfume that I loved was replaced by the odour of tobacco. It had clung to her hair, no doubt.

It was also that day that she announced that she had written a poem and produced it, neatly written upon a sheet of pale blue paper. It had four verses that alternated in French and English, a feat in itself, and she handed it as a gift to Tennyson, saying in French, "Monsieur Alfred, vous m'avez inclus dans vos pensées et avez bien voulu écouter les miennes et je me sens transformé."

I was there to hear this and also, later in the day, his parting remark to her, "Mademoiselle Mercier, I wish I could rewrite my Mariana, because, for you, I would give it a happy ending."

Mariana in the South was never re-written and its theme, set down 30 years before, was to hold fast. The transformation, for which Mariana had thanked the poet, would live on in her capacity to write and to imagine, but there was much of her that was unchanged and that still belonged to Marguerite and now also to Don Angel, the Marques de Mansura.

CHAPTER SIX

The Comte de St Germain

Three weeks after the appearance of the Marques de Mansura, and a week after the far more welcome visit of Alfred Tennyson, Crawfy was again summoned to the front door, this time by a single loud knock. She opened the door wide as she was expecting a delivery, only to find herself hauled back in time. Once again, a strange man stood with his back towards her, contemplating the opposite terrace of houses. For a moment, she believed, with some alarm, that the Marques, Don Angel, had returned. And once more, there was a strange sensation of time, though now there was a difference. With the Marques, it had been as if time had no measurement, so that a moment could feel like an eternity.

This new experience of time was completely different. Rather than extended, the natural sequence seemed compressed into seconds, and as the stranger turned towards her, she was filled with anticipation and an absolute sense of urgency.

Despite this, the man was standing completely still and with no expression, though his calm demeanour was not matched by his opening statement.

"I am the Comte de St Germain and I am here on a matter of the utmost importance."

Crawfy could not remember inviting him in. What she did recall was that from standing motionless he was in a moment striding past her into the reception hall, and that she felt incapable of impeding his entrance.

Standing in the hall, he declared, "I must see your master immediately."

To be addressed this way and positioned as the servant would not normally have gone down at all well with Crawfy. Even now, in the disorientation caused by the Count's appearance and entrance, she began to prickle. Yet, there was also something that felt sincere about this man, so that she believed his business could indeed be important.

My father had heard the knock at the door, followed by the unknown voice of a man, and he was already making his way to the front of the house.

Crawfy had formed a little game for her own amusement in which she would guess what colour paint would be on his fingers, and as was often the case upon his forehead. He had a habit when working of pushing his hair back from his forehead. On this day, there was a streak of crimson across his brow and even some hairs upon his head that were tinged with the same colour.

He entered the hall, the expression on his face making the enquiry. "This is Count Germany." Crawfy had already forgotten his name in her confusion.

"Monsieur, I am the Comte de St Germain," and with a glance at the crimson streak, "And I apologise for the great rudeness of my visit—completely unarranged—to my shame—and also, Monsieur, for disturbing you at your work."

For a moment, Crawfy, still immersed in the mysteries of time, experienced the strange phenomenon known as the "deja vu," as she recalled the Marques, Don Angel, using almost exactly the same words.

But the voice of the Count was different. It was quiet, but distinct, and was elegant without flourish. The use of English had been perfect, delivered with a slight, French accent.

Crawfy, a great observer and recorder of these times in her diaries, now had the opportunity to take in the appearance of yet another European aristocrat who had descended upon us completely unknown and unannounced.

The Comte de St Germain was of medium height, with a slight build, and facial features that were fine, but that would go quite unnoticed in a crowd. His hair was dark, as was his thin moustache. He had a pleasant face with no irregular features, nor any distinguished ones, except for a slight dimple in his chin. His eyes showed that he was observant and open to what he saw.

There was something, though, that overruled the understated nature of his appearance. The only way that Crawfy could describe it was that he seemed "important." His clothes were all in shades of grey, and without any overt declaration of style, yet on close examination they were of the finest materials. Indeed, she wondered whether it was the very exactness and expertise in the cut of the cloth that caused them to seem so deceptively unexceptional. One phrase that came to her, though she could not pin it to any one factor, was that he looked "old-fashioned."

This estimation, though, was put into some disarray when she noticed his hands, one of which was now proffered towards my father in formal greeting. On each finger was a ring, and each glittering ring could only have been of immense quality and value.

My father had formed the same immediate confidence in this man as had Crawfy, and without hesitation, and sensing the seriousness of his business, he beckoned him into the drawing room, from where, in my 17-year-old state, I had been listening to the conversation, and where I now remained, sitting in a corner, a book, open, upon my lap. Indeed, I remember, it was a book of ghost stories.

By now, the Count had realised his mistake in addressing Crawfy as a servant, and when my father introduced her as "Miss Jane Crawford," he made her an especially gracious bow, as if to make amends.

My father knew that he had no need to introduce himself. The man had clearly travelled far to specifically come to his house.

It was, though, not my father that he had come to see. "There are two sisters, they are twin girls, young women, Marguerite and Mariana Mercier. Monsieur, I pray that they are still here."

"Sadly," said my father, "They are gone. They left just days ago and returned to Paris after a long stay with us. It is a misfortune for you, sir, as you have arrived only just too late."

"Yes, this is indeed a misfortune."

"Sir, you know their family?" asked my father. His own links to the family were tenuous and archaic and had barely justified the girls' visit.

"I hardly know the family," answered the Count, "And they are of small concern to me. I am here solely for the safety of the girls. It is damnable that my life is again disrupted because of his latest concoction of evil. Once he gets his hands on twins, the whole thing starts up again."

"Forgive me sir," said my father, looking at this strange visitor with incredulity and beginning to wonder whether he had made a grave error and invited a lunatic into his home.

But Crawfy had understood the reference, or at any rate, had guessed it. I was pleased that it had entered my mind too. "You refer to the Marques de Mansura, the Spanish gentleman who came here to visit the twins."

"Yes, of course." The Count gave this an emphasis that was quite misplaced, given his lack of explanation. Something he now tried to correct.

The three adults were still standing, I being the only one in a seat. I remained quietly in the corner, my eyes upon the book, but my ears, more actively, upon the conversation.

My father gestured to the Count to sit, and he and Crawfy did the same. Though the Count had accepted that the twins had gone and he had failed to head them off—from something we as yet knew nothing of—there was still an air of anxiety in the room. He had inferred that there was danger for the twins and we had grown close enough to them, my father especially, for this to matter.

St Germain had become engrossed in his own thoughts, so that for a few minutes we sat in silence.

My father asked the obvious question. "Sir, if you require to see the Mercier girls so urgently, we can only assume that some misfortune has occurred or is imminent. It is a strain upon us not to know the nature of this and I pray for you to tell us more."

The Count reacted to my father's question as someone interrupted from a reverie. It seemed to me that he had strangely gone on to think of some completely different subject. Now that I know more about the man, I can venture to understand this. A brilliant mind can be distracted to the point of eccentricity by the sheer volume of its own thoughts.

Having been brought back into the room, he focused intently upon my father and upon his question. "The young ladies will be corrupted Monsieur. It is something that I do not wish for, but I fear there will be worse to follow.

"You see, it is because they are twins, and twins of an identical nature. It is a fascination for him."

I began here to become engrossed by the scene before me and the statements of this remarkable man. It was also beginning to touch upon the nature of the ghost stories that I was reading, with pleasure and fear, and I sensed that something uncanny was emerging.

"He will find the twins and destroy them—or, more specifically, one of them. It has become his aim in life, his ideal—though in that I overestimate his capacity. Such a creature can have no ideals. Let us say, instead, it is how he entertains himself.

"First he will make them his own. They can be male or female—in fact he does best with males, as he can bring out their violence. But females will certainly do. He is very powerful you see, very charming sometimes, and he has magic, and he knows many things and places and is a master of history. He claims much and much of it is true. He will charm, fascinate, and own the twins, whilst he decides which one to elevate and which to destroy. And if the destruction is carried out by one twin upon the other, he is at his most content. It is an ancient story, and it comes down to us in myth and legend, and he happily enacts it."

It was then that I amazed the room, and myself, with a sudden utterance. "Sir—Are you a twin to him?"

I expect that Crawfy might have asked the same question. She looked at me with approval. My father turned towards me with surprise and clearly liked the question too.

And so did the Count.

"Young Monsieur, there you are sitting quietly in a corner pretending to read your book, but eagerly taking in everything that we strange adults say. And we have not been introduced."

I felt very proud that my question had been received so well. My father warmly introduced me. "This is my son James, and I apologise to you both. I have been so much taken up by your business, Monsieur St Germain, that I forgot the requirements. My son will indeed have been listening carefully to us—and yes, he gives you an excellent question."

"Young Monsieur, you dive deeply into the essence of the matter. Your question teases at the very roots of it all, and if I had a complete answer for you, then it could well be that I would be free of him. No, I am not his twin. Let us say, that he is my shadow, and, as such, I am called to combat him whenever I can."

The Count now turned back to my father and Crawfy. "There has always been this fascination and fear of twins. As if they were not meant to exist, or perhaps, most relevant for me, it is their representation of opposites. One might say that my service to humanity is that

33

I must contain this so-called 'twin' of mine and when I cannot counter his own evil, I can at least combat such forces elsewhere."

"And is it for you to act now?" asked Crawfy.

"Madame, I have been cast as the saviour in many situations and you will be surprised, even disappointed, when I say that this matter is trifling next to others that have required my response. In one, especially, I was needed to save many thousands of lives—not just two sisters—and, in that, I failed—though at other times I have succeeded."

I was feeling well included in the conversation and even that I might again add something of value. I also remained fascinated. The Count spoke quietly in a measured way. He had a clear diction and the slight French accent gave a musicality to his voice and this, in turn, added a quality that is best described as hypnotic.

I asked my next question, "Sir, what is the event that effected a thousand lives?"

"It was thousands, Monsieur James. If I were to tell you that I gave warnings to the monarchy of France well before 1789, but that these were ignored, you would understand—as you have, no doubt, done you history lessons."

I was completely ready to believe anything the Count said, no matter how fantastic. I saw, though, that the expression that was now on my father's face was a distorted compromise between humour, indulgence and sheer incredulity.

"Sir, you cannot refer to the Revolution in France—it was almost a hundred years ago!"

"Quite so," answered the Count as if he was responding to the simplest of comments. And he continued in the same vein. "It was, indeed, a good few years ago and it has been time enough for the Mercier family to recover. They were aristocracy back then and some of them went to the guillotine. I knew one of the murdered ones, but I had begun to lose interest—until the advent of the twins."

"I expect that you then became concerned …" ventured Crawfy.

"Regrettably, he can sniff out identicals, even over continents—and these two—so talented, beautiful, and intelligent—and also known to me! What a catch!"

For a moment, it seemed as if St Germain, in his enthusiasm for the twins, might even identify with the aims of his cruel "shadow."

"We must act Messieurs!" And I do believe that I was included in this. And to Crawfy, "And Madame, you have sensed something of this man. You have great perception—this I can tell—and if I may extend this, you are able to penetrate those malignant facades that so often influence the masses and give them false hope. A quality needed of a great leader—perhaps not in this life Madame, but maybe the next."

There was absolute silence since there could be no ready reply to a statement that inferred such consequence upon our dear Jane Crawford, and that compelled our attention not to the present, or even the ordinary future, but to a subsequent life in which she might rule a nation!

And compelled we were, as the Count's voice had increasingly taken on a tone that was so relaxed and assured that a warm atmosphere was forming about us, and at the same time a mist seemed to be filling the room so that, as I looked across, it was as if through a soft, transparent gauze. I could see Crawfy, still sitting upon the settee, yet the physical grace which was always hers had been enhanced ten-fold and I can only describe my vision of her as in the realm of those Renaissance paintings that depict the Coronation of the Virgin. And I could see an aura of sparkling white that gave the appearance of a beautiful robe that covered her from head to toe and from which her face, uncovered, looked out with complete serenity.

And then the marvellous vision faded and all was as before. Yet, no one was speaking and it was as if we had all been transported to another time and place.

Later on, when this remarkable man had left us, we shared our experiences of those few minutes. My father had felt sure that he was no longer in the presence of the Count, but was, instead, sitting and speaking with an old man who was surely Leonardo de Vinci, and that the two of them were conversing so well that the great genius wished to entrust him with a secret—one that would draw together art, science, philosophy, and religion, and that would encapsulate and define the absolute essence of existence.

Were the words actually spoken? He could not tell; yet there was no frustration in this. For the rest of his life, and he was to especially need succour in the coming months, the sense of having been close to the greatest genius, and to the most profound of insights, filled him with a pleasure that he later likened to the explorer who has at last come upon a great inland sea, and gazing upon it, rests, and is simply content with the vision of his discovery.

Though he would, at times, curse the Count for the role that was about to be assigned him, he never ceased to declare that the magic of that moment had been the Count's gift to him and that its value transcended all the misfortune that was to follow.

For Crawfy, there was also an experience that would never lose its power or its capacity to bring comfort during the hardest times. She believed that she was with the mother who had died giving birth to her, and her mother, for she was sure it must be she, lay across her lap and was feeding from her breast, and she was young and beautiful, and she looked up at Crawfy as the feeding infant looks up at the maternal face and Crawfy felt blessed; and then she was unsure which of them was the mother and which the daughter and it made no difference and the dissolution became a union of joy.

It was the voice of the Count that had brought the three of us back from our reveries. He might just as well have been the hypnotist calling time on the trance of his subjects. His words were gentle but firm, "I wished very much to find the Mercier sisters here because my time is short. It would have been enough for me to talk to them in your house, though one of them is already close to him and would have been hard to bring round.

"I have no time to continue with this. I am expected in India and, regrettably, my involvement there matters to me more than the Mercier girls. It is not to do with choice, but necessity. My work demands that I leave you now and so I must ask you Monsieur," and here he focused solely upon my father, "to take up this matter. You will need to travel to France very soon."

The dismay of Mariana at the visit of the Marques and the wanton eagerness with which Marguerite had greeted him; the hour in which he and Crawfy had left the Marques alone with the sisters—something he now deeply regretted; the intuition that had caused him to say to Mariana, "Does he own you?" and the realisation of how right he had been; all these memories came flooding into my father's mind to meet and gather with his great affection for the twins.

"Of course, I will prepare myself immediately."

And Crawfy was already thinking of the clothes and other items that he would need, whilst trying to ignore a hint of disquiet as she imagined him, alone, with the two young women.

The main concerns of the Count, ones that we now shared, had been met. My father would travel to Paris to meet the sisters and to use all his influence to dissuade them from any further contact with the Marques de Mansura. How naïve it seems now to have believed that my father would be a match for this man and the powers that he possessed. Whatever his urgent business was in India, some alchemical experiments I would imagine, the Count was placing my father in a most vulnerable position. I can only assume that he truly believed there was some chance of success.

With a remarkable change of tact, the Count abandoned the subject of the sisters and for the rest of his visit spoke of matters far more general, and ones that my father could certainly engage with: politics, the arts, developments in science; his knowledge seemed unlimited. When speaking of the arts, he spoke convincingly of the work of contemporary painters, many of whom he had apparently met. By the time he came to speak of his conversations with the great French artist Géricault, who had died 40 years previously, my father had abandoned his incredulity and relaxed into the pleasures of the many anecdotes. The Count also showed great interest in my father's art and inevitably the subject came round of his portrait of the twins, something that he insisted, with enormous enthusiasm, he must see. The two men then disappeared into the studio, to leave Crawfy and I so stunned by the afternoon's events that we could only sit and speak of quite ordinary things.

The main consequence of the long period of time spent by my father and the Count in the studio, was that the Count, who also professed credentials as an artist, shared a secret: a special way of mixing certain colours with a unique ingredient that was his own invention. My father was sworn to secrecy as to this formidable mixture, and kept the secret to the end of his life. It was also the case that his fellow artists, as well as some of his patrons, began to notice a new and indefinable element that added a most subtle lustre to his paintings.

When the Count departed, we all gathered in the reception hall to say goodbye. I had lost none of the sense of inclusion I had enjoyed earlier. In fact, the Count compounded my pleasure by endorsing the book of ghost stories that had earlier been on my lap and by saying that he knew the volume well. He might as well have said that he had written it. And, of course, the Gustave Moreau painting in the hall was favourably remarked on. Perhaps he was too much of a gentleman to mention my father's nude study of Crawfy, but I know that he saw it, and now that I look back, I believe that it may well have added to the considerable warmth of his farewells.

37

CHAPTER SEVEN

Alexandria

When the Marques de Mansura, Don Angel, had paid us his deeply unwelcome visit, he had sat in our drawing room and boasted of the occasions on which he had spent time with the twins: in Almeria, where he had made his first introduction, and then Rome to which he had invited them, and then his greatest achievement, Alexandria. When he declared the latter, Mariana had been visibly distressed whereas Marguerite had sunk back into the silk cushions of our settee, as if luxuriating in the memory.

My father was now embarking upon his journey to Paris to do all he could to separate the girls from the Marques' influence. The Comte de St Germain had provided enough details to set him on his way and had instilled in him the same sense of urgency which had brought the Count himself to our home in Whitby. But my father was travelling with little knowledge of what had gone before—the times already spent by the twins with the Marques. In these, Alexandria had clearly been the greatest influence. In short, he knew nothing of the damage already done.

Eventually, I did come to know about Alexandria and the events that had caused Mariana such distress and that had nourished the roots of a future Godless life for her sister.

Even with Marguerite's lust for new experience, I don't believe the twins would have reached as far as Alexandria if it were not for the influence of the Marques. Certainly not as young women travelling alone. But the young women were to be chaperoned by a Spanish aristocrat who had a home there; a gentleman who had befriended them in Almeria, then Rome, and who now wished to show them the more exotic culture of a great Egyptian city; a visit that could introduce them to the Arab world and to a centre seeped in history: ruled by Kings, Pharaohs, Emperors, and Emirs.

After a calm, firm request from Marguerite, which was more of a statement, their father gave them his blessing along with a substantial sum of money that would cover all their financial needs and ward off the dangers of a locality, which, in his ignorance, he could only view as primitive. Mariana's views were not considered, as all was subsumed by the enthusiasm of her sister.

Later on, when Mariana and I became lovers, she told me the tale of Alexandria. By then, I was 20, and the age difference far less a factor than when the sisters had first come to Whitby and I was a blushing 17-year-old.

Mariana had rented an apartment in Almeria, the very city in which she and Marguerite had first met the Marques. It was as if she had been drawn back to the starting point of a long ordeal, with that strange force that can compel one who is damaged by fate to repeat their agonies, as if such repetition will undo all that followed.

As a young man seeking experience, I was on my own European travels, and I called upon her, and then stayed. I do believe that her wish that I should stay and the intimacy that developed through the next six months, was more a result of her profound loneliness than any great love she had for me. It is sad for me to realise this, as I felt great love for her. But then, men did feel great love for Mariana, though such love could never assuage her need.

It was early summer when I arrived and the heat was already intense. We did very little in those months. We read and she wrote, because now she was indeed a writer of poetry. Our movements were slow and measured and each hour seemed to drift into the next, until, as the light began to fade, we would stroll through the outskirts of the city towards the fort of the Alcazaba to reach a small restaurant, and there, each evening, we would dine, with one candle upon the table, and the warm indulgence of the patron and the gruff, but sincere, attention of his wife.

And then, the return; the air of the night soft and warm around us, and the great, dark silhouette of the Alcazaba there to be seen if we should turn to look; and back to the apartment, that yes, was even in that same quiet square in which, four years before, the sisters had first met the Marques.

For Mariana, the plaza in Almeria was the source of an experience through which she had lost her sister and her reason for living. She was drawn back there, and to the place where the hands of the clock had once been stilled. Perhaps she wished to start time again and for it to allow her a new life. Or was it the melancholy of the poet, insisting beyond all practicality, that sadness be forever expressed?

On our return from the bar, we would make love, because Mariana desired it, and her desire had a fervour that was beyond passion, as if she were striving to maintain the instinct to live.

It was one night, as we lay in the darkness, the windows open to the warmth of the night and all completely still, that in her soft, lyrical voice she told me of that first meeting with the Marques in Almeria, and then in Rome, and then the events in Alexandria.

After his self-introduction in the plaza, the sisters had met Don Angel, as arranged, the following evening. They were surprised as they had expected to dine in a grand restaurant, but they received a message that their meal should be taken in the dining room of their hotel, and that he would meet them there. It added to the mystery of the man, since they still had no physical place with which to identify him.

Nevertheless, the meal in the hotel was lavish and he insisted that they select the finest items on the menu and the most expensive wines. The young women drank more wine than they had ever done before. The following morning brought with it a pulsating headache for Mariana and a wish for wine with her lunch for Marguerite. During the meal, both sisters had been warmed and coaxed by the delightful vintages, brought to them with each new course, and they were also filled with Don Angel's sumptuous speech, his verbosity unabated throughout the evening. He told tales of nations and dynasties, cultures alive and dead, cities that were flourishing, crumbling, or that were drowned by the sea. All these he knew, had travelled to, and in many, and this with a gesture and tone that would dispel all disbelief, he had lived.

The Marques dominated the evening to such an extent that Mariana's usual dread of losing her sister to another did not arise. Marguerite had found little space to verbally engage with him and had sat silently in awe.

There was also, once more, an uncanny experience of time, as for both sisters, the evening, though overflowing with the many stories of the Marques, had passed in a moment.

In some invisible fashion, the meal was paid for and the Marques departed with a great flourish, insisting that the three should meet next in Rome, and having obtained their address in Paris, declared that he would write to their father, to ask his permission for his delightful daughters to pay him a short visit to that wonderful Italian city—where he also had a home.

In describing the farewell of the Marques, Mariana, who had been speaking to me in English, reverted to French, skilfully mimicking his flattery and grandeur. "Maintenant, mes chères Mesdemoiselles, la plus intéressante des jeunes femmes et des sœurs! Au revoir!"

Rome had followed with great fanfare, and though, again, he professed residence there, all contact was through his display to them of the magnificent sights of the city, and they always dined, though not this time in their hotel, in a restaurant near to it. After dinner, he would disappear and return to meet them the next day, after breakfast, for sightseeing throughout the day. And he was, indeed, the most energetic, theatrical, and knowledgeable of guides.

There had been Almeria and then Rome, but Alexandria, he assured them, would be the experience of their lives.

As Mariana began the story of Alexandria, she paused for a moment, rose from the bed, and in the darkness, walked naked across the room to where a chemise hung upon a hook on the wall. I saw the white shape of the garment as it was lifted, before it fell around her body. The shape then drifted to a cupboard. My eyes were adjusting to watching her in the darkness and I saw her reach into the cupboard to take something out and then move to a table. She leant over the table and there was the flare of a match as a candle was lit. She sat at a chair, next to the table, and was intent on performing an action that I could not see, though I could hear a rustling, and then, again, she struck a match. She blew out the candle and returned to the bed and to my amazement, she was holding a pipe to her lips. There was now a strong, acrid smell in the room. For a moment, the bowl of the pipe brightened, lighting her face with a red glow. She exhaled and a curl of hashish smoke rose and disappeared into the darkness.

Nothing was said about her action. She felt no need to explain and there was such surety in this that it made any questions redundant.

42

"He made it very easy for us. All the travel was arranged by him—though it was father who paid. Marguerite usually made our arrangements and had always been pleased to do so, but to the Marques she always gave way. He could bring out a passivity in her which was quite abnormal. So, we were just sent—more or less—our itinerary. We could see from this that we would not be staying with him, but in a hotel in which he had reserved us rooms. Indeed, the letter from him strangely bore no sender's address at all. Of course, our father, in his careless way, simply treated that as an oversite.

"We travelled the main distance by steamer. I would have enjoyed the journey, despite some sea-sickness, but there was a change in Marguerite's mood. My dear sister—we had been so close—often conversation was not needed; it was enough that we sat or walked, or lay together. Such times made me so happy. I never liked it when she became distracted, and I could get so jealous if she ignored me for someone else. There was no one else like that on the boat, but I still started to lose her. It had been happening since we first met the Marques and now it was starting again before we were even with him. But, of course, he would be waiting at the port for us, ready to show us the city and I believed Marguerite would be ever closer to him and further from me. It was not that he had chosen her over me. I think, really, he was still deciding which of us to prefer. But I knew that Marguerite had chosen him, and she could never be deterred.

"And there he was, ready to welcome us to Egypt and to the ancient and fabled city of Alexandria. He was resplendent in a brilliant white suit and hat and his dark eyes glittered with anticipation. We disembarked and he gathered us up, spoke the most charming words of greeting, and having assured us of his delight at our arrival, hailed a rickshaw to take us to our hotel."

Mariana paused for a moment. She needed to relight her pipe. She left the bed again and relit the candle. The night was very warm and she raised the shift over her head and discarded it so that she sat naked in the chair. Once again, the bowl of the pipe glowed and for a moment some little sparks lifted from it. One must have touched her as she quickly brushed it away from her thigh. The smoke curled in strands which separated, hovered, and then slowly rose into the darkness. She did not return to the bed, and continued her story from where she sat.

To continue to repeat the speech of Mariana, who by then was a consummate poet and who was able to express her thoughts and feelings in words that would have satisfied Tennyson, is hard for me. I fear that I cannot do her justice and it would be best for me to resume her story in my own words, using the fullness of my memory and applying my wish to at least retain something of the quality of her own narration.

They had arrived at the great, bustling port of Alexandria in the early afternoon. On reaching their hotel, a grand building that had been built by the British and that offered the finest of services, they went to their room. Or rather to their rooms. They found it strange that the Marques had reserved them separate rooms. He seemed, so much, to enjoy the fact that they were twins and had known them in Almeria and Rome to share a room. Now his planning served to separate them. It was not the way of the sisters though, and having left their luggage in one room, they made to share the other one in their usual way. Each room had only one bed, but they were of a size that could accommodate even three.

They were to dine at seven and the Marques had shown great foresight in arranging for them to eat in a restaurant of French ownership and with cuisine that was largely in the French style. He had, with careful wording, told them that he did not wish the digestions of fine young ladies to be overwhelmed by strange and exotic foods, it would be no way to begin their holiday.

Feeling refreshed after an afternoon's rest and with the growing excitement from being in a completely new and different environment, the sisters descended from their third-floor room to the ground and from there to the hotel lounge where the Marques awaited them.

In the subdued light of the lounge, all was still except for the turning of the great ceiling propellers, softly humming above them. The dark and ornate furniture seemed to embody the timelessness of quiet afternoons that denied the brightness and hubbub of the streets outside. And again, Mariana experienced the strange deception of time that so often accompanied a visit from the Marques. It felt as if their meeting in the lounge took place in slow motion. She watched Marguerite and recognised those mannerisms of her sister that could so easily captivate a room. She observed very carefully. She recognised her own feelings— her envy that her sister could instantly switch to a way of being that could fascinate men and intrigue women. She knew, as well, that she should feel jealous; that here, again, was Marguerite about to captivate a man and leave her feeling jettisoned and worthless. Yet, as she watched her sister greet this man, she had a novel feeling; it was an inkling of her own strength, for the Marques had not responded only to Marguerite, but was greeting them both with an equal warmth, and she knew that any preference between them was still undecided.

The French restaurant, chosen by Don Angel, was close by and they were able to walk. The décor of the restaurant was refined, yet simple, and made no concessions to Egyptian culture that was, otherwise, all around them. Marguerite sighed, and ventured that she would have preferred to eat in surroundings that were true to the location.

"But we could be in France!" She protested.

The Marques was unmoved. "Dear Mesdemoiselles, I have tried hard to choose a place where the cuisine can be trusted. I have no wish to see such elegant ladies disfigured by the physical trauma of bad digestion. Later, we can try the local food, but first you must settle in and be ready for a restful night's sleep after your long journey. And anyway, you shall have no lack of the ways and pleasures of Alexandria. You may be sure of that. I have much planned for your visit.

"But first you must know something of this wonderful, ancient city, one that you now grace with your European delicacy and manners."

Mariana could never identify her sister with such qualities and she saw Marguerite hide a smile behind a risen handkerchief.

The food was ordered and the meal began. The Marques chatted somewhat aimlessly, as he really had more important things to say, but was reserving these for the interval that would come after the main course.

That stage of the evening having arrived, he dabbed at the corners of his mouth with a serviette, tossed it to one side, leant back in his chair and began to take them far back in time and into the ancient history of the city.

"It was over three hundred years before Christ when Alexander the Great, and so he really was, came upon the little island out there in the bay—you sailed past it—and decided, 'Ah yes! Here I will build my city!' And so, he did, but on the mainland, here where we are. Later they built a jetty that meant that you could walk across to the island. Alexander did not live to see much of this, but he had a friend; a fellow warrior and wise man called Ptolemy who continued the work, and it was he who started building the great—the enormous—lighthouse. Have you heard of it!?"

The Marques paused with an air of severe expectation. The girls nodded, for indeed they knew of the great lighthouse. "A wonder of the ancient world, over a hundred metres high, with a great furnace at the top, and all destroyed by earthquakes. But then, after 1,500 years, what can you expect, especially here. Here the land shifts and buildings collapse. It is the fragility of a building as opposed to the resilience of a human being." At this point, the Marques looked very pleased with himself, and it was clear to Mariana that it was his own longevity that he was admiring.

"You see, the land shifts—there are earthquakes and in rushes the sea. And then there are wars. So much is destroyed. And where does it all go? Well, there can be rubble, and then more destruction as the broken stones of ancient buildings are pilfered to build new ones. But not everything is reduced to rubble. Over centuries, the land sinks. There is so much of this in Egypt. So much of digging up of tombs. But it is here, more than anywhere that there are sunken treasures. Beneath the sea, but also ..." and here he rose out of his seat as if declaring the greatest of facts, "Under the ground!"

The restaurant being largely empty, the Marques now began to pace up and down as if he was delivering a lecture in an auditorium. The sisters felt obliged to follow him with their eyes.

"In Alexandria, people say—'Where is this, where is that? Where is Alexander's tomb, where is the temple of Isis, where is Cleopatra's tomb?' They are under the ground. They've built everything over the top as if they wished to hide it all. But really, they were just being careless—over the centuries. And people come to search—Napoleon comes—'Where is the tomb?' He wants to know. Explorers come from all over the world—and they find next to nothing—just a few stones, a few ruins here and there. Because it is all down there!" And at this, he stamped his foot upon the polished wooden floor, to emphasise what lay buried beneath them.

The sound was so loud that a waiter anxiously appeared fearing some displeasure in his customers. The Marques waved him away. "I tell you this, dear Mariana and Marguerite, because you need to know about this place where you are. A city that you will never forget. And it is timeless, and all buried beneath us, and Don Angel will take you there!"

Marguerite was growing in assertiveness and becoming less under the spell of the Marques. She risked raising her eyebrows to her sister as well as tapping Mariana's shin with a foot beneath the table.

Mariana told me that the Marques noticed this, and indeed he probably noticed everything. But he was in full flow and, as events turned out, he had reasons for his surety.

"And, of course, the library! The greatest library there has ever been—because they loved knowledge and they wished to know everything! Filled with hundreds of thousands of books. Though really—scrolls—because that was their way then. Can you imagine them? Countless scrolls piled upon shelves from floor to ceiling, in room after room, amongst walkways and gardens and magnificent pillars?"

The sisters nodded in obedience, but Mariana told me that she could see the growing scepticism of her sister. She, though, was feeling the magnetism of the Marques and was increasingly being taken up by his visions of the ancient city.

"Every room, for a different subject—the sciences, the stars, philosophy, religion, magic, and alchemy—everything studied in the School of Alexandria and all encased in the most magnificent building. The library—another wonder of the world. All gone. It is a sad thing."

It surprised Mariana that the Marques did, indeed, look very sad. She realised that she had not expected him to show even the slightest sign of humanity.

For a moment, he was thoughtful and withdrawn and then, suddenly looking up, the dark eyes sparkled again. "But maybe I can arrange a little journey into the past."

He had, for the time being, completed his verbal tour of the ancient sites. He assured them that he would have much more to tell them and even to show them during the next days.

When the sisters returned to their hotel, they shared their confusion, but also their interest in the glaring contradictions in the declarations of their host. Everything ruined and most of it drowned or buried—and yet there was much that he intended to show them.

Mariana had left the candle flame to burn so that a soft light gently lit one half of her body. She laid down the pipe. The very first hint of daylight could be seen through the open window. In a few hours we would rise to a morning of clear blue sky and the brightness of an Andalusian day, with the sun already hot upon the stones of the plaza and the rooftops of the buildings. But before that Mariana would sleep some more. She looked tired and perhaps the effects of the drug were making her sleepy. She stretched and as I watched her, I marvelled at her beauty. It is always in the eye of the beholder, but I knew that it was now, at the age she was, that she had never been so beautiful, and to this was added the look of a maturity drawn from deep experience. Experience that I was still to know more about. And I also wondered about Marguerite. If this was Mariana, how would I now see her twin, if I should meet her again.

There was much more to be told of the story of Alexandria, but for now, Mariana wished to sleep, whilst I could only lay awake, imagining the splendours of the greatest city of the ancient world.

CHAPTER EIGHT

Alexandria—the descent

Though, the next day, I urged Mariana to continue the story of Alexandria and tried every trick of manipulation: from teasing, to seduction, to mock sulks, she was just not ready to do so. She had to be in the mood. I can easily see why, since she was not only recounting a sequence of events, but also recalling and evoking a time of the most intense and mysterious emotions, and all set in what I can only describe as a dimension that defied all the normality that we rely on for our surety and even sanity. I also wondered whether the hashish was a necessary requisite. I could see why that might be, as the drug could calm the distress that might accompany her recollections. But what I realised afterwards, was that the hashish could also serve to recreate some of the utter strangeness that the twins were about to experience, so that it was not just a matter of mitigating distress: there was a mood that Mariana wished to recreate that still held fascination for her and which, indeed, held her captive. Beyond any control she may have had, she had been ordained by the Marques into his timeless world, in which ancient rituals of religion and the products of magicians and soothsayers had complete ascendance.

With my experience now as a doctor of the mind and with the help of some of the great writers who inform us and inspire us as professionals, as well as the occasional experience with a patient that has been truly remarkable, I understand that the long history of mankind lives on, deeply buried, in every human psyche. It has been shown to me that some will have access to this, whether through drugs, or madness, or esoteric disciplines, and sometimes even by accident. This is very rare, but I know the potential. But whatever my experience as a doctor, the absolute foundations of these assumptions comes from the story of Mariana and Marguerite Mercier in Alexandria, in which strange forces, the kind that most find hard to credit, but which a few have always attested to, held sway, and when the deep seams of history that lie dormant in the psyche were brought to life by what I will conveniently call magic: convenient, because the concept of magic saves us from the shame of our ignorance in these matters.

So, I had to wait a week for Mariana to continue her story. Then, one evening, she declared that she wished us not to walk to our usual restaurant, but that she would cook for us and that we would have our supper in her apartment.

The windows were wide open and a slight breeze stirred the blinds. One window had no cover, and as I looked out onto the now-deserted plaza, I could just see the face of the clock, softly lit by the lights of the square.

Before a delectable dish made from locally caught fish, we were to drink a special broth of Mariana's own recipe and for a special occasion. Or, so she joked. Indeed, the broth did have special qualities. I do not know what her selected ingredients were: I had been innocently gazing through the window and enjoying the breeze upon my face, so I will never know, and anyway I will never have such broth again. There were herbs and vegetables, but the identity of the drug that she included was never told to me.

Though its effects did undermine, rather pleasantly, my normal assumptions of reality, it was not needed, since the very presence of Mariana was sufficient to dispel normal reality and to happily exchange it for a world of imagination, dream and poetry.

After the meal, she made tea, and we sat in two cane chairs. The room was lit by one candle which was on a table beside her. Perhaps the drug was already working because, in the gentle golden light, she looked unworldly and her pallid beauty caused me to think of Echo from the myth of Narcissus. The breeze was still gently rustling the blinds. The uncovered window was an empty, black space. She wore grey: a very simple and light dress, hanging loosely from straps over her shoulders. She was much thinner now than in the days when the twins had stayed with us in Whitby. She pulled the hem of the dress up and rested it on her knees to be cooler. Her freckles showed up in the candlelight, making a little bridge over her nose. Her light brown hair was very long now and she took little trouble over it. Sometimes she would loosely pile and pin it upon her head, but in the evenings it would hang freely over her shoulders and down to her waist. It was how my father had painted her, whereas he had painted Marguerite's hair as carefully curled and groomed.

She leant back in the chair and in the candlelight I could see that her eyes were half closed and that she was descending into memory. She addressed me directly at first, but after that she spoke as one who is observing and describing ever-changing scenes as they pass before the eyes.

"I have told no one else this story, James, though I have never ceased to live it. Really, it lives in me. Maybe when I tell it, it may no longer do that, but I believe it has claimed me forever. You know how nuns take holy vows for life. This is not the story of a nun, far from that, but it tells how I entered a world that can never be shaken off and to which I fear I must always belong."

For a few minutes she was silent, and then, "I may sometimes speak in French—will you mind?"

I told her that I would be happy to listen, in English or in French, as the mood should take her.

I will now continue with her story and tell the tale as truly as I can. The drug we had taken could have clouded my memory, but the effect was the opposite, as my awareness was heightened, and I felt open, even exposed to the events she was about to describe.

The next two days for the sisters were spent visiting the sites of the city, with the Marques as their guide. Where there was no physical evidence of what had once been before, the Marques created visions of the palaces and temples through his words. He was indulgent and courteous, and was meticulous in his planning, but he seemed more distracted than usual. Mariana had the feeling that the sightseeing was filling in the time and that he had something in store for them that would be of far greater consequence.

This became evident after lunch on the third day. They had graduated to a fully Egyptian restaurant and the Marques had persuaded them to try the foie gras, which he assured them had been eaten in Egypt for thousands of years. Mariana had been reticent, but neither sister could deny the rich taste of the delicacy, or its allure as a food that had once been served to the Pharaohs.

Having completed the courses of their lunch, they were drinking tea and the Marques, who had airily been comparing the cuisines of different nations, suddenly moved the conversation into a new and far more intense place.

"I can show you wonders." The dark pupils of his eyes glimmered as he gazed into their faces. And then he looked away, as if thinking to himself, and his eyes softened.

"It is hard to conceive, but it is true—the great mass of humanity knows so little of pleasure. Oh—they think they do, but they set up great barriers to curtail their instincts—their laws, and their religions. They so greatly fear the overspill that will sweep them to satisfaction. I refer, Mesdemoiselles, to the pleasures and desires of the senses, of which the honest citizen knows so little. You will forgive me; I speak here with young ladies who have been taught to behave with manners and with dignity and it is not my wish to in any way undermine the fine ways that you have derived from your excellent education. You will know from my speech and my actions that finesse is the beacon that lights my way through the rough darkness of the common world. Standards must always be maintained! But maintained, too, in the cultivation of the senses. You see, I speak of the sensual, but Mesdemoiselles, I do so without wish to offend, and I do so in the knowledge that my aim is only to add to its refinement.

"Marguerite and Mariana, dear young ladies, you have travelled and visited great cities with all the wonders that rest within their magnificent museums of art and you have gazed upon the voluptuous glory of the Titians, the soft and sensitive beauties of Correggio—his 'Jupiter and Io' surely one of the wonders of art. You have seen the gentle curves and the vibrant colours that display the poetry and dance of Botticelli—and many others. And Mademoiselle Marguerite, though it is not for a gentleman to comment, I will exempt myself from decorum and say to you that your perfume is exquisite. And I will make further inroads into this exclusive domain of the lady and say that I know exactly where it comes from. I was even acquainted with the gentleman who created it—the late Monsieur Guerlain of Paris. And let me not exclude you Mariana as you, too, sometimes wear this same perfume, though less so than your sister, from which I presume that you do so to follow her excellent taste. All this, I say, to show that I know that you are ladies of refinement and also refinement of the senses, and in this I wish to help you rise yet further, indeed, to levels of pleasure that most cannot imagine. And for this, I have invited you to Alexandria. What better place than an ancient city that has nurtured the most exquisite and ruthless pleasures? We will go forward, you will see, but we will draw from an antiquity when such pleasures and devotion to the deities were as one."

And with complete confidence that the sisters would follow, he strode to the door, put on his hat, adjusted the sleeves of his white linen jacket, glanced at his reflection in the glass before swinging the door open for the twins to exit.

The young women emerged blinking into the searing light and tumultuous bustle of the street. Assuming that Don Angel was behind them, they began to walk, but were confused as to which direction to take and so turned to seek the reassurance of their guide, only to find him not there.

They stood in the melee of the street. All around was activity: men running, traders shouting, women sweeping past, their bodies and faces hidden beneath the niqab, yet their eyes active and enquiring of the two Europeans, who now stood motionless, exposed in their bright, white dresses. Already, beggars, including children, were moving in on this likely source of a handful of coins. Mariana looked to Marguerite and saw the familiar expression and toughness of body that came upon her sister when a challenge arose. She saw the curl of the lip and the flash of the eyes and knew that the beggars would soon be receiving nothing but scorn. Her anxiety at their abandoned state was now compounded with expectation that her sister's hostility would incur the wrath of those, who with outstretched arms, increasingly besieged them.

She turned away from Marguerite and looked about in despair, only to see a man with a mischievous grin and sparkling dark eyes watching them from the other side of the street. He stood at an intersection with another street that was far narrower. He was dressed in the traditional clothes of the city, yet much brighter than those worn by others nearby. He wore a red fez upon his head, and robes of white, patterned with blue and yellow, and he seemed to glow in the sunlight. It was the Marques.

By now, the disorientation of the sisters was so considerable, that his impossible change of dress, from European to Alexandrian, and within minutes, was not questioned. The uncanny was becoming his expected companion. Even across the busy street they could hear him laughing at the mischief of his transformation and as he beckoned the girls to follow, Mariana felt sure that there was more mischief afoot.

They followed the red fez as it bobbed before them. He had taken the narrow road and it became increasingly narrow. There were many people too, so that the bustle was almost unbearable and made worse since everyone seemed to be walking towards them. The awnings of the shops and the cafés on each side of the street met in the middle and all was in shadow except for occasional, razor-sharp piercings of sunlight. Marguerite strode ahead through the din and the heat and the pungent air, though Mariana knew that even she would be exhausted and that it was determination that drove her forward. She also knew that it was her sister's energy that she, herself, was drawing on and without it and the sight of her just ahead, she would surely have collapsed.

The street, quite suddenly, became so narrow that it was only a pathway. The shops and the traders were gone and so, too, were the people. Only one or two hurried past and always heading towards the main street. On either side were plain stone walls and these became steadily higher, so that Mariana had to press back the brim of her hat and lean backwards to see the top. They were now completely in shadow and the pathway was so narrow that she grazed her bare arms upon the stone.

The Marques seemed nonchalant as he walked before them, his arms swinging freely, his hands tapping the walls, and his hips swaying from side to side, as if he were about to begin a little dance.

And then, abruptly, he stopped, turned around to face them and pointed to a tiny doorway. It was so small that they could easily have passed it without noticing. It was clearly old and of weathered, unvarnished wood, yet it fitted the door frame exactly. The Marques produced a key as does the magician when he pulls out some amazing object from his hat: with flourish and with all the expectations of the magic that will follow.

The key turned noiselessly in the lock, the door smoothly swung open, and moving sideways so that he remained full face to the sisters, the Marques crossed the threshold. And there, on the other side, he stood, his arms outstretched to welcome them.

Mariana surprised herself by being the one to enter first, though she felt that she was already in a state that verged upon the hypnotic. The intensity of the streets, their strange host, the sudden change as they had entered the narrow and deserted pathway, as well as the heat of the day, had worn away her fragile equilibrium and left her feeling open and exposed.

Don Angel was now walking backwards, his intense gaze upon the sisters and his smile expressing his pleasure that they had accepted his invitation and were following him.

They were in a garden. It was, indeed, a beautiful garden. They were surrounded by grasses that towered above them, with tall, graceful stems tipped by exuberant sprays of foliage. They had to brush some aside as they walked. Above these, the crowns of the date palms sent out the spines of their leaves like long tresses, festooning outwards and downwards. In clearer spaces there were short stubby trees with wide twisted trunks and branches leading to thick clusters of leaves, and beneath one of these flat green leaves floated upon the still surface of a pond topped by multi-petalled lotus blooms in shades from pale to deepest blue and purple, their star shapes radiating out from cores of pink and yellow. Throughout the garden was the tinkling sound of water as it spilled through different levels to become a narrow stream that wound its way beneath the trees to somewhere out of sight, where it once again began its glittering circular flow. They walked close to the stream and Mariana reached down and loosened a sandal to free her foot and dip her toes into the cool water.

When she told me this, she said that it reminded her of my father's painting of her and her sister, and how he had depicted her standing at the edge of a lake with her feet submerged and bending down as if reaching for something in the water.

She looked around her in the garden and thought, "All this hidden behind giant walls and preserved for ever from the chaos of the city." And then she wondered from where had come the idea of "forever."

And now she felt a growing happiness and she instinctively reached out and took hold of Marguerite's hand.

The Marques saw this and looked at the two with pleasure, and as always, with interest. And then he turned and walked more quickly along the path, between the tall grasses, making a little gesture with one arm for them to follow.

They came to another door and this one was larger and open. Strips of fine white material hung loosely from the top to the floor; the strips swayed in the breeze showing glimpses of the darkness within. By the side of the doorway sat a man who was enormously fat. He was in traditional dress and slouched back in his chair and beneath his tunic his knees were wide apart. He seemed nonchalant, even sleeping, until Mariana saw the glint and movement of a pupil beneath a hooded eyelid. There was just the slightest communication between the two men, but enough to satisfy them both, so that the Marques swept aside the material and held it back for the girls to enter.

Immediately, there were stairs. They were narrow and of stone and as the three descended into darkness, the radiance of the garden slipped away as when the golden flame of a lamp is snuffed out by uncaring fingers. The reality, now, came from the hundreds of steps. There were candles, with just enough light from each to reach to the next, denying complete blackness but exchanging it for huge shadows that swept across the narrow walls and the low ceiling. The air became stale and damp and puddles gathered on the steps to splash over their feet. There was no pause, no place to rest, or to find orientation, and the Marques, rather than slowing, was increasing the speed of their descent. Mariana reached out her arm to place her hand upon Marguerite's shoulder. Without the reassuring presence of her sister, she felt sure she would have turned back; and yet turned back to what? They had already passed through two doorways and descended deep underground. The light and life of the world had been left far behind. To climb back up the steps was inconceivable.

Then she slipped. She fell and was hurt and cried out, but Marguerite took no notice and was being drawn with increasing speed into the darkness below. The space between the candles had increased, so that just there, where Mariana fell, it was pitch black. Like a disappearing ghost, the pale shape of her sister had faded and was gone. In the dark, without definition, she reached out to find the cold, damp hardness of the wall and there was a little protrusion of sharp stone for her fingers to clutch and steady her as she raised herself. She called out again to her sister, but the sound of her voice seemed to go no further than her eyesight. The darkness offered nothing. Again, she thought to escape, but the hundreds of steps seemed insurmountable. And who would be above to meet her and guide her back to the hotel in this increasingly forbidding city? She could only continue downwards, and so this she did, holding out her hand, as if Marguerite's shoulder was still there to steady her. She felt her body to be no longer her own. Her mind forced her to stare ahead, searching for the slightest reassurance of light, whilst her legs and feet made their own repetitive motion that was now an uncontrolled reflex upon the stone steps. She seemed to be sliding, even floating, ever downwards.

And then, light did come. Gradually, the darkness softened. She began to see the walls that were so close on either side and the stone roof above. The air was changing too and no longer had the thick, stale smell of wet stone. It was hard to believe at first, but there was a new smell. It grew in strength and it was of perfume, and as she continued to descend, she knew that this was no smell she had known before and was not a perfume of the salons and drawing rooms of Europe, but far stronger. She thought of the incense that they burnt in her church in Paris, but this was sweeter than that. And now, there was increasing light and warmth. Warm air flowed up towards her. She felt it around her ankles and then upon her legs as a breeze lifted the hem of her skirt, and then upon her bare arms and it bathed her face and ruffled her hair.

There were only a few steps left and she slowed. There was a soft radiance of light around her and the anguish of her descent was dissipated as if blown away by the warm breeze. And there waiting, looking with upturned faces as she descended to join them, were the Marques and Marguerite.

Mariana paused. Her whole concentration had been on the story itself, her attention completely upon the memories she wished to recall. There had been no concern for me as the listener, though I knew that my presence was essential. But now, she spoke to me directly.

"It was as if I had been sent away as a child, abandoned and scared, and that I was at last welcomed home by my parents."

She rose and walked to a small basin into which she poured some water. She dipped her hands into the water to moisten and cool her face. The night was very hot. Then she moved to the open window and looked out. All was still outside. Gazing into the darkness, she continued her story.

CHAPTER NINE

The ancient city

"I felt that I was welcomed home by loving parents and that they were so pleased to have me close to them. The smiles of welcome I saw on the upturned faces of Marguerite and Don Angel turned my despair into a warm sense of salvation. It was truly as if they were the most loving parents welcoming me home and, in that moment, I saw them as a couple, and I was happy to see them as such."

She turned from the window to face me. "But I know now that something had changed. I was not only feeling my relief at being again with my sister and our host. In that period of bleakness, when I had been left behind and Marguerite had stayed close to the Marques, and they together had reached the warmth and light at the end of the steps, they had indeed united, so that they were now a couple, whilst I just stumbled alone in the dark.

"The Marques took his time to decide which of us to choose; it was never to be us both. His elevation of one would mean the dismissal of the other. This was his design and it was Marguerite who had passed the test and arrived with him far underground in his strange terrain. I imagine him now, reaching to the foot of the stairs, turning to greet which of us should first emerge, and waiting there with open arms, and Marguerite, who was most surely ready, falling into his embrace. I believe that embrace still holds her and always will. Perhaps, I should be glad that it was not me, but I lost my sister and I would have even allowed an embrace of the three of us if it had stopped the aloneness that I now feel."

As I listened, my feelings for the despair of Mariana, became mixed with my own sadness that I, as her lover, made no difference to her loneliness. Yet her emotions were so strong, I was, perhaps, being made to feel as she did.

"I have tried to understand this," she said. "Why to split us apart was his purpose. What was the gain for this creature? Separation from another is life's most profound event. It can cause the greatest anguish. And there is jealousy—I know it so well, the most awful of monsters, searching every nuance with eyes that will always see the agonising worst. And then the loneliness. The terrible emptiness of being by oneself, of being only oneself, of being—no—it is of not being at all—Marguerite was my being. In our first year of life, our mother died; I never knew her. It was only and always, Marguerite. And she felt nothing of this. As much as I needed her, she needed others. But she had always been there, and there was love between us and I cling to this—that it had been so. But now, the Marques had chosen her and to me she was lost.

"But what was his purpose? If only he had existed to spread love. He knew of desire, and of the passions of the senses, but not about loving and being loved. That was not his calling. He is the angel of dismay, of destruction—he lives to divide—to tear like creatures apart."

"Was—is he an angel?" I asked.

"One of Lucifer's, perhaps."

"But why twins?"

"Heaven and hell—are they not twins who have been torn apart? He defies unity. His triumph is to defeat it. Mythology has always been fascinated by twins, but has not allowed the love of twins to survive. Usually, one good, one bad, even one that kills the other. The tribes that we call primitive—they have been fascinated too, and scared—that there should be two who are the same—so dangerous that they were either to be sacred and revered, or persecuted. Some twins were killed at birth."

Mariana rose from her chair and walked to the dressing table. Her hair was around her face and it bothered her so that she took a clasp and swept it back. She fastened it so that her face was free. She sat there and now she spoke to her reflection in the mirror and completely in French. It was always her language for the most intimate moments. My own

French was good and she had taught me many nuances. I will continue her story as faithfully as I can.

The couple who were Don Angel and her sister, now held hands and with his free hand, Don Angel beckoned her to follow them. "Of course," she said, "I followed."

They were in a small chamber. There were slender pillars of pale stone, gilded with gold, supporting the roof, and all above was covered with paintings. The paintings were of the softest tones of pinks, greens and blues and were of the creatures and plants of the sea, and all bordered by a cornice into which were carved the many curves and open mouths of seashells. Beneath the cornice, waves lapped and sometimes rose above it with a froth of gold and silver leaf, so that the three humans seemed submerged and to be looking up at the surface. The walls around them were of the palest blue, bearing the faintest shapes of sea creatures and plants, in subtle greens for the plants and gold and silver for the fish.

In the centre of the chamber was a table of pure white marble. It reminded Mariana of an altar in a Christian church. There were two couches on either side covered in material that was sheer and as white as the marble, and upon the couches were silk cushions, some in turquoise and some in a deeper blue with golden thread. Upon the table lay two necklaces. They were stretched across the marble to expose their magnificence. Heavy strips of gold held lapis lazuli and precious stones, in green, turquoise, and dark, luminous red.

In front of the chamber, hung a curtain of finest silk, so fine that the slightest movement caused it to tremble, and so transparent that brightness flowed through to touch and bring to life the light that lay within each stone and that reflected as a sultry glow upon the surface of the gold.

The stones were threaded amongst a thousand beads of tiny pearls and coloured glass, woven together with fine golden clasps to make a collar deep enough to cover the chest, and below that, for each necklace, there was a large pendant that would rest upon the breast bone. The pendant of one necklace was in turquoise and the other in the soft, orangey red of carnelian.

I have read much of Mariana's poetry, and I draw from some of her verses that describe these objects of beauty. Despite the growing tragedy of her Egyptian experience, the beauty that surrounded her was never lost to her sensibility and to her imagination.

61

The Marques, Don Angel, stepped lightly to the table and took from it the necklace with the carnelian. Gently, he raised it and carefully placed it over one forearm. He then moved towards Marguerite. She was wearing the lightest of summer dresses secured with thin straps upon her shoulders. With his free hand he deftly removed the strap from one shoulder and then the other, so that the dress above the waist collapsed to hang down, the neck hem just touching the floor. The lightest of petticoats was loosened in the same way and then the laces that secured the silk chemise were gently pulled so that the material could be freed from her shoulders. As if there could be no divergence between her naked upper body and that below the waist, Marguerite herself completed the undressing. As she did this, the Marques held the necklace with both hands and with her standing naked before him, placed it upon her shoulders, gently securing it behind her neck with a thong of soft, white leather that ended in two golden clasps. The great clusters of beads, pearls, and precious stones rested flat upon her breasts, and between them the golden links from which hung the pendant that rested upon her breast bone. It was, said Mariana, like a coronation, and indeed, the Marques declared, "Now you are my Egyptian Queen."

He returned to the table. There were two, neatly folded pieces of white material resting upon one corner. He took one and held it so that its folds fell free and it hung, suspended, between his hands. Facing Marguerite, he passed it to her, so that she received it with her two hands. She knew exactly what to do and wrapped it around her waist. There was ample of the fine material to allow her to gather and secure it with a bow.

The Marques now turned to Mariana. The other necklace, with the pendant of turquoise, was resting upon his forearm and he performed the same movements with her so that she too, in a moment, stood barebreasted. She felt her mind and body drifting apart. Somewhere, still in her mind, was the voice of decorum, but the exposure of her body brought a new feeling. She felt the cool air upon her skin and a strange sense of freedom, and it seemed ridiculous to stand, still clothed below the waist. So, like Marguerite, she continued to undress until all her garments lay in a little crumpled pile of cotton and silk around her feet.

The Marques placed the necklace around her shoulders, secured it and adjusted the rows of pearls, coloured beads and jewels so that they rested flat. The turquoise pendant, with a pleasing coolness, lay against her skin.

He fetched the other piece of material from the table, and, as had Marguerite, she secured it around her waist.

He stepped back, "The Pharaohs welcome you, too, Mariana."

They sat; the twins on one couch and the Marques on the other. Between themselves, the young women were no strangers to nakedness and, as well, Mariana knew of the physical experiments of her sister, though for herself, to have been naked in front of another, let alone a man, had been unthinkable. There was, though, a surprising feeling of security. There was something in the manner of their host, a man who had just taken the greatest liberty in unclothing them, that left her feeling that there would be nothing done against her will and that all these strange events were part of a grand design. A grand design of the Marques, no doubt, but in its strangeness and its exotic excess, its purpose, whatever that may be, swept all before it. Mariana, who was to become the poet, felt elevated and that she had been taken up into a grand, poetic narrative. Marguerite, she could tell, was completely comfortable, though to say, relaxed, would have been incorrect, as there was an air of excitement that had permeated the chamber. They sat, resting upon the cushions, surrounded by the exotic sea creatures and plants that floated in imagery around them. The white silk curtains swayed and were ruffled expectantly by the breeze, and a tiny little opening between the curtains showed dashes of bright daylight.

Mariana felt her sister's warm arm around her and was filled with a feeling that she could only describe as bliss. She rested her head upon Marguerite's shoulder. From the other couch, the Marques looked smilingly upon them. She now saw him as a benevolent guardian, watching over them like a parent, and she felt regressed into her childhood when shame was an uninvited stranger.

Marguerite had lifted the pendant of orange-red carnelian from her chest. She looked carefully at it and then, turning to Mariana, lifted hers, the pendant of turquoise.

"They have different designs."

Mariana also compared the two. Both bore etched designs upon the stones. Her own was a simple image. Upon the turquoise was a semi-circular shape that was placed with the straight line as its base, and the curved line, slightly flattened at its crescent, above it. Descending from the base were two perpendicular lines, the left one shorter than the right.

Marguerite's design, upon the red carnelian, was engraved upon the stone with great delicacy and skill. It was of a female figure, standing and wearing flowing robes. "My sister's looks Egyptian, and mine looks Greek." Marguerite gave the Marques a questioning glance.

"Twin cultures, Marguerite. The Greeks created Alexandria, but they built it upon the bedrock of thousands of Egyptian years. Your necklace is all Egyptian except for the lady who is Greek and who is Aphrodite. The new Greek Pharaohs knew how to mix their own gods with those of the Egyptians—so no one would be upset. They even created a new god for that purpose, but they did not forget their own and there are temples here to Aphrodite—you will see. And Mariana, what do you see in your image?"

At this point, Mariana turned from addressing the mirror and spoke to me directly. "The necklace was exquisite, but the image displeased me. It was not beautiful like Marguerite's, but was a sombre group of lines and a curve. I said to Don Angel, without hesitation, and even without thought—'I see the sun setting below the horizon.' He clapped his hands and seemed delighted. 'Mariana, you have the gift,' he said, 'It is exactly so—Amenta.' And though his congratulations seemed sincere, I felt the warm feeling of love and acceptance begin to fade. In the imagery upon the pendants, I again saw his choice of Marguerite over me. He had chosen for her, the goddess of love, whilst I had the symbol of nightfall."

I could see the sadness in Mariana, and I knew her well enough to understand how much she was defined by love, given or withheld, and how quickly she could move between happiness and despair. She rose and stepped away from the mirror to sit facing me. I wished to embrace and comfort her, but knew that at this moment it would not be welcome. She was deeply immersed in the memories that needed to be spoken and they were of a nature that would have reduced my sympathy to no more than interference. And, I must confess, my own interest in the story was such that, I too, wished for no interruption.

She continued with eyes closed, as one revisiting and viewing a scene of which every tiny detail must be remembered, and her need etched the words of her story into my own memory.

Don Angel, having bestowed his gifts upon the twins, crossed the chamber to a table that was close to the white curtain. A light breeze moved the curtain from without and reached into the room to cool the bodies of the twins as they sat upon the couch. Marguerite had removed her arm from her sister and her hands lay upon her lap. Mariana had one hand within her own lap and with the other, still held the pendant that had so dismayed her.

The wall paintings of the chamber were gentle frescoes of Greek design, but the table by which the Marques now stood bore all the opulence of the Egyptian. The legs and frame were of a pale wood with an angular criss-crossing of slim supports. He beckoned the twins to join him. Mariana was astounded by what she saw. A huge, scarab beetle stretched wings of gold and turquoise across the surface, and between the curved wings and the six legs were lapis lazuli and shards of multi-coloured glass. The great body of the scarab was in turquoise and its horns were filaments of gold.

Upon the table, were two goblets of pale blue, shaped and engraved like the blue lotus opening its petals to the morning sun, and next to them an alabaster vessel, its slender neck above a swollen body that caused Mariana to think of the swollen belly of pregnancy, and with a handle that gracefully curved from the body to the neck.

Don Angel lifted the jug and poured liquid into the two goblets. He handed them to the twins. "My dear Egyptian Queens. Here is a drink, especially known to those who wish access to the finest sensibilities and to the ambitions of great dynasties. It was created for the courts of the Pharaohs, where it facilitated their most sacred ceremonies, as well as celebrations of a more secret and intimate nature. It is a necessary prerequisite for the little tour on which we will soon embark."

He returned to his couch and gestured the sisters to return to theirs. They both sat holding the goblets. Marguerite drank first. She took a sip, and then reached to the marble table that was in front of them and placed the goblet upon it. Her clear and decisive action was emphasised by the sharp sound of the ceramic meeting the marble. The reflection of the goblet upon the pure white of the surface made a soft blue glow. Mariana could see that her sister would take her time to enjoy the ritual of drinking this very special drink. She had sat back and was resting comfortably amongst the cushions, and was treating the contents of the goblet as a fine wine that needed time to savour.

Mariana took her first sip. The taste was of a rich and sweet wine, yet there was a bitterness within in it and an aftertaste that made her shudder. The Marques noticed and laughed. "Enjoy the drink, Mariana. It can be a little sharp I know, but it has been so carefully blended to allow you some pleasure in the taste, and any displeasure will soon be allayed by the qualities it brings to your sensibilities and to your emotions. Trust me."

"You are not drinking yourself, Don Angel," replied Mariana.

"I cannot indulge, dear ladies, as I am your host and your guide, so sadly I must curtail any excess of pleasure in order to be completely ready for your needs. And anyway, some would say that the effects of this potion are always with me!" And his smile was benevolent and completely self-assured.

And so, they sat, and they drank, and the Marques spoke airily about the many topics that interested him, though not about Alexandria, as this, for the moment, he was saving. As he spoke, the warming effect of the drink began to be felt. It rose up through Mariana's legs and to her body and then her neck until she felt her face grow hot and flushed, and in a most pleasing way, so that all she could do was laugh. She turned to Marguerite who looked exquisite as she languished amongst the cushions of their couch. It seemed to her that her sister even sur-passed the ideal visions of the orient that had become so popular in art. And then, she remembered—they were twins. She looked down at her own body. "I am as beautiful as she."

She wasn't sure whether she had said this aloud, but perhaps she had, as she heard the voice of the Marques, as if from a distance, but clear, "So much the same—and so different."

All was now changing. She felt a numbness in her body and won-dered whether she could walk, but the Marques was standing and she felt Marguerite rising from their couch. She watched her sister step lightly across the room to the ornate Egyptian table. Marguerite gazed at it and stroked the surface with her hand. Mariana, still in her seat, felt the cool surface of the turquoise scarab beetle as if her sister's hand was transmitting it to hers. She rose up herself. Her body felt hardly her own. Marguerite was now standing by the curtain and was reaching out to it.

Again, there was the voice of Don Angel, as if from a great distance. "Yes, Marguerite, open the curtain."

And Marguerite did so and the chamber was flooded with light. The curtain hung from ceiling to floor and was almost the width of a whole wall, so that the sisters beheld a vista that was spread out before them, brilliant in the sun. Marguerite stood in the centre of the great aperture like a graceful statue overlooking the city. And indeed, the panorama of the shoreline, with its palaces, and the sea and the island of Pharos beyond, was stretched out before them.

The twins stood side-by-side, gazing out in wonder, and the Marques came from behind and standing between them, placed one hand behind the back of each, so that the three stood in line, and declared, "Now we will see Ancient Alexandria."

And with a hand upon each, he guided them towards a set of many, wide marble steps, and slowly, in unison, they descended until, after some minutes, they had reached the level of the ground. Mariana turned and looked up, but could see no sign of the chamber from which they had emerged. The steps above them disappeared amongst a cluster of trees and grasses.

The streets seemed to be laid out in an immaculate grid and they walked upon one that led straight to the shore and to the line of grand buildings that faced the sea.

They came to the quayside and there before them were two great harbours divided by a causeway that stretched for a thousand metres until it reached the island. And on the island, they could see, to their right, upon a thin promontory, a construction of enormous size. It raised itself like an extended telescope, reaching up to a fine tip from which threads of white smoke rose to slowly join the tiny white clouds in the sky.

It was at least a 100 metres high. Its great base was square, and upon that was the next section, which had many sides, and above that, it was circular until it reached to the pinnacle where an enormous mirror caught the rays of the sun and sent them blazing towards the horizon.

About the base, and at each corner, were statues of figures holding tridents, and other statues could be seen upon the different elevations, and crowning all, silhouetted against the blue sky, and surely massive in its size, another figure, and all were statues of deities for sure. The pale walls of the building glowed and shimmered in the sunshine and around its base were gardens, the softness of the greens giving relief to the great, bright edifice that defied all that mankind had built before.

It was Marguerite who whispered to her sister in astonishment, "It is the lighthouse of Alexandria—it is a wonder of the world."

The Marques heard her. "Yes, it is a wonder—and we will see more. Come, we will walk along the quayside. It is a fine day for ancient Alexandrians and one also to be enjoyed by two of their guests."

CHAPTER TEN

The library and the temple

Around the island of the lighthouse, the sea was a gently undulating surface upon which the tip of every wave flashed and sparkled in the sun. Beyond the island, the azure of the sea reached to the horizon to become lost as it mingled with the pale blue of a sky that deepened into a rich blue canopy that rose above their heads.

The palaces and temples that faced the sea glowed in yellow stone and glistened in white marble. They were built in the Greek style, with pillars and porticoes. Some were decorated with Egyptian motifs, with highly coloured lines that zigzagged around the pillars or circled them with profiles of warriors, temple beauties, and deities. Some rested in their plain elegance. Everywhere were statues.

For a while they strolled and then the Marques stopped and stood surveying the scene. He had decided that it was time to offer some orientation to his two young guests.

Mariana also decided to pause here, and to break into her account of this remarkable experience. She had summoned up every detail with her eyes closed and with complete submission to her memory. She now needed to take stock to make sure that I was, in my own way, still with her. She wished to explain how it had felt to be there amongst the magnificence of the greatest city of the ancient world. For a while, to return to the present time and her little apartment in Almeria and to the presence of her English lover, she spoke again in English. But this was only for a moment. It was her mother tongue that was required, and for myself, I was happy with this, as the fluency and articulation of her language so matched the beauty of the scenes that she was describing. It was, she said, as if she was watching a play in a vast open-air theatre and had been invited to step upon the stage.

And as well as the scenery, there was the cast. Around them passed the people of Alexandria, some strolling, some hurrying. In her amazement at the scenery, she had ceased to be conscious that she was semi-naked. She was brought back to an awareness by seeing that they were not alone. There was one who wore nothing but necklaces and a profundity of bangles that circled both arms and ankles. She was walking alone and away from them. Most, though, wore light tunics of linen held by straps across the shoulders. The tunics, for men and for women, either rose above the chest or left the chest and breasts exposed. Some of the men simply wore a linen skirt. Occasionally, a man or woman hurried purposefully past, with no clothes and no jewellery. The Marques noticed Marguerite's eyes follow one naked and perfectly proportioned youth.

"He is a slave Marguerite. The slaves are often unclothed."

Marguerite had answered with a coquettishness that Mariana knew well. "So, are we your slaves, Don Angel?"

"Mademoiselle, how could you ask such a thing, when you wear such a necklace."

The Marques rested himself, leaning upon a balustrade at the mouth of the causeway. "We will not visit the island of Pharos, not even the lighthouse. There are other wonders that I wish to show you. And anyway, for the lighthouse, what could be better than to see it from here as it stands upon its island and to view its wonderful profile against the sea. It was built by Ptolemy the Second, the second of the Greek Pharaohs. The Egyptians had welcomed these heirs of Alexander as they had freed them from the rule of the Persians, and they really did not like the Persians—no sympathy for the Egyptian culture—one that had bloomed and prospered for thousands of years!"

The thought of such a dynasty clearly filled the Marques with vigour. He left his resting place and began to pace up and down, just as he had when he lectured them in the restaurant. He gestured to the line of buildings, receding into the distance.

"The Ptolemies built this city and they knew how to both rule and to fit in. They were wise—well—such were the early ones—but, alas, with time, it is always the same—nothing lasts." And with his usual extravagance of expression, his excitement at the achievements of the Ptolemies collapsed into his despair at the failure of their heirs.

As they stood, attending to his soliloquy, Mariana had continued to observe the people around them and her interest had grown at the sight of two young women who were slowly moving towards them. She had noticed them at a distance, and even then, from the outlines of their figures and their movements, she had been quite certain. She looked at Marguerite and saw that she had noticed too. The twins were viewing twins. Two, identical, fair skinned, and light-haired young women were viewing two who matched them in exactness, but whose skins were dark and whose features could only be Egyptian.

Now, the Marques, a little disquieted at losing their attention, also noticed the two women, who continued to approach them.

Their hair was raven black, full, and completely straight. Mariana had already noticed that wigs were the custom for some, and thought this must be so for these. For one, the shining hair was threaded with gold, whilst for the other, there nestled clusters of precious stones. Their skin had a lustre of the deepest brown and their eyes were as close to black as brown could be with their contours painted in blue and green. Even from a distance, she had seen the length of the dark eyelashes. Their dresses of fine, transparent linen were close fitting and woven with threads of yellow and blue. Upon bare arms, they wore bracelets and bangles of many colours, including gold. Beneath each dress, ankles were exposed to show fine gold chains, and for one, the links included tiny silver bells. Mariana could hear the faint tinkling at each approaching step.

Marguerite was staring hard at the two young women, completely fascinated, so that Mariana became anxious that her sister's scrutiny would cause offence, and she touched her upon the arm. "It is alright," said Marguerite, "They cannot see us." And she looked around. "No one can see us—only we can see them."

"It is true," added the Marques. "To bring us into their vision requires a little more from me. Actually, quite a lot more and it really is very tiring. This, I will need to provide later, but I must conserve myself. So, for now—we are just observers. We stroll unseen amongst these wonderful people—and" (nodding to the Egyptian twins), "these two

71

I know—and we share a story, but theirs is a very different one to yours and, anyway, we see them now as when I first met them."

Mariana now felt free to look around. She could see that those who passed them by were of different races. The twins they were observing were surely Egyptian, yet many others were of lighter skin, and from the Marques she knew that Alexandria was ruled by the Greeks. Some of these even wore the flowing white robes that she had seen in picture books. There were others, all men, who wore turbans, or head bands around their hair and she wondered if these were Jews.

Further along the quay, was the intense activity of the port. There were many boats moored, and crowds of men loading and unloading the goods. Crates of all sizes and many sacks were piled upon one another. Some sacks had burst and spilled their golden grain around them. Amongst the bodies of the men, were some that were as black as ebony and that glistened in the heat of the sun.

The Egyptian twins had moved away from the quay towards the inner city.

The Marques watched them with interest. He spoke, and it was with affection. "They are returning home. Later on, they will shop. They do this every day. There is still wealth here amongst the Egyptians—as well as some customs that defy the purity of the Greeks." And at this he glanced towards the naked and bejewelled woman whom Mariana had first noticed and who was now far away in the distance.

"For the shopping, there is the greatest market in the world. You can buy the most beautiful materials, and spices, perfumes, oils and wonderful foods. And to think that a few hours ago, we had lunch in a modern restaurant!" And the Marques laughed with pleasure at his playfulness with time. "And now we must visit the library."

The building they approached was so imposing that, even from a distance, Mariana was in awe. It rose up in stone and marble in Greek and Egyptian design, so that pillars, porticoes, and colonnades vied with massive pharaonic statues. Two male figures towered on each side of the doorway. They were seated upon their thrones, bare chested with their hands upon their huge knees, and they wore the headdress of the Pharaohs, spreading wide behind their ears and down upon their shoulders. Each headdress was brightly painted with horizontal stripes of red, blue, and green and between each colour was a strip of pure gold. From the forehead of one reared a cobra. Its flared hood was in gold and the sun caught its forked tongue so that it flickered in silver. From the forehead of the other rose a hawk, with blue and green wings, and its curved and cruel beak glinted in gold. Upon their thrones were engraved and painted a multitude of designs and symbols. Mariana saw amongst them the symbol that was upon her pendant.

Above the entrance, as if in a marriage of opposites, there was a great frieze, in the style of the Greeks. Female figures in flowing robes reclined in calm conversation, or stood, each with an arm resting on the shoulder of the next. By the side of one, leant a stringed instrument, two of them held scrolls and one held an instrument of measurement. Marguerite had counted them. "There are nine, so they are the muses."

And the Marques replied, "Indeed, it is a museum. The greatest place of learning the world has ever known. Come."

And they climbed the wide, white marble steps, passed the statues that guarded the entrance, and entered.

Inside was an expanse of gardens and buildings that reached so far that Mariana could not to see to the end. At the very centre, was a raised structure that, in its magnificence, claimed its place as the heart and soul of all that was around it. Its elegant roof was supported by pillars on every side. Many were carved as women, standing serenely in long flowing robes, or as bare-chested men with curled hair and great beards who clutched to their bodies the scrolls and instruments that were the symbols of their knowledge.

"And here they keep the books," declared the Marques.

They walked amongst the pillars and under the deep shadow of the pediment and felt the coolness emanating from the stone of the walls. "As befits a great library," thought Mariana.

The Marques found the entrance of his preference and they stood within a chamber that was lined from ceiling to floor with shelves upon which papyrus scrolls were squeezed into every recess.

Mariana had gasped in wonder. "There must be a thousand scrolls."

The Marques smiled and led them through the chamber to another doorway. Before them was a great hall that stretched to a large arch, behind which could be seen another hall and then again, an archway that led to another. And above them were galleries, two stories deep, with their walls covered by the protruding wooden handles of papyrus scrolls, and on the ground floor, where they stood, antechambers branched off showing glimpses of shelf upon laden shelf. There were thousands upon thousands of books.

"The Ptolemies wished to have every book in the world. They bought, borrowed, and stole them. The knowledge of the whole world was their ambition and they believed it to be their entitlement."

The twins were now used to being invisible and were comfortable to gaze around them. Men were quietly moving between rooms or standing reading. Two were in conversation, a scroll laid out before them on a table.

They walked through the arch to the next hall. At one side, upon its pedestal and towering above, was the statue of an enthroned figure. Upon his great head was fastened a cylindrical container and in one hand he held a sceptre upon a long staff. By his side, stood a three headed dog. "It is Serapis," muttered the Marques, but he was now making off at a pace towards the next hall and from there to a doorway.

They had walked through the whole length of the library, past countless books, but also rooms to each side, some of which were large enough for many people to gather. In one, there were close on a hundred, gathered around a speaker who stood beside a large papyrus that was pinned to a frame. Upon it were drawn shapes that reminded Mariana of the lessons in geometry they had received as girls from their home tutor. She heard a dismissive grunt from Marguerite, who had always hated mathematics. In another room, a group were intently studying an image of the stars with lines linking them and creating the shapes of earthly figures in the sky.

The Marques was moving with a speed and determination which conveyed that their tour of the great museum and its library was now complete, and on passing through the doorway, they emerged into an open expanse of gardens. All was cultivated with immaculate care and design. There were many palm trees, shrubs, and grasses and a pathway leading through these to a high wall with a large gate. On either side of this were two, slim obelisks, reaching high into the sky and covered in hieroglyphs and designs. Again, Mariana saw the sign of the Amenta.

Marguerite seemed fascinated as she gazed upwards. "We have one, just the same, in la Place de la Concorde."

"Indeed Marguerite," replied the Marques. "But it is not one of these."

As they paused to study the obelisks there was a startling sound that came from behind a thick group of trees. It was the roar of a large cat. They turned and saw, walking towards them, two people, both in young adulthood. The man was dressed in the Greek style in voluminous white linen that hung down to his sandaled feet. It was drawn up and fastened beneath his chest and one stretch of material rested upon his shoulder and was tucked beneath an arm. His hair was cut short and curled and was of a light brown. Though tanned by the sun, his complexion was fairer than his female companion, whose skin was almost as dark as of the men who had been labouring at the quayside. They had seemed of low cast, perhaps even slaves, whilst she had all the bearing of aristocracy. The shining black hair of her wig was laced with golden thread and lay full upon her shoulders. A blue lotus flower was in her hair, a blue that matched the colour of her partner's eyes. She wore a robe of white linen that descended from one shoulder, so that one breast was covered whilst the other was bare. The garment flowed down to her jewelled sandals and was softly contoured by the outline of her legs as she walked. Her deep brown eyes were made vivid with painted colours of blue, emerald and gold upon the eyelids and the curved black line of her eyebrows met a tiny upward curl at the corner of each eye.

The features of the two, were strong and refined and their movement, as they strolled, was of an accustomed grace and dignity. Mariana felt that they were the most beautiful couple she had ever seen and that their human beauty even matched the magnificence of the great buildings and artefacts around them.

As the two walked, still moving towards them, they each held in one hand a long leash that was restraining the muscular pull of a large, black cat.

"It might have been the source of the roar I had heard," said Mariana, "But I think that was a lion. The Marques had told us that within the gardens they kept wild animals and I had heard such a sound in our Paris Zoo. But I believe that this before us was a young panther. Though each held it by their own leash, I could see it was the man who was restraining the beast. The tension showed within the muscles of his arm. The woman's leash was like a soft thing in her palm."

They walked past and it took all of Mariana's courage to stay standing close to the animal. She wondered if it would notice them; whether it had some catlike sense which would pick up their presence, but it stalked past, the leash held by the man stretched tightly, the woman's swaying, loosely.

"To be so close to such a creature was both wonderful and frightening and for a moment, like the couple, joined together through their cat,

75

I felt close to my sister again, for I knew that she was feeling the same. She even moved towards it and I do believe that she would have embraced it if she could."

It was also the cue for some more words from Don Angel. "One Greek, one Egyptian—you probably realised."

Mariana had wanted to ask a question. "What happened to this great library, for I know it was destroyed?"

"The old gods were many and they were only jealous of each other, but the new ones were the 'One Gods' and they were jealous of knowledge. The Christians came and then the Muslims, and there were wars as well. The library was worn away."

The three passed through the gateway. The length of the museum and its gardens was so great that they had emerged into a different part of the city. The buildings were smaller, though still of a fine design. They continued along the straight road until the villas began to thin out.

The road ended, and spread out before them, was a vast lake. The breeze stirred its heavy waters and the sun was reflected upon the surface in a myriad of tiny shafts of light.

Don Angel lead them downwards between trees, shrubs, and long grasses and by the lakeside was a building that nestled in a clearing. Though its pillars and portico were of smaller size than others they had seen, the structure had great elegance and dignity so that, in its setting, it seemed a location for the gods. And indeed, it was surely a temple, as at its forefront was the statue of a robed female figure. It was exactly the figure inscribed upon the pendant worn by Marguerite.

Two women were standing outside. One wore similar robes to the statue. The other wore a simple smock.

The Marques halted and turned to the twins. "It is now that you are visible to others." And he indicated towards the two women who were standing calmly before the temple and who were watching them. And then he turned towards Mariana, "And now Mariana, we must bid you farewell."

Here Mariana paused in her story. The shock that she had felt then was reverberating through the years. It shook me, the listener to the core, but my feeling was nothing compared to her own devastation.

Her words to me were thus. "I was to be torn away from my sister. I was to be sent away, and I knew not where. And to Marguerite, the temple was open, but to me, it was closed."

76

CHAPTER ELEVEN

The parting

When the Comte de Saint Germain called on us in Whitby, hoping to find that the twins were still our guests and that he might protect them from the pernicious whims of the Marques, he could not have known the damage that was already done. I doubt that with such knowledge he would have dispatched my father on a rescue mission to Paris.

The influence of Don Angel, the Marques de Mansura, was such that the twins were already cast to play parts in the dark theatre of his metaphysical world.

Though we realised that the twins' visit to Alexandria was of consequence, we could never have imagined what had occurred and neither could we realise its aftermath.

I will now return to that night in Mariana's Almeria apartment, and to her describing, as she had never before, the experience of visiting a city as it was in the second century BC.

Of course, there have been times over the years when I have discussed Mariana's tale with friends and colleagues. Not many, I should say—to some, the content would be too bizarre to warrant their attention, and who wants to be ridiculed as a laughing stock? But as a doctor of the mind, I have a few colleagues whose attitudes to the human psyche are less constricted, and who believe that human experience cannot be limited to the tried and tested mores of reality and that it can reach into areas, so wide ranging and of such depth, as to make our desperate attempts at explanation an irrelevance.

I have found that speaking of these matters to such sympathetic minds, and I am tempted to say "souls," has provoked great interest and debate. But even then, most have been able to go no further than the chamber that the twins reached, deep underground, and the liquid concoction that was then handed to them by the Marques. Given his mercurial persona and a gift of conjuring, and very probably, being a hypnotist of the first order, they conclude that the girls were made to drink a most powerful drug and that they were then transported, not through Ancient Alexandria, but through the mind of the Marques.

We have, in recent years, heard much about hypnotism and hysteria and indeed, the research of the late Professor Charcot at the Salpêtrière Hospital demonstrated the most extreme and remarkable states caused by the hypnotic trance.

It is even, and perhaps a related fact, that Marguerite Mercier, much later in her life when she became the Countess de Bolvoir, would come to know Charcot and, as a gifted lay person, be allowed into his clinical inner sanctum. But that is another story.

We also know that there are drugs that can cause the most intense and long-lasting hallucinations. In this context, Ancient Alexandria was a mirage for the twins, a product of intoxication and hypnotic suggestion.

My view is that it can be so—but only if one cannot allow the existence of the *truly* unknown; unknown because it is of a dimension of time and space that few can access. My experience of both the Comte de Saint Germain and the Marques de Mansura pulls me towards believing that they were two such people—with access to different realities and for whom time could be customised and personal age could be unlimited.

In my own enquiries about these matters, I have spoken with senior members of the Theosophical Society in London; wise figures who have deeply researched such matters. Some of them have taken a great interest in the Comte de Saint Germain, believing him to be a soul of the highest spiritual and metaphysical order. One whom I spoke to, believed that she had even met him and I have no reason to disbelieve her. As to the Marques de Mansura, they either know nothing of him or prefer not to disclose what they do know. My guess is that the truth lies in the latter.

At any rate, the Theosophists are most aware of the importance of opposites, a factor which I find takes on increasing significance in my story. One might well assume that the concepts of "twinship" and of "difference" are at opposite ends of a spectrum, so to find so much difference within twinship itself, creates a particularly rich pair of opposites.

But we must return to Alexandria.

The Marques had made his statement that Mariana was to accompany them no further. He had done so with a voice that was completely flat and without the slightest show of concern for its obvious effect. Nor was there anything from her sister, who did not even look at her, but was gazing with anticipation towards the temple.

The only other words from the Marques, delivered as one relating simple, factual information, was that she would be guided back to the great staircase. To Mariana, at that moment, the enormity of the prospect of climbing the hundreds of steps was nothing compared with the devastation she felt at the enforced and completely unexpected separation.

One of the two women who had been watching them, now approached. It was the one with the simple dress. She looked like a servant girl. The other, with the flowing garments, remained to receive the Marques and Marguerite, who were already walking towards her.

The girl spoke to Mariana, but in a language she could not understand, and realising that verbal communication was not possible, she took hold of Mariana's hand and began to lead her away.

Mariana said to me, "The holding of my hand was the one thing that stopped me from collapsing; it was a tiny bit of life in the midst of desolation."

She followed the girl, but after a few steps, turned to look back. Had it all been a terrible joke? She could imagine such from Don Angel, and even her sister joining in. Or maybe she was the victim of a ruthless experiment that was now complete. But the two figures, and the woman, who was surely a priestess, had disappeared and the temple door was shut. No one else was around, just Mariana and the girl who was now leading her down to the great lake.

It was evening, and a cool breeze had begun to stroke the water, so that gentle drifts crossed and re-crossed the surface. The sun was low on the horizon and as they walked, its light flickered from behind the trees, their shapes reduced to dark silhouettes. The darkness that was spreading across the lake seemed to speak of its great depths and the unknown creatures that swam beneath. The temple was still in view, and just one corner of its pale walls was flushed with pink. Within that building was her sister, and perhaps, the Marques, certainly the priestess woman, and maybe others who were like her, and Mariana could only think that they were greeting Marguerite, and that her sister must be a specially chosen guest. There could even be a ceremony, an occasion of the richest experience, and none of it would be hers.

As she stood, overwhelmed by the loss, she felt a gentle pull upon her hand and she allowed herself to be led through the trees and away from the lake. They climbed a hill and entered a place of more trees and many tall grasses, and amongst these was hidden a set of stone steps. They took the steps, Mariana stumbling upon one of them, so that there was dirt upon her white skirt and grazing on her bare arm. The shrubs seemed eager to hinder them and sharp stems leant across to scratch her arms and body.

There was a small stone platform at the top and from there a pathway that led to the wide opening to the chamber from which, that afternoon, they had gazed out across the expanse of Alexandria. The curtain was drawn across and the servant girl drew it open so that they could enter. Mariana recognised just one thing—the great white marble table that had reminded her of a Christian altar. The beautiful Egyptian table with its inlays and its scarab beetle of gold was gone.

She felt the girl unfasten the fabulous necklace and untie the bow that held her skirt, so that, just as in that moment she had stood before the Marques, she was naked. The surge of freedom and the stirring of excitement at her nakedness was now reduced to her sense that to stand there unclothed was a true expression of her shame and destitution. The girl stood in front of her holding her clothes, all neatly folded; the undergarments and the dress that in her ordinary life, that morning, she had been wearing. And she began to realise that the losses she felt were not only for her sister, but also for the necklace, for the fabulous ancient city she had walked through with its villas, palaces, and temples, for the great museum and its library of countless thousands of books, and for the beautiful couple who had, as their pet, a panther. And she grew steadily aware that it was also the loss of a prospect, a potential source of wonder that could have been the greatest experience of a lifetime, and that would now never be hers—admission to a temple of Aphrodite.

The girl had laid the necklace across the marble table, so that it rested just as it had when she first saw it, when it lay next to the necklace of Marguerite with its pendant of the goddess. And she could still only compare—that hers was the symbol of sunset and the oncoming of night.

And night was approaching. She looked out through the large opening and on to the city of Alexandria and the island of Pharos with its massive lighthouse. A mist was descending so that outlines became unclear and beyond the island, the sea and the sky had merged into a background blanket of pale grey. The island was now just a dark strip, and only the lighthouse stood out, crowned by flames as the great furnace that was its beacon had been lit. Its brilliance stirred in her a modicum of hope, and then, as the flame of a candle can splutter and die, that too was taken, and there was nothing there at all. Alexandria was gone.

She dressed, and when she was ready the girl led her to the steps. She was speaking to her again and her words seemed kind. This time, Mariana spoke back, though there could be no understanding.

One thing was certain: that a great set of steps rose above, barely lit and encased in damp walls and low ceilings, and filled with ancient air that had known little movement to lift it from its years of stagnation.

The girl stood quietly by the bottom step. For the first time, Mariana looked at her properly. She was very young, no more than 12 or 13. She had been kind and Mariana felt a warmth of gratitude rise through her body, so that she reached out and held her and pulled her towards her. The girl's body was pressed tightly against hers and she wrapped her arms around her and wept upon her small shoulder, her tears dampening the girl's long, soft hair. Just a fraction of the closeness she had needed from her sister was being found with a young servant whose language she could not speak and whom she would never see again.

And here, Mariana paused in her story to say to me, "And did she ever exist—did any of it really exist—if it did not, my loss is all the greater."

At that moment, it felt like the whole mood and impetus of her story had changed and I could no longer restrain myself. Without any feeling that I was interrupting or imposing, I crossed to where Mariana was sitting and held her close to me. I wished to offer my own shoulder for her tears, but though she accepted my embrace, I believe that she had passed the point of crying. After a while, she gently pushed me away and sat back in her chair.

To recall climbing the staircase was to revive fear and despair and an experience of time as a never-ending wheel that could offer no resolution of arrival. The girl had wanted her to lead the way and she had done so, with the reassurance of hearing some footsteps behind her. She knew, though, that it would not last, and the time came when she could hear nothing but the sounds of her own painful ascent. She chose not even to look round, knowing that she was now alone and would only be staring into darkness.

At last, hope came through the slightest movement in the air around her and a hint of the freshness of open space and she knew that she was nearing the summit. There would be no sign of daylight as, by now, it would be night-time.

Looking up, she at first saw stars, and then, as the exit before her grew larger, the bright shard of a fine crescent moon.

She stumbled into the open and fell flat upon the ground. She cared nothing for the dirt upon her dress, or the bruising upon her arms and legs, the earth felt so firm and welcoming, and she could smell the night scents of the beautiful garden that she had traversed with Marguerite and the Marques, just hours before. She could hear the tinkling of the ornamental stream and she breathed deeply and filled her lungs with the sweet air and exhaled the stagnation of the staircase.

And then a great shape loomed above her. She struggled to her knees and looked up. There could be no escape from the towering figure that was silhouetted against the sky. It had a mouth that was moving and making guttural sounds. The mouth became part of a face and the body beneath the face became more distinct. A great, obese body and she began to recognise the man who had been seated in the garden next to the entrance to the staircase. He had seemed, then, like a picture book genie from a bottle, and more so now, and monstrous in the darkness.

Still kneeling, she placed her arms around her head to, at least, protect that most vulnerable part. She waited for the attack which seemed inevitable. There were still the guttural sounds which she could now hear to be words. But the tone was one of instruction and she felt his foot kick one of her legs. She dared to look up and saw that he had moved away. He was standing, watching her, and then making a gesture for her to follow, he strode along the pathway, his great bulk rhythmically swinging from side to side. She clambered up, stumbled again, and then righting herself, followed him, now hoping that rather than her attacker, he might just be the guide for her escape. The crescent moon was so fine that it gave little light to the garden, yet its clear presence in the sky now brought an expectation that the ordinary world might still be found.

They reached the gate. He opened it and waited for her to pass through. She heard him mutter some words and then it was closed behind her, fitting exactly, smoothly, and tightly into its frame. Once again, as when they had followed the Marques in the daylight of that fateful afternoon, the wall of the garden towered above her and she remembered how she had pushed back the brim of her hat in order to look up and see its full height. And then she realised that she no longer had her hat.

At one end of the pathway there was complete darkness, at the other, some feint light, so that she chose that as her direction and knew she was correct as she began to hear sounds and then glimpses of people moving ahead. She came to the street and remembered that she was on the corner at which the Marques had materialised, resplendent in his miraculous change of costume. It was a point from which she could retrace the steps of the afternoon, back to the restaurant where they had lunched and where he had delivered his verbal introduction to the fine sensibilities they were soon to encounter. From there it was only a few yards to the hotel in which he had reserved them separate rooms. They had scoffed at his presumption of them not sharing a room and they had used one room for their luggage and the other for themselves. But now Mariana had the strangest of feelings that she had no right to share with her sister. That her sister had been chosen, and that they were now to be separate and she was simply to observe the progress of one who had entered a place that was denied to her. And so, she let herself into the room where they had stored their luggage and moved the suitcase and bags from the bed. She placed her sister's belongings on the floor near to the door, and left her own where they lay. Without even undressing, she laid upon the bed and entered a sleep that was so filled with dreams, that on waking, she felt barely returned to the ordinary world, and what existed of that return offered only a cold and hard reality.

She rose and washed. She had stumbled several times and each fall had left its marks of cuts and bruises upon her skin.

Her dress was stained and torn and was creased from her night's sleep. She stepped out of it, kicking it away. It was only fit for rags. She put on a new dress, brushed her hair, and then made the only move possible; she made her way to her sister's room.

At this point in her story, Mariana rose and came to me. She looked down at me and smiled as if she was grateful to me for staying with her through the telling of her tale. It was full of adventure and of woe and she looked tired and I believe she expected me to feel the same. She wanted to rest now and she took my hand and moved us towards the bed. As she undressed I glimpsed a sad smile upon her face and she whispered, "Then my hat must still be there."

CHAPTER TWELVE

To Paris

Thus, was Mariana's tale of the ancient city of Alexandria. She was, in fact, to visit there again, one more time.

But now I should return to my previous narrative.

Having been requisitioned and blessed by the Comte de St Germain, my father set off for Paris. He fondly had in mind that he would find the girls, counsel them about their bad company, and even offer some friendly advice to their father.

He had also planned, whilst in Paris, to call upon his friend and fellow artist, Gustave Moreau, whose little watercolour was always admired by our guests as they passed through our entrance hall. Both the Marques and Saint Germain had remarked upon it, and both had intimated some acquaintance with the upcoming artist.

I am indebted now to the splendid writing of Crawfy, who recorded the most detailed accounts of the events befalling my family. Her diaries encompassed each and every day, and all noted down in her expressive, yet clear, hand. To the details were added her own thoughts and observations, all of which were insightful and pertinent. She wasted not a word.

Crawfy had first begun to write things down, years before, when her involvement with my father became romantic. At that time, she just wished to record and celebrate his success as an artist, knowing that his work was significant enough to need and deserve a place in the archives of British art. This bare-bones account developed into a far more expansive project, particularly when she discovered that she really enjoyed writing and guessed that she had an aptitude for it as well. Unlike some of her contemporary "stunners," back in London when she was my father's much envied model, she was not an uneducated working-class girl who had been "discovered" in the street. In fact, she came from a lower middleclass family that greatly valued education. Her father, who had adored her, had seen to it that she was taught well and was so liberal minded and loving towards his daughter that he even found a place for her to attend art classes, where, through her teacher, she was introduced to my father. He, with his youthful charm, coaxed her into becoming his special model.

As to her own art, it became apparent that drawing and painting was not where her talents lay and her life within the arts became more one of modelling and enjoying the company of a charismatic bunch of young artists, whilst, at the same time, she cared, dutifully, for her widowed father.

I should mention that her friend and fellow model, Elizabeth Siddal, did become a most adept artist, and it was on Lizzie's tragic death that Crawfy wrote one of her fullest and most emotional diary entries. That, however, pre-dates our story here.

I will not even attempt a precis, or to give my own rendition of the narrative that evolves in her diaries, but will present the account exactly as she wrote it.

It will be clear that the "Edward" referred to is the Christian name of my father, and sometimes "Eddy." I will exclude any days from the diary that do not concern this present narrative.

Saturday, 12th November 1864

I have just seen Edward off in his cab. It will take him to the docks and from there he will take the steamer to Calais.

We cannot tell how long this mission will take, but we have assumed no longer than a few days. He must make contact with the Mercier girls and now that we are acquainted with the influence of the Marques de Mansura, he will do everything within his power to shield the girls from such a dangerous man. My memory of this gentleman's visit leaves me sure that it will be no easy task. He exudes a sense of ownership of the twins; something that seems to excite Marguerite, but leaves Mariana in fear and despair.

My view is that the Comte de St Germain, despite his good intentions and apparent clairvoyance, has pitched Edward headfirst into a project that he should have seen to himself. He professes his care for the girls and it is he who knows the full, dangerous power of his nemesis. But off he rushes on more important business, leaving us "holding the baby."

I would feel more anger towards him if it were not for his great gifts. Those wonderful and blissful dreams that he spun around us. Eddy truly believed that he was in deep conversation with his hero, Leonardo. And for me—to embrace the mother that I had never known—what greater and more loving gift could there be? I can still savour her sweet smell and feel the warmth of her body. That will be mine for ever. Even young James was transported to a special place that he will remember all his life.

Edward will call upon the girls' father. A wise move, I think, and we should surely enlist true, parental authority and patronage against the dark father that is the Marques. If only this actual father had shown more interest in the welfare and safety of his daughters. His liberal attitude feels more like negligence. As a girl, I suppose I too enjoyed an unusual freedom, but I knew that my father always had me completely in mind.

So, Edward departs, and I might well enjoy some time to myself, though James will need my attention. I think we will have some outings. He never tires of visiting the ruined Abbey and I am sure he will pull me along there, and probably, once again, he will insist that we go after dark. I think he likes to see how much it scares me—poor woman that I am. I am sure that one day someone will use the Whitby Abbey for a terrific, scary story.

Monday, 14th November 1864

A telegram from Edward. He is in Paris and settled in his hotel. He says that the Channel gave his ship a merciless crossing so that many of the passengers spent their time leaning over the railings. Not him though—rather proudly—according to his brief message.

He had already sent ahead to the Mercier father from Whitby, and though there was no reply, he expects to be received there tomorrow.

Decorum would allow no less, though M. Mercier seems to be an ever-absent character. I do hope that he is not complicit in some way with the Marques. That idea has just come to me! I feel shocked to have even thought it. Surely my imagination has got the better of me. But all is so unknown.

And why did Edward not include his hotel address in the telegram? He would usually do so. Well, I must wait to hear more.

I know that he expects the twins to be at their family home, since we heard no mention from them of newly planned trips. Despite the circumstances, he will be so pleased to see them. Will all go to plan? If it were not for what we know about the Marques de Mansura, I would expect so. Eddy also wants to visit some artist and writer friends in Paris. It is a little reward for him for his good deed towards the girls. For that he will extend his stay for a week and then he will return.

So why do I feel such unease? So much has changed since the visits of those two gentlemen. They forced us into the unexpected and cast us into the unexplained. Our sure-footed family life has been well and truly made to stumble.

Tuesday, 22nd November 1864

Nothing more from Edward. This really is strange and he should know better. I do not fret easily—well, I don't make it a habit—but he will surely realise that I need to hear something. Perhaps he has quickly seen to the business with the Merciers and is now indulging himself in the studios of his friends. He had already arranged his visit to Monsieur Moreau. He admires him greatly as an artist and believes that he will have a great future. We both saw his "Oedipus and the Sphinx" this year at the French Salon and it truly is a magnificent piece of work. I have seen the same from Ingres, which was very good too, but much more about thoughtfulness, whereas Moreau's is all about strangeness!— which seems better to me. In the Moreau, the Sphinx seems to be an altogether feminine challenge to the handsome, male Oedipus and I rather like that. I wonder what it says about M. Moreau? Eddy then told me all about "chimeras." And now I think about it, he probably sees the twins as the chimera twins! Or is it just Marguerite? But then Mariana has her unworldliness. Now, Dear Private Diary, I shall risk telling you that I had a vivid dream of myself with Marguerite and we were extremely, physically intimate, and I awoke quite shaken by the pleasure of it. Then, as the day wore on, I became less sure whether it had been Marguerite who caressed me, or whether it was Mariana. I have had to conclude that there may not be a concrete answer to that and I am happy to leave it that way. Perhaps I'm becoming used to uncertainty!

Not with Eddy though—and I feel very cross with him.

Thursday, 24th November 1864

A letter has arrived—not from Edward—but from Tennyson.

In his normal fashion, he has announced that he will be arriving to visit us and has stated the date—a week from now! I immediately wrote back to him to ward off his visit. We certainly get on and I'm quite aware that he appreciates me as a woman, but I do not think that I would be the main reason for his visit. I expect that he is still on the Isle of Wight and I just hope that my letter reaches there in time. Otherwise, it will just have to be him and me. Perhaps young James could act as a chaperone!

But I have no news from Edward. I should, at least, have had another telegram and even, by now, a letter.

Does a lack of trust come into my thoughts? I know that Edward gets easily carried away—and he likes the girls very much—and they are very pretty—and Paris! And his artist friends there, some of whom only seem to live for their senses!

No. I will trust him. My worry is far more about that dreadful Marques. Cunning black eyes and such superiority. I dislike him the more I think about him.

Friday, 2nd December 1864

Tennyson arrived! My letter failed to reach him—apparently—and if it did, he clearly felt it was still worth coming. And so, here he is.

I have to say that I know well when men find me interesting—and when it is not only their liking for my personality! But Mr Tennyson, Alfred, acts with all the decorum proper to a gentleman.

He seems not troubled at all by the lack of Edward, and he has taken over the smaller drawing room and has even been working there. James is completely thrilled. He finds the poet, with his wild and gypsy-like appearance, quite fascinating. In thrall to him really, and he feels so honoured that the Poet Laureate shares with him his thoughts and ideas.

And, I admit, that I too have enjoyed the privilege of sitting next to our fireside, in the comfort of my home, and receiving a private rendition of his verses, delivered in such a delightful deep voice and with the liveliest of presentation. Perhaps, in this, he and I enjoy the pleasures of romance in a way that puts no pressure on his marital status, or mine as Edward's special partner. Anyway, I expect that he is most content in his marriage to Emily, and if we do ever visit them on the Isle of Wight, I shall be very pleased to meet her.

His visit has also given me the chance to speak about my anxieties about Edward. There has still been no communication. I really cannot talk to James about this as I know it would worry him.

Tennyson though, has been very good. Full of reassurance. He does, though, have some concern, but it is for Mariana. His last visit coincided with the stay of the twins and he was quite taken by them, especially Mariana, who had shown a naïve, but sincere affinity towards his poetry and had even ventured to show him some of hers. Her first attempts, I believe.

But at the heart of it, is her name, and he felt there were too many coincidences. He just couldn't break free from his belief that the deeply mournful and tragic Mariana of his poem, written before this one was even born, had doomed her to the same tragic end, and he found too much in her disposition to match the melancholic subject of his creation. He confessed that "our" Mariana was exactly as he had imagined his own.

I would, more readily, have countered such wild assertions and scolded him for being the victim of his own imagination, if it were not for the recent events that have shaken my belief in the "normal" and undermined my dependence on any sense of time that tick-tocks along in the expected way.

Friday, 9th December 1864

Another week and still no news. Tennyson left three days ago. He could tell how worried I was and realised reassurances were now past their date of value. He has offered to write to some Paris contacts to see if they have heard anything within the artists' circle and even to see if someone will go to the Mercier house.

But he also shook me with a flat statement. It was his parting remark. "Why not go to Paris yourself? Go and find him."

Here I was, forlorn and helpless, in the most passive state, anxiously waiting for even a modicum of news, when actually—yes—I can go and look for him! Alfred Tennyson's statement gave me the confidence, and though I'd rather not admit it, the permission.

Our maid will look after the daily needs of James. I shall declare to him that I wish to spend a few days in Paris with his father as a holiday—though he is a bright boy and I expect he knows that my anxiety is playing its part. He, too, has witnessed our weird and provocative guests and had to join us in the twists and turns of a road that hitherto had been so straight (though I would never wish to say, narrow!).

I shall begin to make arrangements for my departure. If a letter comes, all this may be stopped. I would be hugely relieved to find that all was well and my anxieties unfounded. And yet I can feel something new. It flies in the face of all my concerns. I realise that a cancellation of my trip would leave me very disappointed. It has begun to excite me.

Tuesday, 13th December 1864
Paris

My crossing was easier than Edward's. That was the main news in his only telegram. His rather smug satisfaction at being the only one not to be sea-sick.

I am sure that I am right in my wish to find him and give him any support that he needs. Assuming that I do find him. He knows Paris well and some of the artists' communities, and indeed there will be some there who remember me, though my visits are rare now. But my main destination is the Mercier family home. Surely there is some certainty to that.

I feel proud to have made this trip and for not subsiding into the expected role of the "distressed wife," wringing her hands and dutifully submitting to uncertainty, whilst the man in question may well be up to high jinks. I love him very much and I know that he loves me, but he is so much in thrall to romance and to aesthetics and he absolutely loves women. Indeed, they *are* his aesthetic. And I know I've been the beneficiary of that, and in ways I admire him for it. God knows how he has put up with painting all those portraits of crusty old men. I suppose because they eventually get him to paint their young wives and daughters. They certainly are his best pictures. But his best work

91

ever was that one of the twins. Poor Edward, perhaps he should have stayed with the Rossetti gang, but he was just so good at renditions and they pay so well.

If he is erring at the moment, I will soon enough forgive him, but I will certainly put a stop to it.

I have a nice room in the Hotel du Vieux, near enough to the cafés where he may be having his morning coffee. Assuming that he is safe— I am quite forgetting how worried I have been.

The Mercier house is not close, but in the morning I will take a cab and begin my search right there, at their front door. I am most interested to see inside the home that produced such intriguing daughters.

CHAPTER THIRTEEN

La Maison Mercier

Continuing from the diary of Jane Crawford
Wednesday, 14th December 1864
Paris

T his is going to be hard. I can see it. All the excitement of travelling alone to Paris made me far too frivolous. My visit to the Mercier house has put a stop to that.

I arrived there at mid-morning. That was my plan—to give the occupants time to rise, but to catch them before they went out.

The house clearly belongs to a wealthy family. I was struck, though, by its bare face. Everything at the front all flat, as if the architect had suffered an especially austere mood when he made the design. And no doubt that my first impression was increased by my reception.

Which was nothing. The bell sounded—harshly—and my knock upon the door gave that empty echoing sound that never bodes well for a visitor. No response. I lingered by the door and then despairing of such a fruitless visit, I went back down the steps and onto the street. And then I heard, and only just, a rapping upon glass. I looked back at the house and could see nothing. The great windows returned my gaze with a blank stare. But then, high up, from a tiny window on the very top floor, I caught some movement. There was the face of a woman, and though just a misty apparition through the glass, I could see that it was indeed she who was knocking. She was moving her arm as if beckoning me and so, with a vestige of hope, I climbed back up the steps and stood stationary in front of the great, black, front door.

There was the echo, which grew louder, of footfall upon hard floors and then much rasping of bolts and of the turning of keys in locks, before the door swung open. It was Mariana.

I had forgotten what a lovely girl she is. But then part of that loveliness was in the sheer pleasure we had in seeing each other. I was so relieved that my journey was not to be wasted, a relief that was mirrored in her own expression.

But such enjoyment was to be brought to an end when we spoke. The house that I entered was luxurious with fine furniture, paintings, and oriental rugs, but amongst all that abundance was a lack of warmth. A dour aesthetic that repeated the building's blank façade and it reminded me that the twin girls had lost their mother at a very early age, and as I stepped forward and looked around I felt that I was seeing the evidence of a lack; the lack of a maternal eye and hand.

A wave of compassion swept through me, as I too, had grown up without a mother, though I had been much compensated by the love of my father, a love and care that did not exist for these girls. Their father, as was clearly the case just then, was always away.

Mariana in her soft voice and in her excellent English, with its lilting accent, told me that she was so pleased to see me. She led me into a reception room and then, as if she had sensed my thoughts, "I apologise—my father cannot be here, and I expect you wanted to speak with him. His work takes him all over Europe. He has been gone for three weeks and will not return for a month." And with a plaintive resignation, which brought tears to my eyes, "And so, it is just me. And Madame Crawfy, I am so glad that you are here. And how bad of us that you were not admitted when you arrived. We have one maid in her sickbed and another who is out now, and is shopping. And I no longer open the door myself—it might be him."

I had no need to ask her who the "him" might be.

"And Marguerite?"

"Perhaps with him. I do not know. She has her own way. I have not seen her for a week—no—even nine days. But have you come for me or are you searching for Monsieur Edward?"

I saw the anxiety in her eyes and her need to know that she played at least some part in my visit. We were still standing in the middle of the room. I reached out and took her hands and was about to reassure her when she continued, "Monsieur Edward came. He knocked and rang—just like you, but I feared to answer and then through the window I saw it was him, but he was already in the street and was walking away. I hit the glass so hard that it almost broke, but he did not hear and he did not look back."

For me, this was bad news indeed. For Mariana, it seemed just another of life's disappointments. She went to make tea. I had no wish to wait sitting in the drawing room and so I followed her. We passed through the dining room which even increased my sense of gloom, as all the curtains were drawn. I expect they look on to the gardens at the rear. Was this a sign of a house hardly lived in, or was it to give extra reassurance against the sudden appearance of the Marques, one who took pleasure in emerging in the most unexpected ways?

When we reached the kitchen, I pulled a chair up to the great scrubbed table and sat. Mariana spoke as she made the tea. "He had already come between us, before our visit to your Whitby. I thought that in your house we would have respite, but he still found us. Maybe Marguerite had told him, but I think he finds us anyway. Marguerite was pleased to see him—so much had already happened—more than you could know. If I told you that he took us to Alexandria as it was when the Pharaohs ruled, would you believe me? That was where he cut us down the middle and did the most terrible unkindness to me. He denied me entrance to a temple into which he welcomed her."

I felt that it would be unkind to show Mariana the disbelief that was my immediate reaction to "Egypt of the Pharaohs" and to a "temple," and yet so much that is strange has already happened. But, surely, in this, there must be some deception, some mind trickery of the Marques. I tried to look encouraging. I wanted her to continue.

"It was there that he cut us apart and did such cruelty to me. He allowed Marguerite an entrance, but he denied it to me. A place that I knew would have beauty—a temple of Aphrodite—of love. I just believe—I cannot know—but all my senses tell me—I think it, but I feel it too …" And here she placed both hands to her abdomen. "For me it would have made a completeness, a fulfilment for my whole life."

As she spoke, I became painfully aware of the separation between the two girls. Her sadness was so profound, as if a rich and vital element had been scooped out of her, especially, and in its most complete way, by whatever happened in Alexandria, and it seemed to me that it mattered little whether it was in our year of 1864 or the time of the Pharaohs and the pyramids.

Yet in no way did it seem that I was talking to a vacuum within an empty shell. Something resides in Mariana which is of great quality. In a mournful way, thinking of his tragic poem, Tennyson sensed it. Edward felt it when he painted Mariana in the water of the lake, whilst Marguerite stood her ground upon the earth. And I felt overwhelmed with a feeling of love, so that without any pause, I rose from my chair—indeed, so suddenly that I heard it fall back behind me, and I went to where she still stood and embraced her, and held her close. Despite her pain, there was no stiffness or resistance in her body, which relaxed into a closeness with my own. Her head was upon my shoulder and as she raised it, her hair brushed my cheek and I felt its softness, mingled with the dampness from her tears.

"Madame Crawfy, you have come to be kind to me. This I know, but you have not only come for that."

My hands still rested upon her shoulders and our faces were close together. "Yes, though it was care for you, it was also for your sister, and it was also to find my Edward."

"You must find Edward, Crawfy. He will be searching for us and I fear where his search may lead him."

I wanted to stay with Mariana. To leave then would have been wrong, even though I shared her worry and knew that I must now search hard for Edward. I wanted to find out more; about her and her sister, and her family. I did not even want to let go of her physically. If one can exude the need for love, then surely she is such a one. She has nothing of that grasping way that so often engenders aversion and repudiation rather than love. Instead, I felt captivated by her need.

Is this, her pliant, loveable self, part of some strange formula? One that requires to be tested to the point of destruction, by the selfishness of Marguerite and the Marques?

I did stay longer; for the rest of the day, until the little windows, high up in the basement kitchen began to darken. She told me how only one child had been expected; how even within the womb, Marguerite had claimed the space. Their mother was not able to feed them from the breast and could hardly muster the strength to care for them. She was a woman beset by illness and pneumonia took her life before her daughters were 1 year old. Amidst the tragedy, there was, within the family, a dark humour, that no one could survive the sheer force of the infant and child that was Marguerite. The twins had separate wet nurses, as Marguerite's would soon flee to escape from a ferociously hungry infant whose bright pink gums would bite deeply into the nipple and who would suck as if the very purpose of her existence required the complete emptying of the breast. Her success in this engendered no sense of guilt, as Marguerite's growing appetite for the offerings of the world retained the same ruthless greed that had sent her nurses to find a more normal infant.

In her teens, she welcomed the realisation of her attractiveness to men, and to women, and took growing delight in extracting as much pleasure and power from her physical attributes as was humanly possible. And it was not only her physical beauty, as she possessed a wit and a sharp intelligence that appealed greatly to men, whether through the challenge thrown down to their potency, or from a latent wish to submit that found in her a perfect domination.

And watching from the wings and just occasionally sharing the stage, was her twin Mariana; just as beautiful and just as clever, but with far less sense of entitlement and power, so that she was regarded as her sister's benign shadow; one who would also have caused fascination, if not for the charisma of Marguerite that reached into every corner of any drawing room, gallery, or ballroom in which the two girls made their graceful appearance. The fascination was at first for the apparition of two young women of striking appearance and so impossibly identical. From that point on, it became evident that one was to be the main voice for the two. Not that Mariana was lacking in conversation or in interest in the world and culture, but she felt no impulse to push aside her sister or to bathe in the tremendous attention that the girls attracted. As well as this, she did not share her sister's delight in flirtation and in the subtle seductions that can fuel a conversation, elements that with a sanguine resignation, she saw as being too evident within their social discourse. She would sometimes long for a conversation that existed solely for its subject matter.

She listened to Marguerite's tales of actual amorous encounters with a fascination, and within the subtle power of their twinship, she enjoyed a vicarious pleasure that she was happy to leave her sister to provide. She was still clinging to all that they shared and this faith kept at bay the anxiety of separation and the jealousy that would, in time, prevail.

As the reality of their difference was increasingly felt, she could fall into times of deep loneliness, though it was no clear thing that Marguerite had abandoned her. The two could still be drawn back into the intimacy of their childhood and at such times would be warmly merged, sharing their discontent or their happiness, lying upon a bed, or slowly strolling, arm in arm, through the streets or parks of Paris.

Perhaps I have become the mother that Mariana lost at such an early age. She spoke to me with such openness about her life and her feelings and with great trust in me. I expect that she became attached when they stayed with us in Whitby. It can be a powerful experience at that age to stay with a family, especially a happy one such as ours.

She had not lit a lamp in the kitchen, so that we sat almost in the dark. It was as if it suited her mood, though I believe there was no conscious intent. She had become lost within the deeply personal history she had shared. We climbed the stairs and found the passage way that led to the front door. I was in front and I turned. Mariana had withdrawn now, as if our parting was yet another sadness. She stood a few feet away. In the dark hallway I could only see the outline of her body and above that the pale oval of her face. Within the oval there was the movement of her lips, though I could not hear the whispered words.

I left her where she was. She made no sign for us to embrace. I pulled the door closed behind me, and tested it for safety. It was firm. And then I descended the few steps to the street and walked a few yards along, before pausing to take stock of where I stood and to turn for a last look at the house. I saw that a lamp had been lit, the pale light just showing through the same small window on the top floor, through which, in the morning, I had seen her face.

CHAPTER FOURTEEN

The artist Gustave Moreau

Continuing from the diary of Jane Crawford
Thursday, 15th December 1864
Paris

So, to the home of Monsieur Moreau. And I was not to be alone. In the morning, after rising, I descended the stairs of my hotel and made my way through the lounge. Protruding above the back of an armchair was a familiar head of hair. The woman sitting there was closely watching the entrance to the breakfast room and clearly waiting for someone to appear. The light brown hair that had caught my notice was the same that had brushed my cheek, dampened by tears, the previous day. It was Mariana.

I placed a hand upon her shoulder and she turned and rose.

"Madame Crawfy—I had to come as you will need me."

Of course, I protested; it had been so evident that Mariana did not feel safe, even locked away in her own home. But what she then said made complete sense. And what a fool I had been since it was something I had refused to think about: not everyone in Paris will speak English! Indeed, most will not—and my own French is—well, I should not put myself down, but it certainly is not fluent. So yes, if I am to find Edward in Paris, I will need an interpreter, and Mariana, with her care and clear thinking, had come to my rescue.

And anyway, I was so pleased to see her. I have a warm feeling that I know is maternal and comes from my childlessness and her lack of a mother—my lack of a mother as well. It is a strong mixture. But there is something else: we are also grown women, and when we embrace I sense another pleasure that merges in with the joy of caring and friendship. And why should this not be? I will not berate myself. There are times when such feeling insists on inclusion. It is unbidden, uninvited. It calls upon one; a silent visitor in the dark of night, in fitful sleep and dream, or it confronts and can shock in full daylight. It makes no introduction and no attempt to explain. If refused entry, it will bide its time. It takes no heed of normal discourse and its source is as free from our will as is nature itself. And if, in our response, we should surrender, our very helplessness pervades and extends the pleasure. And so, I will let my feelings be!

We had breakfast together and I shared with Mariana my plan for the day—that we would visit Gustave Moreau in his home. His studio has the same address, so I felt it most likely that we would find him present. I trusted that Edward would recently have been there and that from Moreau we would discover his whereabouts.

After breakfast, we hailed a cab and set off for the 9th arrondissement and the rue de la Rochefoucauld. Mariana suggested that we exit our cab some distance away as she believed I would enjoy the walk and it is, indeed, an area of great vitality. I loved the glass covered arcades and all the little shops, and the galleries too. I could see that she felt at home there and if it were not for my eagerness to track down Edward, we would have lingered, had coffee and shopped.

We arrived at 11am, an acceptable time to visit since Monsieur Moreau is known to be an extremely industrious worker who would need to make use of every hour of daylight within a mid-winter day.

The door was opened by an elderly lady. Here, I felt blessed by the presence of Mariana and shamefully realised just how hopeless was my task without her. Mariana respectfully turned to me as she spoke and gestured, so that it was clear that she was there to represent me.

There was, however, in the lady's response, no sense of greeting and her face showed only alarm and confusion. I could see that this had nothing to do with me and was completely a reaction to Mariana. It was a most troubling start, and possibly an end, to our visit. Mariana continued to introduce me and seemed to be doing all she could to counter the hard stare that confronted her. Since she was gaining no advance in this, she switched to introducing herself. This brought about a look of even greater scrutiny, though it then changed to uncertainty and eventually to a decision—and only just—to allow us into the house.

We were placed in chairs in the drawing room and a maid was sent to fetch Moreau. The woman sat with us, though clearly begrudgingly, and still with considerable discomfort. Though she did have some English, and I some French, her true conversation could only be with Mariana, but since she still regarded Mariana with suspicion, fluency did not occur and instead she took solace in turning the conversation towards me, so that our attempts to understand each other could offer distraction—until Monsieur Moreau arrived.

A nice-looking man, around 40, with dark hair, beard, and brown eyes. Judging from his smart appearance, he had not, as yet, begun work. It was clear from his words to her that the elderly lady was his mother. Despite her discomfort, I could see the easy warmth between them. As yet, he had not noticed Mariana, as it was only I who was introduced, along with the purpose of my visit. The mother then departed, giving Mariana one last, searching look before she left the room.

Moreau now turned to fully attend to us both and to my utter surprise, gazed at Mariana, and then in words I was just able to understand, "Mademoiselle, you are back! I fear that our conversation has not deterred you."

It was said calmly enough, though the underlying displeasure was clear.

Mariana knew the situation so well it was as simple to deal with as the most commonplace error. "Monsieur, you mistake me for my sister."

Mariana has an air of sincerity that would normally leave no one in doubt, but Moreau's wish to believe her was clearly undermined by the testament of his own eyes. He stood and stared, the strange circumstance allowing a scrutiny that would otherwise have been unacceptable.

His expression then changed from incredulity to interest, and from there to the beginnings of a smile.

With the benefit of Mariana's later exposition, I will attempt here to record his words.

"Well, Mademoiselle, something tells me that if you are not actually the one who called here a week ago, and you are not again attempting to raid my studio through subterfuge, then you are a very different young lady to your sister."

Moreau, had now perched himself on the edge of an armchair and was responding with increasing interest and amusement. "I have to tell you, Mademoiselle …?"

"I am Mariana," she replied.

"… that your sister called upon me, completely unannounced and caused quite a stir. She was also rude to my mother, which, for me, is unforgivable."

And then turning to me, "And Madame, I can tell you, that your husband did indeed visit me and we had a most pleasant time evoking our memories of Italy and sharing our joy in the great Quattrocento artists. We are kindred spirits, Madame, though how he survives painting all those portraits I can hardly believe. I have painted no more than a few and I will keep it that way."

All duly translated by Mariana, who was clearly beginning to enjoy her prowess as a translator. What a wonderful gift to speak many languages. I believe that she has Spanish too. If only I had such skill.

Edward has certainly travelled and loves the 15th century Italians, so I could well imagine the two enthusing about their gods! But where was he now? Apparently, he had called on Moreau just a day after the spectacular visit of Marguerite. He had then told Moreau of his reason for being in Paris, and spoke of his visit to the Mercier home and of receiving no answer. That part, of course, I already knew.

The remarkable coincidence was that Marguerite had called upon Moreau only the day before Edward's visit and had left notice of where she was staying. It was seen as enough by Edward to find her. So, after a splendid visit to his artist friend, he had left with high hopes in the pursuit of his goal.

This gave some reassurance to me, but I was troubled to see the anxiety that came upon Mariana. She was, no doubt, pleased for me, but her concern was for her sister, and so she asked the question that had also been gathering force in my own mind. How had Marguerite caused such offence in the house of Moreau? And what was she doing there anyway?

"Your question, Mademoiselle—I will try to answer—though I fear that, as the young woman is your sister, indeed your twin, I may only cause offence. Nevertheless!"

And so, we now heard the story. Marguerite had called upon the Moreau house, giving no previous notice, and upon Moreau's mother opening the door had introduced herself in the most haughty manner. She next thrust a calling card into the old lady's hand, which was quickly followed by a sealed envelope addressed to her son. She then stood motionless and unyielding upon the door step. The mother felt confronted by an irresistible force and quite mesmerised by eyes, that within the soft contours of a beautiful face, fixed her with the hard, unblinking stare of a serpent about to strike. Confused and shaken by the outlandish manner of the request, she made straight for Moreau's studio and delivered to him the envelope. It was addressed in a surprisingly light and elegant hand. He opened it and read the few words, *Monsieur, I admire you as an artist. And I am your Sphinx. Marguerite Mercier. At present—Hotel Place du Tertre.*

Such a statement, and one so germane to the subject of his celebrated painting, provoked an interest that overcame his irritation. He felt that imbedded in those few words was both an invitation and a challenge, so that the very image of his painting flashed before his eyes—Oedipus and the Sphinx locked together in the lure of their deadly combat.

He made his way from his studio to the front door where he expected to find his visitor, but no one was there. He stepped out so that he could look into the street in both directions, and there were only a few solitary figures going about their business and clearly not the "Sphinx" of the note and the Marguerite Mercier of the calling card. Disappointed, as the audacious message of the note had hit home, he closed the door and made to return to his studio. He was half way along the corridor, when he was arrested by the sound of a woman's voice. It was not his mother's. It was soft and clear and came from the adjacent drawing room and it requested his presence. He turned back, entered the room and there she was.

At this point, he paused and his gaze towards Mariana became especially intense. "I could almost say, Mademoiselle—'there you were,' but I can increasingly tell the difference—though it is not in your looks."

His strange guest sat extremely poised in the largest and most comfortable of the armchairs. As he entered, she rose and the folds of a magnificent cape fell around her to reach and lightly brush the floor. The movement of the garment and of her body lifted the air and the scent of roses reached him. "Dark roses surely," he mused, "peut-être, Les Fleurs du Mal."

In his description, Moreau could hardly contain his artist's enthusiasm. The cape was of silk and of such a deep and lustrous blue that he now felt bound to "include it in his palette." Resting upon the blue silk and glowing in silver were wide embroidered strips of an intricate floral design and the collar, edgings, and hem were of thick, black fur. The cape was fastened at the neck and the fur covered her lower chin, brushed against her cheek, and just touched her earlobes, so that her pearl earrings nestled there as if in two, soft, dark nests. And as she stepped towards him, one bare white arm reached out from beneath the cape to offer him an elegant hand that was as relaxed, yet refined, as the woman herself.

Moreau paused and for a moment his gaze turned inward as he contemplated the beautiful apparition that had graced his home. Mariana, also reflecting upon the image that he had described, looked puzzled and remarked that such a cape was unknown to her and that her sister must have recently acquired it—a gift perhaps. She added that it confirmed that Marguerite was now living in a world that was far from the one they had shared as sisters.

Moreau broke out of his reverie, raised his hands, let them fall, and declared, with some embarrassment, that he believed that for a moment he had been quite hypnotised. "Your Sister, Mademoiselle, has a most powerful way about her. But then of course, she had come as the Sphinx, and felt quite sure that I would be her Oedipus."

He had offered her refreshment, but her only interest was to accompany him to his studio. She wished to have the honour of seeing the surroundings in which the great painting had been produced. Moreau's response was subject to the aesthetic seduction that had gripped him— just as in his painting, the Sphinx has sunk her claws into the torso of Oedipus. Marguerite, her natural charisma enhanced by the precisely calculated manner of her appearance, the bare white arm suggestive that the cape covered nothing but her naked body, had for the moment complete command. There was also an inference that this woman, wearing a garment of considerable quality, might just be a potential collector of his work. And artists survive by selling their paintings. It was no regular thing for him to allow a stranger into his studio and to interrupt him when working, but Marguerite had won access. It was first round to the Sphinx.

It is very recently that Eddy and I saw the painting. He had insisted we travel to the Paris Salon to view it, as it was the greatest success of the show. There are features that I remember well. The painting is rectangular, in the portrait mode rather than the landscape, so that all is very perpendicular. Oedipus has a long staff which accentuates this. He does look magnificent; a fine figure of a man, almost naked of course with a few flimsy bits of material covering one of his legs and hiding his manhood. It is absolutely a depiction of confrontation. The Sphinx is unusually small, with the pale face and breasts of a woman, the great grey wings of an eagle, and the sinewy body and hindquarters of an animal. Strangely, she has a necklace of beads around her abdomen. With her four clawed feet she is climbing up the body of Oedipus to reach his face and stare, so they become transfixed by their mutual gaze. Beneath her, a long tail curls like a brown snake. Oedipus must find the answer to her riddle or she will destroy him. Many have passed that way before and failed.

Moreau led the way to the studio. "I always have much work in progress so there was plenty for your sister to see. Her remarks were good— I heard them as from one who knows and appreciates art. I showed her my drawings. She liked the watercolours."

It was here that it became a little clearer as to how Marguerite had discovered and become interested in the art of Moreau. Perhaps his growing reputation was a factor, but she also told him how much she had appreciated a small watercolour of his that was owned by some friends in England and she gave to him Eddie's name. This of course allowed Moreau to relax a little more before the challenge of this woman, since he well remembered Eddy's purchase of the painting.

After looking at the paintings and drawings, they had sat down and talked. Moreau had surveyed the face with the grey eyes that, disconcertingly, refused to blink. Emerging from the dissociation caused by the sudden arrival of this woman—into his life, his studio, and his routine, and the overwhelming effect of her appearance and manner—he was now trying to work out what exactly she wanted. There was, as yet, no indication of her wish to buy an artwork. His thoughts on this matter stilted his conversation, so that there was suddenly a silence between them.

The white arm appeared again and reached out to adjust the cape which was threatening to fall open. The cape was secured and the arm slipped back within. The two remained seated, with no words. Until, "Monsieur, I offer myself as your model."

I have here, indeed—I wish—to give my own assessment of Monsieur Moreau. And I believe it to be borne out by the interaction that then followed within his studio.

His colours are glorious, but mainly this man is a thinker. Clearly, he is a romantic, and quite able to express emotion. Eddy has seen another work of his—a Pietà, which he described as the most melancholic picture possible, and extremely beautiful in its mournful sadness. But the idea, the ideal, the thinking in a picture is what really matters to Moreau.

This is my view and I believe that it is why Marguerite suddenly found that things were not going her way. Oedipus was about to strike back.

Rather than take the bait and leap to the response which would have been the norm for many artists (Eddy for sure, I'm afraid—though I was always his best model) Moreau became indignant. He actually felt that the proposal of this woman was an affront to his art; as if this queenly female who was now declaring herself as his model and clearly expecting her appearance to carry all before her, felt that her personal alure would matter to him more that the content and the ideas in his painting; that she proposed herself with a sensuality that would only debase his art. He was no painter of pretty nudes for bedrooms.

As he spoke to us, his annoyance at her proposal was still evident. He had refused her point blank. This is something that Marguerite, and Mariana will know this best, does not take well. She haughtily rose and made for the door. Half way along the corridor she came up abruptly to the figure of Madame Moreau, who, hearing raised voices, had thought that her son might be calling her. It was then that Marguerite caused the unforgivable offence of insulting the old lady. She pushed her aside, so that Madame Moreau was left pinned to the wall. An indignant and increasingly angry Moreau, followed Marguerite to the door where she remained standing. Despite her behaviour, she still expected to have the door dutifully opened for her. Moreau was only too pleased to do so. There was a carriage outside that had no doubt brought the richly robed creature, a chimera indeed, and which was awaiting her exit.

The pale face and grey eyes held his gaze, just as his painted Sphinx stared into the eyes of his Oedipus. "Monsieur, you are still a great artist, but I feel that there is something that you lack. Perhaps the answer lies in your mother."

Moreau, now furious at the deprecation of a relationship that was of great affection and quality, answered, "Madame, I suspect you know little of mothers! And do not visit here again. You belong more in the studio of Félicien Rops—go there!"

I do not know of this Félicien Rops, but perhaps I will find out. I suppose he is an artist. I will ask Edward—when I find him.

I will add my own thoughts here. Maybe, it is a woman's insight. Only we can know the range and intricacy of the feelings that men have for us. My goodness, such a range. I suppose I rather pride myself in this. Perhaps, because I have always been happy to be a woman, I can consider these matters from a calm and secure plateau. I believe that

106

Monsieur Moreau may be troubled by a certain aspect of womanhood. It is one that seems to have become rather fashionable in art. In this, our fair sex is perceived as increasingly powerful and dangerous to the men that paint us. They cannot decide whether to adore or to fear us. We become the Sphinx and the chimera, the siren and the seductive assassin. I can see that the startling arrival of the chimera, Marguerite Mercier, may have caused a surge of interest: intellectual, aesthetic, but also, surely, one of desire. A desire that gradually changed to anxiety as Marguerite, with all her charms, truly became the Sphinx.

To us, though, his two female guests, Monsieur Moreau was a gentleman and as helpful as could be.

We were ready to leave and he led us to the front door. As he did so, he spoke as if thinking aloud, "I am still unsure as to what the lady, truly, wanted."

We now stood on the doorstep outside and Mariana addressed him. It was with absolute calmness and clarity. "Monsieur, my sister has left you with a riddle, and one that you have not solved. But I know her well, so I will venture the answer. I believe it to be very simple. She was inspired by your work and came to you—for adventure. One that she would have shared with you—not for long—but with an intensity that would have filled your dreams for years to come. She really did wish to be your Sphinx and to delve with you into mysteries. That is her way. You declined Monsieur, perhaps for the good, though you may also wonder about your loss."

Moreau stood, remaining thoughtful.

In our cab, Mariana sat quietly and contentedly. We bear such contradictions as human beings. The qualities of Marguerite that have caused such anguish for Mariana mix with strivings, aspirations, and practices that she also admires. With Moreau, she had just been her sister's champion.

And soon I will find my Edward. Moreau has given us the whereabouts of Marguerite—the Hotel Place du Tertre. He had told Edward too. They might well be there together.

CHAPTER FIFTEEN

Cora Pearl

Continuing from the diary of Jane Crawford
Thursday, 22nd December 1864
Paris

It is a whole week since my last entry. It will be a boon if writing can now bring some clarity and light. But how to divide this past week? The dates are there, but its time could be compressed into a few intense hours or stretched into a dreamlike expanse of months.

And in the midst of our self-absorption, there is, in London, young James and in three days-time it will be Christmas and we must rush to be with him. We have, shamefully, abandoned him. I have sent a telegram to our neighbours asking for their continued kindness in seeing that he has everything he needs. Never, before, would I have allowed myself to fail so terribly. But I do fear that—yes—I was made helpless.

I remember the first day best and I will start there. From there on, I will strive to find some order, though to make sense will be harder.

All was clear at the start; we knew where to go. Marguerite had given Moreau her address as the Hotel Place du Tertre. Moreau had passed this to us, and also to Edward. I expected we would find Marguerite there, and hopefully Edward too.

From my own hotel, I journeyed by cab to Mariana who was already waiting on the doorstep of her home. She seemed enlivened by the thought of re-joining her sister. Their separation had not been for long, yet I now know how abandoned she can feel.

Her hair was tied behind by a black, silk ribbon, and as she eagerly descended the steps, the bright rays of the winter sun burst from between two buildings and glancing upon her hair, burnished it with gold. Her face was pale from standing in the cold so that her freckles seemed more prominent, but the anticipation of the day had also brought two rosy spots to her cheeks. She threw herself into the seat beside me. It was so pleasing for me to see her smiling excitement that I wrapped my arms tightly around her and kissed her warmly upon both cheeks. And I was quite sure, in that instant, that her soft cheeks, lovely as they were, were only a substitute for her lips. But I had no wish to embarrass her.

We were both excited. She was to be reunited with Marguerite and I with my errant Edward. I was concerned, though, that we may have mis-timed our journey. It was late in the morning and though lunch would be served at the hotel, the two, either together or singly, would have many alternative venues for their mid-day meal. Edward is certainly a lover of lunch and will extend it for as long as he can. We hoped to find them, if not in the hotel, at least in a restaurant nearby.

The Hotel Place du Tertre was small but luxurious and far nicer than my own. In the reception hall everything was red, a colour that, by chance, would continue to surround us throughout the day. There was much brass, beautifully polished: candelabras, decorative objects, and upon the walls, small relief plaques that showed mythological scenes. Above us, the great propellor, dormant now in winter, reflected the light from a large crystal chandelier with a lustrous glow that reminded me of Mariana's hair in the sunlight. The richness of the décor and the warmth inside added to our anticipation and Mariana rushed to the receptionist who stood waiting to greet us.

My French was good enough for me to understand their exchange and its content was also clear from the disappointment that clouded Mariana's face. "The Englishman and Mademoiselle Mercier left for luncheon with a gentleman and lady who called for them this morning."

Mariana asked for more details. Who were the two others and did he know their destination?

"The lady, I recognise as Madame Pearl. The gentleman, who was dark haired and I believe, not French, I do not know. Nor Mademoiselle, do I know their chosen place for lunch, but Madame Pearl is well known to favour the Café Anglais."

I saw Mariana's flush of expectation turn to pallor as she heard of the dark haired and "not French" gentleman. She seemed to wilt and I felt a churning in my own stomach.

And the questions now arose. Edward was in Paris to warn the girls of the danger of the Marques, yet was about to have lunch with him. And one of those he had come to protect was to be there too. And who was this Madame Pearl? The name sounded English.

At least we knew that the Café Anglais was a likely place to find them and we set off immediately. It was in walking distance and we strode purposefully, though we shared an unhappy silence, each of us absorbed in our troubled thoughts.

The restaurant was located in a large building on the corner of the Boulevard des Italiens and the rue de Marivaux. There were four stories with attic rooms and a wild array of chimneys upon the roof. Though some upper windows benefitted from the decorative addition of shutters, the structure seemed austere. Not so, the interior; the furniture in dark, lustrous mahogany and softer shades of walnut, gleamed beneath the dazzle of chandeliers and the reflected light from giant, gilded mirrors.

We were immediately confronted by the restaurant's host. He looked delighted to see us, as if we were his most favoured guests, though neither of us were known to him. I did, though, catch the moment of surprise and partial recognition as he glanced at Mariana before supressing his wish to look more closely. I am becoming familiar with this reaction and I know that it means that her sister has recently been present. Recovering from his momentary lapse, he was again efflorescent with welcome. He would, with great pleasure, find us a table—"Madame and Mademoiselle"—and he ventured that we must surely be sisters and so it must be a family occasion. The over-familiarity was delivered with such panache that its flattery overcame the offence.

Mariana was only intent on finding her sister. She interrupted him whilst he was in full flow—we were not there to have lunch—but we were intent on finding some family members who may be his guests. She gave the description, along with the name of Madame Pearl.

The host's delight in seeing us was in no way diminished by our wish not to dine. In fact, there was much compensation in Mariana's description of the four we were seeking, and especially in the mention of Madame Pearl. With another glance at Mariana, this time with open recognition, all seemed complete, and requesting us to follow, he turned swiftly with the elegance of a dancer and guided us to a doorway set apart from the dining room.

We had already seen the luxury of the restaurant and this was continued, even in the staircase that rose before us. Though the space was narrow, it had not prevented the hanging of paintings, some large and all with heavy ornate frames. Our shoulders brushed against them as we ascended. They were mostly of women, resting upon couches or within leafy bowers, hardly clothed or naked, and all in the rococo style. The carpet was red and of the deepest pile so that each footfall sunk into a cushion from which it sprung lightly to the next step. If we had made any sound, it would surely have been muffled to silence within the closed space. Light came from high above; a chandelier upon the top floor perhaps, so that a soft light descended, just enough to allow the paintings to be viewed.

At the first floor, we entered a corridor with several doors. The host seemed sure of his destination, and reaching a door that was half way along, he grasped with one hand it's highly polished handle and with the other knocked gently but firmly. As he paused for the response, he looked round to us and I saw in his face an easing of formality and an invitation to intimacy, even collusion. It was unwelcome, and it filled me with discomfort and unease.

From inside came the call, "Entrée!"

Mariana recognised the voice. She turned to me with an imploring look. A longing for a relief that could in no way be given. We had sought this meeting and there was no turning back.

The door swung open. The host gestured towards the interior and with a nod of his head, stepped back into the corridor. We were not to see him again.

The doorway was a place of impasse, as if to cross into the room was to make a long journey to a destination no longer desired. The two of us stood motionless, looking in. And in that moment, I had the strangest impulsive thought. It came and went in an instant, but in those seconds I knew that I loved Mariana more than Edward. And then, I surveyed the scene before us.

The room was large enough for dining. An elegant, mahogany table was covered with white linen and lace. Ornate dining chairs surrounded it and their seats were of red silk. There was much red in the wall covering too, with floral patterns in green and gold. There were no windows and there was an intense smell of fine perfume. The paintings on the walls remained in the rococo style, and whilst the staircase paintings had suggested the erotic these had no ambiguity. The Classical romances of mythology provided the content.

A chandelier, far too large for the room, hung from the centre of the ceiling. Only some of its candles were lit, so the light was soft, barely reaching to the corners.

There were two couches, both in powder blue silk with gold brocade and with pink cushions. They were against adjacent walls and each faced the door, as did the four people who sat upon them. All four were staring at us in complete silence.

Upon one couch sat Marguerite and Don Angel, the Marques de Mansura. Marguerite's arm was around him. On the other, sat Edward and a woman. She was in her 30s and had red hair. In that opening moment I noticed her more than the others. I am not sure why. Perhaps, because she was sitting with Edward, though she was not the one I had come to see.

It was, of course, the Marques who spoke first—always in control. "Mariana, how wonderful! You have come to see us. Such a surprise— and you have discovered us here in our special haunt!"

Marguerite Mercier rose from the couch. She was wearing a dress of emerald green. Her arms and shoulders were bare and it was no dress for the cold of winter. The room, though, was warm and Mariana and I were wearing our heavy coats. The contrast was striking. Marguerite walked easily to her sister and embraced her. Mariana could hardly respond and stood stiff within the embrace, her hands moving only to clasp her sister's waist.

The Marques remained relaxed upon the couch. His black eyes were alive with interest. He was dressed as a gentleman of the highest society.

He beckoned to Mariana to join him upon the couch and, as one hypnotised, and surely against her free will, she complied. Her sister was content to take a dining chair to sit beside them. She looked completely at ease.

Such could not be said of Edward. The shock of our sudden entry had left him spell-bound. I was dismayed to find that I felt no pleasure in our reunion. I had expected to fall into his arms. If I felt anything, it was anger.

There was no discomfort in the woman who sat beside him. She rested easily upon the cushions. I saw that she had freckles, just like the twins. What a thing to notice in that moment.

Her hair was a dark red, almost auburn, and her face pale and powdered, and can I say beautiful? No, I believe not, yet as soon as she spoke, it was filled with such warm expression that it was hard to look away. Her body seemed completely relaxed, absolutely known and lived in. If one knows physicality, and I do, one can tell these things in an instant. The mind and the body are one.

She was the next to speak. A bare arm separated from the deep blue abundance of her dress and a diamond bracelet slipped along her wrist just enough to catch the light from the chandelier. She turned her head and the diamond pendants of her earrings swung and there was the flash of their reflected light. The head, poised above a long neck, also bedecked with diamonds, turned towards us, and with a look of pleasure at the unexpected, she asked, "And who will introduce us?"

I knew that this was an English woman. The French was good, but the accent was there.

Edward now found his voice and with it a relative composure. I could see that he was trying hard to recover. I could also see that there were the beginnings of a pleasure in seeing me—and, no doubt, in seeing Mariana as well. He cleared his throat and began to speak, probably to make the introductions, but he was resolutely interrupted by the Marques, who seemed to be revelling in the unforeseen events and the discomfort that some of us were feeling. He assumed the authority of the host, or perhaps, more evocatively, the ring master. I can well imagine him standing grandly in the ring, cracking the whip and having lesser creatures perform to his will.

He now spoke in English, delivered in a Spanish accent that was so pronounced that I was sure that it was mannered. All part of the game, I expect. "We have three English here, two French, and one Spanish. With respect to our dear ladies of Paris," and he turned to the twins, "though we are guests in your native city, let the language be English. It is one we can all speak and understand—and is it not so, Cora, that the customs of the English are the toast of Paris, a trait that you have no doubt enhanced?"

Madame Pearl replied in English, "Angel, the language that I understand so well, is that of flattery, since all around me speak it. A language in which you sir, are most fluent."

I was surprised. Her voice had a distinct west country burr. So strange from a woman who seemed to embody the very verve and style of Paris.

The Marques clearly enjoyed the touché of his English friend. He then returned to the formalities. "Mainly, we have already met. Madame Crawford, I remember you so well and you welcomed me so warmly, when I landed on your doorstep, like a bird from the sky. And you allowed me into your home to visit my good friends the twins Mercier." And as he turned again towards them, he grasped the hand of Mariana who still sat beside him.

My own thoughts were of complete resistance to his assumptions of a warm welcome. We had been overcome by the suddenness of his visit. I was also aware, as I considered his overture to me, that he would surely have in mind my unclothed figure in the painting he had admired so much in our vestibule.

Returning his gaze to me and then to Madame Pearl, "And here, Madame Crawford, is Madame Cora Pearl, an English lady like yourself and one, whom I might say, is also blessed by those qualities of beauty and grace that fate has so kindly bestowed upon you.

"And Cora, my dear, meet Madame Crawford who is the wife of our splendid resident artist, Monsieur Edward."

It made little difference to me that the Marques had assumed Edward and I were married. I expect he knew the true status anyway. I was more concerned about the term "resident artist." I looked towards Edward with an alarm that was surely evident.

The Marques noticed, and continued, "Madame Crawford has been an inspiration to Monsieur Edward," and I knew then that he was, indeed, thinking of the painting, "As, my dear Cora, you will be an inspiration to him now."

The Marques, a master of timing as well as of time, allowed the implication to hover. Then, before either Edward or I could find words, he reduced the tension. "Because Edward has agreed to paint our beautiful Cora. The renowned painter of portraits has descended upon Paris at the perfect time. At least two gentlemen of great wealth are longing for a portrait. Will it be the Duc de Rivoli, or Prince Achille Murat, or someone else!? Perhaps Edward, you can paint several portraits and retire on the proceeds! And what a pleasure for you to paint the most famous woman in Paris."

It was clear to me now that Cora Pearl was a courtesan of the highest strata, and judging from the fortune in diamonds that were strewn upon her person, I could see that in the Paris of the "Demi-monde," she might well be the most famous woman.

I have a keen sense of those feminine qualities that appeal to men. Sometimes, I, too, find them appealing. I could see that this self-assured woman could summon a man to her bedroom with the slightest of gestures. Partly by sophisticated design and partly by inherent ability. I have heard, as well, how such courtesans, through their very indifference, can reduce great men to puppies and bring great fortunes to ruin. I feared for Edward—and for us.

Edward was now standing. His absence and non-communication had been given a little credence by the Marques. Clearly, he had been conducting business of a kind, though he still had much to explain. He slid two dining chairs away from the table so that we could sit upon them together. "Jane, I am so sorry. I have lost myself these past few days. I have begun Cora's portrait and you know how I become when I am working."

My response was crisp, and as yet, unforgiving. "And where do you paint? You have no studio here."

He coloured. "Madame Pearl has kindly allowed me a room in her home. It is the easiest way—a convenience for us both."

We had now become as the central figures upon a stage.

"And does Marguerite visit you there?"

Marguerite now interjected in such a way that I remembered how charming she could be. "Madame Crawfy, it is such a delight to see you here and with my darling sister. I think that you have been caring for her. I am so pleased that you have found us. But please do not chide Monsieur Edward. He has been offered a huge sum to paint a very famous lady—how could he say no? And yes, I do see him as I am often now the guest of Madame Cora. And you must stay with us too. We will have a wonderful adventure. Don Angel has a splendid idea and you could have a special part in it."

With little understanding of what I was saying, the words spilled out, "An adventure like Alexandria?"

Even the Marques looked surprised, but Marguerite showed no reaction. "I can only hope so Madame Crawfy, and I know that you will enjoy it."

Unlike Edward, who seemed already in a trance, I was not impressed by the proposal and had no wish to be caught up in it. I did not realise that the first coils of influence were already circling around me.

My reply to Marguerite was more than straight forward and also conveyed a sharp rebuke to Edward. "Marguerite, Edward came to Paris to give you advice. He did not come for adventure. He has also left his seventeen-year-old son alone in England and it will soon be Christmas!"

I did not look at Edward, but I knew that my words would have collided with his plans. This was not the Edward that I have loved and admired. For him to have forgotten about James and Christmas showed me that he had already profoundly, lost his way.

If the Count St Germain could spin us into different worlds—marvellous ones, this nemesis of his, the Marques de Mansura, could do the same; yet into places that were far darker—and would he bring us back? Marguerite was now his handmaiden, and Edward—some kind of servant?

Cora Pearl then addressed me. "Madame Crawford—I believe it is 'Crawfy' n'est-ce-pas? Come and join us tomorrow. Don Angel has rented a most interesting and unusual house and we will have a wonderful party there. You must come—it is so good for me to have a woman from England to talk to. Please, Crawfy, you must!"

As she was speaking, she rose. I saw the full figure of the courtesan: the more than ample breast, the slim waist, the graceful, ease of movement. She came to me and placed a hand on each of my shoulders. She leant forward and her face was close to mine and she looked me directly in the eyes. Hers were smiling and they sparkled like the diamonds that gently swung from her ears. Her hair was held back from her face and the eyes, set far apart, confirmed a look of complete openness. She was so close that it seemed that I was only breathing her perfume and then it was no longer just perfume, but the very essence of the woman.

I heard words and saw that her lips were moving. "But I cannot let you have your Edward tonight. He will paint me by candlelight. And then tomorrow he will paint me in the morning and we will see which we prefer—Cora by day, or Cora by night. And maybe one can go to my dear Plon-Plon* and the other to—well, whoever will pay the most."

There was no will in me to resist. And if I could be so overwhelmed in an instant, what hope was there for Edward? That night he would be with Cora Pearl, and probably Marguerite too.

I felt a growing weariness; a great heaviness came upon me. I gazed at the couches with their soft cushions and could have laid myself down and just lightly slept—and perhaps Cora would stroke my hair—such a lovely woman. I wondered whether all the room's paintings contained visions of her. My eyes rested upon one that was of a sunset. Nymphs were resting on the grass. Nearby, a shepherd played a flute. And there was a satyr amongst them. Not soft and beautiful like the nymphs, or like Cora, and yes, of course, not like Mariana, but dark and rough and with a great shaggy main. It sniffed the air—almost an animal—and, without doubt, as I felt desire, there was thrust into my mind the figure of the Marques.

It was the very shock of my vision and of its wish that brought me back from my strange dream.

And I could hear the voice of Marguerite. Such an ordinary statement, "Crawfy, will you join us now for lunch?"

A new person had entered the room. It was a waiter. There was the clink of glasses and the rattle of cutlery. Perhaps it was the waiter who made the difference, someone from the outside world. The trance was broken. I remembered that there was a world to return to.

I looked to Mariana. "Shall we go now? Will you come?"

She did not move. She still sat beside the Marques. Marguerite had leant towards her and was holding her hand.

Was the Marques watching me in triumph? I believe so. I knew that Edward was no match for him, but I had just an inkling that in some way I may be, and that this interested him. His power, though, is very great, and that of the Pearl woman too.

"Tomorrow my carriage will come for you," she said and laughed. "It is so lovely to have met you."

I gave the address of my hotel and made for the door. There was no sound from Edward. My aloneness felt shameful. They were there, enclosed in their special room with their collusive wishes and thoughts, and I just an awkward creature in a foreign city. My legs trembled as I descended the stairs. My knees were weak. Half way down, I stumbled and for steadiness, grasped the heavy frame of a painting. From the canvas, the cool face of a naked courtesan observed me. And the perfume of Cora Pearl was still in the air, and in my hair, and my clothes.

*Plon-Plon—the nickname of Napoléon-Jérôme Bonaparte.

CHAPTER SIXTEEN

The green fairy

Continuing from the diary of Jane Crawford
Friday, 23rd December 1864
Paris

I slept well last night. It was impossible for me to continue writing yesterday; I was exhausted. But now, after a good night's sleep I can continue with my account of the events of these last few days. It helps me to remember and it is important to write these memories down as I fear that otherwise they could disappear, just like forgotten dreams.

I shall continue from where I left off.

Since I had no indication as to when Cora's carriage might arrive, I spent a listless morning. I was at least able to jot down some memories and impressions of the previous day and my encounters with the five who are now becoming the main protagonists of a story. Both Edward and Mariana had allowed me to leave the Café Anglais alone. A cruelty—particularly on the part of Edward, and it rankles still.

I am grateful for those notes that I made, as the events that have followed have increasingly defied reason and there are few clear memories to guide me, or, more exactly, to denote dream from reality.

At three in the afternoon the carriage at last arrived. I had seen many draw-up to the hotel and had frequently risen and hurried to the door, believing that "This one is for me." But there was no mistaking Cora's carriage. Without hesitation, I gathered up my coat and travel bag and made ready to exit. The carriage was a shining black coupé and was pulled by the most distinctive horses. No gentleman would have dared associate himself with the two coiffured ponies that now stood outside the hotel. They were identical in size and in the silky, dappled, black and white of their coats. The driver, who was in the outfit of a groom, opened the door, and all inside was the brightest yellow with cushions plumped and piled upon the seats.

The groom spoke, and it was in English. Indeed, the English of an Englishman. "Madame Crawford, greetings from Madame Pearl. We are to journey to just outside the city. We will ride for an hour and Madame has provided refreshments for you within."

"Within" was delightful. The upholstery, rather than the usual leather or robust cloth, was in yellow silk. The cushions were stuffed full of the softest feathers, and a rug of thick white fur was ready for me to place upon my knees. And there in a container, also lined with yellow silk and resting upon the seat, was a crystal decanter. It was filled to the brim with a liquid of ruby red, and surrounded by a variety of cakes and biscuits all with sugar coatings that were, of course, bright yellow.

And then we were off. I rested back upon the cushions and through the window watched the city buildings disappear, to be replaced by countryside, sometimes of open fields, sometimes thickly wooded. On at least two occasions we crossed the undulations of the great river Seine. It was a cloudy day and I believed it might even snow. This jarred, as the thought of snow at Christmas made me think again of our terrible abandonment of James. And here I was in France, in the carriage of a famous courtesan, reclining amongst her yellow silk cushions and heading for a house inhabited by the Marques.

We came off the road and onto a track that was to lead us to our destination. At the end, we drove through an archway and pulled into a wide and open courtyard. I could see a house through the window, surrounded by huge trees. It was old, built with bricks darkened with age. A section with a lower roof was attached and I could tell from the windows that it was a chapel. The house itself had three stories. It was a large building, yet the great trees seemed to clasp it in their embrace and smother it in a cloak of shadows.

The coach which had paused, now moved forward, closer to the house, and the hooves of the ponies crunched the gravel and I heard and felt the stones ricochet against the floor beneath me.

Our arrival sounded so loud, yet when we halted, all was silent. Despite the trees, there was no bird song.

The driver must have sat for a while, taking his time, as it was several minutes before the springs groaned and the carriage shuddered as he climbed down from his seat. The gravel crunched again and the door was opened. He said nothing, just waiting for me to step down.

There were other coaches there, parked at a distance and all beneath the overhang of enormous branches. Though made indistinct by the shadows, I could see that there was a coach identical to the one that had brought me. It must have brought Cora Pearl.

I stood waiting in the open. I only had a small travel bag and then I wondered if I would be there for the night? We seemed so far from anywhere and Paris was already just a memory. I felt again the disorientation that now, so often, pursues me.

I was alone, standing in the large, open space of the courtyard. There was no greeting, so my only course was to head for the door and hope for at least some welcome.

There was a trembling in my legs as I walked. I remembered the previous day and my wobbling descent and stumble upon the stairs of the Café Anglais. It was fear, though with an addition. There was excitement too. I was loath to recall it, but its strength cared nothing for my resistance. An unacceptable pleasure—I felt again the anticipation that mingled with disgust as I studied the Arcadian painting in the room at the Café Anglais. In that moment, I had been as in a trance. I had gazed at the shepherd, and at the nymphs, who surely the shepherd could not see; and there lurking too, taking his time, enjoying the breeze and the heat of the sun, was the satyr. And as I looked at this primaeval creature, so self-assured, so devoted to the senses, I knew that I was also watching the Marques and despite my inner protest, had felt a surge of pleasure.

Then I had fled. I had left Mariana amongst them—though it was her wish, if wish it could be called. She had surely lost her will; as has my Edward … My Edward?

And now again—against my own will, a tingling of expectation and a tremor of fear.

When I reached the door, I leant against it. The walk across the courtyard had tired me. I needed, as well, to find a vestige of composure. I lifted the heavy door knocker and let it fall.

It is from here on that my memory cannot be trusted. I will try to write down the events and find for them some framework of time. But time became bent, distorted, even non-existent, though my calendar tells me that I was in that house for three days.

I knew that it would not be Edward who answered the door. At this time, he was gone to me; perhaps as disorientated as I—trapped within the influence of Don Angel, and of Marguerite too. And I knew, as well, that Cora Pearl needed only to incline her head. Though does such a woman do anything if not for payment, and though Edward is a wealthy man, he does not have the income of Emperors and Princes.

The door swung open, and it was Mariana. But should I say—it was meant to be Mariana? She spoke as Mariana, yet it could have been Marguerite. From then on, all was to be mixed in confusion. Beginnings and endings would coincide in one continuous event; ecstasy would mingle with the fear of the unknown; where each of us began and the other ended would no longer be defined.

Now, I realise that this was his game: to remove difference for each of us and to reduce all to a central theme, an overarching concept—the phenomenon of identical twins whom one cannot tell apart. And now I can see why Mariana would join the game, even though it was the creation of the Marques. For her it was an offering of joy. She was not to be distinguished from her sister—they were to be as one.

So, did Mariana or Marguerite answer the door? The voice and tone were of Mariana, but in the next days I watched each become the other. I saw the enormous pleasure that Mariana felt in becoming her more adventurous and ruthless sister and how Marguerite could withdraw into a poetic soul. And was it, anyway, all my illusion and were they just being themselves? Of one thing I was certain. During these three days, the twins were almost always together and I saw the intimacies and the tiniest nuances of communication; ones they would have shared as children, and that in young adulthood had been lost.

And for the first time, I saw them dressed in identical clothes. The garments were of the greatest simplicity and they had both allowed their hair to be loose. It cascaded over their shoulders, to fall between their shoulder blades, and even to reach their waists, and the colour and length was exactly the same for them both.

I passed through that door into another world—though at first it was ordinary. We were in a small reception room. The light that came

122

through the window, shaded by the great trees, was acceding to the dusk. The chandelier in the room had no candles and the light came from the soft glow of two oil lamps. Edward was standing in shadow, alone against a wall. Cora Pearl was sitting next to the Marques at a small ornate table. I could see that the table legs were inlaid with patterns of ivory. The top was covered by a white linen cloth and upon this were drinking glasses and silver spoons.

The twins were also standing, very close to Cora and the Marques. Whichever one had let me in was now standing with the other.

Cora rose in greeting. "You came—I am so pleased. Can I call you Crawfy as the girls do? No! Surely you have a proper name and an English one too."

And I answered, "It is Jane."

"Then Jane it is. So much nicer—and you will call me Cora, of course."

It was a long time since I had been called Jane. I realised that even Edward now called me Crawfy. It was so nice to hear my real name. It was already warm in the room and I felt a new warmth inside me.

She returned to her seat next to the Marques. Don Angel was no longer dressed as the smartest man in the city. He wore a purple garment in linen. It was fastened above one shoulder by a golden clasp. It bloomed around his body and above a belt embroidered with silver and gold. His arms were bare, as were his legs from the knees downwards. His leather sandals also had golden clasps. I have seen such costumes in images from ancient Greece and Rome.

It made a great contrast to the outfit of Madame Pearl. Her colour too was purple, but her dress, in the peak of Parisian fashion and surely from the house of the greatest couturier, was as elaborate as could be. From an exceedingly narrow waist, its great mass of silk flared out to brush the floor with lilac frills. The neck line was low and the dress rested upon the edges of her shoulders where there were two great bows in black silk. A matching bow marked the centre of her waist and an even larger one rested in the curve of her back. The shape of the dress was enhanced with a profuse layering of material, all trimmed and decorated with strips of lilac.

I now realised the significance of the clothing of the twins. They wore plain tunics in white linen. Their arms were bare and the cloth fell from shoulder to ankle, resting upon their bodies in such a way as to show that there was no clothing beneath. My intuition took over from here—the scenario was becoming clearer—despite the outfit of Madame Pearl,

123

I could see that we were in Classical days and that the clothes of the girls were of the women of the temple, the priestesses.

Beside this, the plumage of Cora was laughably out of place, though she would soon be making a dramatic change to her attire.

The Marques was studying the paraphernalia upon the table. He called across to Edward. "Monsieur the Artist. Do you know about the lovely, green fairy who has inspired so many of your colleagues?"

Edward seemed to know the nature of the thing, though his expression showed no direct experience. This was clearly not the case for the Marques.

Cora spoke directly to the twins. "My dear girls, you will soon partake of a pleasure that Angel has placed as the first amongst many we will enjoy."

And Don Angel added, "And it will be something new for you all, except of course, for our illustrious lady of Paris."

Cora acknowledged the truth of the statement with the simple gesture of one well used to all pleasures.

The Marques continued, "But we will leave the preparation for one who is a master at creating the finest foods and the most exquisite drinks, and also, with the help of myself, the most dramatic potions! Madame Pearl has lent us her faithful and famous chef."

At which, Cora opened a door that looked out upon the corridor and called out a name. A middle-aged man entered the room. He made a gesture of respect to Cora and murmured, "Madame."

"Ah!," declared the Marques. "Monsieur Salé, let us now mix up the magic. We have here all that we need and I have brought with me a little additive, a very special extra, only known to me and maybe a few friends. A little extra that Marguerite and Mariana have already savoured."

He made no explanation for this last remark, but I immediately wondered about Alexandria. "Now Salé, we will begin and we will say a little prayer as you do your work."

At which, the Marques sat back, still erect, and lowered the lids of his eyes, though I suspect not enough to entirely reduce his vision.

I believe that we all felt bound to be silent after such a statement and such an expression of reverence to whoever, or whatever, the Marques de Mansura might pray to.

But it was only for a minute. The eyes suddenly and alarmingly opened and the black eye balls flicked from side to side as he resumed command of the room. "I jest a little. But let us revere the potion so that she knows that she is truly loved. She will repay us by finding our most secret desires and serving them well."

Salé had brought with him a large crystal decanter and a larger glass container that had a metal lid and a long metal stem. The decanter was full to the brim with a pale green liquid.

He moved the six glasses that were on the table so that they were close to each other and then poured a measure of the liquid into each glass. At their top the glasses were of the usual shape, yet they swelled out to make a bulb towards their base. Each glass was filled to just above the bulb. He then moved the large container to the centre of the table. Its stem raised it above the lips of the glasses which he gathered closely around it, so that they just touched its body. At the top of its stem, where the metal widened to receive its main glass body, were a number of tiny taps. Each glass was placed so that it was beneath its own tap.

Salé then reached for a collection of silver spoons that rested nearby. They were beautifully designed and I could see that each one was different, though all bore a number of perforations. He placed a spoon flat across the opening of each glass and upon every spoon he placed a sugar lump. He then turned on the taps. From the taps, a clear liquid dripped upon each sugar lump and then trickled slowly into its glass. Gradually the green liquid blossomed and bloomed and became milky white. It was here that Don Angel passed to him a small ivory container, no larger than a snuff box. From the container, Salé sprinkled a small amount of powder into each glass.

Whilst all were intent on watching the alchemical process, I looked across at the twins. They were still standing side-by-side. One held the hand of the other and they seemed like ethereal beings who were about to enact a monumental ceremony. In a way, this was true. The Marques beckoned them to come closer. The preparation of the drinks was complete. Salé had performed his duty and with a final glance at his concoction and a respectful, yet knowing look towards his mistress, he left the room.

The twins were to serve the drinks and they came to each of us with a full glass.

During the silence and attention which had accompanied the making of the absinthe, I had retrieved something of my own being. I found that, at least for a moment, I could again distinguish between the two twins. I was baffled as to how my confusion had occurred, especially

125

given my growing affection for Mariana, and my growing distrust of Marguerite. But though I again looked for discomfort in Mariana, I saw no such thing. She was transformed by the physical closeness to her sister and there was a re-found intimacy as they were both serving the Marques.

And in that lucid moment, I could see his game. I do believe that I have some insight into this man—if man he is. When he came upon us at Whitby, he declared his fascination with "twins." I know now, from Mariana, that he had torn them apart, probably in Alexandria— and now he was putting them back together. It was his power and his pleasure. And I could see that he wished to mingle us all together, to blend us into his own concoction as he blended the absinthe with his special powders.

There was a new silence as we sipped from our glasses. The power of our host ensured that no glass would remain empty. I liked the taste. It was strange, like nothing I have had before. There was a complexity and I could tell that several elements had been expertly mixed together.

It was the Marques himself who was the last to finish. He had been holding his glass and gently swirling the content as he watched the room.

He placed his empty glass upon the table. "Now, my dear guests, we will exit this dingy, horrible room, for which I take no blame, and enter one which is far more to my own liking, and indeed is of my own design. And Cora, you will wish to change. You will know where to find us." Cora leant towards him and kissed him upon the forehead. "Mes amis. Au revoir. And do not begin the games without me."

The rest of us stood for a moment, in due respect to her elegant exit, and then followed the Marques along the corridor to a set of large doors.

He threw them open and the contrast was astounding. The room was enormous and had probably once served as a ballroom. He took several paces, and turned to beckon us. I was the first to enter. It was brilliantly lit with three massive crystal chandeliers. There were many oriental rugs upon the floor, and some hung upon the walls. There were tapestries too. Not faded, but in the brightest of colours and designs. Some showed Egyptian figures and were in the style of ancient Egypt; all in profile and many in which men and women were offering and seeking love. There were strange symbols as well and against one wall, and as high as the ceiling, were two enormous black statues of cats.

Upon a great table there was laid a profusion of the finest food. Clearly the chef Salé had already been to work and not just with the making of absinthe.

And amongst the Egyptian art and artefacts, there was also the Greek. Distinctly not angular like the Egyptian, but flowing. Two beautiful marble statues were positioned near to the great cats, as if to play with the difference. They were both of women, elegantly posed and gathering around them the many folds of their robes. The far wall was almost covered by a fresco. The soft tones showed a lake surrounded by trees and near the shore of the lake a building in the Classical style. It had a small portico and pillars that surrounded it. Two figures stood outside, one in the same garment now worn by the twins, the other in a shorter smock. A priestess and a slave, I thought, outside a temple. I saw the twins gazing at the painting in amazement.

The voice of the Marques rang out, filling the great hall. "Let me tell you about Aphrodite." And having our attention, his voice softened. "We all need to have a god—or a goddess—and she is mine. And a goddess is to be served, and this I try, in my own feeble way, to do. One, of course, hopes for some kind of reward, but I have found that to wait for such a thing will only end in disappointment. And anyway, I have always known that the pleasure is in the serving. It is why we must be very careful which god we choose!"

And finding his own remark very funny, he laughed aloud. I noticed that Edward laughed too, and then I also began to laugh, and I knew that the potion we had gently sipped was to have its way, and that this was just the beginning.

"She came from the sea," proclaimed the Marques. "Born from the froth of the waves. There are different versions of course—the poets could each have their own Aphrodite, as I have mine! But all agree—she was born a fully formed woman! Straight into being the goddess of love and fully equipped. And really, not so modest as in the Botticelli, beautiful as his painting is."

And as if responding to a pre-ordained cue, Cora Pearl suddenly appeared. She had shed her purple satins and silks and all the frills and bows. She now wore only a diamond bracelet and a band of gold around her neck. The band of gold was faced with an enormous ruby. The magnificent body emerged from a doorway and with complete assurance and pleasure in its own movement, walked slowly towards us.

"And here she is." The voice of the Marques was now low, but perfectly clear. "We now have the goddess herself," and turning to the twins, "and we have her priestesses," and turning to me, "and who will you be Jane?"

I was now unsure of everything, let alone my role in the house of Aphrodite. My vision was becoming misty. Not so that it was hard to see, but that all objects seemed softened and surrounded by their own aura.

The voice of Don Angel was there again. "I do believe, Jane, that you could be Aphrodite yourself, but there can only be one, and for now it is Cora who claims the crown."

"But we do need the High Priestess."

It was Cora's voice and she had come close to me and was holding out a garment. It rested within her arms and beneath her breasts. The breasts were beautiful and, on an impulse, I touched them.

She spoke softly, in almost a whisper, "That is right Jane."

I took the garment. One of the twins, I know not which, hastened towards me to help me to undress and put the new garment on. When all my clothes were discarded, she placed it over my head and let it fall. It slipped easily from my shoulders to my ankles. It was like hers, but there was embroidery and it was edged with gold. Across the room I saw that Edward was now dressed in the same style as the Marques.

I must soon return to the events that were to follow. It was clear from that point that the promised "adventure" would contain much physicality and that since we were in the domain of Aphrodite the goddess of love, the erotic would supersede all else. But first, I must attend to the bizarre surroundings in which our adventure was to take place.

It was probably the next day that the miracles began. We were all in the great room. I think we had just had one of our delightful breakfasts.

Don Angel had risen from his seat and crossed to the wall in which there were several windows, all of which had remained shuttered since our arrival. The windows were large as befitted the room and arched so that the rectangular shutters allowed the curved area at the top to be free to let in the daylight. So far this had sufficed, though the light in the great room was muted. At night, the chandeliers were lit and, in the daytime, extra light came from the two huge fireplaces, within which logs glowed and spat and threw out enormous heat. From time to time, to tend to the fire, a servant entered, always averting his eyes. No doubt, he was trained to do so. We were indeed extremely snug and warm despite wearing clothes designed for the islands of Greece in ancient, bucolic Summers. Cora was not to allow her nakedness to become too habitual, and so, lose its impact. In the mornings she would wear a loose smock, though of material so fine that the suggestions and hints of her body were always present.

Don Angel stood before the largest of the windows. There were two shutters. He grasped the handles of each and pulled them towards him. They were so large that his arms could not stretch widely enough, so he completed the opening of one side and then moved to the other. The shutters swung flat back upon the wall with a bang and the light streamed in.

Not the mid-winter light of rural France in a house circled by trees. It was the light of summer and of wide-open spaces.

Both Edward and I rushed to the window in amazement. Cora followed us, whilst the twins looked without moving. We were gazing out to sea. The ocean was the most beautiful azure and the horizon was so distant that it could only be told from the finest strip of pale yellow which then became blue again, lighter in tone, but deepening as it rose and as the sky soared towards and above us. Before us were grassy fields with many cypress trees; the light green and the dark. The fields gently undulated as they sloped down towards the sea and upon the coastline was a white strip of buildings shining in the sunlight. Beyond, and seeming to rise out of the water and touch the sky was a great tower. The reflected light of the sun was blazing from its summit.

I heard Edward gasp and I instinctively reached for his hand. He too was reaching for mine. It is in these moments, shocked out of our resentments, that love can be remembered and sometimes, re-found.

He gasped, "This is … the lighthouse of Alexandria … How can this be?" He stared at the scene before us, turned and stared at the Marques, and then back to the window. "It must be Alexandria!"

Don Angel, stood beside us. "Aphrodite travelled well. She made it easily over the sea to Egypt, where the Greek and the Egyptian made a nice mix. She has some lovely temples here. Smaller that in Crete, Cythera, and Athens, but they are more intimate and are my favourites. And anyway, I can't be everywhere and this is my favourite city—until the Romans come. Then sadly, its end begins.

"You will of course wish to go down there and walk the streets and visit the great library and the gardens and harbour and the greatest market in the world. But alas, this I cannot do for you. Even Don Angel has his limits. The energy needed is so great and I am still recovering from our last trip."

And at this, he turned towards the twins, and I realised that the girls had indeed walked those ancient streets with the Marques.

We came time and again to gaze through the great window at the wonderful sight. But Don Angel was true to his word; we were not to visit the city and could only look; the window remained closed and locked. It was also as if some unspoken decree had come down upon us. For three days we remained in the house and I had no notion of stepping out, even for a moment. Perhaps the spell was maintained by Angel's strength of will and no doubt it was helped by his very special recipe for absinthe. The green liquid was always there and we were constantly urged to drink it, and this was no struggle, as the results were endlessly pleasing. They were the foundation for the sensual pleasures that were built upon them. Angel would not magic us into the ancient city, but he could bring something of the city to us.

On one afternoon, I came to the ballroom to eat. The table there was always covered with the most wonderful foods and silver bowls were piled high with exotic fruits. Some were unknown to me and it was my wish to discover yet more new tastes.

The twins were there in the ballroom. They were together, sitting on cushions upon the floor, their backs against the panelled wall. They were looking across to the far end of the room which had the painting of the lake and the temple. In front of the painting there were two human figures. They were walking towards us, yet they came no closer, as if they were walking upon air. The man was magnificent, as handsome as could be. He was wrapped around in white linen and with a swathe of cloth that gathered upon his shoulder. His light brown hair was cropped short, but with enough length for the curls to fall upon his tanned forehead. His female companion was of a far darker skin and with more pronounced facial features; a strong, aquiline nose and a wide mouth beneath high cheekbones. She was wearing a wig that was black but with a hint of purple and laced through it were coloured beads and jewels. The lids of her eyes were painted with blue and gold and glittered as if encrusted with the powder of diamonds. She wore white too, and her robes were the same as her partner, though one breast was exposed whilst the other was covered. And pacing beside them, its skin gleaming black and rippling as it moved, was a panther.

I have dreamed, just occasionally, of wild beasts. I wish it were more often. Mainly it has been lions and once there was a tiger. These are my favourite dreams. They seem to offer so much; some rekindling of an essence that rules the wild beasts and that we have lost. I fear these creatures in my dreams and love them too, and my fear is only my awe at their presence; they never attack me.

And all this I felt, as the two magnificent humans with their beast of a pet walked towards us, but never came closer. And then very gradually the vision faded and was gone.

I looked to the twins. There were no words to say, only my look of amazement. One of the girls said, and it was in French, "Maintenant Crawfy, tu as vu ce que nous avons vu. Votre vie peut-elle jamais être la même?"

On one afternoon, perhaps half way through our stay, the sound of music came from the ballroom. I was with Cora, and we both went to discover the source. Standing near to the table was a woman in white robes. A diamond studded blindfold covered her eyes. Her arms were bare and her fingers were stroking the strings of a harp. The harp itself was an item of wonder; it was so large that it required the player to stand. Its frame curved downwards and widened as it met the floor. Extending from its foot was the golden head of a pharaoh. Upon the pinnacle of the instrument, higher even than the musician, was the painted head of a bird, its cruel beak belying the gentle beauty of the music. All along the bowed frame were designs painted in blue and red, and pressed into the wood were bands of gold, with one great sheath of gold as the curve neared the floor. The music was melodious, but strange to my ears. Each note was carefully plucked and the sound did not reverberate as in the instrument that we know, but was puckered; each note a pure entity in itself.

I said to Cora, "Is she real?" As I believed she was another apparition. Cora was as unsure as I, and went across to where she stood and reached out and touched her arm. It was real flesh and in surprise, the woman froze. The music stopped and then Cora whispered in her ear and I saw her body relax and the playing resumed.

But now to return to our first evening. It was for Cora Pearl, on behalf of Don Angel, to announce the form of our "adventure" and the rules of the game. She had just made her spectacular entrance as the naked Aphrodite. Don Angel had clapped his hands and cried out in appreciation. Cora had stood before us and her hand had risen to the fabulous gold band around her neck. "Mon chère Angel. Je l'aime complètement. What a wonderful gift!"

The Marques in response had looked a trifle put out. It was most unusual to see him loose his composure, if even for a moment.

His voice was lowered, as if it were only to be heard by her—yet it was full of expression. He hissed, "Cora, it is just a loan!"

She ignored his comment. No doubt, Madame Pearl expected to leave any house she entered with at least one treasure.

The Marques resumed his affirmative manner. "Madame Pearl, you are a goddess indeed and you reign over us tonight and throughout this visit of my most welcome guests." And his arm swung widely to encompass us all.

"The Pearl is now the Aphrodite, the deity of love and beauty, and we are all in her command."

The goddess then declared the rules of our stay. "And my command is that we do not leave this house until all have known and savoured the love of each other."

And so it was. Over the days, we were to make love to each person who was there.

As I think about it now, the permutations are considerable! I, for one, performed my obligations. Perhaps we all did. Or maybe, in the dreamlike intensity of those days, anything can be imagined. But in my memory, my intimacy was, indeed, with each, and as I look back I am amazed at the increasing ease in which I could partake of the very real pleasures that ensued.

Cora initiated the proceedings by walking over to Edward, taking him by the hand, and leading him out of the ballroom and to one of the many bedrooms on the floors above.

I believe that Edward departed somewhat in shock; it was certainly a state that I shared, though the sheer atmosphere that surrounded us, no doubt enhanced by the intake of Don Angel's potions, was filling me with a feeling that was warm and carefree. I could no longer be sure as to Mariana's feelings, but, no doubt, Marguerite would now be savouring the occasion.

The food was on the table, and we commenced to eat and to drink, whilst Don Angel continued in his invocations to Aphrodite, describing in the most theatrical manner the many mythological stories that pertain to the goddess.

It was about an hour after Cora's disappearance with Edward, that she returned alone, and walking straight towards me, now took me by the hand and led me away. I could feel no resistance to this, but once again I felt the wobble in my legs and an acute onset of what are normally described as "butterflies."

Over the next three days, sometimes spontaneously, and sometimes with the encouragement of Cora, we all engaged in the game. This included Don Angel though he remained aloof of any organising.

I suppose, really, it is like an endless erotic dream, and that is how I remember it, though I was awake enough to be aware of my preferences.

With Cora Pearl—there was some indifference—on her part, I think. I do believe that with me she was only performing. I imagine—no—I can tell that women do not inspire her to her best endeavours. Her greatest skills are kept for men; no doubt, this was to Edward's advantage. Perhaps, one day, he will tell me.

And the twins? I was not sure which one was which; at times I was with one, at other times with the other, and sometimes with both. What is clear is the overwhelming pleasure.

And my allotted time with Edward did remind me of how enjoyable it could be for us—something rather lost over the years and subsumed under a life of routine.

Gradually, there became an erotic mingling between us all, and the collective became a thing in itself. Couplings were repeated and we no longer retired to individual bedrooms but lay upon the couches in the ballroom. I increasingly felt at one with every other present.

And throughout each evening, the harpist, always with the diamond studded blindfold, would take up her position and play.

But I can say little of my time with Don Angel. It has been erased, just as the hypnotist declares to his subject—"You will awake, and remember nothing." There is a sense, though, despite my amnesia, that there was a whole night in which I was filled completely with sensual delight and which was a consummation into a realm in which one joins with the most fundamental yet mystical elements of the universe. I had made love to Pan.

CHAPTER SEVENTEEN

Mariana in the house at Poissy

For our story to have been passed down through the spoken word, many years later, would not have been the same. The very nature of the events defies definition and their context was so abnormal that time would have faded and distorted them. What we have instead, gifted from her diaries, is Crawfy's direct experience, laid down as it happened.

Just for now, we will be leaving her writing, though we will return to it later.

There was one other person who could recall these events dramatically, and through absolute, first-hand experience, and who had the narrative skill with which to describe them, and that was Mariana and we will now revisit the Poissy house, as remembered by her.

I have already described the account that she gave me, one warm night in Almeria, about the remarkable events that occurred when the Marques invited the twins to Alexandria. A vivid and emotional tale of events that I can only see as being profoundly shaped by magic.

So, when she also told me about Paris, and about my father and Crawfy; about the Marques and the force of nature that was Cora Pearl, I was ready to hear more about a world in which the uncanny pervades our, so-called, "normal" reality.

In the months after we parted, I felt duty bound to write a personal account of our six months together. Partly, to mark a time in my life which I knew would be unique, but also to try to think through and understand the stories that she told me. On reading Crawfy's diaries, so many years later, I have been able to compare her experiences to Mariana's. There are similarities, of course, but also some profound difference. I will therefore return to December 1864, and this time from the memory of Mariana. I believe that it can only add to and enrich the account that was laid down so well by Crawfy.

It was another warm night, about a month after her recounting to me the tale of Alexandria, that Mariana described those days spent in Paris and in the house on its outskirts.

We had been to our little restaurant on the edge of Almeria. It was not a well-known destination and was rarely crowded. Mariana and I were so regular in our attendance that we had a table set and reserved for us each evening. If we were not there by 10pm, the patron would simply remove the sign and make the table available. It was a lovely, friendly understanding. He and his wife were clearly fond of us. And Mariana, with her great aptitude for languages, had become fluent in Spanish and she conversed with them with great charm.

As we walked back along empty streets, in the soft warmth of the Southern Spanish night, Mariana told me about flamenco and that it was the natural music of where we were living, and how there can be a moment of elevation in which the dancer or singer becomes filled with sublime energy, so that they are uplifted and become at one with the essence of their music. Indeed, it becomes an experience of the soul, in which movement, emotion, purpose, and song become merged. This cannot happen without great skill, but when it happens, all lessons are forgotten.

I do believe that this led her to speak about the merger of the six at Poissy. For Mariana, it had been a dance of Eros; over three days and nights, a sublime mixing of bodies and selves.

On our return, she sat before the table, near to the open window, with myself and the large, silent square outside as her audience, and she spoke of the house on the outskirts of Paris, that Christmas period of 1864, three years before.

It was as if she could only enter into such memories if she had drugs that could replicate the feeling experience. In the soft and spare light of one candle, I could see her, once again, filling her pipe. She lit it and the smell was different to the usual hashish. I had smelt it before and knew that after smoking it she would be deeply withdrawn and happy just to dream. Strangely, I never questioned Mariana about the drugs: why they were so important; where they came from; how they made her feel. I suppose, because it seemed so private and personal, and anyway I never lost the feeling that I was her house guest and that there were boundaries not to be crossed. With hindsight, it seems certain to me that the drug that night was opium. And so, let us call it opium. And having inhaled from her pipe, she came and lay down upon the bed where I was sitting and she pulled me to her so that I lay next to her. The rest of the story was told as if she was speaking from within a dream and almost as a whisper in my ear.

All remained quiet in the square outside. The candle had only been a stub and the little flame died with a puff of smoke. We lay in the dark, though it was a darkness that my eyes became used to. I felt her warm breath as she spoke into my ear and my eyes rested upon the faintest patch of light that was upon the ceiling and that came from, I know-not-where. Perhaps a lamp in the square.

I will not repeat details that I have already given from Crawfy's diary. Mariana's description of the house was much as was hers and anyway, it was the events that took place within that Mariana wished to speak of, and most of all, that the Aphrodite temple was to become manifest again.

She described the scene with the absinthe and how the Marques had mixed in the powerful ingredient from his own formidable supply. Mariana mused that it could have come from anywhere in the world— and from any century! She laughed a little at the thought.

They had then moved into the great ballroom that was filled with statues and artefacts from ancient times. There were the two huge, Egyptian, cat statues and all around were ornate tables bearing vases in black and gold, their bellies crowded with images of warriors and lovers. The largest table was covered with silver dishes full of exotic fruits and sweetmeats.

The far wall was completely covered by a wall painting and she recognised the scene immediately. It was just as Crawfy has described in her diary, but was of far greater significance for Mariana. There, by the lake, was the temple, quite small, but utterly elegant in its Classical Greek design. And standing outside in the painting were the two women, the priestess who had welcomed Marguerite into the temple

137

and the slave girl who was there to escort Mariana back to loneliness, and to a modern, foreign city.

As she looked, she saw a drift cross the surface of the lake and the branches of the trees gently swayed. She wondered if there was a breeze and then felt it upon her cheeks. She knew then that the magic had begun.

As Mariana spoke, I sensed a drift in her too, in the tone of her words and her story, and there were pauses when I believed that she would fall asleep. But it did not happen until the end, and then she slept through until the next evening.

She described Cora. She had liked her, but found her unlike anyone she had ever known. Her history, her background, and her life were alien to Mariana, who had been brought up within the middle-classes of Paris. Yet, amongst all the strangeness and the metaphysical nature of their time there, Cora was the one who had seemed the most normal, the one who still kept an elegant foot in the ordinary world. And unlike all the others, she clearly did not fear the Marques. She treated him instead as an affectionate combatant. To Cora, who could dangle the richest and most powerful men from her little finger, it was perhaps a relief to have a friend who was far beyond such influence. And Mariana, by now, also knew that Don Angel was a dark prince of Eros, whilst in her Paris demi-monde Cora reigned as Queen. A regal partnership, then.

On that first evening, Cora had completely entered into the role of the love goddess. She had discarded her clothes and displayed the reasons why men had ruined themselves for her favours, perhaps even for a single night.

"But it was not only the body," mused Mariana—"Something else, as well."

Cora had begun the three days and nights of love by taking my father to one of the many bedrooms. There were so many rooms. It was, thought Mariana, so much of the experience—that great big house, with three floors. Perhaps 20 rooms or more, so that one could be utterly lost. And who would one be with in that room, or the next room? The partners changed; the time spent with each was incalculable, indistinct, as if the very sexual climax and its expectation became stretched out to infinity.

Cora had returned without my father, who, presumably, was left to regain his strength. It was then that the Marques had stepped across to the twins. They were sitting close together, still enjoying their newly regained closeness.

Mariana whispered to me, "I knew exactly what would happen. And I was happy for it. Indeed, I was very happy since I knew that we would be together, and that he would love us together."

And so it was, and she had no regrets. In fact, in those moments she felt a creature born within her that could speak of the ancient spirits of the forest, and of the rivers and the sea, and of the singing of nature that could become a rapturous roar. And she knew that the erotic was now as much a part of her life as the happiness of friendships, and that it would drive her love of poetry, and her joy in nature, and that she had also merged with the voluptuous tastes of the sister she lay entwined with and the man who now seemed more of the elements than of humanity.

That night, she and Marguerite had slept together, holding each other in intimacy and as I now imagine, regressing to even before their birth, sharing the warm, close confines of their mother's womb.

The next two days and nights were under the divine instructions of Cora; no doubt, as well, in accord with the wishes of their host. The aim was for each of them to know the other with complete intimacy. Though there could be nothing to compare with the experience with her sister and Don Angel, Mariana's time with Crawfy was completely satisfying and full of love, and she knew that this was the same for them both.

Perhaps, even within the influence of the opium, Mariana felt to spare me any knowledge of her and my father, as it was not mentioned. It would have had to happen though, as would his time with Don Angel. One can only imagine that Don Angel was adept at giving satisfaction to all, not withstanding, their gender.

Though it reached a pleasurable conclusion, her time with Cora seems to have been similar to Crawfy's experience. She was left with the feeling that Cora much preferred to make love to men. She had, in fact, during a phase with both the twins, broken off to offer them a verbal lecture with full demonstrations of how they could achieve the greatest sexual pleasure along with some remarkable tips as to how to completely captivate the erotic senses of a man. This rather academic guide to love making had formed an interlude, after which she returned to the more practical and physical applications of all that she had described.

It was on their final evening in the house, and before the final night, that Don Angel had summoned the twins to the ballroom and had guided them towards the far wall on which was the great painting of the temple with its lake and trees. The two women, standing outside the temple, had already seemed real to Mariana and the movement of the trees had become so pronounced that she could hear the soft sound of the breeze slipping between the branches. Now, upon the drifting surface of the lake, there were tiny splashes as fish jumped, and circles spread outwards as insects rose and descended.

To their side, the great window was free of its shutters, and just as Crawfy has written, Ancient Alexandria lay in the distance, its white buildings now flushed red by the lowering sun. The great furnace at the peak of the lighthouse had been lit and she could smell the wood smoke as the flames leaped towards the sky.

The sight was so magnificent that she gazed at it, transfixed, and for a moment was distracted from the temple scene that was before them. She turned back to look again at the painting, but there was no longer a wall, no longer the ballroom in which they had stood, and instead, her feet were resting upon soft and cool grass. She could feel the blades of grass between her toes and a breeze ruffled her hair and the tunic that she wore, and before her, as she stood with Marguerite and Don Angel, was the temple, real and resplendent in solid pale stone and white marble.

Mariana's excitement was immediately doused by the expectation that, just as before, here at the entrance, she would be refused entry. She looked to the slave girl who would lead her away. The girl was there, but this time, she was standing apart. The priestess came towards them, smiling and holding out a hand to each twin. Her words, in a strange language, were spoken with warmth and were surely a welcome. She led them between the pillars of the small portico and into a garden. They walked beneath palm trees and between scented shrubs and grasses and Mariana remembered the garden in Alexandria, through the little wooden door and behind the high walls, when the Marques had taken them to the stone staircase that had been a portal to the ancient city. This garden was smaller, just a small enclosure shaded by palms, but full of the blooms of corn flowers and the scent, that can be greater in the stillness of dusk, from shrubs of jasmine and henna. There was a pond and upon it lay the flat green leaves of lotus plants. The pointed petals of their blooms were blue and purple and were open wide to display the stamens at their heart in red and gold. Mariana knew that at night the petals would retract and keep their fragile centre safe until the dawn and she thought that this temple must be like that, a beautiful protective layer to the soft, female centre within.

The twins had reached the main entrance to the temple and Mariana looked around and saw that Don Angel was no longer there. Then she saw him standing at the entrance of the garden. He spoke softly, yet she heard him clearly. "This is only for you. I may not enter."

And Mariana noted this with pleasure. That the feminine power inside the temple was a match for the Marques and she felt a new courage within her as she entered.

The woman, who was her guide, stood by her as she gazed around in wonder. Then she took her by the hand and led her to a large, free-standing marble trough that was filled with clear water. There were yellow flowers floating in the water surrounded by purple and white lotus blossoms, and the priestess picked some of the yellow flowers from the water and gently shook them. She laughed as the cool drops splashed into her face and moistened the gauze that surrounded her body. Some drops fell upon Mariana and she laughed too and then the priestess threaded the stems of the flowers through Mariana's hair and made a little necklace of them to place around her neck and Mariana felt that she had been anointed.

Then other women gave her wine to drink and sweet foods, more delicious than any she had tasted before. There was music played by a harp and the harp was played by a young girl, exquisitely pretty. Women drifted past, all dressed in the simplest of transparent gauze and in the middle of the temple, resting upon the mosaic floor with depictions of the goddess, was the goddess herself, sculpted in the smoothest, gleaming white marble.

Except that there were two of them. Beside the white Aphrodite, was another, just as large, but whereas the one rested on her plinth, poised and motionless, the other was painted, covered in colour and was advancing, a spear held aloft, as if to challenge anyone who dared enter her domain. The faces and bodies of the two were identical, but not in their expressions, nor in the movement of their bodies. Both naked, one gracefully standing, the other expressing her body as if that too was a weapon. Mariana saw and was filled with the poise and peace of the one and felt the warlike excitement of the other. And she knew, "It is I, and Marguerite." And as she looked at the white marble statue which seemed so cool and restful in a pose that could last for centuries, protected here in its temple, by the lakeside in the shade of trees—as she studied it—she realised that she was as beautiful as Marguerite, that she was as beautiful as her sister, but she would never use her beauty as a weapon; she could feel the excitement of doing so, but that was for her twin. And Mariana felt that she had found herself.

She walked alone between the pillars of the temple. The women whom she passed smiled warmly. The music of the harp still floated in the air and the young harpist had been joined by a singer—her exact twin. Mariana gazed at the walls. They were covered with painted scenes from the tales of Aphrodite. They showed her with her lovers. She could tell from his warrior appearance that one was Ares, though the god of war was sleeping like a lamb within her arms. Another must have been Poseidon, as the two made tumultuous love within a huge vortex, a great whirlpool that rose out of the sea. There was the messenger god, Hermes, with wings upon his feet and the two bodies entwined, yet launched and flying through the air in ecstasy. And surely one was Adonis; a man of great beauty, but without the trappings of a god and earthbound and making love to her upon a bed of lush grass and crushed primroses. On another wall, Aphrodite rested in a clearing surrounded by trees, and fauns lay near and around her as if to make a protective guard of honour and worship. On yet another, she was bathing and playing in the water with the naiads who were there to honour her and every single one of them reflecting her beauty. And on the last wall was Aphrodite the warrior—magnificent and ferocious. No longer the soft embodiment of the breeze and the warm Cyprus evenings, or the clear, sparkling waters in which she bathed, but rushing to the earth from the sky with sword and spear. And above were depictions of the zephyrs, the winds that were at the command of the gods and that could blow helpless mortals to and fro at their command.

She slowly turned to take in all that surrounded her. There was no sense of unreality. No feeling that she was in the house of a religion or culture that was not hers. All was as it should be. And it was then that she realised that each woman in the temple had another who was identical to her and that all who were there were twins. And she realised then, that within a union of two, the "I" could still remain distinct and unassailable, and indeed it could be enhanced. Her happiness was complete.

So complete that she looked around for Marguerite, to share this wonderful knowledge and to share her happiness with her own twin. And she saw her sister there and Marguerite was standing alone and was gazing at her with absolute hatred. The look had all the piercing malevolence of a spear flung towards her heart. And she knew

142

immediately, "It is my happiness she cannot bear. She believes all this can only belong to her."

And all that had been wonderful and kind to her, began to fade. It was like a magnificent dream, a dream of joy that the morning waking infiltrates and discards into the pale light of an ordinary day.

The walls, with their colours and their tales of love and deity, began to fade. Beneath her feet the floor trembled and then undulated, becoming stone waves that would toss her aside. The figures around her, the timeless priestesses of Aphrodite, were no longer physical beings but became hollow phantoms, ghostly spirits, disappearing into the air. She looked for the statues and it was as if they had shrunk or become far off, out of reach. The roof above seemed to fly away, and instead there was only the sky above and it had become night and all she could see were thousands of stars, beautiful but remote in their cold, endless space.

Mariana became quiet for a while. I could feel her warm breath as she lay beside me, her lips almost touching my ear. I feared that she may have fallen asleep, or lost consciousness because of the drug. But she continued.

"Would it have been better if I had never entered the temple? To have known and felt so much and then, at the point of climax, to have lost it; never, fully, to receive what had already been given to Marguerite. My joy in the temple, my belief that I belonged there, had just begun. She could not bear me to have it, and she willed it that I should not. Nothing can ever match what had been offered and nothing can ever make up for what was denied."

It was at that point, listening to the despair in her voice, that I understood her loneliness and how it could never be assuaged. To accept less than the joyful unions she had tasted was unacceptable. She had known a magnificent communion, and to long for it was her only way of holding on. To settle for less was to give up that which mattered more than anything. Mariana's longing for union was inborn, just as I now believe a recoil against twinship was inborn in her sister. What Mariana depended on for her existence, Marguerite refused, in order to save her own.

CHAPTER EIGHTEEN

The city at night

After the dissolution of the temple, Mariana found herself once again standing outside it, and though, now deserted, it was completely intact. All around, there was silence. She was by the lakeside and the lake was a flat, black expanse that reached out and disappeared into the darkness of the night. There was no moon, but the sky was brilliant with stars. She turned towards the city and to the sea beyond it. The flames from the furnace of the lighthouse reached up into the sky lighting up the island of Pharos from which the great construction rose. She felt dazed and shocked by the loss of bliss, for it was indeed such a state that had been hers in the temple. She needed to walk, to try to salvage at least something of the extraordinary, and so she walked towards the city. There were fields to cross and clusters of trees where it was very dark, but as she came out of the shadows, the night was lit up by the stars. There were so many that she believed they must either merge together or collide. Despite the loss of the temple, this made Mariana laugh, and really it was a laugh of wonder.

She came upon the roads on the outskirts of the city, all laid out in a meticulous plan. It was easy to make her way to the waterfront, and she also had the great lighthouse to guide her. Arriving at the quayside, she paused. There was no one to be seen. The only sounds were of the waves as they struck the harbour walls and from across the island the sounds of the massive combustion at the top of the lighthouse. She gazed at it. Its fire created a halo that expanded from the island over the sea and at the centre of the halo the smoke from the furnace curled and rose up towards the stars. Mariana thought of dragons. There was a causeway that led to the island, but she chose not to take it and instead walked towards the main quay where, with her sister and Don Angel, on their fateful first visit, she had watched with wonder the great hustle and bustle of the ships being loaded and unloaded and the bodies of the semi-naked men, some with skin darker than she had ever seen before. Now there was no one.

Mariana was surprised at her own courage: to have turned away from the lake and the temple that had so cruelly excluded her and to have entered into the ancient city. Was this entrance forbidden? If all these miraculous events were created by the Marques, was he allowing her to do this, or had she, for a moment, escaped from his thoughts? Would he suddenly, with fury, appear and reclaim her? Would the wonder of her stroll through the empty streets of the ancient city also be ripped away from her? Would he deny her everything? She turned around to survey the whole scene, and now she began to fear.

There were two figures who were approaching. Both wore long, flowing garments in the Greek style. She was sure that they would have seen her. She felt panic. Should she continue walking towards them, turn and walk away, or just stand and wait?

The two moved slowly and they were speaking to each other as they walked. She could see now that one was a man and the other a woman. It was the woman who noticed her first. She paused in her conversation and then said something more to the man, so that he continued on his way whilst she approached Mariana until she stood before her.

Nothing was said. Everything that then passed between them, though it had the most sensitive articulation, was through emotion. At that moment Mariana knew that she need feel no fear. The woman took her by the hand, and they walked together, and to a part of the city where there were gardens. The smell of shrubs and flowers was all around them and the grass was soft underneath her feet. The woman sat down upon the grass and Mariana joined her and she felt sure that the woman knew all that had happened and knew that she had been cast out of the Aphrodite temple and that the goddess could be as cruel

146

as she could be loving. But this woman, Mariana knew, was a person of kindness.

"She has come to save me, she thought. But for how long?"

And she felt such a tiredness that the need to sleep overwhelmed her. She lay back upon the grass and the woman lay beside her and placed her arm around her and let Mariana's head rest upon her breast. Mariana felt a great peace, and a gratitude welled up, so that, in the moment before sleep, she raised her head and for the first time looked fully into the face of the woman. And, for sure, the face was of Jane Crawford.

When she awoke, the city of Alexandria was gone and she was once more in the Poissy house and was lying upon a bed in one of the rooms. She felt the bed move as someone rose from it. She opened her eyes to see who had been lying there. Crawfy was standing by the bed and was looking down at her. She leant over Mariana and kissed her upon the forehead and for a while she just looked into Mariana's eyes. Then standing up, she smiled, turned, and quietly left the room.

The next day, they all departed the house. Don Angel with Cora Pearl, her chef, Salé, and with Marguerite. Mariana left with my father and Crawfy, who travelled with her to her family house in Paris, before making haste in their onward journey to Calais and from there to England and Whitby, where this narrator, at 17 years old, eagerly awaited a family celebration of Christmas.

Mariana had completed her story.

I had imagined that the narration would give her relief from her increasingly mournful nature. Perhaps she thought so too, but it was not the case. If anything, she fell into even greater melancholy and her affection and need for me became so reduced that it felt as if we were estranged. At least, I knew that it was nothing that I had done, no way in which I had personally disappointed her. Nothing was really about me. A relief in some ways, but also deeply disappointing that I should mean so little to her. I had always tried to show my attraction, even my love for her and had felt honoured to have an older and beautiful lover whose gentle nature could feel as poetic as the verses that she wrote down. And she was never cruel to me. She just increasingly withdrew into her own world. I thought of Eurydice and her descent into the underworld, and these things are so often about thwarted or disastrous love.

I could tell that our time together was over. I also knew, with regret, that she could let me go with little emotion. And to protect myself, I resolved to supress my own. So, our parting had no more ceremony than the parting of acquaintances after a chance meeting. What a waste as I think of it now. But I do not hold it against her. I can easily imagine that, after my leaving, she sat in her favourite chair, in her little apartment, maybe with her pipe and its special contents and was immediately away into memories of ecstasies begun but not completed, and mergers joined and then torn apart.

And it was probably time for me to move on. At 20 years old, I needed to consider my future career. My stay with Mariana was of long hot days extending into vast amounts of time in which little happened. Just my constant awareness of her, and the love making, which was fulfilling for me, but which, for her, seemed like the desperate searching for something that was already lost.

And now, too, the autumn had arrived. I asked Mariana what she planned to do.

"I will move away from the city. I like our Almeria square and usually it is quiet, but I need something quieter still. I want to forget about time. We have that clock in the square. It was the one that stopped when my sister and I first met Don Angel. He left and it started again. Now every day I see it and it reminds me of then. And I feel that time has stopped for me now. I see nothing ahead, so I will just be with the present. The days will turn into nights, but each day will be the same, as will each night. And I will stay the same too. I will find a small place in the Tabernas desert, where nothing can disturb me … and no one find me."

That made me ask. "Might he still come looking for you?"

"He has taken so much of my life. Taken my sister. Taken away happiness just as I had found it. Destroyed my ability to love and have joy. There is only my actual life still to take. And he may wish to do that. Perhaps, he would find me, even in the desert; he has his ways. He may send my sister. It would be his greatest triumph to have Marguerite kill me. For him, the complete consummation—the one elevated, even to the point of taking the life of the other."

"Then you cannot go there. You still have family in Paris. In England there is my father and Crawfy. They love you—they would help you."

"And these are easy places for him to find me. And James, I am fond of your father, and Crawfy too. Especially, I love Crawfy, but we have all been part of Don Angel's game. We are all compromised. Perhaps, if

Crawfy came to me, I would have her stay with me ... just as you have stayed, James—and now have to leave. Yes, Crawfy is the only one, but perhaps she would then be in danger too.

"You must give her my love when you return to England."

In fact, my journey to England would not be for almost two years. I felt unable to return. I spent the next months wondering haplessly through Europe and even the Middle East, trying to recover from the separation. I kept in touch with my father and Crawfy by letter, though I could never bring myself to mention Mariana, though she was ever in my thoughts. And always, I returned to our final conversation. It was as if she, who had so often felt abandoned, was now abandoning herself. And not only to a life of complete aloneness, but also, and the thought was at first incredible though utterly persistent, the chance of her physical destruction by the hand of another. The ultimate cessation of time. I feared that she was viewing this as her destiny.

Eventually, I did return to Whitby. It was now with the knowledge of my father and Crawfy's fateful days in Paris, and I realised how much those events had affected the happiness of our home. I was 17 then and had feared that they would not return by Christmas and that I would be compelled to spend it with our neighbours. It sounds ungrateful, since they had shown great kindness in looking after me whilst father and Crawfy were away. But, of course, I wished to be with my loved ones at Christmas. And we had, indeed, been a very happy family and household. But on their return, I could tell that something had changed. Now that I look back, I realise that I sensed a new self-consciousness between them. A previous ease of intimacy had been lost and I believe that it was usurped by intimacy of a different kind. The way a species might live contentedly in its habitat for centuries until an invader, fiercer and more predatory, moves in and destroys it. This new species of intimacy was paradoxical because the physical and emotional sharing was still there, but it had lost—I think the word is—its innocence, so that they who knew each other so well, also surveyed each other from a distance. And I can see that that distance was created in the house outside Paris, when they had shared their intimacy so completely with others: with the twins, with Cora Pearl, and with Don Angel.

And though Crawfy seemed, as an individual, to have gained an inner strength and assertiveness, my father's usual, jovial extroversion was tempered by periods that I can only describe as depression. Fortunately, as the months went by, his spirits rose, though there was

149

a new quietness about him that sometimes troubled me and, as a son feels towards a loved parent, I wanted to make it better, but with no idea how I could.

On returning to them now, after my two years living away, I viewed the "loss of innocence" in the light of my knowledge of the history. And now I also shared in that loss of innocence as I knew what they knew, and, indeed, they must have easily assumed that after my sojourn with Mariana that would be the case, though nothing was said. And Mariana's account had also brought me to a new awareness of my father's and Crawfy's sexuality. This awareness was more easily put to one side in respect to my father, but it was not so easily done with Crawfy. This woman, who in my childhood had been a safe and loving mother figure, was in truth, not my mother, and was an undeniably desirable woman, who had physically loved my own lover, Mariana, who herself had been loved by my father, who remained the lover of Crawfy. I felt drawn down into an incestuous whirlpool. Innocence had indeed been lost.

I began to see my forthcoming career as a chance of a much simpler life. I also needed to detach myself from the intense aura of melancholy that had clung to me so pervasively during my time with Mariana.

Of course, my father and Crawfy still wanted to ask about Mariana and how she was. I also felt the urgent need to talk to them about her, not so much to share details of my time with her, but to have them know of the fear that had been increasingly growing within me. Ever since, in a quiet and resigned voice, Mariana had spoken of her death, even at the hands of her own sister, the unimaginable horror of this had forged its way into my worst fantasies. Though I railed against myself and declared that such a thing was not possible, the idea would do nothing but insist and grow.

It was on my first evening back in our Whitby home that after dinner I told them of my fear. We were in our main living room and the three of us were sitting before the log fire. The autumn days were growing shorter and it was dark outside, though the curtains had not been closed. For a while we sat silently, the only sounds being the crackling of the burning wood and the sound of the wind. The weather had deteriorated that day and Crawfy had felt sure that there was a gale on the way. There was a new rattling as hail began to strike the glass of the windows.

The silence between us seemed to insist that I should now speak of Mariana. I surprised myself. I gave no gentle lead in and I made no reference to uncertainty. "Mariana now lives in the Almeria desert. She has been there more than a year. She will be alone. She doesn't care about anything. And she is beset with an idea. This idea is that the Marques, and her sister, might come to kill her."

My father had been leaning forward, poking at the logs in the fire. He became transfixed in that position. Crawfy, who had a lace cloth upon her lap that she was embroidering, dropped her hand into her lap and gazed at me. Both were shocked at what I had said, as was I, by the way I had said it. Yet I had plainly stated the essence of my fear. What I could not convey was the starkness with which Mariana had said the words, "He may send my sister. It would be his greatest triumph to have Marguerite kill me."

My father spoke first, "It cannot be!"

But Crawfy remained silent.

My father dropped the brass poker into its container and sat back. He turned directly towards me. I saw that though he had exclaimed against the horror that I had foretold, there could be no absolute denial. He returned his gaze to the fire and the three of us watched the flames as if longing for them to bring relief. In the room there was complete silence. Outside the wind howled, before suddenly becoming mysteriously quiet and then rising again to violently cast the hailstones against the widows. Crawfy stood up and walked to the nearest. For a moment she looked out as if expecting to see some awful creature emerge from the darkness. She hurriedly drew the curtains and then moved to the other widow to do the same. She returned to where we were, tightly holding her body with crossed arms as if the outside chill had seeped into her bones.

She sat again, and still we were in silence until my father said, "When the two girls came to us, here in Whitby, for a vacation, they had already been marked by Don Angel. One was bold and the other scared, but they were still together. I painted them as twins, yet wished to show the difference as it intrigued me. But who could possibly know that such difference could turn into murderous hatred!"

And as he spoke, the anger in his voice began to grow until it was a match for the raging of the wind outside. Never had I seen him in such fury. He rose so suddenly that his armchair shot backwards across the carpet. Pacing up and down he launched into a soliloquy of hatred for the Marques de Mansura. His "sheer evil," "his seductions," his drugs, and his "disgusting harlot," Cora Pearl. And his black magic and "filthy spells." A suppressed rage, grown more poisonous over the years, was, at last, spewing forth in words of the most utter hatred. And though I had never seen him like this, I felt that I was getting my father back, and that such outpouring of fury and scorn was, at last, his liberation.

And then there was that which lay most deeply at its core; he stopped pacing and stared hard at Crawfy, "And you made love to him!"

Perhaps Crawfy felt as I, that this outpouring must be allowed, though his accusation of her was ridiculous. She had indeed made love to the Marques, but, over those fateful days, all in that house had made love with each other. Nevertheless, for my father, it had been a victory for the Marques that left him a vanquished cuckold.

His jealous fury towards Crawfy would dissipate. My father was a man of integrity and he would regret the outpouring, but I believe that both Crawfy and I could see his need. He abruptly left the room and headed for a place of solace and of calmer thinking; his studio.

It left Crawfy and I together. So far, she had said nothing. I was surprised by her first words.

"I'm not sure why or how, but I feel that I have some insight into Don Angel—more than your father has. I also have a great fondness for Mariana, though I have not seen her for these last five years and I fear that she has greatly changed. She has been the victim, that is for sure, but does she now persecute herself? To wish for such a retreat, to live in the desert, seems an abandonment of life—of the life force."

She paused, "And does she even crave death? I am astounded by what I think—but might she even wish Marguerite to kill her? That in death by the hand of her twin she in some terrible, dark way, reunites with her.

"And as to Don Angel. Yes, I believe he would facilitate this. He would find fulfilment in the killing of Mariana by her sister."

It was then that Crawfy asked me to tell her much more about my stay with Mariana, and she listened with such intent that I knew that as much as she loved me and wished to know about my time away, she wanted most of all to hear of Mariana, and I knew then how much she loved her.

I had much to say and the fire that had been burning with such vigour was only glowing embers when my father returned.

He was calm now, and he had indeed been thinking. Perhaps he had been sitting in his studio, contemplating his portrait of the twins that still hung in its usual place.

He spoke immediately of his decision, "There is only one option—unless we declare Mariana a figure from the past who is no longer our concern—and that we cannot do. In my first attempt to help the twins—I failed. Failed terribly. I even helped create the failure. It cannot be so again. This time if I fail it will not be from my own weakness. I shall journey to Spain; I shall find Mariana, and if she is willing, I will bring her with me to England. She can live with us and we can give her as much protection as we can.

"I will leave tomorrow."

CHAPTER NINETEEN

The return of St Germain

M y father was ready to leave. But it was not to be.
His travel cases, so carefully packed over-night by Crawfy, were almost immediately abandoned, with the clothes and personal items left to find their mournful way back to their respective draws and cupboards. A remarkable turn-around given the great expectations and the fraught excitement that had kept us awake the previous night.

We had all gone to bed expecting that the coming day would see my father depart on a long trip that could only be open ended, since we could not foretell what protection Mariana would require and how long it might take to persuade her to come to live with us in England—if, indeed, she would allow it. Her wish to live in isolation had become so profound and her view of the dangers she faced seemed embedded in a morbid fatalism.

The event that was to completely upset my father's ambition was a visit which brought back memories of one that preceded it by five years. As usual it was Crawfy who answered the knock at the door, and there she encountered a figure whom she immediately recognised.

"Madame Crawford, who last time I mistook for a maid servant. Have you found time to forgive my foolish error?"

I have no doubt that Crawfy surveyed the Comte de St Germain with pleasure. She, of course, could never forget his presence and the wonderful scenarios with which he had blessed us. Needless to say, she found his appearance completely unchanged by the intervening years. There was, perhaps, a slight adjustment to his dress, given any minor change in fashion; otherwise, all was the same, including the precious rings which encircled each of his fingers.

It was, though, a complete surprise that he should come upon us then, and I believe that we all, in that instant, connected his appearance with the perilous position that we believed Mariana to be facing. The fact that he had arrived just before my father's departure impressed itself as far more than mere coincidence, yet he insisted that it was no such thing. It was indeed, though, his concern for Mariana that had caused his visit.

I was so excited to see him again. Generous as ever, he made a great fuss of how I had grown and that I would now be "even cleverer than the brilliant seventeen-year-old" he had met before.

He stood in our living room and I felt a warmth that surely came from his presence and that seemed to join the four of us together.

Crawfy called for the maid to bring tea, and then we all sat. I have described the calm nature of the Count, but that is not to say he was unhurried. I remembered from his visit before that he had had little time to stay with us. On that occasion it was an important matter that awaited him in India.

Now was no different, and he at once gave excuses for this being a visit of only an hour or so. He was involved in a most problematic political situation in which he hoped to be a help. It would involve his immediate travel to America.

He then declared the reason for his visit. "My dear friends. I laid a heavy burden upon you before. You may well believe that I was inconsiderate and unkind in doing so. Perhaps, even selfish. Should I not have performed the protection of the twins myself? You may well think that now. It is the case, though, that in these matters, it can often require the help of ordinary humanity for us to win through. This is my justification, as well as the very great demands that press upon my time."

The Count paused and rose from his seat. He walked to one of the large drawing room windows and stood there looking out at the garden, his hands clasped behind his back. The storm of the previous night had ceased and all was very still outside. There was a sparkling of frost upon the lawn and upon the leaves of the shrubs. He continued, still with his back towards us.

"We have not met since then and I cannot know all that transpired, though I have some knowledge. You travelled to France with the best intentions and events took their course. And we did fail, didn't we?"

I expect that my father felt at least a little relief that the Count generously used the collective pronoun in respect to the failure.

The maid brought tea and the Count returned to his chair. Crawfy carefully poured the tea into each cup as if it was a procedure that facilitated her thoughts. She too, seemed remarkably calm and for the first time, I got the strangest of feelings that she was, in some indefinable way, linked to the Count, and then—might that also mean—to the Marques de Mansura as well? I soon discarded such thoughts.

"Sadly, the twin called Marguerite is now lost to us. She will never be saved. For a while, she was under the tutelage of the courtesan, Cora Pearl. No doubt, she is thriving now on her own account. And, of course, she will still be under the patronage of Angel—damn him!" And for a moment the demeanour and appearance of the Count became completely changed. I suddenly believed that I was viewing a different entity. He had risen again from the chair and his size seemed immensely increased, his voice far louder, his eyes glaring, and there was a disturbance of the air around his body the like I have never seen, but which could only be caused by a massive vibration of energy.

And then the storm passed, as quickly as it had arisen. He turned directly to Crawfy. "Excuse my language Madame. When it comes to Angel, I fall prey to anger. But my thinking must remain clear!"

And then to us all, "You see, I know the trajectory. He has deeply drawn each twin into his life; he has pitched them into his world of sensuality and unbridled emotion; he has separated them—he has brought them back together; he has indulged them and shared carnal discourse with them and he has showed them wonders that mortals rarely see. But they are wonders he has promised to one and torn away from the other. He has elevated the sister Marguerite and cast Mariana into misery. My friends, he has sheared them apart, and we know what this means to Mariana. We know that it was her very needs and her longing for love and union that attracted his malice. This is the entity that he serves. And they are not the first. He has cursed twins like this over generations. But the Merciers are the current victims and I have my connection with their family. It requires my special sympathy and care.

157

I believe, too, that Mariana Mercier has qualities that we must especially endeavour to preserve."

The Count returned to his seat. He was calm again and his next words were all the more shocking for the flatness of their tone. "I fear now, even more for Mariana. Her extinction would provide him his fulfilment."

I had to interject here: first with a mixture of relief that my intuitions had been correct, quickly followed by utter dismay that they should be so. But here, from the Count, was complete confirmation. "Monsieur, I have recently been with Mariana, and this too was my belief. A terrible sense that she was in increasing danger. And she seems not to care."

"Indeed, James, I believe you are correct. And you would appear to have been in an excellent place to have your awareness. And for how long was your visit to Mariana?"

How strange and unexpected can be our reactions. I must admit that as I replied, "It was for six months," I felt myself blushing terribly and am sure that I turned crimson. Such was the power and authority that I gave to the gentleman before me. However, St Germain was not of such forbidding and punitive authority. He seemed perfectly happy in the recognition that Mariana and I had been lovers.

"Indeed, James, you are right. I have made my own conclusions from sources one might describe as from the occult, but more concretely from his past behaviour. The complete annihilation of one twin is his perversity and ultimate gain. And his unspeakable method is to have the deed done by one twin upon the other."

Again, I interjected, "And it is just what Mariana expects!"

"Indeed, she has completely been drawn into the entrails of his plan. But you say, James, that she can still see clearly, and this offers us some hope. She has, though, lost the actual will to save herself.

"So, once again, family of the artist, I look to you for your assistance."

"This time," said my father, "It is well placed. I shall not suffer seductions again. My resolve and my anger will see me through to do everything I can to save the girl. I am to leave for France in two-hours-time and then onwards to Spain."

"But Monsieur," said the Count, and his voice was calm but with absolute authority. "It is not for you to do this. It is for Madame Crawford."

We were stunned. It flew completely in the face of our intense expectations of my father's journey. We had been filled with thoughts about his trip and the danger he was undertaking and of his new confidence and determination. We were also aware of his need for atonement.

So, for a full minute, we sat without speaking.

The Count broke the silence. "Monsieur, I am most terribly sorry. I see that I do you a great disservice. I cannot commend you enough for your plan to save the girl. I must say, Monsieur, that I had no prior knowledge of your plan. It is cruel for me to now snatch it away. I can well imagine the resolve and courage that was to accompany you on your journey. And, no doubt, you love the girl—in which, Monsieur, you are clearly not alone. However, it cannot be you who travels to Mariana, nor you Monsieur James—it can only be Madame Crawford."

I felt a great sympathy for my father then, even, I must add, pity. It was his chance to redeem himself, to be the hero he had once intended to be and now it was being snatched from his grasp—just as he claimed the quest. But the Count was adamant.

"How can this be?" It was almost a gasp from my father. "Jane is just a woman; she cannot have the strength to make combat with the Marques."

"But just think Monsieur." The Count's voice was exceedingly calm. "Just think. What is the enemy here? What is the essence of the foe that we now make combat with? There is nothing here that is to do with physical strength. In this battle such factors are irrelevant. There is the need for other qualities, and I should say—carefully—other powers. We must be so careful in the use of 'powers'—they can so terribly corrupt. You are a great artist Monsieur. And I can see as well, a compassionate and brave man. No doubt, as well, you are of the highest intelligence, and I remember," and here the Count spoke most gently, and with a slight smile, "I remember you had conversation with De Vinci. You, of course, believe that it was only I that made that happen, but I can assure you, it required something from you as well. But Monsieur, despite these qualities, the trip to Mariana must only be for your Jane."

I could see that, despite the kind and generous words, my father's pride was smitten, but such was the certainty of the Count, he could make no more objections.

To finalise this, the Count then declared, "And now I must spend some time with Madame Jane. I beg of you Monsieur, and you James, to allow us some time to converse as there are matters of great importance that I must convey to her."

159

And so, my father and I left the room. I placed my hand upon his shoulder and I believe that there were tears in his eyes. We were silent, but I trusted that he would still find ways to regain his honour and, for sure, he was not diminished in my own eyes.

And as to Crawfy: I was beginning to view her in a way that went far beyond her surrogate motherhood of me, her maternal presence in the home, and her loving companionship to my father. She was beginning to inhabit a very different place.

I retired to my room to give thought to the situation and to try to imagine what was then passing between the Count and Crawfy. I was hardly able to do so.

My father retired to his studio. He would work now upon whatever current painting was upon his easel and his portrait of the twins would be hanging in its ever-present place upon the wall behind him.

When I returned to the drawing room, Crawfy was alone and the Comte de St Germain had departed.

CHAPTER TWENTY

The Château Beauséjour

Once again, through the pages of her diary, Crawfy must take up the narration. If I should need to insert an extra sentence in order to clarify, then I will do so and I will make clear that the words are my own. This may not be needed. Crawfy was scrupulous about detail and she was not willing to let any moment of importance have time to escape her memory.

She told us nothing of the conversation she had had with St Germain and we were so imbued by its exclusiveness that we felt that questions were forbidden. An unspoken decree had descended which divided us from any details of why it could only be Crawfy to take on the mission. We were then reduced to being helpers only in the practical sense, making sure that she had everything she needed for her journey, and repeatedly telling her of our love for her and imploring her to take the utmost care.

Her own demeanour was grave, and I could sense that it was not just my father and I who feared for her wellbeing. There was an unusual pallor to her skin and a tautness to her features that betrayed the dread that she tried not to show. Whatever the Count had said to prepare her for her task, it had not included a guarantee of success, nor of Mariana's survival, and perhaps, not even her own.

Despite our ignorance of the finer details of Crawfy's mission, we did understand that she was confronted by both a worldly danger and an occult one. If it were the case that Marguerite had been enlisted—persuaded—seduced, or even mesmerised into murdering her sister, an act of the plainest, physical brutality, there were also the malevolent powers of the Marques; an occultist of the highest order who had a far greater weaponry at his disposal. At least we knew that, on our own side, St Germain was also a man of occult power. I could only wish, that in some way, he had transmuted at least a portion of that to Crawfy.

I will now continue with the pages from Crawfy's diary, beginning with the day that followed her departure. One can ascertain that she wrote her entries at the very end of the day before retiring to bed, though, there were times when events made that impossible. She would then continue her entries as best she could, and as soon she was able.

From the Diary of Jane Crawford
Friday, 12th November 1869
Paris

I came to Paris yesterday with the aim of continuing to Spain within the next two days. I kept it to myself that the Count has passed to me a sum of money that allows me to vary my travel arrangements and timetable if events should require so. As it was a practical offer and not made from generosity, I accepted. Already, I have needed space to manoeuvre, and it is in Paris that I have focused my first efforts.

St Germain believes that Marguerite is utterly lost to any redemption and will now only lead a life that that does homage to her metaphysical mentor, the Marques. However, the Count believes that the Marques will not gift her with any occult learning. He has no need to, and no wish to share his powers. Marguerite can easily carry out his destructive intent with the considerable strength of personality and physical capacities she has been endowed with.

Five years have elapsed and Marguerite will have moved on from the tutelage of Cora Pearl and will have set herself up, either as a courtesan in her own right, or will have found some alternative way towards wealth and status. We expected that whatever incubation had occurred for Marguerite (who would now be 27), she would soon be emerging, fully bedecked, in her latest plumage.

So, Marguerite will not be returning to the fold of ordinary, loving, and caring humanity. The Count, though, recommended I visit her first—as long as she can be found. He wished that I show that we are ready for any malevolence that she might harbour towards her sister and that wherever Mariana might isolate herself, we will be watching over her. There are, after all, the laws of the land which can protect its citizens, as well as the laws of hate and dark magic. And as to the latter, the Count insisted that I should mention his own interest in the wellbeing of Mariana. That, no doubt, would be relayed to the Marques and would give, at least, some strength to our cause.

My first attempt to locate Marguerite was at the Mercier family home. If questioned by a member of the family, it was quite in order that I should make such a visit, as I would claim to be, for just a few days, in Paris. I had, after all, been the hostess to the twins' visit to Whitby five years before. There would, of course, be no need to mention the stay in the house in Poissy that followed soon after!

If that failed, I would go to Cora Pearl's house, though she may well have moved. But, if so, a forwarding address would no doubt be supplied by the occupants.

So, this morning, I took a cab to la maison Mercier. Arriving, I stepped up to the front door to knock loudly. I still had in mind my previous visit and the way that the only occupant, Mariana herself, had been hiding in a room at the top of the building. As before, the large facia of the house returned my gaze with a blank stare whilst the sound of my knocking echoed inside, as in a completely empty space.

I waited, and at last there were footsteps. They grew louder as the occupant walked along the tiled hallway. There was a rattling and shuffling of locks and the door swung open.

It was a maid servant. A young girl who lifted her pinafore to wipe the sweat from her brow before gazing at me searchingly. Clearly, she had been cleaning. It seemed evident that visits were not a common occurrence.

I made my introduction in French and said that I had come to visit Madame Marguerite who was a friend of my family.

The maid was apologetic. Madame had stayed in the house for two nights the previous week, but she had not seen her since. She could not say when she would return.

"And in any case, Madame, the family are moving house. Perhaps even as soon as next week. I am alone here, Madame."

And she opened the door wider to make more visible the long and wide hallway from which much of the furniture had been removed. It looked dark and forlorn.

"She may return Madame, but I believe she is in the country."

"Where in the country?"

"I know not Madame. I'm sorry. She said only those words."

The girl was eager to get away and I thanked her and left my name and the address of my hotel, though it seemed unlikely that Marguerite would seek me out.

"In the country," was so vague that I was left empty of ideas. The only other contact was Cora, so I straight away headed for the address that Edward had given me. It was where he had begun to paint her—and whatever else they had got up to—and where he and the twins had stayed, just before Poissy.

A cab was easily hailed and I made for the rue de Ponthieu. I had felt anxiety about my visit to the Mercier house and now, travelling to Cora's home, a place that would in no way be empty and forlorn, I felt an even greater anxiety. Though was it really that? I allowed myself to sink into the feeling and was surprised. I perceived that hidden within the anxiety, there was also a stirring of excitement.

The cab swung into the rue de Ponthieu and stopped outside the address. Being unsure that Cora still lived there, I asked the driver to wait (my French was so far proving sufficient). The door was opened and I was informed, though in a most weary manner, "No Madame, Madame Pearl no longer resides here. Yes, we do have an address for her, indeed I have come to know it by heart. It is rue de Chaillot, number 101."

I thanked the man for his help and for the new address he had given me, and was sure I heard him mutter as I turned away, "You and many others Madame."

No doubt, a number of Cora's old calling cards are still in circulation.

And so, to the rue de Chaillot, number 101 which was just a short trip away, still in the northwest of the city.

Number 101—which is a rather distinctive number, is also, a very distinctive house. Indeed, "mansion" would be the truer description. Once again, I asked the driver to wait and repeated my now habitual action of rapping on the door. Here there was also a door-bell, so I energetically used both methods.

Such a difference to the bleak house of the Merciers. I immediately heard footsteps scuttling towards the door and their muted sound suggested the luxury of fine carpets.

The door was opened by a woman of middle age wearing a black dress and with a white cap upon her head. She regarded me quizzically, but with a not unfriendly interest.

Again, my French was sufficient and I had a good sense that, this time, I had come to the right house. But, once more, there was disappointment. It was, though, a measure of the warmth of the reception, that the woman, immediately recognising that I was English, attempted to speak to me in my own language. "I am so sorry, but Madame has gone to the country. She stays there in her country house. Who are you Madame please?"

I explained, with a rueful feeling, which, of course, I kept hidden, that I had once spent a most enjoyable few days with Madame Pearl and some other friends, and now, being on a short trip to France, I had hoped, once more, to have the pleasure of her company.

I am quite sure that the woman, who was clearly Cora's housekeeper, was far more used to dealing with callers who were men, and no doubt having to make snap decisions as to whom to allow access and whom to turn away. I believe that Cora is an excellent business woman and no doubt keeps a tight diary, yet the amorous male in pursuit of the most desired woman in Paris might not stick to his allotted appointment. For the housekeeper, to deal instead with a mild-mannered English woman, would therefore have been a relief. Indeed, I was invited to enter the house.

I still retained my cab, as I was just to wait for the housekeeper to write down Cora's address in the country. It was then that a head looked round from one of the inner doors. For both of us, it was that tantalising moment of seeing and thinking that we know, yet given the suddenness, with complete uncertainty; and then, the simultaneous and celebratory recognition that follows. It was Cora's chef Salé.

Salé, of course, is no ordinary member of staff. Cora herself had told me that she was extremely fortunate to have his services and that he stayed with her most faithfully and would go to no other household, despite many attempts to lure him away, especially by the women of Paris who were her greatest rivals.

But there was far more to our recognition than that. Salé had been a presence throughout those days of concourse in Poissy. He had begun the whole venture for us with his preparation of the absinthe which he had mixed, most potently, with Don Angel's special ingredient. And then, in the days that followed, he had floated in and out of the rooms, serving drinks and exquisite food, and had done so in such a way as to cause no one embarrassment even when in the most intimate congress or state of undress. Though not a direct participant, he had played an essential role. And my memory of this brought not the delayed embarrassment that it might have done, but instead, a warm feeling of an intimate occasion shared. He was also pleased to see me and we conversed as well as our different languages could allow. Indeed, our meeting brought forth even greater fruit. He was, that next day, journeying to Beauséjour, Madame Cora's house in the country. If I intended to meet with her, I should surely accompany him.

And so, I relieved the cab driver of his wait and enjoyed a very pleasant lunch with Salé and the housekeeper, whose name was Madame Laforêt. Salé, who clearly knows her well, calls her Eugénie. I discovered that she too has served Cora for a number of years and it was clear that Cora inspires a great loyalty, even devotion, in those who work for her, and that this is a loyalty that she generously gives in return. Both Eugénie and Salé were full of praise for their mistress, and even spoke of her as a highly respected friend.

I thanked them both for their hospitality and arranged to return, early in the morning, for the long journey to Cora's house in Olivet. A cab was easily found and I have returned to my hotel.

I will now cease to write, I believe that everything has been covered, and I must sleep soon. I am to rise early.

Saturday, 13th November 1869
Olivet, the Loire Valley

We were to travel to Beauséjour in one of Cora's own carriages. It was similar to the highly polished coupé that had collected me from my hotel to take me to Poissy those five years ago. On that occasion, the upholstery had been in primrose yellow silk and I had hardly dared to sit, fearing that I might spoil its pristine, elegance. On this occasion, all was in purple, a colour that Cora seems to favour. By now, I could relax and feel more confident as I knew that however expensively luxurious were Cora's possessions, they were made to be thoroughly used and enjoyed. I also had the lively presence of Salé for the long journey. We could speak little, as language posed a barrier, but he did manage to tell me, and I to understand, something of his background. He said, without modesty, that he had been a chef of renown even before he entered Cora's household and that she had first engaged him whilst she was under the protection of the Duc de Rivoli. The meals that he had prepared for her dinner parties were described in extreme detail and in words that matched the fantastic extravagance of their cost. For this he could only speak in French and I believe that any lack of understanding on my part was easily compensated by his gestures and tonality. French is such an expressive language. Salé seems to be a man well fulfilled in his position and by the end of our journey I saw him as a very different character to the respectful shadow that had served our needs in Poissy.

Beauséjour translates as "a beautiful place to stay." It is indeed, and even in the winter, Cora's residence, which is really a château, is a delight. The old building, with its great shuttered windows, is surrounded by a large expense of land and nearby flows the river Loire. The gardens are, of course, perfection. A sumptuous place of character and, no doubt, a most sensual one for Cora and her guests in the summer months. The woman seems to be riding at the height of her powers.

Riding is a relevant term. As we entered the driveway, we saw ahead of us a figure seated most comfortably upon a splendid horse: bare headed, with hair tied back, and immaculately clothed in a long, dark, riding dress. Hearing our carriage approach, the rider turned her horse and came towards us at a gallop. The carriage continued on its way, and the rider now turned to trot alongside us before leaning from her steed to peer through the window. It was Cora.

Her face lit up as she recognised me.

She called out in English, "It is surely Jane. You have come to see me!" and at that, with a flick to the horse of her riding crop, she sped ahead of us to the château.

She disappeared from view and must have headed straight for the stables. It was Salé who escorted me into the house and arranged for refreshments to be brought. He then departed to assume his duties. When the refreshments arrived, they were not brought by a maid, but by Cora herself.

She sat down opposite me. She was still wearing her most impressive riding outfit. She leant forward, resting an elbow upon one knee and her chin upon her open palm and gazed at me with cool grey eyes. Her face was completely open. Then, after a moment's scrutiny, she sat back and smiled broadly, "Jane, it is lovely to see you—and I can now practice

167

my native tongue, before I forget all my English. And you have found your way to my hideout in the country. Here, I can ride as much as I like. I have six horses and two English grooms. What do you think of that?!

"And Salé has brought you. He is a dear and I really need him here as I have guests. And now, one more, as you have arrived out of nowhere!"

It was time for me to confess at least something of the reason for my visit. "Cora, it is so lovely to see you." And I really meant it. "But this is just a happy coincidence. In this moment, I feel that my trip to France could be made entirely for the pleasure of seeing you and helping you to remember that you were once from England. And we did share a special, few days in that Poissy house—and with the mirage of old Alexandria on the horizon. Was it all just a dream, Cora? We recognise each other now—so we must have been there!"

"That rascal, Angel!" Cora tossed her head back and smiled broadly. "He has all these tricks. It's drugs I think—he carries with him all these potions. My goodness, he has given me some that have allowed me the most considerable offerings to my male patrons. And then, sometimes— just for relaxing. He mixes it, I think, with hypnotism. Who knows? When we party together it is always remarkable and I have no cause to complain. Far from it! And I do not bother to think about why or how. It is what it is—and whenever he is here—and I haven't seen him for two years. If he comes—he comes." And she gave the shrug of one whose present life is so full that there is no space, or indeed, need, to anticipate the future.

"To be sure, Cora," I said, "I have no expectation or wish to see Don Angel. But I came to Paris to seek out the Mercier twin, Marguerite, and I do believe you might help me in this."

"But, of course, Jane. I will forgive you for not making me your main port of call. So, it is Marguerite—and she is here! She stays with me now for a few days. You have accomplished your mission!

"We will seek out Marguerite later. She is staying here with one of her artist friends. A very nice man called Félicien Rops. Do you know him?" I shook my head. "He is a young artist from Belgium and he likes to make pictures that are rather risqué. I have yet to pose for him."

There was though a memory that suddenly came back to me. I remembered that when Mariana and I had visited the artist Gustave Moreau, he had told us of his fraught encounter with Marguerite and how, as she had departed, he had flung after her the disparaging remark that she would be better off with—Félicien Rops. It had meant nothing to me at the time, but now I was intrigued to meet this man whom Moreau saw as a just pairing for Marguerite.

But I was brought out of my thoughts by Cora loudly proclaiming, "But here is the greatest artist, and the one whom I really love to pose for!" The words rang out as a man entered the room. He was in his 30s, with a pleasant appearance, quite small and with light brown hair and moustache. He moved lightly on his feet.

"Now Jane, this one you must surely have heard of—Jane Crawford, meet Gustave Doré."

I was, indeed, impressed. Eddy has often spoken of Doré, and always with great admiration. An artist known mainly for his illustrations, but who is also a fine painter. And there was much more that I could say, though some translation by Cora was required.

"Monsieur Doré, what a great pleasure."

Doré seemed absolutely affable and I could ascertain immediately from his expression and tone of voice that he is a playful man.

"Madame Crawford, the pleasure is mine."

Cora interjected, "Jane is the, well, how do we put it Jane—the consort? Of the artist Edward—*."

"Madame I know of him. He creates fine portraits."

I was eager to say, "And our friend is the poet Alfred Tennyson—and I am quite sure, Monsieur, that you are making the illustrations for his poem on King Arthur."

"What a wonderful coincidence Madame! And to be with one who is so close to the great poet. Sadly, I have yet to meet him and fear that I may not. I am only visited by the assistants to the publisher. I have to trust that my imagination will not stray too far from his."

And so, we talked—Cora enjoying the translating when needed, and inserting her own lively comments—in French to Doré, and to me in English. I have said that Doré had impressed me as being playful and clearly this was bound out as there was much humour in the conversation; Cora, herself, being completely of that nature.

I could see, too, that he adores her and that she reciprocates. At times they held hands and kissed and on two occasions she affectionately ruffled his hair. It seems to me, most unlikely that the artist is seen professionally by Cora, (though most unusual for her), and that there

---

* Because the name of my late father is well known to the public I still wish to retain his privacy within this narrative.

really is affection, even love; certainly, from him to her. Perhaps, all part of her relaxation in her country house.

We had now reached the late afternoon and the light outside was fading. A maid came in and lit the lamps and also many candles that were interspersed around the room. She then attended to the fire in the large fireplace, so that it crackled and roared before settling into a nest of red-hot, glowing logs.

Doré, who clearly felt at home, had poured us glasses of sweet wine, and with the warmth of the fire and of the fine wine, the thought of returning to my hotel in Paris felt increasingly alien. Indeed, the journey by now, was nigh impossible. I had no need to worry. Cora was only too pleased to have me stay the night. There were many rooms and I would be well looked after.

In fact, I had become so comfortable that I had completely lost sight of my mission.

My true aims now fiercely retaliated against my temporary denial. As we moved to the dining room, the recognition that I was really there to encounter Marguerite most forcibly returned and my happiness was replaced by fear. I have realised that, in the years without seeing her, and especially in the preceding weeks, she has become a figure of dread.

"Come," said Cora, "Let us reunite you with the twin."

I can write no more, and I will return to these pages in the morning. I am exhausted and need time to think about the remarkable events that followed.

CHAPTER TWENTY ONE

The dinner party

From the diary of Jane Crawford
Sunday, 14th November 1869
Olivet, The Loire Valley

It is now mid-morning and I will continue with my account of the events of last night. My sleep was fitful and full of dreams. One especially unpleasant one had me in its grip throughout the night. In other circumstances I would have slept well; the room is comfortable—lovely in fact, with homely and tasteful furnishings, and looks out onto the gardens. All very different to the chaotic nature of my feelings.

Downstairs, I can hear voices and there are the sounds of breakfast being served. I will not go down though. I will claim a headache and the need to rest until a carriage has been made ready for me. I need time to think. The strength of purpose that I carried with me from England has dissolved into uncertainty and confusion.

It is all from the dinner last night and the hour that followed. I hope that my recording of the events might now help me to find clarity, as the cause of my mission has been thrown into doubt.

I had been with Cora and the artist Gustave Doré. All very light and amiable, and then we made our way to the dining room with Cora in a fine mood and the amorous Doré frisking at her side.

My own mood in no way matched such jollity. I was about to encounter Marguerite and I had become truly scared of her.

I forced my thoughts to counter this—"She is just a young woman—and has no magical powers," but I was unable to convince myself.

Despite my attempted denials, I could not free myself from the sense, that though Marguerite may not have access to the occult, she still has the power of an immense force of will—and added to this—I doubt that she feels remorse. Nor is she inhibited by the normal human restrictions that come from ambivalence. She knows only certainty.

We entered the dining room which was ablaze with light from two huge chandeliers. Too large for even that elegant room, but then Cora needs to be seen as extravagant: it attracts even greater rewards from her patrons.

There were many paintings upon the walls. Some were of the sensual rococo kind that I associate with her, but not only these. There were landscapes, very fine and Dutch I would think. But most of all, there were the paintings of horses—all dominated by one spectacular portrait of Cora upon a fine black steed.

I give these impressions now, but they were not immediate. They came later, when I studied the inanimate objects in an attempt to calm myself.

When I entered the room, I looked immediately at Marguerite. There could be no pretence of ease or nonchalance. I was drawn, straight away, to her face and figure. She was gazing back at me. I averted my eyes, believing that my face betrayed my fear.

There were three others already waiting to dine. One was sitting so close to Marguerite that he had to be Félicien Rops. Their arms were touching and no doubt there was a similar, but invisible contact, under the table.

The two others were middle-aged men, meticulously dressed for dinner and of the most affluent appearance. I cannot remember their names, though one was a Count and the other was also titled.

They looked at me with open approval, presumably because we were in the house of Cora, but she soon dismissed any unworthy expectations by introducing me as Madame Crawfy, consort of the great English portrait painter Edward—.

"Madame Crawfy" and "consort" were fine by me (and Edward is, indeed, a very good painter).

I imagine that any declaration of my official attachment to a man would not have deterred Monsieur Rops, but he was far too taken up with Marguerite.

He has the appearance of a "Félicien." The look of a flamboyant artist, an aesthete, and undoubtably handsome. His has a full head of wavy, dark hair and a moustache that turns up at its tips. His dark eyes were sparkling with humour and the kind of self-confidence that can easily slip into arrogance.

And then expectations forced me to return my gaze to Marguerite. I had the uneasy feeling that her own eyes had never left me. I know that I blushed.

Of course, I broke into the expected greetings that pass between those who have not met for years.

In contrast, her own greeting was effortless and I believe now that it may have been genuine. She had, after all, no prior knowledge of my arrival and surely no knowledge of why I was there. For her, then, a happy coincidence, though Marguerite knows exactly how to be in any circumstance.

I think it was the first time that she has called me Jane. Perhaps a declaration of her maturity at age 27 and that she now considers us as equals. "Jane, it is truly a great pleasure to see you. How long has it been? Six years? Oh—five. Nevertheless, a long time, in which much can change."

This last remark was made in such a positive tone that, for a moment, I felt a dash of hope and relief that Marguerite herself had changed. I then scolded myself for allowing such wishful fantasies. How easy my task would be if it were so.

She looked leaner. A little older, and, if anything, more beautiful. Her hair which has always fallen in curls around her face was drawn back. Severely, in fact, but this did nothing to detract. It allowed the high cheek bones and the finely delineated nose and lips a clearer display. The slight bridge of freckles was still there above her nose. I thought then of Mariana and wondered if the twins even shared the exact number of freckles. Unlike Cora, Marguerite seemed to have no addition of cosmetics at all.

Her eyes are clear and grey, and I really believe that they never blink. Is this possible? Perhaps just my metaphor. I am quite sure my own eye-lids were lowered for much of the evening as my acute discomfort turned to confusion, though it became increasingly interspersed with moments of self-conscious pleasure, all of which was in response to Marguerite.

The jauntiness of Cora became increasingly annoying, as did her mutual indulgence with Doré. The two became more and more intimate, at first teasing and then giggling, kissing, and whispering into each other's ears. By the time of the third course and after several glasses of wine, Doré had managed to completely free one of Cora's breasts from her low-cut gown. This seemed to create no surprise, but only approval amongst the men and drew from Rops the comment, "Ah, the most famous breasts in Paris."

He had claimed much of the vocal space with amusing stories that caused great mirth in the two noblemen, but they were told with such speed that my own French could not keep up. Cora, by then, had become bored with having to translate for me.

Marguerite, who could also have translated, never offered, and it seemed that she designated her companion's stories to be hardly worth repeating. Despite his clear focus upon her, she seemed quite aloof and, in her near to perfect English, she increasingly only addressed me, so that I felt that she and I were creating our own little private enclave which we were sharing with growing intimacy. With some misgivings, I noticed that it was a pleasing place to be.

The two noblemen were clearly disconcerted by Cora's attention to Doré, though this may have mitigated against any rivalry that could exist between themselves. They increasingly turned their focus upon each other.

Salé was sending his creations through from the kitchen. They were perfectly served by two pretty maids in black and white uniforms. No doubt the dishes were splendid, but I was so taken up by my emotions, as to hardly notice one course moving into the next. I am just glad the master chef is unaware of the degree to which I was wasting such exquisite flavours.

Though I, at least, went through the motions of eating, Marguerite hardly touched her food and this seemed to be not out of discomfort, but from choice. I wondered what nourishments she preferred.

She spoke to me of her stay with us in Whitby and how much she had enjoyed it. I was amazed by the accuracy of her memory about the weeks she and Mariana had been with us and about the town and the surrounding countryside. She particularly loved the ruined Abbey. That got her talking about art and how the great, German Romantic, Caspar Friedrich would have made such an excellent painting of the Abbey—such a spectacular gothic subject.

It is most strange how the very words we must not say can by-pass all resistance and drive themselves into our speech despite our intense,

174

internal protestations. To myself, I had declared that, surely, I must never mention the artist, Gustave Moreau.

And then, I heard my voice, "It was five years ago that I visited another great painter, Gustave Moreau. And I was with your sister. Edward had seen him too—he is such an admirer of his work."

Marguerite remained completely composed. "But Jane, did you not know? I too called upon him. In fact, I even offered my services as a model. And he declined. I have often pictured myself in one of his paintings. In fact, I believed at the time that I really belonged in one!"

Here Monsieur Rops loudly interjected.

Marguerite turned back to me and translated.

"Félicien says that Moreau is planning to paint images of Salomé, so I should definitely be his model. Well, I agree! But the foolish man has missed his chance!"

There was something about the absolute clarity and confidence with which she said this that caused me to laugh, and I was not alone. The two gentlemen guffawed loudly and Félicien Rops looked very merry. Marguerite seemed pleased to have entertained us.

My unconsciousness of the food had also included my intake of wine. My glass had been repeatedly filled by the serving girls whenever I automatically emptied it. The luxurious, red wine warmly seeped through my body and melted away my painful, physical anxiety, and my conversation with Marguerite increasingly became a source of pleasure.

I do, of course, love her sister, her identical twin, and there were times, those five years ago, when I loved her deeply. And now, here was her replica, but with the added fascination of other and rare attributes. The same face and body; the same clear, melodic sound to the voice, and yet with such different words and intonations. Such sameness and difference mingling so enticingly together. I was becoming entranced.

Now that I look at my own writing and the phrase that I have just used, I have to ask—was I really in a trance? Has Marguerite been gifted of the occult by the Marques? All I know is that during the evening I became increasingly fond of her, and yes, I do now trust her.

It was at the end of the meal, when for a rare moment there was silence in the room, that Marguerite looked directly at me and asked, as if certain that I would know, "And how is my sister?"

Félicien Rops immediately interrupted. "Marguerite, you have a sister?"

Cora then joined in, "A perfect twin!"

Rops could hardly conceal his delight at the erotic possibility.

Marguerite was calm, unsmiling, and ignored the others. This was only between her and me. I believe that she had begun to wonder, just a little more, as to why I had appeared after so many years.

My first answer was completely honest. "I have not seen her. Not for all these years Marguerite—not since I last saw you. After Poissy, we took her to your family house and that was it. We returned straight to England."

I paused and Marguerite said nothing. The room remained quiet. Her silence was a command for more details. "But I know someone who has seen her … I believe she is well."

My statement was utterly inadequate and had such a ring of falseness that Marguerite immediately responded with concern. Her hitherto calmness changed completely into anxiety. "Jane—are you so sure of her wellbeing? Is she unwell or in trouble? Is she still in Spain?"

I was now thrown back into the stressful state with which I had first sat down at the table. All present were focused on the two of us, and just at that moment, only on me. And yet I could not speak. I was so utterly caught between my growing sense that we had misjudged Marguerite and my earlier certitude that Mariana should be protected from her at all costs. Her whole demeanour in that moment was of the desperately concerned sister.

My voice seemed very quiet to me and strained. "Yes, Spain still. Near Almeria."

"Yes," said Marguerite. "She got fixated on that place and went to live there. But why for so long? You know that it was there that we first met Don Angel. Dear Angel, whom I haven't seen for so long. I got on with him so well, and Mariana was so jealous. She really couldn't bear us being together. And he offered many wonderful things to us as twins, but always she would leave herself out and then sulk terribly. Oh dear, Jane, I know I shouldn't say such things, but her jealousy really tore us apart—I felt I couldn't do anything of my own."

As if it was an annoying incumbrance, Marguerite pushed away the arm of Félicien Rops which had remained steadfastly attached to hers. She raised a hand to her face and for a moment her fingers fluttered upon her forehead. Then she dropped the hand in a gesture of despair. "But I have neglected her, and I fear that she is in trouble. Jane is this really why you have come? Have you come to tell me that something terrible is happening to Mariana?"

Of course, this is the case. Yet Marguerite's manner was now bringing such distortion to the planned content of my mission, that I was speechless. I could hardly say, "Yes, and you are the terrible thing we fear will happen." Nor would I want to when my judgement of her was changing and I was beginning to see her concern for her sister and her sadness at their separation as heart-felt and genuine.

I fell back to a truth that was easy to express. "I believe that she is unhappy. She chooses isolation."

Marguerite had already made up her mind. "I must go to her. I will go to Spain, to Almeria. Is she still in the square?"

Again, I felt blocked. Was I to help Marguerite to do the very thing that I have come here to prevent? I have come to warn her off—to tell her of our suspicions and that any outrageous act would be accounted for. Yet she only seemed to wish her sister well. "Jane, why don't you say? Is it a secret? We are twins. Do you wish to come between us?"

"Marguerite, I am sorry. I must tell you. I have come to tell you that Mariana wishes to see no one and that she fears a visit from you. She fears the Marques too and that the two of you will seek her out. She is frightened Marguerite. It is perhaps a part of the sickness of her melancholy."

Marguerite considered. "Sometimes, when the mind goes, those who are most loved become the greatest threat. I have heard of this. I think that this is what you are telling me Jane. My sister has become sick in spirit and in mind."

The interaction between myself and Marguerite had changed the whole nature of Cora's dinner party. She was looking increasingly uncomfortable. Doré, no longer able to be playful, was attending to the napkin in front of him and was twisting it into shapes as if he wished to wrench it into a sculpture. Rops was adapting rather better to the change. His affectionate arm had been brushed aside by Marguerite, but he altered his position so that he reclined back in his chair and the fingers of one hand attended to the fine upturned tips of his moustache. He seemed to be deeply immersed in his own thoughts. The two noblemen had ceased to converse. My conversation with Marguerite and the emotions expressed, allowed for no ordinary chat or banter. They were compelled to quietly observe, and did so.

The tension was broken by the opportune appearance of Salé. In fact, we had completed all the courses, and he had come to receive his just acclaim. Cora looked immensely relieved. She rose to her feet adjusting her dress as she did so. "Mon Cher, you have done wonders as ever."

Salé looked very pleased. The two noblemen, who were probably not used to such affection and praise being given to one they would consider a servant, gruffly echoed Cora's words. After all, having waited so patiently, they would not wish to lose her favour.

And their patience was about to be rewarded. Cora clearly felt that she needed an exit and the inevitable expectations of these gentlemen could expiate this perfectly. And they were to be freed from any rivalrous discomforts since Cora's beckoning look clearly included them both. Appearing as nonchalant as they could, they followed her from the room.

Marguerite's voice was completely clear and authoritative, "I believe that the remaining gentlemen now go for a smoke—and to talk about art. Whilst I must speak more with Madame Crawford."

Doré did not seem disconcerted by Cora's disappearance with the two noblemen. Presumably, he can rest easy that when she makes a distinction between work and pleasure, he finds himself in the latter category. A distinction that he would share with very few others. I have surmised that the playful and extrovert Cora Pearl is also a cast iron business woman.

He had, though, clearly not expected to be commanded thus by Marguerite. He may also not have wished to find himself smoking and conversing with Rops—on art or any other subject.

Rops' own response to Marguerite was an elegant shrug of the shoulders. I dare say that to submit to her whims was not too great a threat to him and was all part of their mutual game. He would, no doubt, find ways to re-assert himself.

We were, therefore, alone. Despite the attentions of the serving girls, the table, which stretched between us, was strewn with debris from the meal, along with empty and half full dishes, goblets, and an assortment of exotic fruits that had escaped from a giant silver bowl. One maid did attempt to enter, but an imperious wave from Marguerite caused her immediate retreat.

Marguerite's focus was completely on the subject of her sister. She rose and walked around the table so that we could sit together. We were close enough for me to catch a hint of an exquisite rose perfume. Just a hint, yet all the more powerful in its reserve. The clear eyes gazed searchingly into mine with a complete sincerity of need. "Please be honest with me Jane."

Close to us, in the huge fireplace, stabs of yellow flame flashed and flickered before retreating into a fierce red mass of smouldering logs.

Marguerite, knowing of the warmth of the room, wore only a silk blowse above a grey cotton skirt. The blowse was lilac and it was embroidered with pretty floral motifs. She looked so at home in Cora's château—and so cool. Though my top coat and cloak had been discarded on arrival, I was still dressed underneath for the November journey.

She could see my discomfort. "Come, Jane, you will boil in here with those winter clothes. We will go to my room."

She took my hand and led me through a long corridor that opened into a spacious vestibule. There were plants in stone containers and small statues of nymphs surrounding a pool with a fountain that made little splashing sounds. Arising from there was a wide marble staircase that gently curved as we climbed it to the first floor. The sound of my outdoor shoes on the marble echoed in the stairwell, but at the top the carpet was thick and luxurious so that my feet were suddenly silent. Marguerite had made no sound at all. I saw that she wore silver slippers, the kind that I had seen in paintings of oriental scenes.

She spoke as we entered her room. "You can see Jane, that I feel very at home here. And in Cora's houses in Paris as well. She makes me very welcome and somehow we get on together. She is not sophisticated. Well, that is not true, in some ways she is sublimely accomplished."

And at that, Marguerite put a finger to her lips and bade me listen. From a room nearby, came the exuberant sounds of love making. She smiled and turned her attention back to me.

"And when it comes to decorating a house—or a château, she is in her element. And if she can have her horses nearby, she can feel complete. I have no interest in riding, but she forgives me that. She has many gentlemen friends who ride with her and gift her with even more horses. She even has English grooms to look after them. She needs them. But we are so different—no doubt. Let us say that I am more reticent than her."

My own view of Marguerite is that she is of such strong character that the word "reticent" can hardly apply.

"And I share with Cora a friendship with the Marques. Whenever he is in France, the two of them make sure to create adventure. They play, and then he is gone, and she plays her games elsewhere. Though, no doubt, none are quite like the creations of Don Angel."

I was sitting upon Marguerite's bed. She had pulled up a small armchair and was sitting so near to me that our knees almost touched. At her mention of Don Angel, and perhaps, as well, due to the closeness of her body, I felt my anxiety return. I was sure, too, that a chill draft had entered the room. I looked to see if a window was open, but all were closed and the curtains were drawn. I interjected, and my anxiety was clear to hear.

"Don Angel—is he here now, Marguerite?"

She laughed, "Jane, you are getting like my sister. She came to dread him. And for no account other than his fondness for me. Well—is he here?"

She looked enigmatic and with a mischief that troubled me even more. "Sometimes I think he is everywhere. So, perhaps he is—and he appears whenever it suits him. I admire this, but Mariana came to hate it. She felt we could never be free of him and was quite sure that he preferred me to her, and once she had decided that she invested everything in proving it right."

I felt cast in the role of Mariana. As I looked at Marguerite, she seemed magnificent and utterly superior to me. She had risen and walked to a little table from which she lifted a silver cigarette case. "Do you smoke cigarettes Jane?" I shook my head. She lit one for herself and returned to her chair.

"But you must tell me now—all that is happening. We must try to help her together."

I had been warm when we had entered the room, but now I felt so cold that I began to shiver.

Marguerite, of course, noticed, but she saw it as my anxiety. "Really, Jane, Don Angel is a good man, you really should not fear him. And he might help us find Mariana and bring her back to us."

She had only lit one lamp which barely lit the room. She still sat close, and the smoke from her cigarette drifted around her face like a misty, blue veil.

I looked through the smoke and over her shoulder. There, sitting in an armchair, in the corner of the room, was the Marques. He was completely still and watching us.

Marguerite continued, "And Jane, in a week's time it is our birthday. We would always celebrate it together—what else would we do? But now—for years—there has been nothing, not even a greeting

180

between us. This year we will put it right. We will go to Mariana and we will have our special day. We will make it like no other."

I could only stare at the Marques, as if it were just he and I in the room. I heard Marguerite's voice. "Jane, what is the matter?"

Her face was close to mine. I could not take my eyes off the apparition in the chair. He was so still that he might only have been an image; except for his eyes. Looking straight into mine, they were widening with surprise.

My look was so transfixed that Marguerite turned to follow my gaze.

"Jane, what is it? Do you know that you are staring? What is it over there?"

She broke into French which I did not understand. She turned and looked again.

My eyes, still locked to his, I murmured, "Don Angel sits in the chair."

Marguerite rose and her own eyes searched the room. "Jane, he is not here. No one else is here—it is only the two of us." My words were just a whisper. "He is here. He sits there."

Mariana sat next to me on the bed so that we were both facing the chair in which he sat. But I could see him and she could not. For a moment she was quiet, considering the situation. "Then he wishes you to see him and that I should not ... or ... he thought that neither of us could ... but you can."

And I could tell from the look on his face, that it was the latter. He was astounded that I could see him.

Marguerite rose. She still looked at the chair that to her was empty, but she did not approach it. I could tell that there was no doubt in her mind that in some astral form, he was indeed there. Nor did she doubt that I could see him.

She spoke to me, knowing that he could hear and would be attentive to her words. "He can travel like this. You do not see his real body. Who knows where that is. It could be anywhere in the world. But his mind can travel and it can take on a physical form. Sometimes I have felt his presence, but never seen the form—like you are seeing Jane. And how can that be?"

And with a chiding voice, "So, Angel, am I no longer your best friend that Jane Crawford can see you and I cannot?"

But I could well see that there was no favouritism. The Marques had not expected to be seen at all.

181

As Marguerite spoke, his image began to fade. He paid no heed to her, and all the time, until he was completely gone, his gaze was upon me, and the dark eyes staring at mine were the last of him to disappear, and the gleam that was always there had gone: they were as two pieces of black coal.

I said, "He has gone now Marguerite."

She had been taken aback, surprised, even offended, yet in a moment she was composed, her thoughts overruling her feelings. "Well, Jane, he must have come for a reason. He can sense things from a thousand miles away. Perhaps he knows of our visit to Mariana—he might want to help—he will be so sad that we are estranged. Yes, he will want to help us put things right. Perhaps he will conjure some wonderful scene for our birthday. Yes, that must be it! What a wonderful thing that will be."

And now, warm feelings returned to Marguerite and she looked so happy at the prospect of the reunion, and once more I felt the sincerity of her love for her sister. And perhaps the Marques might indeed wish to help us and to see a transformed and happy Mariana.

I had no more words to say. Tiredness overwhelmed me, and to be sure, it was my experience of Don Angel that had been the most exacting challenge of many that day. I can hardly believe now that that same morning I had been in Paris, at the town house of Cora and boarding a carriage for the countryside with Salé.

Marguerite guided me to my room and embraced me warmly. "Thank you so much Jane. You have made such a difference. You have joined me again to my sister and, together, we will hasten to see her."

And now it is the next morning and I write these lines which only increase my confusion. I had hoped they would bring clarity. I have been away from Marguerite for long enough for the aim of my mission to come back to me, and especially my instructions—and guidance— from St Germain. But has he seduced me? Am I caught up in some terrible, enduring feud between two supernatural beings—and why should this happen to me?

I hear steps approaching. Marguerite will surely want to seek me out. I will end here.

CHAPTER TWENTY TWO

Farewell to Beauséjour

From the diary of Jane Crawford
Sunday, 14th November 1869. Night-time.
Rue de Chaillot, Paris

My room was close to Marguerite's; just two doors along the corridor. Seeing how tired I was, she had practically put me to bed, but as soon as she left, I felt compelled to sit at the table, open my diary, and record the first part of the evening. Then, on waking, I had the energy to finish my account. Now, a day has passed and I can, once again, make the hour before sleeping my diary time.

When I wrote this morning, I had hoped to make, at least, some sense of the evening's events and to write myself into a calmer and more thoughtful place. I had little success and am still beset by doubt. One thing I will declare: I believe now that Marguerite is a friend and not a foe and this, at least, has brought a wondrous relief. How could we have imagined her to nurse and succour such malevolence. I believe that young James must take some of the blame. Whatever he was told by Mariana, her words became subject to his own imagination: he was surely morbid and distressed that she could end their love affair and do so with such ease.

Three powerful figures, Don Angel, St Germain, Marguerite, circle Mariana, either to protect or destroy her. And yes, I too, am now part of the fray. But I am also shaken by my experience of those around me. I have stepped into another world; the world of Cora Pearl—utterly immoral and profligate—only in Paris under their emperor could it happen—and for how long? Those in high office abandon their dignity, throw self-respect to the winds, risk their fortunes, all for her favours.

And I am now a friend of Marguerite, yet I am in awe of her. For a moment I felt I would do anything for her friendship and favour. Does this diminish me?

But lurking, most frighteningly, is the Marques de Mansura. If it is truly years since Marguerite last met him, he has located her, and me, for a special reason. And surely, that cannot be for the good.

Yet Marguerite admires him deeply and is so grateful to him. And can we really trust all that St Germain has said? Is Mariana just a pawn in their own ancient struggle—a piece in their contest to move and to eventually discard forever from the board?

Am I and Edward, also pawns?

And now, as well, there is Félicien Rops—the elegant, embodiment of sin.

This morning, I ceased to write when I heard footsteps on the marble stairs. Then there was silence as the feet met the carpet of the corridor; a silence that lasted too long—someone was surely listening at my door. Then the knock.

I had expected Marguerite, but it was not her. It was Rops.

His English is poor, but he was surely making the effort. In the main, I will record it as the English should have been. "Good morning, Jane. May I call you Jane? Thank you. And you have not joined us downstairs. Are you unwell? I trust your sleep was not full of horrid dreams."

He laughed; quite sure, I suppose that a disturbed night might well follow a dinner with Cora and her friends. "Madame Jane, I should not just appear at your door. I know this. But I so wish to speak with you and you have not joined us for breakfast. And yes! I also have a message from Marguerite."

I was prepared to let him in. I felt I had his measure, and his wish to talk seemed sincere enough. Most importantly, he had a message from Marguerite. "You may enter, Monsieur, but it cannot be for long. I wish to return soon to Paris."

He entered and I could see his enthusiasm for the task was in no way dampened by my ambivalence. I knew full well that, notwithstanding the message from Marguerite, his intention was to seduce me.

He slipped gracefully across the room and looked through the window at the garden. "Madame Pearl makes a wonderful house.

You know it is the first time I have met her—though, of course, I have heard much. And Marguerite loves to tell me of her escapades."

I was in no mood to give encouragement to this man. I brought him back to business. "And you have a message from her. Could she not tell me herself?"

"But Jane—she has gone. She left this morning in a rush. I thought I must have upset her—it is like that between us—but I believe it was something else. And can you help me in this? You spent much time together in her room."

I imagine that his genuine need to understand her departure had since become mixed with more subjective imaginings about the two of us in her room.

I brushed such thoughts aside. "Monsieur, do you know the Marques de Mansura?"

"I do not know this Marques. From the title he is Spanish. Should I know him? A past lover of Marguerite perhaps—or of Cora?"

He looked interested. I suppose that I was searching for anything, any reference to the Marques that might help me understand the visitation. "It matters not. But please tell me this message from Marguerite."

He gave a look of mock concentration, as if delving deep into his memory. "Ah yes! She arranges your journey to Spain for tomorrow. You will go together to find this twin of hers, this Mariana. You must meet her at Cora's Paris house in rue de Chaillot. Tonight, you stay there and tomorrow your long journey begins."

Again, Rops looked to be enjoying colourful thoughts. But he also wished to enquire more deeply into the subject of identical twins. "Jane, please tell me about this Mariana. This other Marguerite who exists. How wonderful it would be to see them together. Are they the same in their nature? Surely there can be no other like Marguerite."

Rops was being playful, but I could also see an enquiring mind that was not completely taken up by the carnal. And his question opened a space for me that was the antidote to the forced thinking and reactive emotions that had governed me since I arrived at Cora's. As Rops watched me with keen expectation, I began to reflect. With all the events, the emotions, the fears, the intense affects swirling around the object of Mariana, it had been a long time since I had really thought about her as the person that she is.

I gestured to him to sit and placed myself in the other chair. I was going to give him a serious and thoughtful reply. I spoke as

I thought, and the thinking was fresh, and in that process, I realised that Mariana, my Mariana, had become lost to me. Then gradually, as I talked to Félicien Rops, she began to return. "Mariana is a poet." This was my first remark and it surprised me, though the use of the term opened a gateway to a garden that, for too long, had languished in the shade.

"She has great grace and also, generosity. She is kind. Like her sister, she can be a muse to the artist, yet whilst Marguerite excites, Mariana strokes and sooths. Marguerite is of the land and the city, and Mariana is of the seas. And there is sadness. Often, she is melancholic; yet when she smiles, her face is transformed and all around her share the radiance and are made happy. She has depth. She cares nothing for the material. The world around her has no precedence over that which lives within. She is deeply passionate. She loves. She is a child of Aphrodite."

The last sentence was not thought, just spoken, as if it came from another part of my being, and it heralded the strangest of feelings, like a forgotten dream whose memory is tantalising in its closeness and whose impact still remains in one's whole being. There was the glimmer of Ancient Alexandria on a warm night, the slightest sea breeze refreshing the quayside and then, lying upon the soft grass of a garden. The night sky was stupendous with stars.

Rops was different now. "Madame Jane—I have a terrible reputation—a seducer of women. And, too often, I believe my reputation." He laughed, very entertained by his own joke. "Yes, I do. And I came to you this morning—no longer attached to Marguerite—and Madame Jane, you are a beautiful woman. And of course, we are also in the house of La Grande Horizontale, Madame Pearl. I mean her no disrespect; she makes it a form of art. Here, one might say, 'anything goes.'

"But Madame—I see that it does not. A lady with integrity such as yours ..."

Rops was struggling with his English. I thought it best to wait quietly.

"A lady such as you ... is not so easy to persuade—if persuade at all. Please forgive Félicien for his hopes and for his impertinence.

"But, as well, Madame, any such effort would be misplaced, as I see that it is women whom you prefer." He paused, as if to deliver something of great value. "Especially this one—this twin of Marguerite—this Mariana.

"You must indeed join Marguerite and go to her. It is their birthday. What joy you will have."

As we sat together, I saw in Rops, not the decadent aesthete. Not even the artist. All mannerisms, all arrogance, all affectations, had ceased. He was completely open and sincere and I felt for him only affection. "Monsieur Rops, perhaps you are right, and if you see in me a lover of women, I believe you do so as one who shares such love."

The mood had changed so much during Rops' short visit. By the time he left to return downstairs, we were both quietly self-reflective.

I had not made arrangements for a carriage back to Paris and just hoped that one of Cora's would be available. Somehow, I had assumed it would be; with Cora, everything seems possible.

Rops reassured me. A ride to Paris could surely be arranged, and he would see to it. He was staying another night, but would then be journeying home to Belgium, "Though, increasingly, I am a being of Paris."

He added a sombre note, almost musing to himself, "Yet clouds of war are forming."

Before I left, Eddy had told me of the rumours of conflict between France and Prussia. What havoc a Prussian victory might cause to the extravagance of Paris; to the profligate lives of the nobility—and to their queenly courtesans.

There is little to say about my journey back to Paris. Even amongst the luxurious upholstery of a Cora carriage, the long ride was uncomfortable and cold. I was sustained, though, by an event that occurred straight after our departure.

I made myself ready and descended to the ground floor. All was now very quiet in the building and I feared that Rops might have failed to arrange for my carriage, but when I looked through one of the giant windows and onto the courtyard, there it was, with the driver already in his seat.

He got down to help me with my bag and to see that I was comfortable. My destination was simply the one that Rops had delivered in his message. In this there was no will of my own and the words felt tenuous.

"Rue de Chaillot, the house of Madame Pearl?"

"Of course, Madame." And I could tell from his accent that he was English. One of Cora's English grooms perhaps.

With a crack of the whip, we set off along the driveway, rattled through the gates, and turning a corner, the château was lost from site. I mouthed the words to myself, "Farewell, Beauséjour. I doubt that I will see you or your like again."

The day was bright, cold, and fresh. The morning's frost still sparkled amongst the evergreen shrubs that bordered the road. There was a thick rug and I placed it over my body, right up to my neck. From the rug came the scent of a magnificent perfume. Cora's of course, and from the finest perfumer. Despite the cold, I opened a window. The breeze blew back my hair, and tingled my forehead and cheeks. We were now amongst fields and the winter sun was bright and low in a cloudless, pale blue sky. Still the frost sparkled. I closed my eyes against the sun and its rays penetrated my eyelids so that I was immersed in a deep orange glow.

I opened my eyes. Framed within a halo of brilliant light, was the shape of a figure upon a horse. It disappeared in the glare and then returned as a silhouette, disappearing again, then quickly gaining size. It seemed to float. There was now the pounding of hooves, distinct and overriding the sounds of the carriage. Still, I was dazzled by the sun, so that horse and rider seemed only half real, half imagined.

Then, they were free of the sun, and absolutely clear to behold. This time Cora rode a chestnut horse that seemed as golden as the light from which it emerged. She rode with great ease. She slowed to keep pace with the carriage and called out to the driver. He called back and they laughed. The words were in English and were blown away by the wind.

Still alongside, she leant forward to look through the window. She did not ride side saddle and instead of the usual, long, riding habit, she wore a tight dark jacket with white breeches and black leather boots. In the rays of the sun, the leather glowed and the buckles and stir-rups gleamed and flickered. The mane of her horse flowed in the wind and was full and white, and her hair was loose and free with strands stretched by the wind across her face. She gave a large smile; then with a touch of the reins, she veered away, and the sound of galloping hooves was gradually lost to the mundane noise of our own horses and the rat-tling of our carriage wheels upon the rough surface of the road.

Cora upon a golden steed. Completely herself. I hope to remember her, just like this.

It was night-time when we arrived here. A servant welcomed me and took me to my room. A supper has been served and a message con-veyed, "Madame Mercier gives her apologies, but has decided to retire early. She hopes you will understand. She wishes to be fresh for your long journey that begins tomorrow. She wishes you a restful night."

188

I am content to have seen no one and have had much writing to do. It is strange, though, to hear no sounds in this house of banquets and parties. Even the city home of Cora Pearl can sometimes rest quietly, and I do believe that tonight I will do the same; and as sleep draws me in and thoughts are freed to stray and to mingle with dream, I will expect a vision of Cora, astride a galloping horse, resplendent, happy, and fulfilled.

CHAPTER TWENTY THREE

An unexpected encounter

From the diary of Jane Crawford
Monday, 15th November 1869. Night-time.
Hôtel Louvre et Paix
Marseille

"Jane—you are not telling me all that you know."

We were on the train, and so began the first proper conversation of our long journey. There was no hesitation for Marguerite, no waiting for the right moment. "You say that Mariana fears Don Angel. Well, that I can understand. But to fear me as well—her sister, her twin! What has been done? What has been said to cause this? And why do you believe it?"

The last remark was delivered sharply and I feared that I had given her great offence. I realised too that beneath the aggression was her pain and her dismay at the gulf that had opened between them.

We were travelling by train to Marseille. From Marseille we will sail directly to the port of Almeria. The journey will take us three days in all, and we are now spending the night in a most luxurious Marseille hotel—paid for by Marguerite.

On the train we had as much comfort as possible. Marguerite had insisted we travel first class and had paid the fair for us both, having refused my contribution. Our journey has become her great endeavour to reunite with her twin, and I am now, simply, her travelling companion. Her manner is of one undertaking a mission of great importance that will, hopefully, lead to a happy event.

And, after my conversation with Félicien Rops, my thoughts have stayed with Mariana and I feel the full return of my love for her, and I know that whatever are the instructions of the Comte de St Germain, and the warnings of danger from him and from James, I am travelling not just to rescue her, but to be with her. It is five years since we bade farewell to her in Paris, still reeling from our sojourn at Poissy. Truly, the most intense days of my life, and also my closest time with her. Five years that had seen her sister grow more beautiful and fascinating, and surely it will be the same for her.

It was amongst these thoughts and feelings that I searched to clear the space to find the answer that Marguerite so urgently required.

To gain time, I asked a question of my own. "Marguerite, how will we manage? We will be travelling for days, much of it in discomfort."

"Jane, our arrival will be the recompense for any hardships. I will be reunited with my sister. I thank you forever, for it is your search that has awakened me. I realise that our time apart has done me great damage. It will have done the same to her. I believed that I was free, but I now know that it has not been so.

"Because Mariana's need was greater, it seemed that it resided only in her. It was so easy to think like that. My need for her—I forgot it. How selfish I have been. To Mariana—and to myself."

If tears should ever seep through and glisten the eyes of Marguerite, this was such a time. She raised a handkerchief, wiping one eye and then the other. For a moment, the absolute self-sufficiency, the utter force of character, melted away, and along with it the quality that defined her so severely from her sister. I could, just then, have been sitting with Mariana.

I was sure that I should give her the complete answer to her question. Marguerite cannot be the danger and if we truly need to save Mariana, it is from Don Angel, and for that we must work together.

I told her everything. I began with their visit to Whitby. A time that she remembers so well and with such affection. Then how we had suffered the appearance, completely unannounced, of the Marques. And I let her know that we had seen her great pleasure at his arrival, and the abject dismay that was felt by her sister. And how, soon after, there came St Germain, full of florid warnings of danger. He had missed them by only days, but could no longer pursue them and instead charged Edward to be his ambassador in Paris. Edward was to carry a warning in words that would persuade the girls to never see the Marques again.

And what a sorry mess he made of his charge. And I, trying to pick up the gauntlet, was also sucked into the charisma of Don Angel and the seductive charms of Madame Pearl. And instead, there we were, all of us, spending three days and nights in a French country house, gazing through the windows at Ancient Alexandria and enjoying an indulgence of the senses that would have graced any ancient, decadent palace, or indeed, the celebrations of that temple of Aphrodite that was painted upon a wall of the great ball room.

Much of this is known to her and so was easy to tell. But not the part with St Germain. I was embarrassed that I could say so little about the Count. Just the power within his calm being, and the joyful experience he bestowed on us.

I had been looking down as I spoke, concentrating and collecting my memories. At one time I looked up and saw that her face was filled with anger. It made me hesitate. Was this a terrible mistake? I looked down and then up again. But as suddenly as it had come, the expression was gone. She was smiling, wishing to give me the full reassurance to continue. I was committed now, and knew that I must continue. I would speak just as she would: with no reticence, with absolute clarity and no apology.

"Last week, St Germain, came to us again. A complete surprise. Once more, he was full of warnings. Even, that you, Marguerite, would try to kill your sister. That you will do this in the service of Don Angel, as it is his great satisfaction, the complete perversion of love and trust. The ultimate murder, the killing of one twin by another."

Marguerite sat motionless. Her face, completely without expression. Just the eyelids moved; not a blink, but a slow closure before opening again, like a curtain drawn and quickly pulled back. She repeated my words exactly. "The ultimate act of murder—the killing of one twin by another."

I stumbled over my next words as I was so shocked by her calm.

"And James, Eddy's son. He is a young man now and for six months he lived with Mariana—they were lovers."

There was the faintest response; an eyebrow slightly raised.

"And it came from Mariana too—she told him that she feared Don Angel—and you—that you would find her and destroy her. And Marguerite, in her melancholy, she seemed ready to allow it."

She turned to look through the train window. We were travelling through a forest. The morning's clear winter sky was now full of clouds and outside the high trees flew past, their forms blending with the speed into an endless dark wall.

In the silence, I followed her gaze. Against the impenetrable face of the forest, there was little to see, and instead I watched her reflection in the glass. Her face was completely clear, and how to interpret this I cannot know. I felt oddly that she was no longer with me, but had entered a place of imagination that would not be shared and I had the strangest feeling that Marguerite was gone and had been replaced by another.

There was no more for me to say and we sat in silence until, at last, her view still through the window, she spoke. And it was not about her sister. "Your Count seems to have a quarrel with my Marques."

Her remark, containing a dash of humour, along with thoughts that have matched my own, brought me some relief.

But silence returned and the noise of our train, with its great engine, seemed to grow in volume, and as we raced over the tracks, the predictable sound became harsh and hostile.

And then, once more, she changed everything. It was as if, with a magic spell, with a wave of an invisible wand, she could colour the mood from light to dark and back again. Did the sun break through the clouds? I cannot say, but in my memory, it did. Marguerite turned back to look me fully in the face and her expression was brimming with warmth and affection. She spoke in French, knowing that I would understand the simple sentence. "Then Jane, we must stop these men meddling with our lives—and the life of our sister."

She spoke calmly but with such surety and I knew that whatever she would decide to do she would accomplish. If St Germain's warnings were true, it would make Marguerite the greatest danger, but I believe she is to be trusted. We are on the same side—and I am now an honorary sister!

Tuesday, 16th November 1869. Mid-morning.
Hôtel Louvre et Paix
Marseille

I cannot leave my entry until tonight. I write now because I must order my thoughts. Not just my thoughts but my feelings. I feel my centre has been lost, sucked up into some dreadful vortex that will cast me down, I know-not-where.

It is now mid-morning. Soon we will embark upon our ship and finally reach Almeria. Marguerite had told me that she would not be taking breakfast, so, this morning, I left my room, ready to sit alone in the dining room.

The room was large, magnificent, and exceedingly busy. Not due to a surfeit of guests, but because it was filled with the intense activity of numerous waiters who were so much in command that I felt anxious my order for breakfast might seem like an impertinence. I took a breath, summoned up my best French and made the order. I would have a selection of fruit with pains viennois and chocolate to drink. I seemed to have ordered well and after looking at me directly for the first time, and with just a hint of flirtation, my waiter pivoted on one foot and was away and calling loudly across the room.

I was so deeply in thought, that if an overt incident had occurred at a nearby table, or anywhere else in the dining room, I would not in that moment have noticed. So how can it be that I did notice one lone figure who was standing, motionless, in the entrance?

His eyes had searched and found me and he was now walking towards my table. He could only be coming for me, and who else would this gentleman have business with at this time? He stood in front of me. His appearance was as elegant and subdued as ever and I doubt that the other guests even noticed him. There was just his one exception to reticence—the many rings upon his fingers. He made no introduction, no words of greeting, and his look was grave.

It is not for a lady to stand when a gentleman arrives, but without thinking I began to rise. He made his first communication, a gesture that I should surely not get up. And then, "Madame Jane, I must ask you first, where is the Mercier twin you travel with?"

"Monsieur le Comte, I am astounded that you are here. Please, allow me a moment to check that I am not dreaming."

"Jane, tell me. Where is the Mercier woman?"

"She declines breakfast. Soon I will join her in her room."

"And then you are onwards to Spain."

This was not given as a question, but as his certain knowledge.

"Good—she is not here—so I can join you. But Madame Jane I forget my manners. Forgive me, please, for I am full of great concerns and we have little time. May I sit?"

I was still too shocked to give a response. As I had not refused him, he drew up a chair. He was almost opposite, but was still positioned to keep sight of the stairs that led down from the rooms. "Madame Jane, I cannot be everywhere and my time in Marseille was not expected. I know of your journey. Some of this remains as we planned, but you were never meant to travel with Marguerite. Jane, remember what I told you."

I have never written down what St Germain did tell me back in Whitby; those things he felt that I should know, and I alone. Through all the struggles that force me one way then another; to think and feel and believe in something that is then turned on its head and is made to be false; through all of this, those words of the Count have almost become lost.

Now, in a clear, quiet voice, he was to remind me. "Jane, remember what I told you. The Marques de Mansura, despicable and corrupt as he is, is not the threat. Oh yes, he was once, but is no longer—because he now knows, you, Jane. You have become a principal player in this drama of ours. He knows you now and what you are, but, especially, what you will become. He has seen, and he knows you better than you can know yourself. One day, you will know it too. Time is so relative, Jane. To you, there is just one life and then—what happens? But you believe your earthly life will stop. We believe and know about lifetimes, how the soul goes on and how some, and such a one is you, can grow ever-more powerful. He fears that if he does you great offence in this lifetime, sometime, maybe a century hence or more, he will meet you again and you will require his penance. And by then you may be his equal, even his superior. He fears the loss of his own power. He fears that he will die. He already declines. Corruption will always wear itself out. And he made a grave mistake with you, Jane. In his celebration of the senses, in that house outside Paris, he allowed a physical union with you. He must have realised then that he had already ceded power to you. You are a rare person, Jane—extremely rare. I sensed it when I first met you. I made a remark then, but now, I sense the future even more; as does the Marques. You will go on to be a force in this world, and one for great good. Indeed Madame, I am honoured to know you—even now.

"But I digress—we must first look to the present. The Marques is no longer a danger. Marguerite Mercier, absolutely is."

Perhaps it was my only way of escaping the confusion that now overwhelmed me. It is not in my nature and certainly not to one such as the Count—but I became furious. "Monsieur St Germain!

You appear—unannounced as ever! You set off your explosions of mistrust and danger. You enlist me in your own vendetta—with this other mystical creature—and then, no doubt, you will leave me alone with it—abandoned—whilst you rush off to some other cause on the far side of the world. Sir, shame on you! And I have had enough!"

I was astounded at my own anger and my ability to express it. St Germain was not in the slightest taken aback. "Madame Crawford, I no longer simply enlist you. There was, at first, much of that—but all has changed. You are, no more, my volunteer. In this scenario—you are embedded. As much as Mariana, Marguerite, and the Marques. You have been intimate with them all, and you love Mariana. This, I can tell, and you wish to save her; not to help me, but for your love of her, and Jane—believe me—her sister will kill her if she can.

"She has charmed you of course. She is a remarkable woman. Now you travel with her, and you, yourself, escort her to Mariana. And, perhaps, it is I who has now become the villain. But remember, the Marques fears you. I have told you why. Marguerite knows nothing of this, and fears you not. My goodness—such a woman. I believe that I fear her myself. She has been well versed in the ways of the Marques and in her role in the destruction of one twin by another. His own intent has changed, but it lives on in her. We can only hope that he has not endowed her with powers of the supernatural."

The waiter had returned to our table, his presence and look as arrogant as before. I cannot tell how it was done, because I noticed not the slightest movement from the Count who did not even give him a glance. Yet, the waiter was dismissed in such a fashion that he seemed to slink away, as if in disgrace. Such is the authority of an aristocracy that has lasted for centuries.

And then he was gone. There was no promise of help or a future meeting. I can see that I am alone and it is for me to decide whom to believe.

I have come quickly to my room to write this down. I know not how the day will pass, but it will be with Marguerite. Soon she will knock upon my door. Later we sail for Almeria.

CHAPTER TWENTY FOUR

A conversation with Marguerite

From the diary of Jane Crawford
Wednesday, 17th November, 1869.
The very early hours.
"The Louis Martens." The Balearic Sea.

There was a knock on my cabin door. Surprisingly loud since it was past midnight. I had been restless and unable to sleep and the strange intrusion would have been welcome but for my immediate expectation of another unwanted visitation. It made no difference that we were somewhere upon the Balearic Sea and that all onboard had retired for the night. The Count and the Marques have proved that there is no obstacle to finding me, or us, if they wish to do so. I dreaded that it might be either of them—the Count with some final instructions, or the Marques just to terrify me. It was, in fact, Marguerite.

I had least expected that it be her, though as my travelling companion, she was the most likely. But two hours before, she had given me a very firm "goodnight," and left me sure that she was gone until the morning.

Clearly, she had just risen from her bed, as her hair was loose and tussled and she wore a night gown. Her feet were bare. "Jane, I am so sorry. I am unable to sleep. Too many thoughts and visions trouble me. Can anyone really wish such terrible ill to Mariana?"

I have written before that vulnerability is not something to disrupt the poise of Marguerite, but here, at this time, the poise was gone and her face showed only anxiety and her eyes were beseeching me for help.

It is in my nature: without a thought, I responded by wrapping my arms around her in a wish to give any comfort that I could. "You must come in, Marguerite. Please do not concern yourself. It is fine. I was not asleep and my own mind is full of the same disbeliefs and worry. I believe that we are tossed around by the most violent of seas."

I hoped that my allusion to the movements of our ship might bring some relief of humour, but her expression remained grim.

"Come—I have a small flask of brandy. It will help."

Edward had thoughtfully slipped the flask into my luggage. Now, there it was, just waiting for the right time. I poured out two large measures. "We are still in this together Marguerite—we will find Mariana and we will bring her back to France. What is she doing anyway—alone in the desert and in winter?"

What had happened to all those warnings from St Germain, just the day before. In that moment—gone—all of it.

"I have a need now."

Her tone was so much softer than usual. She sat upon the narrow bed, whilst I sat in the small armchair. She leant forward, so that her elbows were upon her knees, and she was looking down. Her hair hung on either side so that I could hardly see her face.

Then she looked up. With a sudden movement she brushed the hair from her face and the cool grey eyes were fixed upon me. Clear, but moist. "I think I need to tell you—to be able to speak of ..."

She paused and then, "My sister and myself. How we grew up. Can I tell you Jane?"

"Marguerite, anything you say about yourself and your sister can help me to understand her deep unhappiness and desperate need. Please speak. Say anything you wish. We are alone together, Marguerite, at sea, and we have the whole night."

I was filled with compassion for her. For a while, she stayed silent and then she began. "Soon after we were born, our mother died. We have no memory of her. It was too soon. Jane, we never had a mother. There were nurses of course. They came and went so quickly. There was a family joke. It was about me—not Mariana. They said that I was the hungriest baby that had ever lived. Well, according to the wet nurses. Apparently, I drained them all and sent them packing. How can an infant have such power? Just a funny story."

I said nothing, but I could well imagine the depleted nurses escaping from the voracious infant before being swallowed whole. I thought—and what about Mariana? But said nothing.

"The governesses came next. One or two stayed the course, but they were not there for us. They were there for our father. And now I have to tell you about him."

Right from the beginning, Eddy and I had wondered about this unknown and mysterious man. A father who seemed to exist in name only. Eddy had written to him before his mission to Paris. He had urged the father in his letter to watch over his girls, to be alert to the danger that was the Marques de Mansura. But, of course, there was no reply. Here was a man of complete absence and the space he left seemed filled by the Marques. For Marguerite, at least.

"My father is a diplomat. Very successful in his career, and he travels everywhere. By the time we had grown up, we hardly saw him. And he was very free with us. As young women, he let us travel. I was the one who wanted it. I wanted to be everywhere, to see everything. Poor Mariana: I dragged her around all over Europe. Not that she was dead to it, or even lacked interest. She was just not as hungry as I.

"And my father, our father, gave us much money. Huge allowances for us both. What lucky girls! And he gave us the freedom to use it as we wished.

"Yes, he was very liberal, but you see, he had been so in other ways.

"Poor Papa. He had lost his wife. You are a woman of the world Jane. You will know that there are men who need lots and lots of love from a woman—or women. Such was my father. And so, those governesses. Those women who were there to guide and to teach us—to give us the moral codes and the certitudes that growing girls need—to be splendid examples of womanhood—these women were really his mistresses. And they served his purpose well.

"There was one, his favourite, who left our home just as we were growing into young women. When she left, he turned his attention to us."

The implication was already horribly there. I could see the ghastly revelation that was coming. I was already too shocked to respond, to mutter even a word. So, I just stared. And she seemed to expect no response. In fact, the whole tone of her delivery had become flat and without expression.

"And so, it went on. It was with us both. Sometimes together; sometimes he would choose one or the other. And then when we grew a little older, he introduced us to his friends."

All I could say was, "Marguerite ..." Just her name. I felt frozen, unable to react. I wished I was not there, or that she would go, but I knew that now she had begun, she would need to tell everything.

"It was then that his work trips began, and he was away for long periods, even a month or two at a time."

It was a chance for me to say something, "Thank God, Marguerite. There was at least some respite from your ordeal."

My statement felt innocuous, my words an empty offering. And she made no response, just continued in a voice that had become simply matter of fact. "Sometimes, his friends would still come. Just two or three of them. Special friends. They had keys to the front door."

I thought, then, of when I visited the family house. And Mariana, peering through the window, lodged in an upper room for safety.

"He had employed a new governess. This one was not to be his mistress. She was older and was like a stick. She took no interest in us. Only to make sure that we had our meals, our clean clothes, our schooling. And there was not much school since I refused to go. Then it ended completely—because I decided so.

"Can you believe that Jane? The daughters make the decisions. And Mariana did not wish to go to school alone and to be there without me. Sure, she would otherwise have stayed there. Our father said nothing. You know, he had become scared of me. And do you know why Jane, why he feared me?"

Something had changed in Marguerite's demeanour. It was no longer with the matter of fact, emotionless expression of before. A new vigour was rising in her; it even brought a flush to her face, and to the cheeks that had seemed so pallid.

"It was because I came to enjoy his attentions. Sometimes, it was even I who invited him. The shoe of power had moved, quite subtly, onto the other foot. And of course, I had so much knowledge of his misdemeanours, and of his friends. One of whom, Jane, was your Comte de St Germain."

I nearly fainted just then. A mist seemed to fill the cabin. And it felt that our ship had become embroiled in some massive upheaval of the sea. Perhaps this was so. I increasingly think that the forces of nature sense our moods and act them out. I have come to know about magic and elemental powers. I knew, though, that I must stay conscious. I looked down and then forcefully up and grasped my knees with my hands. I did not allow my gaze upon Marguerite to waver. My sensibilities had already been stretched to the limit by her confession—if confession it was. But now, the inclusion of St Germain—all the residues of belief and of trust were being snatched away from me.

Perhaps it was a desperate search for a remedy. I forced into my mind the memories of my own father. How I too, had lost my mother, and how he had cared for me, adored me, loved me as his daughter, and always, even when I was small, with the greatest respect. And how, in his old age, with immense gratitude, I had cared for him.

In absolute contrast, I was now hearing a tale of the primaeval, of the lowest animal instincts. No! Not even animal, for animals protect their young—this was from the lowest of human instincts.

And I think of Mariana. How did she bear all that? How did she survive? I said, "And Mariana?"

"For a while she did as she was told. She was too young to say no. And she looked to me for guidance, and saw that I made no protest. But then, when father's friends began to come, she refused. She would even lock herself in her room at the top of the house. It was the first of our real separations. And we ceased even to speak of it."

My capacity for thought was returning and I found the words. "Marguerite—does this father still visit you?"

"It is three years since I saw him. Just the allowance—always there."

"He is a terrible man, Marguerite. He deserves no longer to live. And who is he damaging now?"

"But Jane, you speak thus of my father, but then you believe the words of your Comte de St Germain. Perhaps it is he who truly wishes to destroy us. Mariana and I; we know so much to shame and disgrace him. He will fear us for that."

I knew that I must ward off despair, and out of all my confusion came one certain thought: that I should not react, that I should make no conclusion, no decisions until I had time, just by myself, to search through all my thoughts and feelings. Indeed, as I write now, I do this very thing.

And I needed some time just then. The brandy had no appeal. There was water and I poured two glasses. Marguerite ignored hers.

A slight calm settled, as after the storm.

"Marguerite, why do you tell me this, and why now?"

"We go to reclaim my sister. To save her from whatever danger pursues her. And you need to know, Jane, that this Count of yours, this St Germain, is not the knight of rescue you believe him to be. I remember him. He is a man devoted to the senses, to perversion, a ruthless man. I know he is powerful Jane, perhaps like Don Angel, and he will have convinced you utterly. He uses you now for his purpose. He seems to hate Don Angel—a man of absolute culture and wisdom. A man who has taken my life and enriched it with his knowledge and his love of the world and all its history. A man with such heavenly powers that he transported me to a temple in Ancient Alexandria where I met the priestesses of Aphrodite. Can you imagine that Jane? Can you imagine how wonderful that was? You, yourself, saw the city from a distance and you were full of wonder.

"So, I tell you about our childhood because your St Germain is part of the story. And I tell you because you worry so much about my sister. Yes, she can have the greatest melancholy, and this may at least show you some of the cause."

Marguerite's whole presence now seemed to fill the room. She was full of conviction, of the power of thought and the rapture that she felt about her own life and her sadness about that of Mariana. I felt drawn to look only at her eyes and I lost myself in the gaze.

"People are so different, aren't they Jane? Yet nobody expects that twins, identical at birth, should be so. Yet when they are, when the difference cannot be denied, how fascinating that can be. It even fascinates me. These events caused much anguish to Mariana, yes, even damage. But, for me—I embraced them. I used them. I discovered much about men, and I found that if I met their challenge, by neither showing nor feeling fear, I gained power—indeed, that my power was the greater.

"It is why I get on so well with Cora. We are the same in this. But I have no wish to be a courtesan. I could of course, if I wished. I could be the richest and most famous ever. But this is not my plan. I will marry an aristocrat of great wealth. As well as the riches, I desire a title. It will happen. I will make it so.

"And what power does Mariana have? She writes poetry and becomes a recluse, a hermit in the desert. Whilst I live my life, satisfy my hungers, and feel that none can defeat me. And, most of all I have freedom. Some might say that those who defy the rules of society, the so-called rules of life, will become captive and ruined by their own decadence.

They may even be seen as villainous, but if we can embrace our villainy, we know the greatest freedom. This, I believe. This, I know."

I was completely weighed down by her argument. My own energy was draining away, or maybe she was drawing it into herself. I could only feel her utter command and presence. And then I began to feel mad, and to actually see her words as well as hear them. They were like little blocks of letters that floated in the air between us. And she kept drawing me into her gaze. Those grey eyes that never blink. All doors within me had closed, the access to hope and love and care, had been slammed shut. I struggled with the tiny bit of resolve that still remained and with all my will, pushed one door open. Just enough. It was a desperate protest.

"You denigrate Mariana as a lost creature. A lone waif in the desert who is pining into non-existence. A victim of those people and events whom you met and embraced. She is your twin, Marguerite, yet, right now, I believe I know her far more than you do."

Energy was returning. I felt it rise throughout my body and its hot flush was upon my cheeks. My thoughts were now solely on Mariana, and it was her presence, as if in complete contrast, that was filling the room. "She has warmth. She cares. She loves. She believes in others. People feel happy when they are with her. They may not even know why. It is just as it is, and it is welcome. Nothing else is required except, perhaps, a few words. A few words can count for so much if they are well meant. She thinks too, but her thoughts are not like yours. Often, she needs quietness—for her soul. Unlike you. Indeed Marguerite, do you ever have the capacity to be alone?"

The spell had been broken. Mariana had been the antidote.

The phenomenon of Marguerite had subsided. Like an enormous ariel balloon from which the gas escapes. And like such a balloon, she was now descended to the ground. Once more, a mere mortal, though I hope I can always be ready to resist a Marguerite who has certainly been endowed with at least a portion of the powers of her mentor. I have no doubt, that for some moments, I was entranced, and it took all my willpower to escape.

But I cannot account for her history of St Germain. I have swung wildly from my own doubts and suspicions to deep respect and gratitude. He gave me a vision and experience of my mother with such power that it filled the crucial years of her absence. What greater gift could there be. But if his indulgence with the twins was as Mariana described, he was as villainous as the rest. With his occult powers, even more so. I feel in my deepest intuition that much of her story is true. I can sense it. But of him? I know not.

She was, now, as she had been when she entered. She looked ruffled, anxious, concerned. The eyes that had penetrated my very being, were now beseeching me for care and understanding. "Jane. I have entrusted you with my story—with our story. I have craved your indulgence. I wished not to shock you, but stories must be told. And most of all, I wished to warn you about your Count. I am hurt Jane, that you have turned against me, as if some choice must be made. That it is either me or my sister. It is both of us, Jane. We are twins and we will reunite. It is my wish. I believe you wish for it too."

There was no more that either of us could say.

Had the sea been stormy? It had felt so, yet now, all was calm. Just the slight motion of the waves. After she left, there was a sharp rattle of rain upon the cabin window. I opened it. The wind blew through and wet my face with raindrops. It felt wonderful. How could anything feel wonderful after Marguerite's story? Yet it did, and I have an inkling that I have found some power within myself. Something new. Perhaps, something that I have been told will come to me; in this life, or the next, or the next. I realise that I have survived a considerable force that sought to control me. So, Marguerite cannot be trusted. But who can be? Does she seek to save or to destroy. There is no way but to travel together to our destiny. We will find Mariana, and then we will see.

CHAPTER TWENTY FIVE

Disembarkment at Almeria

*From the diary of Jane Crawford
Friday, 19th November 1869. Before breakfast.
Hotel Regente. Almeria*

I am alone and must make my entry for yesterday.

It was already dark when we sailed into the port of Almeria.

We had no hotel reservation and had simply hoped that in the winter month of November, there would be rooms available. The accompanying concern was that at this time of year, most hotels would be closed.

Our family had always been able to converse with the Mercier twins, thanks to our valiant attempts at French and their fluent ability with English. However, in Spain, we had no such facility. We had hardly a word of Spanish between us. And then we had to ask for the whereabouts of a young French woman, who is existing somewhere in the Tabernas desert. We just hoped that, given the strangeness of the situation, we could convey the essence of our search.

Our doubts about finding a hotel seemed confirmed. The coachman, whom we were lucky to find at the port, could only be bothered to give us a massive shrug. It could have meant that all hotels were indeed closed, or that he simply did not understand our request. Yet he loaded our luggage and then waited for us to be seated. In a spirit of helpless unknowing, we could only assume that he would take us and deliver us, at least, to somewhere! He climbed into his position, cracked his whip and we trundled off.

We could see that there were hotels near to the port—of a kind—though our driver must have assumed that they were not suitable for ladies of our appearance. Seedy places, and no doubt their dockland rooms were frequented by women of a different sort.

As we rode, Marguerite suddenly abandoned her seat in the open carriage, and with considerable agility climbed forward to the driver's seat and placed herself, fairly and squarely, next to him. She then pulled from her bag a sheet of paper that was covered in handwriting.

What a remarkable woman she is. Such foresight! Turning to the driver who had obstinately refused to look at her, she read out, completely in Spanish, what was obviously a most pertinent question. Where she had found such a script, I cannot tell. Perhaps, even before she left Cora's château, or maybe in the Paris mansion. It was such an open house there, with men entering and leaving, and there might have been one who was fluent enough in Spanish.

Anyway, the planning was impressive and the delivery imperious, and matters moved on dramatically.

The driver's whole demeanour changed. He was immediately full of interest and enthusiasm. I remember his words because he loudly repeated them several times, "Ah! La dama del desierto!"

Well, I can understand that.

This was followed by a mass of words of great expression and colour which was impossible for us to understand, except for one phrase, "La dama Mariana!"

Then, using very slow speech, with much physical expression, and from a discourse of suggestion and insinuation, a possibility emerged. Even a probability, if we should allow it. Our surly Spanish coachman, who was now affable in the most volatile way, would take us to Mariana himself, the very next day!

Clearly, the hermit woman, who would still need supplies in order to live, had become a known figure, celebrated for her strangeness. And our driver welcomed with delight his chance to take us to her. Presumably, the chance for a closer view of the peculiar young woman of the desert.

It was a tremendous relief and so encouraging. But we were, by now, feeling the chill of the November night and to add to our discomfort, it had begun to rain. I have not known such rain before. Was it because we were near the sea? It was the finest spray, so that I could hardly feel its touch upon my face and hands, yet within minutes, my clothing and hair were wet through.

The coachman found this very jolly. He was, of course, in his own clothing, completely prepared. He was now speaking non-stop, all interspersed with guffaws of laughter and I could see that Marguerite was giving him her full, skilful presentation of attention, so that he believed she understood his every word. And she let it continue so.

He must now have thought us worthy of a fine hotel, so that we drew up outside a building that looked far less forbidding than those murky places by the harbour.

The hotel was small and full of blues and greens: the walls, the cushions and upholstery, the carpet and the curtains. And it was warm. The receptionist spoke some French, and a little English, and with a combination of both, we made the reservation of two rooms for one night with the possibility of more nights, if needed. I had insisted on this as I hoped that we would be returning to Almeria and thence to Marseilles and Paris with a revived and restored Mariana. Though she had shown such foresight, this part of the plan had not occurred to Marguerite.

Our driver had been delighted to bring our travel bags into the hotel and would have continued their delivery into our rooms if it were not for the resistance of the receptionist who rang a bell to summon her own porter. With celebratory farewells, he departed. Through the translations of the receptionist, we made a clear arrangement for him to collect us at 10 O'clock the next morning.

A light supper was brought to us and we eat it together in my room. Neither of us were hungry, though a carafe of wine was welcome and warming and was soon emptied.

With the wine, the warmth, and now in dry clothes, and with the certainty of seeing Mariana the next day, I began to have a fine feeling, so pleasing to both my mind and my body, that I can only call it euphoria.

And this seemed to be shared by Marguerite. She was so relaxed, and her keen edge of energy and certainty that had looked after us so well that day, was now softened into an ease of being and into her pleasure at our successful arrival.

CHAPTER TWENTY SIX

The plaza in Almeria
and a new presence

From the diary of Jane Crawford
Friday, 19th November 1869. Evening, before dinner.
Hotel Regente. Almeria

This morning, after dressing, I used the time to write my journal and record the events following our arrival in Almeria. I am still astounded by Marguerite's charming of the coachman!

This current entry I am writing before our evening meal, and have yet another day of strange events to record. It should not be the case, but instead of being in the desert home of Mariana, I am, once more, writing from my hotel room.

When I finished writing this morning, I went downstairs for breakfast. I decided not to knock on Marguerite's door, but to let her take her own time to rise and get dressed. In fact, she was already in the dining room and drinking coffee.

She allowed me to walk to the table where she sat, watching me with that cool gaze as I crossed the floor. She had bad news. "Our carriage driver will not be coming. He called here very early and left a message. Today, he must help his brother on his farm. He will come instead tomorrow. So, Jane, today we are just ordinary tourists in Almeria."

I was deeply disappointed. I had expected to be seeing Mariana within hours. My feelings showed and Marguerite took me by the hand. Her grasp was warm and reassuring. "I know you long for Mariana so much, and I do too. And think, Jane, how wonderful it will be when the three of us are together."

I had coffee as well, and neither of us were interested in breakfast, so, soon after, we went back to our rooms to get ready for the day and to be relatively normal Almeria tourists, though there would be few of those in November.

Of course, Marguerite has been to Almeria before, with her sister. She told me a little about the city. It is the driest area in Spain, but in November it can rain, and that we knew from yesterday. And today she wanted to show me round and said that we would be starting at a very special place.

Our hotel was close to the cathedral, which, as always, is at the centre of the city. It is large and imposing, though has no tall tower or spire. Marguerite said that this might get us lost, since little protrudes above the rooftops to use as a marker. But she believed that she could trust her memory and anyway, any chance of losing our way would be seen as a challenge to be defeated. "So, Jane, let us go!"

The weather was mild, even pleasant; nothing like the stormy Whitby that I had left just a week before. That is amazing in itself. It feels that it is an age ago. St Germain had suddenly appeared and then he sent me here, on this mission, and alone. In Marseille, he appeared again and told me that I should in no way be travelling with Marguerite. But there it is—it has happened and clearly not even someone with his abilities can foretell everything. Indeed, if he really does fear for the safety of Mariana, her actual future can surely not be known to him.

This morning, in Almeria, there was a clear sky and there was warmth from the sun. Despite my disappointment that we would not be travelling into the Tabernas to find Mariana, in the easy temperature and the clear and fresh air, for we are not far from the sea, I thought I would allow a day as a tourist. And Marguerite had firmly placed herself in the role of guide, even the historian. As we set out, she told me of Almeria's past: Its great wealth as a port in the Muslim era, when the huge fort of the Alcazaba was built upon the hillside to overlook the city; the production of silk; the trading of textiles and copper, and of slaves; the battles and sieges for its possession; the raids of the Barbary pirates, and then in the 15th century, the conquest by the Christian monarchs. And it has been rocked by earthquakes, one of which devastated the city.

There was little for me to say. She was so happy teaching me, and described things in such a colourful way, that it was exciting and a pleasure for me to listen.

It was not long before we walked through an archway and so entered a large square. We stood at the edge, looking in. No one else was there. It was strange, because until then we had been passing others, mainly locals going about their business. And now there was no one, just we two. And all was completely silent. Perhaps the surrounding buildings act as a shield against the sounds from outside. All around the square is a covered walkway, its roof just above head high and supported every few yards by pillars. Beneath the walkway there were deep shadows as the sun could not penetrate and it was only just possible to see that, set back, there were doorways.

The sun was very bright and its glare was in our eyes, and it caused a sharp contrast between the open square and the darkness of the walkway. We both shielded our eyes.

For a few minutes it was like this, and then there was a change. It felt uncanny as it was so unexpected. All morning, the sky had been clear and blue, but now a great cloud appeared. As we stood, it passed across the sun and the brilliance was gone and so was the warmth. Without the sun, I felt the chill in the breeze and feared that my clothes would not keep me warm. Indeed, the chill turned into cold and then the sun, after reappearing for an instant, was gone and the sky turned to slate grey.

I looked at Marguerite, but she was only gazing into the square and made no response. The breeze had increased and she had taken off her hat and loosened her hair to be caught and lifted by the cold air.

I wanted then to leave this square, but she stood motionless. At last, she moved. There were seats in the square: wooden slats in iron frames. They were placed at the edge, but there was just one near the centre. She walked towards it, and I had no option but to follow.

When she reached it, she remained standing, just holding on to the iron arm of the seat with one hand. "You see Jane, there are certain places that are special. Can you feel it about this one? Everything has changed, hasn't it? We entered as two women sightseeing on a sunny day. But this place was not going to allow us to be so complacent. Life is governed by the most magnificent, yet unexpected, forces and this is one place where they gather. It is a place where he could first meet us, where he could find us, and we find him. I believe that he really feels that identical twins are a force of nature themselves, and that we will always serve up the unique and the unexpected, the aberrations of nature that he likes. He collects twins like us. But I do believe that we have been special to him. And then he likes to play. He uses us to test out the most unexpected human elements. Especially, on each other. And he has not finished yet. How wonderful, that he can allow us to do exactly what we want. To go far and even further, to reach into the most unknown and forbidden places."

"It was here that you first met the Marques?"

"Indeed, it was, so I brought you here to see it—and for the sake of my own memories."

Now, she sat down upon the seat and gestured to me to join her. Her hand took hold of mine, and she kissed me upon the cheek, and despite the cold, I felt a warmth rise within me. I thought, "Can she change moods? Can she even change the atmosphere of a city square? Is she beginning to effect nature itself?"

But then I thought—"No, at least, not yet. It is the strength of her character."

"Do you see, Jane, the clock upon the building there?"

I followed her gaze and saw the clock. It was high upon the pediment of a building that was the most prominent in the plaza.

"Look at the time, Jane. We will now look away and wait for what happens."

I was remembering now all that Mariana had told me as we sat in the kitchen of her Paris home. The way that she and Marguerite had met the Marques, in this very same square. How he had walked towards them, spoken, charmed Marguerite, caused Mariana to feel fear and invited them to dine with him. It was, in a way, the very beginning of the story. And then, after he left them, they had gathered themselves and made their own way to the archway and the streets beyond, and how she had looked up at the clock and seen that time had stopped; that since the Marques came upon them the hands had been fixed and still. She had tried to discount this as her imagination, but truly, she knew better.

And I thought of my own encounters with Don Angel. Always, time was disturbed, as if a force, circling around him, corrupted all its certainty.

Marguerite was talking. She hardly paused for beath. I knew that I was not to look at the clock again for some minutes, so, instead, I had looked within, into my memory of Mariana's story and my own encounters with—magic. What else can I call it?

There was an even greater coldness to the air and the light had darkened so much that underneath the walkway there was only the darkness of night. And I felt, "Is this now the evening? Is night-time nearly upon us? We must get back to our hotel before all is dark." And still Marguerite was speaking, and then I heard the name, Aphrodite, and I began to listen.

She was speaking of the history of the goddess. But it was not in terms of love or beauty. Well perhaps, beauty, but a terrible beauty, and I thought, that is also the beauty of Marguerite. She spoke of the bitter revenge of Aphrodite: upon her enemies in love and against those that might challenge her grandeur. And the cruel punishments that befell women who had the audacity to show beauty that might match her own. Like Psyche, who challenged her, though without intent, and who vastly increased the insult by gaining the love of Cupid, Aphrodite's own beautiful and incestuous son. How Psyche had to suffer for that.

There was Phryne who bathed naked near to Aphrodite's temple, so that people wondered, "Does her beauty even match that of the goddess?" And to increase the outrage, it was on the day of Aphrodite's own festival. Phryne missed the penalty of death by a hairsbreadth.

Aphrodite's fury at insult was so great, and the slights so frequent, the rivals so numerous, she could be called the goddess of revenge and her punishments were of the most imaginative torture.

"Yes!," declared Marguerite, "She is magnificent in her jealousy. You see, Jane, nearly all struggle with jealousy and they fear it. It leaves them feeling so weak. My sister has had terrible jealousy. She hated it when others took interest in me, and especially, when I took interest in them. She always feared she would lose me.

"I, too, can know the feeling of jealousy, but like Aphrodite, I know that those who cause it must be conquered. It is not something to leave me weakened, weeping like a child. Instead, it means the resurgence of my powers. It is simply, another challenge to be met with and to win. I am like the mediaeval knight. I ride in full armour, my plumed helmet upon my head, my sword, shield, and lance at the ready, and I ride through the hills and forests waiting for any who might dare to challenge me. I will meet their challenge then and there, and will leave them unhorsed, wounded, even dying.

"Do I speak as a man? You know well, Jane that beneath the chain male and the iron breast plate, there is a woman's body. One that can always bring me victory."

It now felt like night. A blast of cold wind swept across the square so that I shivered and crossed my arms to hug myself warm. I had not looked at Marguerite as she spoke, but now I turned to see her and it was not the person that I knew. She was now standing, and seemed taller, and her whole body was stretched and thin. Her face was gaunt. Was she still beautiful? The wind was whipping the hair around hollow cheeks. The pupils of her eyes had darkened and seemed only to be looking at her own, strange vision. A peculiar beauty, an awful beauty, and with the ugliness of brutality. In the completeness of the triumph of her being, and in the cruelty of her thoughts, she no longer paid heed to me.

And then, in a moment, all changed again. The sun burst through the clouds and a dazzling light filled the plaza. I was so surprised that I looked away from Marguerite to see the square so filled with brilliance. I looked back at her and it was the Marguerite whom I knew, and she was smiling at me and the warmth that came from her matched the warmth of the sun.

"Jane, you are so good to put up with my dreadful musings. You really are my darling. And not just my friend, not only my travelling companion, but the one who has made me see that I have to find Mariana. And Jane, we will be there together—darling Jane."

And she kissed me upon the lips. "Come, we will leave here now. Enough of mysterious forces. I will show you more of Almeria."

And she took me by the hand, and I felt as compliant as a little girl walking by the side of her mother. We crossed the square and entered the shadows of the archway, and then through that into the sunlit street.

And I had forgotten to look at the clock.

Marguerite was full of energy and an enthusiasm that seemed charged by our time in the plaza and by her soliloquy—thrown out to me, to the wind and to the dark, elemental sky. She no longer held my hand and speedily led the way, assuming that I would be close behind. But we were now in more crowded streets. There were shops and outside some there were queues. We met and mingled with a bustling crowd of people, perhaps coming from church. There was much talking, people calling each other and shouts from within the shops. There were carriages in the street too, so that people had to stop and squeeze close to the buildings as they passed.

And then, suddenly, and with a feeling of shock, I could no longer see Marguerite. I searched frantically with my eyes. There were many people, but none of them were her. No longer was I the compliant child walking safely, hand in hand, with mother. She was gone and I was lost.

My anxiety stopped me from thinking. I saw the entrance to another road, and as I could not see her ahead, I entered it. Immediately, it was quieter; silent in fact. There were no shops and no people. This street was very narrow, and very shaded, with the buildings joined together and closely facing. All had blinds that were drawn against whatever time of day the sun would penetrate. But that was not now. The paving stones seemed polished and softly glowed, but in places, were replaced by rough cobbles.

With no sign of anyone in the narrow street, let alone, Marguerite, I should surely have turned and retraced my steps. But some force kept me going and, given what followed, I now understand this.

On my left-hand side were the houses, joined together except for occasional alleyways, all deeply basked in shadow. On my other side was a wall, perhaps 10 feet high. This too was in shadow, except that its top was just catching the sun. The wall was long and I walked by its side and looking up, could see the occasional burst of foliage rising above, so that I could tell that it enclosed a garden.

The wall was plain and of dark bricks, but in one place, set in a small square of cement, was a painted shield in black and white bearing three stars. I recognised it, as the same was upon the gateway of a monastery close to my childhood home. It is the emblem of the Carmelites. I continued along the wall. Then the wall joined onto a building that was even higher, three stories at least. There were small windows, all protected by vertical iron bars and the upper windows were tiny. The glass was in leaded diamond shapes. All behind the windows was dark, so that I could see nothing within, except that through one, high up, there was the faintest, soft glow of light.

I could see ahead the large doorway of weathered wood. I thought that it would be a rare chance to see anyone enter or leave this building. So, it was a shock, that as I approached, there was the rattling of metal fastenings and the door swung open.

217

I thought, "This is the home of Carmelite nuns, I must just look ahead, they are utterly private and will not wish to be seen." And so, averting my eyes, I quickened my pace. But a female voice said, "Jane."

I had to look round. I had already passed the doorway. I believed I may have been only hearing things, or had misheard something said by one towards another within. I still could not believe that it was I who was addressed, even when the girl standing in the doorway smiled to me and beckoned.

She was not a nun, but a girl in her teenage years who was dressed as a maid. She said my name again, this time in a questioning tone of voice. It was probably the nearest she could get to speaking in English. But clearly, she knew who I was and there was purpose in the way she addressed me.

I said, "Si—I am Jane."

The girl moved backwards into the building, still holding the door open, and it was for me to enter.

The light was dim, but more soft than sombre. There were candles and there was also the light that that came from the street through the nearest of the windows. It made little diamond shapes upon the large, stone slabs of the floor. The walls were a pale white. All felt cool and there seemed to be a haze in the air. Perhaps it was the from the smoke of incense, since the smell was powerful and strong.

The girl led me through a corridor, half turning at intervals to encourage me to follow. She had closed the door behind us and locked it. At the end of the corridor there was an antechamber. The girl gestured that I should wait and disappeared through the next doorway. In a moment she returned and stood to one side.

I walked into a most beautiful chapel. It was lit by at least a hundred candles. There were no windows, but light radiated everywhere. It burnished the gold and silver of the many lovely artefacts. I was beneath a statue of the Virgin. Her crown glittered with jewels and there were precious stones in her hair and sowed into her garments. Her painted eyes looked down upon me with a gracious and kindly pity.

There were no jewels upon Christ, whose statue faced hers across the nave. Mother and Son, wrought by the sculptor as the same age. She, the figure of grace, piety, and spiritual beauty. He, her son, racked with pain, bleeding, his skeletal body hanging from the cross, naked but for a whisp of cloth. Across the room, he eyed her. She looked downwards.

The Virgin was there again, above the altar, cloaked in a deep blue and highlighted with gold. She seemed to float in front of the stone carvings behind her, and on either side were frescoes of female martyrs. I recognised one as St Catherine, as she was depicted with the spiked, breaking wheel, and also with the dove that fed her when imprisoned. Once more, high up, there was Jesus; still upon the cross, and now a small, distant figure, and at the top, in the dome that crowned the chancel, there was painted the great, muscular figure of God, gazing down at his chapel from within a swirl of wind-blown drapery.

I was in awe, my gaze moving from wall paintings to magnificent wooden carvings, and enraptured by the grandeur of the altar and all that surrounded it.

I did not notice the figure, sitting on one of the pews, until I heard her voice. It was so calm. In the instant, a great restfulness came upon me. It was as if I had drunk a magical draft that, straight away, changed everything.

As I think of this now, it is exactly as it was when St Germain placed my mother and I together so that we were joined in the most peaceful union of infant and mother. And, as yet, it was just a voice.

The voice that called my name then spoke to me in English. A slight accent from somewhere; I did not care. It was like listening to a gentle passage of music. "We have pulled you off the street. But I could not let you walk by. And anyway, in truth, this is a visit from you to us. It was only necessary for us to be here and ready to receive you."

Physically, she was small and she spoke without any gesture of expression. All was within the voice. She was sitting upon a pew nearby, her body turned, just enough to be able to comfortably see me. She wore a brown habit with white material around her face and shoulders, and a black veil rested upon her head and descended behind her back. The veil created a dark enclave from within which the white toque framed a face of soft, smooth skin, untouched by any furrows of doubt or distress. She seemed ageless. Only the eyes and the manner of her gaze showed how much she had seen and known.

And how can I, Jane Crawford, know these things? How can I see so much in just a moment? I know, that in some ways, I have a growing ability, and here I was with one who would know this about me. Within my state of surprise and awe, I felt an affinity; even that I had come home.

"I expect you are dazzled by all this grandeur around you. Really, it quite embarrasses me. It isn't necessary at all, but it is the way of our church. We do, at least, modify it by the simplicity of how we live. Come sit with me Jane and let me be with you for a while."

I sat next to her. I could only feel a submission to a power that seemed so much greater than I. There was no strength in my body and all I could do was lean towards her and rest my head upon her lap. It was a gesture of respect to a higher spirit, but it was also to allow a great reservoir of need to burst free. All the strains and excitements and the fears of the years since we met the twins, flooded out as uncontrollable tears, and so it was for many minutes. She said nothing, just rested her hand upon my head.

And I said, with little knowledge of the church, or nuns, or religious practice, "Forgive me, Mother."

How interesting it is that when we need great relief, it is, so often, in the form of forgiveness. From our sins, I suppose. I was not even sure for what I was asking it. There was just such a need to be unburdened.

"Of course, I forgive you Jane, if you so wish. To be able to ask forgiveness is such an important step towards humility. We value it greatly here. But I believe that your visit is not about the past, but about the future."

It made me think again of St Germain. When he had taken me to one side so that we talked alone, he had told me of my future, describing things that I could not even imagine. He spoke of such great things for me that I could only feel embarrassed. Achievements and powers to be gained in lifetimes to come, until I would be like him and life would not be subject to time.

I guessed now that this small woman in the habit of a Carmelite nun, and with the softest voice that was also as clear as a silver bell, was one such as him.

I said, "Do you know St Germain, the Count."

"Oh, St Germain. Yes, we have met." She thought for a moment, then, "I remember him, he amuses me, because he is like this chapel here, bedecked in all its finery. His essence needs no decoration and yet he covers his fingers with all those rings. How interesting that the development of spirit can still allow for these little quirks of display."

She was smiling, and did, indeed, find it amusing.

She said, "So, Jane, you have been in contact with him?"

I was confused now. "I thought you would know that. I thought he must have told you about me. I am on a mission—for him—and for myself too."

"It is many years since I met him, and I do not know your mission. But we are joined together in other ways, as you are becoming joined to us now. And that is why you needed to come here. It is another step for you. I can help a little in that. As to your mission, you can tell me about that if you like. I know that St Germain is always getting mixed up in worldly affairs, so I expect that is in its nature."

And so, I told her all. Not altogether in sequence, but I believe that nothing of importance was left out. When I mentioned Don Angel, the Marques, a little furrow appeared in the brow of her face, which, until then, had looked so untroubled.

"So, he is part of your story."

She spoke in a quiet, matter of fact way, about matters that seemed so strange. "He was a follower of Zarathustra—Zoroaster for the Greeks. He became a great adept, but the temptation of Satan can be so great. In their religion the dark lord is Angra Mainyu and this Don Angel crossed over to him. You will find Jane, that it is when your new powers really emerge, that you become the greatest danger to yourself. You must never be ruled by them, and never be tempted by the route that seems quickest.

"I know that he is still with us, though his powers are waning. One might say that he has been spending his collateral and not wisely investing."

"This is what St Germain told me and said it is why he fears me, as my strength will grow and he will fear my revenge, even a century hence."

"So—St Germain said that? Well, he may be right. A century—or more."

I spent much time speaking of Mariana and she watched me calmly and patiently as I described her. I did not feel that I needed to state my love for her. She would know that anyway. When I told her that Mariana had visited Ancient Alexandria, the calm expression on her face changed completely to one of great interest, even excitement.

She said, "In Alexandria there was a temple to Aphrodite. It was a little away from the city, by a great lake and shaded by trees, and a grassy hill ran down from the temple to the lakeside."

She was radiant, as I answered, "I have seen the picture of this, painted upon a wall in a house where we all stayed. I know, that to Mariana, it had a special meaning."

She said, softly, "Then, she was there."

"But now she is in the desert—alone—and we fear for her."

"Yes, this sister of Mariana, this Marguerite, is a powerful force. Her power is not from magic, she is powered by the darkest human emotions. They can cause terrible damage. St Germain is right; she is your true and most dangerous enemy."

She rose. "Come now, the weather is fair and we can walk in the garden. The sisters just now are at work. When it comes to Vespers, I will need to leave you, but you may stay in the garden as long as you wish. The girl who asked you in will not be far away."

So, we left the chapel and walked through a long corridor lit by just the occasional candle. At the end, she pushed open a door and we were outside. And in this, the driest part of Spain, there was the sound of trickling water flowing beneath the shade of trees. And as she walked ahead, the course brown material of her habit brushed against the many, fragrant shrubs on either side. The summer was long gone, but still, some flowers had their last chance to bloom before resting until the spring. There was a light breeze and the sweet smell of herbs and I thought that, just a little, I was in heaven.

We talked, and it was so easy. I told her lots about my life and the artists I had known as a young woman and how I had modelled for Eddy and that when his wife died, I had become his companion. And how we had brought up James, who is now a young man.

And she told me about her life as a Carmelite nun and how she had come to this monastery in Almeria and begun there as a novice and was now the Reverend Mother. And I had to ask her, why, with her wisdom and her many years of life, did she begin there as a novice, at the bottom, and she told me that for a while, like the Marques, she too had become proud and been governed by her own powers. "I had to re-find my way."

As I think of this now, I believe it was the main thing she wished to impart. Her own special lesson to me, though there was much else that she spoke of with words that will feed my thoughts for ever.

When a bell rang from within the building, she told me that she must go. She made no physical contact, just said that I would be in her prayers and for the next few days, all the sisters would pray for me—and for

Mariana. And then, as she stepped away, she turned back. It was as if she had been considering whether or not to say it. "When you see your Mariana, you can tell her that we have met before. Now I revere Mary, the Mother of Christ. There have been other women before Mary. Once, a very long time ago, I served Aphrodite. That is where Mariana met me, just briefly, in the temple."

I left soon after and the girl was there to guide me. As we entered the street, I could not help but look lost, so she stayed by my side and I only needed to say the name of my hotel. She took me there and then slipped away.

I did not call at Marguerite's room to see if she was there, but went straight to mine and began to write. It is dusk now and I have written my account of the day and must go down to the dining room. I expect Marguerite will be there.

CHAPTER TWENTY SEVEN

The watchman

From the diary of Jane Crawford
Saturday, 20th November 1869. Early morning.
Hotel Regente. Almeria

Dinner last night was dreadful. I had to pretend that all was fine. A whole evening of being utterly false whilst Marguerite chatted in her most charming way. She was completely relaxed. Of course, I could make no mention of the Carmelite Monastery and the woman whom I met there. As to our parting in the street, she apologised profusely for having walked on too quickly. She had at first turned back to find me, but then had to assume that I would manage. "I abandoned you Jane, but well done, you found your way—there was no need for a search party." And she reached across the table and warmly squeezed my hand.

I am clear enough: her transition to that wild creature in the square; the way that the elements resonated to her with wind, darkness, and cold; these would be enough, but I have, as well, the judgement from the Reverend Mother—a woman whose name I do not know, but who knew mine. She said that Marguerite was our greatest enemy, and I cannot doubt this now. I know that Marguerite will be marvellous, gallant, charming, and full of love, but I must not be deceived. She can change a mood as quickly as the weather and light were transformed in the Almeria square. And I must travel with her. How else can it be?

I have woken early, indeed I hardly slept. My night was full of dreams that could not be thrown off when waking. Dreams of being chased and a terror that it is I, not Mariana, who would be killed.

I have sat here watching the light slowly define the objects in my room and now all is clear and still I sit here feeling the beating of my heart and the anxiety that fills my body and arms with pain.

Now I have written this entry, I will pack my journal with the rest of my belongings. Then I will go downstairs where Marguerite will be waiting.

* * * * * *

Thus ends the above entry to Crawfy's diary.

And sadly, it is the very last one.

And this would, therefore, be the end of the narrative.

It is the case, though, that despite the abrupt ending to those pages, the remaining events and their aftermath can be recorded, and perhaps it is appropriate, since it was I who began this long account, that I should also be the one to write the final chapters. And I am able to do so, since I made sure that I was there.

The Comte de St Germain, had explicitly stated that it should be Crawfy who should hear his final instructions and that it should only be she who journeyed to Spain to warn and protect Mariana.

Both my father and I were shocked by St Germain's insistence that the journey should only be taken by her and by his refusal to give us an explanation. His command to Crawfy, that she should not share any of the details, even with us, her family and loved ones, added to our dismay, and I must say that, for my father, this was also a cause for great displeasure. I could see, well enough, the degree to which he was supressing his true feelings as he endeavoured to give Crawfy the support that she needed.

My own feelings were quite different. I did not feel the hurtful insult of being excluded. The intensity of my own response, an intensity which very quickly grew to a pitch, was driven by my renewed fear for Mariana's survival. I had denied my love for her and had done so to recover from her complete and abrupt ending of our relationship. Now this love returned in a surge of protective anxiety. And it seemed that it was only Crawfy, a woman travelling alone, who was to guard her against human, and possibly occult malevolence. This, surely, could not be enough.

I did not wish to discuss this with my father. I could see that despite his own deep feelings, he was prepared to withdraw and summon up enough faith in St Germain, to allow Crawfy to follow his instructions and to make the journey.

But to this, I could not conform. I was due to visit the family of an old school friend in London and I explained to my father that they now expected me and it would be too rude to delay my visit. I packed a case, placed all the ready money I had in my wallet, and headed, not for the train station, but to the port at Whitby. It was the day after Crawfy's departure and I was to follow almost exactly in her tracks.

I had assumed that she would have an uninterrupted journey, by boat to France, train to Marseilles, and then by sea to Almeria, and thus had the continuous worry that being a day behind her, I might still be too late to avert the crisis that we feared. One thing that St Germain had made clear was the need for absolute speed.

But I was not to know that he had directed Crawfy to firstly locate Marguerite in Paris. The intention was to warn Marguerite off and to then, hopefully, bring Mariana to a place of safety: if possible, our home in Whitby. As it turned out, Crawfy's search for Marguerite added an extra night in Paris and then led her to Cora Pearl's country château which added an additional day and night to her journey. Thus, without realising it, I reached Almeria first, by a whole day.

If it were not for the cause of my visit, I would have simply taken pleasure in being there. It was soft and mild November weather and I walked through streets and amongst buildings that were full of memories of my six months with Mariana.

But now, there could only be urgency. I could, though, make use of those memories to help me in my search. There were surely shop-keepers, men and women whom we had come to know, who would be aware of her home in the desert. However reclusive she had become, she would still need food and supplies. And so, I went to the small store that we had so often used for the things that we needed.

The owner and his wife were both there and greeted me warmly. But, when I told them that I was searching for Mariana, I could see their unease. And what were they to do? They knew that Mariana lived alone and so I was no longer her partner, and clearly they knew

227

of her need for aloneness and privacy. It mattered not whether they understood why she should wish to live so. Given her fluent Spanish, her easy charm, the grace with which she conducted the smallest affair, they would only want to protect her needs. And Señora Montes gave the most non-committal answer. After my six months there, my own Spanish was easily sufficient for us to converse, but she had little to say. A shrug and a few words that told me that just occasionally they would see her, but informed me of nothing more.

This caused me real concern. I had imagined that it would be easy to find those who could help, but if these two, the most likely ones, refused, then my task would be much harder.

There were some bars and cafés that we often used and in some the waiters or the barmen remembered me, but they had seen nothing of Mariana. These I believed. In her current mood she would not be visiting them.

My boat trip had been through the night and I had arrived in the port of Almeria in early morning. It was now mid-day. Soon the shops would be closing for the afternoon siesta and I would be left wondering through empty streets in a helpless search. Then it would be evening, and if I should find her whereabouts, it would be too late for any journey outside the city.

With a wave of resolve that was drawing energy from a growing annoyance, I turned back and made my way, in a far more determined fashion, to the original store. Señora Montes was not there, but her husband was. He looked at me warily as I entered, yet there was something in his countenance, some hint of sympathy, which I did not expect from his wife. I was relieved that she was absent. My only course was to be as honest as circumstances would allow.

"Señor Montes, it is no small matter that brings me here to find Señora Mariana. She may not wish to be disturbed, yet I must bring to her attention matters that are of extreme importance and that are for her own wellbeing. I have travelled in great haste from England—just for this. Please Señor, you must help me find her."

He looked behind him, towards the closed doorway. There was no sign of his wife. In a hushed voice, "Señor James. I am pleased to see you again. It has been a long time. Do not be upset about my wife. These women—they protect each other. Sometimes, she talks to Señora Mariana and Mariana says—no visits from anyone. Just the deliveries that we send. But I understand. I can see from your face—it is important."

Again, he looked towards the door. There were sounds from within. From under the counter, he quickly took a pad of bills and a pencil. He pulled off the top sheet, turned it over and wrote down an address. He then took a bag of flour and a bottle of olive oil and placed them in a small box.

"This is the address of Carlos. He makes the deliveries. Tell him this box is to go to Mariana and that you will go too. You will need to walk to his house."

He drew me a little map with the pencil which showed me how to reach him. "He does very little, so he should take you now."

I could see that he was still anxious that his wife might enter, but I needed to speak with him more. I wanted to know more about Mariana. I feared a transformation that might shock me and I wanted to be prepared. "How is she, Señor?"

"Señor James, your Mariana is known as the woman of the desert. Once a priest journeyed out to her. He had heard about her and felt sure that she must need the help of God—living out there all alone—a young woman. When he came back, he would not speak of it, but we know that he went there again—many times. Some said that maybe he needed Mariana more than she needed him—others laughed and said 'Father has forgotten his holy vows.'

"When we deliver to her, she steps out and greets us, but always we leave the goods outside her door. She has a little cabaña; it is very small. On early mornings she sits outside, and then, when the sun begins to rise, she goes inside. No one will see her again until the evening. Then she sits out on the little gravel patch in front of her door. She is very thin Señor, yet people say she is like a beautiful spirit. At night she can still be seen there. Sometimes she is writing."

And he chuckled. "All this, Señor, is from just a few times she has been seen. Deliveries and travellers passing by. Once, there were young men who used to go out there to spy on her, and they told their stories too, but something about your Mariana makes people respect her, strange though she may be."

It was then that I saw his wife standing in the doorway. She had returned so silently that I could not tell for how long she had been there. Montes followed my gaze and looked around to see her. He shrugged in acceptance; the deed and the indiscretion were done. He placed the pad and the pencil back under the counter and busied himself by tidying objects on a nearby shelf.

"There it is Señor, I wish you well."

Señora Montes spoke. Her voice was calm and with no sign now of evasion. "She is special, James. She lives a pure life. The Virgin watches over her. Do not take the sins of the world into her home."

"Señora, I wish to protect her from such sins."

Our communication was now within a very different context. I observed the cross that hung from a fine chain around her neck, resting upon sun-browned skin above the top button of her blouse. On the wall, close by, hung a faded, framed picture of the Virgin. She gazed up at the angels who hovered above her and her hands were clasped in an ecstasy of devotion. I remembered, now, the importance of the church to so many we had known in Almeria. I also knew that the adoration of the Virgin was imbued into the hearts and souls of many Andalusian women. I could see then that I, a man, would be encroaching upon the sanctity of the female soul; that for this woman and mother, who kept a small store and would simply do this and care for her family until death, Mariana had become a kind of emblem. Her unworldliness, perhaps the very existence that now excluded men, was approaching a virtue of female spirituality that was a succour to her life.

"I thank you, Señora, for your affection towards Mariana. I come only to help her."

"She deserves nothing less, Señor James."

It was a long walk to the address that I had been given. I feared that the man, Carlos, may have retired for a siesta and be resolutely determined to be undisturbed.

The road took me past the little café that had been the place of so much pleasure for us on many evenings. I was completely thrown back into my love for Mariana and for the unfathomable depth of her feeling. I had forgotten, and indeed I thought "Did I ever properly, realise?" There can be so many regrets when qualities are recognised too late. What a mismatch of time it can be, when we catch up, but only to a memory.

These thoughts instilled in me an even greater sense of urgency. And now it was not just to save Mariana, it was to be near her again.

It was mid-afternoon when I arrived at the address on the outskirts of the city. The cart that Carlos used for his deliveries was outside and he was next to it making some repairs to its open-seating area. He turned at my approach, saw me, and then with no acknowledgement, turned away, back to his work. With a hammer, he struck loudly on the wooden framework of the seat. Despite my anxiety for as much speed as possible, I could tell that this man was not to be hurried. And so it was that for what seemed an age I stood, feeling conspicuous and foolish, whilst he continued to ignore me and to hammer with considerable force. At last, he paused, surveyed his work, and ran his hand over the joints he had been repairing. I was just about to speak, when he walked away.

I called out, using the best Spanish accent I could manage. It had some effect. He paused, his back towards me and then turned. He was still grasping the hammer. He took a few paces towards me, lifted the hammer, and then threw it. It looped several times before crashing into the recess of the cart. "You are English and you are here to see me—so I can guess your business."

I could tell from the accent that he was born and bred of Almeria. "Señor, I was given your address by Señor Montes. He says you make deliveries and I have some here." I held out the bag with the olive oil and the flour.

He snorted and looked contemptuously at the bag. "I know what you want—you wish me to deliver you to her—and she wants no visitors. Be gone. Go back to your hotel."

"Well, I really don't have one. I have come straight from the port, and to there from England. Señor, I have not come to stare at the woman of the desert, or disturb her in any bad way. But I do know her well and I have such important news for her that it cannot wait. I ask you, most respectfully, to take me to the woman."

He came closer and he leant against the cart. He was of extremely large build, middle aged, with a face weathered and lined, and a countenance that remained, steadfastly unsmiling. This man would give no quarter. For the first time, I noticed that he was blind in one eye. I gazed intently at the eye which I believed to be the good one. I knew that one error in my speech or attitude would finish the business completely. I could also tell that anyone who might force their way into the space of Mariana, would answer to the physical might of this man. He had, surely, become her guardian.

"Señor, I only say that your protection of the woman Mariana is something that I, as one who has known her well, must value, and I thank you for it. But you have no need to protect her from me—indeed my whole reason for being here is to preserve her wellbeing and her safety."

231

"Do you say that she is not safe? What is this danger?"

I had no option but to tell him more. This was a man who had no time for nuances that were simply evasion. He viewed the world with one eye in his judgements as well.

"There may be those visiting, who do not wish her well. They may already be with her. This is the reason for my haste."

"No one is with her—I would know. We will go there now. I will be watching you, Señor, and I will see the way she greets you. It will tell me what I need to know. Be careful, Señor, that you have told me the truth."

My relief was tempered by a new fear that Mariana might show some displeasure at my arrival. It could be enough to move this man to violence against me. And for the first time I really thought through what I was attempting to do. I had been so full of myself as Mariana's saviour. Rushing neck and neck with Crawfy to reach and to warn her. But looking around me, here so far from England and so far from France, these dangers to Mariana seemed incredible. I stood, on the outskirts of Almeria, the great fort of Alcazaba close by on its hill, carefully watching over the city as it had for hundreds of years. The weather was soft and mild, just a breeze moving the occasional cloud across a sky that extended from one distant mountain range to another. A great arc of blue and beneath that the grey green of the cacti and the beginnings of the desert shrubs. And all completely silent except for the sound of dust as a lizard emerged from behind a rock and in a flash was gone behind another. The man with one eye was motionless and staring at me.

I had been so sure of myself, but I had not stopped to think. Was the danger so real? Had we all been caught up in hysteria? All Mariana wanted was her privacy and, in the Tabernas desert, she had found it and around her were those who saw her as some kind of icon. She was fulfilling her own being, and in her strange choice of life, was offering a fulfilment to them. And I, and Crawfy too, wherever she now was, were to butt in on this with warnings of great cruelty and even death. She had ended our affair. That was that. She, certainly, did not look back. I now realised, with a wave of panic, that my arrival might be a source of real displeasure. The thought hurt, and here in front of me, was a man who seemed to embody a straight-forward reality and his one-eyed stare brought me completely down to earth.

There was an additional thought. I hardly noticed it at the time. It flickered in and out and disappeared as fast as the lizard. But I have certainly thought of it since. I had completely denied something that, in truth, I knew to be true. Crawfy loves Mariana: I can tell this, and it is not just friendship, nor the sisterly love of one woman to another. It is a love that surely rivals mine. I had not wished to know this, but was I also racing Crawfy to be the first to reclaim Mariana's love?

"Señor, I cannot tell how the lady Mariana will greet me. It is more than a year since I last saw her. People change. I believe that she has. She has come into the desert to live and I know now that there are those, those in your community, Señor, who admire this woman, and who have great affection for her. I believe that many people in the past have felt the same, though we did not know her as you do. Please understand, that in my own way, I share your feelings and for this reason I am here."

I had no doubt that within the forbidding exterior of this great crag of a man there was a softness. But I also knew that it was narrow and selective and though my words had reached him, his favour did not extend to me. He was ready though, in his watchful and suspicious way, to take me to her home, and then to observe.

He told me to wait and disappeared behind his house. There must have been a small paddock there as, after some time, he returned leading a horse and carrying the equipment needed to attach the horse to the cart. When done, he climbed into his seat. He made no gesture, simply staring ahead, but it was clearly time for me to come aboard. The only seat was next to him, and so we set off, silently, side-by-side.

CHAPTER TWENTY EIGHT

Mariana in the South

The Tabernas desert is the only real desert in Europe. Gradually, we left behind all vegetation, except for occasional shrubs and rough grasses that grew defiantly in the rocky landscape. In the muted light of early evening, the mountains formed distant, grey silhouettes that marked the horizon on three sides. On the other, the land drifted away into a pale distance. Though all was dry, the air was cold, and I pulled my coat close around me and fastened the buttons, from top to bottom.

We rode along a rough track that wound between undulations in the ground and outcrops of rock. All was rock, dust, and scrub, except for occasional luminous patches where white flowers grew. In places, the rocks reared up into massive forms, their shadows plunging us into darkness.

I turned and saw that any signs of Almeria had gone, though in the distance, to our left, the outlying, small white houses of a village, were clustered, far off, upon a hill.

Carlos, had not said a word. He ignored my occasional questions as if they were unworthy of answering. He looked steadfastly ahead and refused to look at me, but there was something that did draw his attention and it caused me to feel that all was not well. I had seen jackdaws perched and flying above the buildings near his house. We had left them behind, but once outside the city and well into the desert they reappeared, their black silhouettes circling above us, or completely still and eyeing us from rocks by the side of the track. One flew down to perch on the edge of the cart and hammered its black beak into the wood. I turned to look. It was joined by two more and then there was a flock above us, chattering with harsh, high-pitched calls. One of those on the cart moved closer. There was a dull gleam to its black feathers, and above the pale grey ruff of its collar, its head twitched from side to side. It moved some more in a sudden sideways lope, its wings slightly extended, until it was almost next to us. Carlos swore and swung his arm. It gave a coarse cry and flew off, but only as far as the next outcrop of rocks from where it eyed us as we approached. As we passed, I heard sounds that were almost human. I strained to listen through the clatter of our horse and cart. But then we were passed and it was gone. If I had been with a more friendly companion, I would have joked that it wished to speak with us.

They have a dark beauty, these birds, but here in the failing light and surrounded by the bleak, elemental landscape, I could only think of malevolence and the expression, "the evil eye." Perhaps Carlos, who would be closer to ancient folk law than I, was thinking the same.

It must have taken us two hours, and it was dusk when I saw the distant shape of two small buildings. Carlos gave a grunt of recognition and steered the horse off the main track and onto a smaller one that led towards them. Here the land was flatter, though it remained barren. I cannot imagine how two such buildings had ever been envisaged, let alone lived in, so far from anywhere.

As we drew closer, I could see that one of them was a ruin, whilst the other was intact. It was very small. We went into a dip in the ground and I could only see the roof with its curved terracotta tiles. They looked cracked and worn, but complete, and a chimney protruded with white smoke curling up. The thought of the fire within brought a moment's feeling of warmth, and then I thought of Mariana, now so close, and the barrenness around me softened and I could only think of her.

And there she was. Just as Montes had said, "In the evening she sits outside." She was wrapped in a cloak. The cloak was dark, and in the twilight, it merged with the dark grey clumps of stone that were the walls of the cabaña, so that her face seemed to float above it.

As we approached, she stood up. The cloak slipped away and the white dress beneath completed the vision of some pale spirit of the desert.

And then she turned, walked inside, and the door closed behind her.

"Bad news for you, Señor," muttered Carlos.

I feared the judgement he would make, but the greater distress was her rejection. We had been close enough for her to recognise me.

Carlos halted the cart. He leant forward, his arms resting upon his knees, whilst he stared at the closed door. We both sat motionless and silent. There was silence all around too. The jackdaws had gone. No movement except for the grey smoke gently rising from the chimney. We continued to sit. I looked at him and his face was impassive, and it seemed as if he had withdrawn completely and was deep within his own thoughts. And then I had the strangest idea that he may have been praying. To a Christian God, I suppose—but maybe not.

And then, with the suddenness of one who suddenly awakens from sleep, he sat upright and grasping the reins made to turn us away and to leave that place.

But the door opened and Mariana stepped out. The large cloak was around her, its hem brushing her bare feet and ankles. It was now deep twilight and she seemed to float towards us. Gradually her face became more visible and she was smiling; though not at me, but at Carlos.

She stopped at the cart and she stroked the head of the horse. Did it know her? It seemed to know her well. She spoke to Carlos and I could tell that the Spanish was perfect and even in the dialect that was his own. "Dear friend, it has been a while. Have you been well? And the family?"

The normal remarks we make at a friendly meeting, but delivered in a voice that had the resonance and soft delicacy of the finest bell.

"Señora, I am well and the family are well, though my son wants to leave us and go to Madrid. This makes us sad, Señora."

"Of course, I feel for you, but he is a young man. If it is wrong for him, he will return. Does your wife feel deeply about this?"

"She does, but I believe that I do, even more."

She reached up and took his hand. "Thank you, Carlos, for so much. Without you, I would, indeed, struggle."

"Señora, others would help, but it is my pleasure." And then he looked at me and back at her.

237

"It is fine, Carlos. I know this young man and I am pleased to see him—though it is some surprise. He may stay."

And so I climbed down from the cart, and still she had not looked at me.

She turned and walked towards the cabaña. I began to follow, but halted when Carlos called out, "Señor!"

For a moment I feared that the calm installed by Mariana's words would be lost and I might still have to face some stern words from her guardian.

I turned. He was holding out the small box with the flour and the olive oil which had been my excuse for his delivery. I believe there was the hint of a smile as he gave them to me. But also, "You told me there was danger. I may be close; I may be far away. If I am away, it is for you to protect her. Make sure you do Señor!"

And I thought to answer, "We may need you tomorrow. Can you come?"

He looked hard at me. His slight nod was confirmation. He then turned the cart to make his slow journey back to Almeria.

Mariana had paused outside the cabaña. She was waiting for me. As I walked towards her, my stomach was tight and my legs were as weak as stalks.

Inside, I sat in a little wicker chair. There were two of them and she sat in the other. There was a small, bamboo table beside her with an oil lamp that barely lit the room. The ceiling was in darkness and the upper walls in shadow. The light caught her face. Around her mouth and the corners of her eyes were lines that I had not seen before, and her skin was dark from the sun. Her hair fell carelessly around her shoulders. It made me think of my father: how he would love to paint her now, and how well he would do so. And did her twin show such changes?

"James, you come to me at dusk, through the desert. You persuade Carlos to bring you. Do you come from England? Such a long way. Few people visit me and few is enough. I had no thought that you would come, or that I would ever see you. And here you are, and surely, you bring bad news—which can only be of my sister. Is she ill, has she died?"

Her tone of voice shocked me. So matter of fact. From our time together, I knew that the vast attachment to her sister had diminished. She had weathered the agonising loss, though the longing for another had still possessed her. It had moved across to that very thing that Marguerite had destroyed: the blissful union with Aphrodite, her temple, and the

238

women who served her. But, now, in an instant, I sensed something further. She was no longer in the grip of such yearning. She was pared down, lean of body, and lean of soul. She had found her strength and rebuilt herself in the desert. She had needs and had gratitude, as I saw when she was with Carlos, but she was her own being; as strong and rooted as the landscape around her little hermit's house.

And I could speak to her so plainly that I was amazed by the words that I used. "Mariana, we were lovers." And ruefully, "Do you remember?

"I have come to you because I love you still, though this is no declaration, for I know that such a thing would be refused. We had our time and I will always be grateful, though there is pain in my heart that such a thing could end. My visit now, is indeed about your sister. Mariana, you told me yourself that you believed she could harm you and that her intent could be greater still: even to remove you completely from this earth. I, we—my father, Crawfy, and the Comte de St Germain, the man who has always wished to protect you—we believe that she will now make her move. She has her own motives, but you know that she carries out the desires of the Marques de Mansura. He has played with you both and his greatest achievement, the exquisite, consummation of his game is the death of one twin by the hand of the other: the ultimate, incestuous murder. You sense this, I know. I have come to warn and protect you. Mariana, please. The time has come. Now is the greatest danger. Carlos will return tomorrow, please come with me then and we will go to England where you will be safe."

"James, you are a kind man, and you were a kind boy. It is why I have always loved you. Even when you were such an embarrassed and awkward young thing, when we stayed with you at your home, I thought— 'Well, perhaps later on.' And it happened. And I could love you still James. But you know, I had to be on my own—absolutely. I have needed others so much, too much, so now I love nature and the desert and they allow me to rest within myself, with no torment. The land outside can be warm and loving, and in winter cold and cruel, but it will always be true to itself and to me. No shocks, no conceit or deception. It knows no jealousy or envy.

"And so, to my sister, she of the terrible envy. All her achievements, and there will be many, will never be enough until she has removed me from her life—one way or another. Yes, I did once tell you that she could try to kill me. And now you say the time has arrived. You know,

I have come to be resigned to this. Really, James, you can take me to England and to your Whitby, and Don Angel will find me without the slightest problem and if he wishes to send Marguerite to complete his work, he will.

"I have found myself here in the Tabernas, and now I can face death. Not that I wish to die and I will fight to live, but I am alone here. Of course, woe betide any mortal who should intrude or wish me harm. If Carlos was nearby, he would destroy them; he keeps an eye out with that one watchful eye. But you have seen, he lives far away, and he would be no match for them, and I have no wish to place him in danger.

"You too, James may have entered into great danger. Really there is so little you can do. Don Angel has enormous power. Whatever is my destiny, it must now come to pass. If Carlos comes tomorrow, you must leave with him. That is my wish."

"But it is not just I, Jane Crawford comes as well. It was she that St Germain charged with the task of finding and warning you. I came, without anyone's knowledge. My own choice, my own need to help you."

When I said the name of Jane Crawford, I watched her poise and self-containment lapse; as if, whilst walking, she had suddenly tripped. She recovered immediately, but I saw her reaction and it filled me with pain. The love was clear, the biggest love, and it was for Crawfy.

She spoke slowly, as if thinking hard and fast. "Jane is coming. So now all is different. Yes, very different!"

She rose, pushing the little wicker armchair to one side. It was light and it fell. The composure was gone. "Can I not be left alone? To be immune? I care not for the evil of my sister, but now you include Jane!"

Her last words were not just to me, but to the room, the desert outside, even to the whole world which now threatened to impinge on the life that sustained her.

There was anger: anger that she could no longer rest calmly with whatever fate decreed. I had spoken of the one she truly loved and she could no longer consider her fate in isolation. Jane would be here, back in her life, after many years, the first time since Poissy, and Jane, too, would be entering into danger.

She walked to the little window and closed the shutters against the darkness outside, then moved across to the small stove that warmed the room.

I was in torment. I was the bringer of awful news, the messenger with the toxic message and I feared that she would hate me for it.

For a while she thought carefully and then seemed reconciled. Her tone softened. "Of course, you had to come. And Jane too. You have travelled far and you have done so for me. Thank you, James. And you will be hungry. I will make some food."

I remembered how little we had cooked when we were together, always preferring to stroll out to our favourite bars and restaurants. I remembered, too, that when Mariana did cook, her special herbs could enter the mix. Enough to cause us to dream and gently fall asleep. Did she still favour such recipes? I knew I should stay completely alert.

I could now study her closely. She was, indeed, very thin. She moved with an ease of movement, though, that showed she was in good health. In fact, there was a gentle physicality that suggested a harmony of mind and body. Her voice was deeper than before. She had always spoken quietly, yet with words completely distinct. Her hair hung loose and was lighter, in tones that suited her tanned skin. And the freckles were there, even more pronounced. I liked the little lines around her mouth and eyes. They had not been there before, but all these changes suited her and perhaps were the measure of the happiness she had found in solitude. Because of the November chill, she had placed a shawl around her shoulders, over the plain cotton dress. Her feet were still bare.

The stove warmed the building and she had lit two more lamps so that it now felt bright and cosy. It seemed a happy little house. In fact, it was just one open room, though there was a curtain drawn across from where I assumed the bed to be. There was a crucifix upon the wall—a gift from the priest who visited? And also, a ceramic Buddha, and a little framed painting. I recognised the Hindu deity from images I have seen. It was Lakshmi. She sat cross legged upon a pink lotus flower, its petals gently curling around her feet with their points circling the green and gold of her tunic. One hand held a golden casket from which spilled gold coins, another hand was open palmed, and in her other two (for Lakshmi has four hands), she held two pink lotus flowers their stalks gently secured aloft, between finger and thumb. Bracelets festooned her arms and necklaces hung from her shoulders to her waist. A goddess of beauty, love and absolute abundance.

And there was Mariana, as unadorned as could be, and to me, even more beautiful. As we ate, I told her of the visit of St Germain and the urgency of his warning. She was thoughtful when I mentioned the Count. "There was a Count who visited us when we were girls—he knew my father."

241

She lowered her face so that it was in shadow. When she looked up, I could see that she was deeply troubled by the memory. I wanted to ask her more, but she moved quickly on to her sister. "What do you know of her now?"

I could tell her nothing, just that she would surely be based in Paris, as only Paris could satisfy her needs and appetites.

"Yes, that is true," she said. "How different these twins are."

I wished to hear more about Alexandria, to take in an experience that was so uncanny and to hear of it from one who had been there, who had travelled back centuries, who had breathed the air and felt the breath of the women of the temple, who had even walked through the great library, a marvel of the ancient world, a pinnacle of its civilisation.

She said, "When will Jane be here?"

"Perhaps it will be tomorrow. She has surely been delayed on her journey."

"Then tonight is for us James."

She took me by the hand and led me to the curtain which she drew back. The little bed was narrow but she had us lie upon it. And then, as once before, she rested her face upon the pillow whilst I lay upon my back and her breath touched my cheek as she told me again of all that had happened in the ancient city and how at the end, when the temple collapsed around her, and when she was lost in spirit, wondering at night by the harbourside, she met a woman who was so like Jane Crawford, and the woman took her hand and led her to a place where there was grass and they had lain looking up at the sky that was phenomenal with its stars, and how this had saved her.

And then we made love. Was she making love to me or just to love itself? It matters not. I look back now, so many years later, and know that there has never been such a night as that, with the woman of the desert.

CHAPTER TWENTY NINE

The uninvited guests

When I awoke, I was alone. Perhaps Mariana had risen during the night. It was not a bed for two, unless the only wish was to be entwined until morning. Or maybe she rose early. That seemed likely in her new life, though it was never so when we lived in the city.

The curtain was across, holding the darkness in the tiny bedroom of the cabaña. From the bed, I reached across to draw it back and leaning round, I looked for her. The little building was empty. All was tidy and the plates and pans from our meal were cleaned and back on their shelves.

I got up from the bed and put on my clothes. It was cold. The little stove was lit but had yet to match the warmth of the evening. What a hard life she led, and she loved it. I supposed that she was already sitting outside on the patch of gravel by the door.

But she was not there, so I sat in the little wooden chair and imagined that I was her. Sitting there alone, with no one else for miles around. Her splendid, calming, fulfilling solitude; her breaking from a twin who had reflected her being only in looks, and whom she had once clung to so desperately.

At first, I had no concerns about her absence. She would be walking somewhere. But then I awoke from my reverie. Mariana was in danger and I had slept whilst I should be completely aware. Marguerite and the Marques could come at any time—and had they already done so?

I abandoned the chair and walked quickly along the track that led from the cabaña.

I came to a group of rocks which were easy enough to scale and that allowed me to look around and see much further. I saw her then, sitting upon a rock. As if she sensed that I had seen her, she turned around. She waved, and I realised, that from where she sat, she could see far along the track to whoever might approach and that she was waiting there for Crawfy. I had slept long and it was probably late morning. If Crawfy had left early, she would be with us soon.

I walked to Mariana and sat with her. For a long time, we were silent and the silence was fine, even the best way, for in that silence rested the intimacy of our shared life in Almeria and now, our night together in her little home.

She looked up at the sun and I guessed that she was gauging the time. "She will be here soon."

And it was soon after that, that we heard the galloping of horse's hooves. Very distant, and eventually a rider came into sight. Something was wrong though, and I felt the tension in her body as she strained to see better. I stood too and the two of us were there, standing on a rock and gazing into the distance along the winding track. It was a lone rider, and making speed, so that it soon became clear that it was a man. A man strangely attired. He was like a visitation from a tale of Arabia: tall in the saddle with a white tunic that billowed in the wind. Upon his head was a white turban and a great length of scarlet cloth was wound around his face with its tail streaming behind.

Mariana had fixed her gaze upon the rider, but for a moment, she looked up. Two large birds, eagles perhaps, were circling above us.

Her words were quietly to herself, "Of course, he would have an escort." She had recognised who it was, and I turned to her for explanation. She just said, again, very quietly, "It is he."

And then he was upon us, pulling his horse to a halt in a cloud of dust that receded to reveal the Marques de Mansura.

I recognised him now. It had been five years since he descended on us at Whitby; uninvited, unexpected, and knowing that the twins were there. I had seen him briefly then, and the aftermath of that visit had remained with us all. Of course, it was only his costume that had changed. Then he had been dressed as a European gentleman. Now, in his gesture to the desert, though a Spanish one, he was dressed as a Bedouin tribesman. A man who enjoyed his theatre. He unwound the headdress and there were the distinctive features: the aquiline nose, the high cheekbones, the thin dark moustache above sensual lips, and the eyes with pupils that were almost black. And not a day older.

He called out in French, "Mariana. You make it so hard for me to visit! The middle of a desert. So uninviting, so unfriendly!"

And to my great surprise, he recognised me. He changed to English. "And you the boy from Whitby, now a young man—and here in the desert with your Aunt Mariana." And he laughed merrily at the thought. "Well Mariana! The things you get up to."

I knew the history, the terror that she had felt about this man and the massive distortions of reality that had brought her unworldly pleasure and earthly pain. She had been drawn into his imagination and the theatre of his life, yet she looked at him steadily and replied with absolute calm.

"Angel, you will find me wherever I am. If only you no longer wished to. Have you not finished with me Angel? Is there still more for you to do?"

He had moved his horse very close and as we stood upon the rock, his own body was level with ours. I could feel the heat from the steaming flanks of the animal rising up from below.

He chose to speak in English, a language that we could all understand. "Mariana—I ride to you through the desert—I come only for the reunion—to enjoy the party, to be there with my twin girls, and you chide me."

I could tell from her voice that Mariana's certainty had faltered. "I know of no reunion, nor wish for one. I may be visited by a friend, that is all."

"Ah yes! Dear Jane is coming." And looking at me, "Your lovely nurse, young man, Crawfy, she is coming—but she will not be alone!"

I think she had already realised, but she asked, "Marguerite?"

"Of course! A reunion—so it must be her! When did you last meet? How could you have fallen so far apart?"

"You should know—you caused it." She had recovered quickly and there was a renewed firmness to her manner.

Don Angel studied her carefully. The horse became restless, but he leant forward and spoke softly in a strange language. In a moment it was still and he resumed his gaze. "You have changed—no more Paris finery. And now a creature of the desert."

He raised himself, standing in the stirrups and surveyed the landscape around him. "A nice desert, and near to Almeria—where we first met. I feel a little honoured that you wish to stay here." Again, he looked around and seemed satisfied.

He looked up. The eagles were still very high. One hovered, whilst the other slowly circled around it. He made the slightest gesture and the two birds veered away and headed for the mountains. He gazed after them. "They help me find the way. Now, Mariana, you can at least look after my horse. She is tired and thirsty."

Mariana had gathered herself and I could see that she was completely focused on the moment. She had been told that there would be more visitors, even her sister. We were in the desert. A place where she could hardly be reached, but if she was it was a place of no escape. She would have to humour and deal, moment to moment, with this invasion into her life. I could only hope that her character, consolidated in solitude, was strong enough for the coming trials.

She stepped carefully to descend from the rock, paused, and then jumped the remaining distance. The movement was athletic and sure-footed. I saw the healthy, wiriness of her body and I imagined her leaping from rock to rock like a creature born to live there.

Don Angel had dismounted and was leading his horse. He walked next to me and placed his free arm around my shoulders. I was amazed, since rather than recoil, I felt a warm feeling of friendship. Was this the man who could harbour such evil intentions—and to Mariana? Yet my consciousness of why I was there, in a foreign country, miles from the city, cried out to me from a far off, receding place. I fought for it and brought it back. I listened to the voice. "This is the Marques de Mansura who plays with destruction."

His arm slipped away as if he had read my thoughts. I was then fearful that he could do just that—know what was in everyone's mind. Could his powers be so great? I believed it possible. I forced a friendly remark. "Sir, how could you know to be here, to know of these visits, to be present for this—reunion?"

246

It sounded hollow and pointless. Of course, he would know, such was his power and his involvement with the twins—his possession of their lives.

Nor did he answer. Having sensed my resistance, he turned instead to his horse, patting and speaking to her in the same strange language.

Mariana was waiting at the door. She held a bucket out to Angel. "Water is precious to me here. I rely on supplies and you are lucky we have had rainfall. This is all your horse can have."

"We thank you, Mariana." He patted the horse. I noticed then that it was magnificent. Not a large horse, but beautiful, in chestnut and white. Should not the Marques be riding a sheer black stallion? But no effect was lost. His hand caressed its white main.

My mind drifted again. I had the strangest sense, as if in a dream, that this was no longer a horse, but some female entity, under his command, trapped in the body of a beautiful animal.

The eagles had gone, but once again, there was a flock of jackdaws. They flew overhead, chattering with sharp calls, and a row of them were lined along the roof. And it was not only the birds. A snake slithered with speed across the path and lizards scuttled on either side. And I was sure I could hear insects. Not just the buzz of them flying, but the sound of earthbound insects gathering, burrowing in teeming thousands. The barren desert was opening itself up to show the life that surged within it.

I heard Don Angel, "Not a bad desert."

I had stopped, completely still, filled with the sounds and the vibrations of countless creatures. I thought, "This is the soul of the desert."

It was Mariana's voice that brought me to. "James. Come here!"

The Marques was now behind the cabaña and caring for his horse.

She seemed to know, "You are feeling the desert, James. And he will make you feel many things, some of them wonderful. But never trust him. Hold on to your mind."

She heard the new sounds first. She had held me by the shoulders as she spoke, gazing into my eyes, but now she looked over my shoulder towards the track. She was completely alert and her eyes were clear, keen and focused. I was still mingled with the creatures of the desert and I thought of the birds of prey, the eagles, with their incredible power of sight. Now, I heard the sounds too and I looked around. A horse and carriage were approaching.

They came over the brow of the hill and there they were. It was an open carriage with the driver at the front, and sitting behind, two women. Mariana dropped her hands from my shoulders. I heard her breath quicken. She made a few steps forward and then stopped. From behind the cabaña, the Marques appeared and he too, stood still, and watched.

The carriage halted a few yards away. I thought, "These friends, these patrons of Mariana, never come close—as if in respect."

"Hola, Señora." The driver got down. He brought not only the two women; there were supplies and pitchers of water. These he attended to first, as if not sure what to do about his passengers. He laid the supplies upon the ground and then he too remained still.

The two women descended from the carriage. One slipped down easily with complete eagerness. She rushed towards Mariana, throwing off her hat as she did so. The shining, light brown locks fell around her shoulders; the hat dropped to the ground. She cared not for that, but only to be with her sister. But then, just before the embrace, a pause; a momentary halt, and it could only have been for the difference. It was surely in all our minds as we watched the scene: the reunion of twins who were, no longer, so alike. Marguerite would have seen the thin, tightness of the body, the lack of cosmetic care, the plainest of clothes, the tanned skin, and perhaps those feint lines upon her face. And yet, something surely remained, a quality that still marked the phenomenon of their twinship.

She circled her sister with her arms. "Darling Mariana." And then, exclaiming, "But you are so thin!"

The laughter of the Marques rang out. "Marguerite, your sister is no longer a lady of Paris! She lives now with the elements. And how very interesting this is."

He spoke in English, asserting that it should be the language of the day.

Marguerite still held her sister, but at a distance, scrutinising, as a mother might examine her new born baby. "Darling, I can feel your bones. Are you starving yourself? We must look after you—we must make you well."

Again, it was the Marques, "But she is very well."

Marguerite must have been as surprised at the presence of the Marques as she was at the appearance of her sister. But Mariana had first to be her full attention. Now she turned to him. "Well, Angel. After all these years you come to us again! As always—without notice." But then her voice changed. It softened and was complicit, as if the two of them were alone.

"And you always know when a special time has come—of course you are here." And then, a change again, and her attention was back to her sister. "Mariana, forgive me for the past. Was it I who drove you to the desert? My selfishness. Oh, I know my faults and wish so much to redeem them. To have a twin, another so like oneself. What a gift of God! What can be more wonderful, more requiring of the greatest celebration, and the most profound ceremony. Tomorrow is our birthday, is it not?"

I was astounded. A birthday had never been mentioned and I believe to my father and Crawfy it was completely unknown. Did St Germain know? And my feeling was not of celebration, but of unease.

And what of Mariana? She accepted the embrace of her sister, even placed her own arms around her waist. But there was no warmth; no visible connection. Though not quite that, because she seemed interested. As if she was thinking anew about her twin, gauging her again in this moment, viewing her not through emotions, but with the coolness of her mind. And she had said nothing.

And we were now joined by Crawfy. She had quietly descended from the carriage. Unlike Marguerite, who despite a desert journey, was richly attired and surrounded by a blue velvet cloak, she was calmly and practically dressed. She wore a bonnet tied under her chin which she loosened and discarded. Her hair was tied behind. Of course, she looked beautiful and I noticed, for the first time, that there were whisps of silver in her hair. She stood, quietly, somewhat apart.

The Marques de Mansura was, naturally, the master of ceremonies. "It is the eve of the birthday! Mariana, you are our host, and how wonderful that we can celebrate, and all be here."

He gestured to us with a wide sweep of his arm, but I noticed a special look towards Crawfy. It was different. It was not the intimate ease which he extended to the rest of us. It was not even friendly; yet it was knowing, as if some understanding was shared.

And I noticed too, that amongst the greetings and the proclamations, no words passed between Crawfy and Mariana. In fact, though Crawfy stared at her, I did not, for a moment, see Mariana return her gaze. How strange that those with the most powerful attraction can show the least attention. But perhaps it was not needed and was simply known.

Mariana thanked the driver. She wished him to return later to collect her guests who would be returning to Almeria. He nodded and raised his cap in respect. He returned to his seat, called to his horse, and they slowly moved off along the track.

Mariana turned and entered the cabaña. We followed. The five us to be squeezed into her little home. I was last to enter, but first I looked around at the great expanse outside. Far away, upon a raised part of the track, was a horse and cart. Not the one that had just left, which still trundled on its way. This one was absolutely still. I could just make out the large form of the man who sat, motionless, upon the driver's seat. The one-eyed watchman had returned.

CHAPTER THIRTY

The birthday party

"James, please bring in the chair from outside."

I responded to Mariana's request and opened the door and carried in the little wooden chair that she kept outside the cabaña. As I did so, I looked up to where I had seen the watchman. He was still there.

With the new chair there were still not enough. The five of us filled the room, so that I found myself standing with my back tight against a wall. Mariana had drawn back the curtain that secluded the bed, so that the bed could be used as a seat. Marguerite had immediately clasped her sister by the arm and drawn her there so that they sat together. She seemed determined to stay close to her and to have a prolonged physical contact. Once seated, she gazed at her with extreme affection, kissed her upon the cheek and placed an arm around her. She had tossed the blue velvet cloak to one end of the bed. Underneath she wore a magnificent black silk dress. It had long arms, with great gatherings of lace around the cuffs. The neck was low enough to show the large silver crucifix that hung there. A dress for an occasion: "A magnificent funeral," I thought.

The Marques and Crawfy sat in the two wicker chairs, so that, at first, they faced each other, their feet almost touching. Again, there was a strange quality, something shared that was unique to them, but by

251

no means comfortable. With Crawfy, Don Angel's usual carefree and self-assured manner seemed held in check.

I heard him quietly say to her. "Madame Jane, I trust your journey was not too tiring." And then, with a little of his normal tone and swagger, "I came on horseback."

And Crawfy replied, "My journey has been mixed. An adventure for sure—one that I undertook for the Comte de St Germain. You know him of course. He cares for Mariana."

To which the Marques, replied, "As do we all, Jane."

Marguerite had been talking loudly and fussing over her sister, but at Crawfy's mention of St Germain, she in the instant, took notice. Mariana rose, and stepped to the little cupboard where she kept her dishes. There were some cups and glasses there. "I live alone. We will have to share the glasses and I have only water or milk."

"Not fit for a party!" cried out Marguerite. "I have something better." She had a small bag with her in the same dark blue velvet as her cloak. It was by her feet and she reached forward and pulled out a bottle. It contained a green liquid. In my youth and inexperience, I had never tasted absinthe but realised from the colour that this was surely it.

"Do you remember Poissy?" declared Marguerite. "We began with this. Mariana, we need two jugs—these you surely have. I have brought the sugar and the spoon. And Angel, you were our host—we no longer have Cora's wonderful chef, but you can surely make us the finest drink."

The Marques seemed relieved at the intervention. He was no longer locked, face to face, and feet to feet, with Crawfy. He swung his chair about. It screeched on the stone floor. He was exuberant. "Marguerite, you are marvellous! You know just what to do. I should have thought of this myself. Of course! I will prepare the drink and we will toast the wonderous twins on the eve of their birthday."

His exuberance was not shared by all. Crawfy was completely still and without expression, but was staring at the bottle that Marguerite still held aloft, as if to penetrate its contents. I thought then—"Is not poison the woman's way of killing?"

And Mariana, whom I knew well to enjoy the most exotic drugs, in her new self, was indifferent. She did, though, fetch the two jugs, one of which she filled with water.

Don Angel chuckled. "It will be made in the most rustic fashion. But we will manage."

He carefully allowed a thin stream from the bottle to enter the jug. He then balanced the spoon so that it straddled its mouth. Then, holding the other jug, he, very slowly, dribbled water from it onto the spoon with the lumps of sugar. Even in the little desert cabaña, the process had mystery and the anticipation of a magic ritual, and the smell of wormwood rose and filled the room. I had heard the odes to the green goddess and thought, "Here she is, she is with us, I can smell her perfume."

And once more, clouded by the prospect of pleasure, I had lost my purpose. Were we the playthings of the Marques and Marguerite? Both adepts at the sensual arts. Were we to lose our hold on reality? Marguerite and the Marques could do their will, whilst we became lost in intoxication. I turned towards Crawfy, my only ally. She still surveyed the scene with complete vigilance. I breathed deeply and felt restored.

Mariana, in collecting the materials for the ritual, had found some relief from the attentions of her sister. But there was now a sudden turn of events.

Marguerite loudly addressed us all. Her voice was clear and commanding. The English was impeccable. "There has been a mis-understanding. No—the wrong word. Its nature is too soft for what has been thought. I know that I am a woman of strong feeling. For this, some admire me, others may fear me.

"My loves can be passionate, and my hates can last forever. I know who I am—that surely is of great worth—is it not? I live in a freedom that most will never know. And why? Because I am not daunted by the useless worries that dog the lives of others."

She rose from the bed. She seemed very tall and her presence filled the little building. "But to believe that I would harm my sister! My twin—the one with whom I shared my childhood—even our mother's womb. Together we became women. How can you understand our intimacy, our knowledge of each other, the knowing that is shared, that is an instinct, a reflex—all that we have together?

"Yes, there is a belief, a vile suspicion that I would harm her. It is why Jane—you are here—and you James—no doubt it has brought you here too. And Mariana, how could you let this be believed? Have you come to fear me so much?

"But Jane, in your needless wish to save Mariana, you came to me first—to warn me away, but I have turned this into what I truly desire. Not damage to my sister—but my wish to show her my love."

253

She turned to face her sister. The black silhouette of her dress shimmered in the soft light, as if moved by the energy of her feelings. She stretched out her arms and the cuffs slipped back to show the white skin of her forearms. "I know that I have hurt you, Mariana. I am so wilful—I know—and you used to follow me so helplessly."

Her tone softened; her voice became quieter; no longer full of declaration, but with poignancy. "I simply took you for granted, I know this now. I have had much time to think—and yes—to change. I am here to mend all that forced us apart. Our birthday will be the re-birth of the twins, in a new and wondrous way. This unique thing we have, we will cherish. Two separate lives, but lives that are enriched by an intimacy that few can ever imagine. In this, Mariana, we can now live. I give you my pledge."

Marguerite fell back onto the bed. She was flushed with the passion of her speech and now I was thrown into uncertainty. It was so easy to attribute villainous wishes to Marguerite. She had confessed that she knew it to be so. No apologies for that. But to endow her with the most evil intentions—we were surely in the grips of hysteria.

Mariana moved back to the bed and sat beside her. She was unsure what to do—surely as amazed at this scene as was I. There was no need for action. Marguerite made the movement, burying her head in the bosom of her sister, her whole body seemed to be racked with sobs. Mariana's arm, at first tentatively, circled her twin's shoulders and then, as if with an expression of enormous relief from a tension that had divided them for years, she clasped her sister to her.

I turned to Crawfy. There were tears in my eyes and I wanted to see if she was as deeply affected as I. I was surprised. Her look was calm and vigilant, just as she had studied the contents of the bottle.

The Marques had broken off from his preparation of the drink, but resumed, though his eagle eyes flitted from the stream of liquid falling upon the spoon to the twins embracing on the bed, whilst his hand remained as unmoving as the rocks of the desert.

It was the drink that allowed us some release from the intense emotion of the sisters. It was ready and the Marques poured it into the collection of glasses and cups. Really, such a lack of refinery only added poignancy to the occasion. Mariana was stroking the head of her sister, their relative power completely reversed: she, firm and strong, whilst Marguerite was helpless in her sorrow and remorse.

It was the turn of the Marques to deliver his own speech. "What a remarkable thing! This love between sisters and especially, between twins. It has fascinated me—well, I must admit—for centuries!"

And his laughter seemed the absolute antidote to Marguerite's grief. She looked up and then reached into her blue velvet bag for a handkerchief. She shook back her hair and raised her face, and it was as the sun rising or breaking through dark clouds. And I watched Mariana, who sat, now holding her sister's hand, her face completely calm.

"Come," declared the Marques. "We are not only celebrating the eve of the birthday, but a reunion that fills our hearts with joy."

We raised our glasses, or a chipped cup in my case, and I had my first taste of absinthe. In the way that laughter can follow tears, Marguerite was now softly laughing, and I shared the sense of relief and of a new peace that I was sure she was feeling.

The Marques circled us again with the jug of absinthe, and I felt the most wonderful warm glow which at first crept through my body and then developed into a surge of pleasure. All were very happy—except for Crawfy.

She sat quietly, as far apart as the little building would allow, and though she looked to be sipping her drink, I do not believe that she swallowed a drop. She stared intensely at the sisters and their display of shared love and I wondered whether she had fallen into jealousy.

Really, it was left to Don Angel, as was clearly his wont, to behave as the host. There was such jollity as he showed himself to be the most playful of men. It was so different to the intrusive and threatening figure who had descended on us in Whitby. And he was full of stories: an amazing fund of facts and tales, about Almeria and the South of Spain, but also about Paris. Here, he and Marguerite had their own knowledge, especially of the latest scandals. Mariana, who had abandoned that life for one so different, listened with interest, though I could see that she was sure in her separation from that life.

But the attention of all was stirred when he began on the recent exploits of Cora Pearl. Cora was now liaising with Prince Napoleon, the cousin of the Emperor. Of course, the prince would still have to share her. Cora was the consummate courtesan. Her wealth was fabulous, her diamonds alone worth a million francs. She could lose a fortune at the tables of Monte Carlo and think nothing of it: it was easily replaced by the next man to give her everything. She had appeared at a ball as

Eve and as naked as the first woman herself. "But then," declared the Marques, with obvious pride, "For us, at Poissy, she was Aphrodite! What could be better?"

And all of his tales poked fun at the men who pursued her, so assiduously, often hopelessly, and sometimes, ruinously. Never did he say a word to undermine his admiration for her. Marguerite, clearly felt the same, and now, having emerged rejuvenated from her outpouring of pain and guilt, clapped her hands in glee at some of Cora's most outrageous acts.

And, as the master of ceremonies, he eventually decided to call time on the proceedings. He drew back the curtain of the cabaña's little window. Perhaps he had already sensed that the carriage would have returned. Indeed, he announced that it was there. I knew from my own experience that these drivers would wait patiently for Mariana's signal before approaching the house.

"And my own horse—she has waited for me with great patience. She will need to be fed and watered and put to bed in Almeria. She must wait no longer.

"James, you have been an excellent guest. How fine it has been to see you here—and of course ..." and this with a knowing twinkle in his dark eyes, "so fitting for you to visit Mariana. I trust that your good fortune continues.

"And dear twins, tomorrow is your birthday; but, at least, you have celebrated today. Marguerite will return to Paris knowing that she has a sister again. And Mariana, such transformation. I am deeply impressed."

Finally, he turned to Crawfy. She had not moved from her seat. Her glass was set down nearby and I felt sure that it remained full. As he stood before her, there was a moment that is hard to describe. Let me put it like this. Though he stood before her, and in that small space might easily have towered over her, she was in no way diminished by his presence.

There is a painting that I have seen since, and I mention it now because whenever I think of it, I think too of this moment in the cabaña between Don Angel and Jane Crawford. It is of Mary, Mother of Jesus, though she is not portrayed with the usual features of the holy Virgin and there is little that is spiritual about the painting. The scene is outdoors and behind her is a simple landscape with trees and blue sky and far off mountains in a deeper blue. She wears the traditional, blue robe, but

256

beneath this is a dress in a soft, muted red that is almost a rustic brown. She rests calmly in a stone chair, an ordinary woman, but upon a little throne that is supported by carved sphinxes. Her husband, Joseph, so much older, stands by her side, and the infant Jesus sits upon her knee, unsupported by her hands, which rest easily by her side. Before her, and we see the scene in profile, kneels a man in the attire of an Islamic warrior. For me, this picture is about the woman and the man who pays homage before her. She sits back in her chair, relaxed and pensive, as if contemplating the fact that he should do this.

This is what I think of when I recall the scene between the Marques and Crawfy.

His words to her were simply, "And Jane Crawford. You perhaps, have not joined in our little party. But then, Jane, we know you are different, and this I have always known. And I assure you, you can rest easily."

And then to us all, "Farewell my friends!" And he was away. As we gathered our own things together, through the open door we heard his words to his horse and then the gradual fading away of the sound of the hooves.

It all seemed very quiet then. Outside was the same carriage that had brought Crawfy and Marguerite.

I wanted so much to have my own last moments with Mariana, to make my own personal farewell. I had no sense of when I would meet her again. She seemed fixed in her life out there in the Tabernas desert, cared for by the local people who thought so much of her, indeed, who believed in her. I had to return quickly to England. I had left with my father believing I was visiting friends. If I was not back soon, he would worry. I knew that I would have to tell him all that had happened, but felt he would forgive my deceit and he would be so pleased to hear that Mariana was safe and that the twins were reunited.

Despite my wish to embrace Mariana, to feel the body that I had known so well and to tell her how much my departure was also my loss, I could not encroach upon the absolute closeness that now joined the sisters. Marguerite embraced Mariana still, whilst she whispered her own good byes into her ear.

And so, I stepped outside and waited. Crawfy followed me and stood there too, though she remained close to the door as if she needed to hear whatever might be said within. It was dusk now and the wind was chill and a fine spray of rare Tabernas rain had begun. Crawfy was fixing her bonnet. She looked anxious, and at one time felt compelled to step back inside. She returned and waited. All was very still.

Then Marguerite emerged. The blue velvet cloak was around her and she had discarded her hat. The rain was in her face and in a moment, her hair was wet, but she seemed not to care and lifted her face to the sky.

Then Crawfy, once more, stepped inside. Marguerite accepted this and walked towards the carriage and I joined her. The carriage was open and before we reached Almeria we would be wet through. There was no doubt about that, yet Crawfy was still in the cabaña and was making her own goodbye. I could only think of the love that existed between the two women. Indeed, it felt more fitting that we should ride off and let Crawfy remain.

But then she emerged and slowly walked to the carriage. She stepped up and joined us and the carriage turned away from the cabaña and we began our departure. I was the only one to look round. Mariana was standing in the doorway. She saw that I had turned and waved. It was our final goodbye.

It was very late when we arrived in Almeria. We headed straight for the hotel where Marguerite and Crawfy had their rooms and I registered there too. The rain had been brief, and our clothes had already dried, but we were cold and very tired. So much had happened, yet there seemed so little to say; we were each enveloped in our own emotions. The next day, we would be returning to our homes. We made our goodnights and resolved to meet for breakfast in the morning.

Perhaps the absinthe was having its last effects, but there were also the emotions of the day, so that my sleep was restless. Full of dreams that were vague in content, but clear in their troubling affect. There had been such happiness between the sisters, such playfulness and fun as we drank and celebrated the forthcoming birthday, and also the reconciliation of two remarkable women, who had forged such a place in our lives. And yet, my sleep was disturbed and on waking I was filled with melancholy. Of course, my separation from Mariana was a factor. I decided that it must be that, yet there was something about my last sight of her, alone in the desert, in the dusk and the rain, the rocks around the cabaña seeming to loom as dark and threatening shapes, that caused me, though I reasoned against it, to feel dread.

I dressed early and then was constantly scanning my watch, waiting for the time when I could descend the stairs for breakfast. At last, the time arrived. The hotel had few guests and Crawfy was alone there. I walked towards her, so pleased to see her. But something was wrong. I could sense it immediately. As soon as she saw me, she rose. Her whole being was filled with anxiety.

"I called on Marguerite—so that we could come down together. James—she is not there. I knocked—no answer. I thought I must wake her and entered. She is gone and all her clothes—everything."

She looked around, distraught. "James, it is the day of the birthday. I think she will do it now. We must go to Mariana."

CHAPTER THIRTY ONE

A desperate journey

The next hours were frantic. Carlos, the one-eyed watchman, was too far away, on the outskirts of town, and would he even be there? We had to have a carriage immediately. The best way was to find our driver of the previous day. There was no one at the hotel desk. I looked around frantically. I had some idea where the kitchen was and so made for there. I found the receptionist chatting easily to the chef. I had burst in and my entry was clearly an interruption.

"Señor?"

"Señora, forgive me, but this is of the greatest urgency. Please, you must help us. We must find again the coach and driver who took my friends to the Tabernas. And, I am sorry, but it must be now!"

"But Señor, how can we find him? He has already taken your friend Señora Mercier."

"To where?"

"They did not say, Señor. Maybe to the port, or maybe to your friend in the desert. They left one hour ago. She has taken all her bags, so she will not return."

"I implore you Señora. Please find someone for us. Anything will do, as long as we can get to our friend in the desert. It is vital that it should be now. We have money. We will pay well."

She considered. Whether it was sympathy for my state of panic, or whether the thought of the money, her manner softened. "My husband has a horse and cart. It is early so you can catch him. Say that I sent you. But you will be uncomfortable Señor—there are no seats. Does the lady go with you?"

"Yes, she does."

"Then you will need cushions. Take them from here, and go to my husband now."

"And where?"

"Very close. I will show you."

Crawfy was waiting anxiously in the hotel lobby. She was already dressed for the journey. She saw and acknowledged my look of relief.

The woman took us into the street and pointed to a nearby road. "You will see Señor, the cart is there."

And so it was, and so was her husband, but not a horse to be seen.

I passed on his wife's instructions and again mentioned payment. He grumbled, but agreed.

We then stood in silence, staring at each other. Did he want payment then? In a harsh whisper, Crawfy urged, "We will pay him on our return. Tell him. We must go—and where is the horse!?"

The driver ambled off, telling us to wait. I called after him, "Please Señor—please hurry, we must depart now!"

There was a slight lengthening to his stride, yet it seemed an age before he returned, leading a pony. The pony already looked the worse for wear. But now, at least, we had transport.

There was no doubt about the discomfort. Crawfy laid the cushions out in the cart and made herself as comfortable as she could. There was a small space next to the driver and this I took so that I could continue to exhort him to go at the utmost speed.

I believe that the little horse had never been driven so hard. The driver declared, "I fear for my horse!"

The distance seemed enormous. We watched the outskirts of the town go past and then it was the start of the desert. The rocks that bordered the track grew larger and more numerous. I feared terribly that a wheel might strike one and be broken and that we would be stranded, with too far to go and too much distance to go back for help. There was a

262

great jolt as we did strike a rock. I watched the driver muster all his concentration to listen for any damage to his cart; there was no time to stop and examine. All was well and he called out to his horse, urging it to go faster.

At last, there was the familiar glimpse of the cabaña and its disappearance as we dipped below the hill before we rose to the crest and saw it in full view.

And the most hopeful sight: the door was open, as if in welcome.

"Crawfy, I believe that all is well."

Even the driver seemed reassured and slowed his horse, allowing it a little relief from the enormous effort of the journey. He leant forward and patted its rump.

We pulled up close. I jumped down and reached up to help Crawfy step down. I was surprised. She showed no haste. She accepted my hand and steadily reached the ground. I was about to rush inside, but her hesitation held me back.

The wind was up and, in our haste to leave, she had forgotten her bonnet. Strands of hair had escaped from their fastening and were blown across her face. She wiped them away.

I said, "Crawfy."

And she just shook her head. She had begun to weep.

All my hopes then crashed. I believed in her intuition, and she had sensed the worst. Of course, Mariana would not leave her door open on a windy morning in November.

I left her then and ran into the little house. As I reached the door, my own recoil sent me falling back as I was struck full in the face. There was the screech of a bird and the wild beating of its black wings. It flew past and then there was another, the tip of its wing striking me as it flew towards the nearby rocks.

They seemed such hateful creatures; the cohorts of death. I was no longer rushing. I stepped inside. Crawfy joined me. We both stood at the centre of the plain little building.

And there she was—alive and well and sitting on the bed.

I cried out, "Mariana—thank God! We were so worried."

It was the familiar cape that had deceived me. Mariana's, but not worn by her. And the voice, different—the voice of Marguerite, "She is not here. She has gone."

Crawfy's words were spoken quietly, but with absolute clarity and with no hesitation, "What have you done with her?"

Marguerite rose from the bed. She tossed away the cape. She was still wearing the black dress and the silver necklace with the crucifix. "Jane, you persist with your vile suspicions. Do you think I have hidden her corpse under the bed? Have a look! Search in the cupboard for a body! There is no Mariana. If anyone has removed her, it is not I."

Crawfy's tone remained calm, but with a hardness that I had never heard before. "We are in the desert. There are a thousand places where you could hide a body. Only the birds and the insects would find it. No one else comes here. Where have you put her Marguerite—your darling sister—where have you hidden this terrible crime?"

"Jane, it is our birthday! I wished only to see her one more time before my return. Yet, you accuse me in the most awful way. I cannot believe that you still think this of me. Were we not friends? Did we not both long to see and cherish my sister? Now you become my enemy. Take care, Jane Crawford!"

She picked up the cape and wrapped it around her. "She has gone—and she gave us no farewells. At least she left her cape to keep me warm. It is freezing here."

It was, indeed, very cold. The stove had not been lit, nor were the lights, and all seemed grey in the little cabaña: the colour of desolation and of the absence of its host.

Crawfy stepped outside, and then called me.

The land surrounding us seemed terribly bleak. There was no sun and the sky was a continuous sheet of steel grey cloud.

"We will have to search James. I see no sign of the Marques and so, as St Germain predicted, she has done this herself. But even Marguerite is not strong enough to move a body far. We will search."

I said, "Crawfy, perhaps Marguerite is telling the truth. Mariana might have left—it is possible."

"And where would she go—and with whom?"

The driver who had brought us was waiting for our instructions. He was clearly impatient to leave, with or without us.

Crawfy sent him away. We would pay him on our return to Almeria. No doubt a carriage would be coming for Marguerite and we would use that.

Without the body and with only our fears, we could not even feel grief or give mutual comfort. We could only search, with our feelings as barren as the rocky landscape that surrounded us. And whilst we searched, Marguerite sat outside the cabaña on the little wooden chair and on the patch of gravel where the rare traveller might sometimes glimpse her sister.

By the time that a carriage came, slowly, rattling along the track, we had given up our search. It was the carriage that had brought Marguerite that morning and it had returned to collect her. There had been much time for her to fulfil her plans.

Our search for signs of Mariana had been fruitless and we came back inside. I think Crawfy had to do something—anything—in there. To clean or to tidy, to make some gesture towards Mariana and her home, or, perhaps, to just delay our departure and the awful feeling that we would never see that place again and that Mariana was lost to us. But there was nothing to do. Everything was in its place. The bed was made, the stove unlit. Crawfy had a final look round and then walked to the carriage. I came out and stood next to where Marguerite was sitting. She was now wearing her own cape, but the cape of Mariana was still there beneath it. She rose and walked to the carriage. I placed the little wooden chair inside and closed the door and joined them.

Marguerite was completely impassive and seemed to have removed us, and all our surroundings, from her consciousness. She remained staring straight ahead. And there were no more words from Crawfy, who was so filled with a cold fury that she was beyond speech. We journeyed that way, in silence.

I tried to broker some conversation, still hoping to find an escape from Crawfy's conviction of Mariana's death and that there must be some other explanation. But the two women remained fixed in silent animosity.

Marguerite's luggage was strapped to the carriage and it was clear that she would now be continuing to the port, and then presumably, to France. Crawfy called out to the driver to take us first to where we could speak to the police, and that was where she and I disembarked. It was her warning to Marguerite that there would be no end to her search for the truth.

In the police station, I translated, as she reported that Mariana Mercier was unaccountably missing from her home and that she suspected that harm had been done to her. She had given no notice that she would be leaving and we had seen her the day before. And then, unable to contain herself, out spilled her accusations against Marguerite. Even I, who had been with Crawfy and who had shared her absolute alarm, heard the words as bizarre as I translated them: a wealthy French tourist had travelled to Almeria to murder her twin sister, a woman who lived like a hermit in the Tabernas desert—the policeman looked at Crawfy as if she was in the grips of the wildest fantasy. Nevertheless, all was duly recorded. A least there would be the register of a missing person.

Though, "Surely, Señora, the lady will soon be back in her home. She may just have been shopping in the city. All will be well, but we will keep your address and send you any information that we have."

We stayed another night and travelled back to Mariana's cabaña the next day, but all was exactly as before.

We then had no choice but to return to Whitby.

Crawfy had said, "There is only one way we can ever know what has happened and that is through the powers of St Germain. In time, he will know—but where is he now? And will we ever see him again?"

In the night, as we sailed from Almeria to Marseilles, I sat in Crawfy's cabin and she told me about herself and Mariana. In Poissy she had fallen deeply in love, and it had never truly diminished. Just lightly shaded by the years when they had not met. And Mariana had told her so much of her life when Crawfy visited her in her Paris home.

"I had knocked and there was no answer. I was leaving, and then, there she was, in a window, at the top of the house, banging the glass for me to return. She was so scared then, frightened of the Marques and she knew she was losing her sister.

"And when we all stayed at Poissy—there were the twins, the Marques, Cora Pearl, and your father, James—we were there and the Marques once more created Alexandria. We could see it through the window."

I said, "Mariana told me of this and that once again he took the twins there and to the Aphrodite temple. And this time she entered, but Marguerite's envy reduced the temple to rubble. Afterwards, Mariana was lost and in despair and had wondered at night in the ancient city, and she told me that she had met you there and that you had saved her."

"I was not there James, but that night I had dreamed of her and when I awoke, she was by my side. Perhaps that was enough.

"We know now that the bounds of life, the limits that we come to accept and even need, can lose their strength, can melt into strands that can be pulled aside. These two—The Marques and St Germain, have showed us this.

"Marguerite tried to poison my trust in St Germain. She said that he had been one of their father's friends: the men who came preying upon them when they were girls. After our so-called party, when I went back inside the cabaña, and you and Marguerite were waiting upon the carriage, it was something I had to ask her. If it were true, who could we ever trust?

"She remembered him. A man who, one day, had visited her father and insisted on seeing the girls. But not as the others. He had been kind and later she had heard loud and angry voices from her father's study. For months after that, the other men ceased to come, but then it started again."

I had not known of Marguerite's deceit, yet I was still relieved to hear that the Count was as fine a man as I believed him to be.

But what was he to think of us now if Mariana was dead?

And then, I, too, spoke of Mariana, sharing with Crawfy the time of our six months in Almeria and the things that had made us happy. It seemed like a wonderful, easy life, as I looked back. And as I spoke of this to Crawfy, I felt the full force that came from a knowledge that we had both been lovers of Mariana, and it was an understanding that filled me with the strangest of feelings, as if, in the sharing of a loved one, the two of us became lovers ourselves. Since Crawfy had been like a mother to me, it was a feeling that I may well have fought and denied. But I did not. I was learning that the boundaries that divide us are not as unyielding as we care to believe.

I returned to my cabin and I believe that sleep came to us both. It is the body's kindness. For a few hours we could escape from the pain that would return with the dawn.

CHAPTER THIRTY TWO

On our return

We had travelled back to England in great sadness. In Whitby, each of us felt helpless. Crawfy remained sure that a terrible crime had been committed, yet the only evidence was that Mariana was no longer in her home. She resolved to return there in a month's time. I gave her the address of the Montes store in Almeria so that she could send a letter in the hope that it would be forwarded to Mariana, but she received no reply. My father, already depressed at his own failure to help the twins, was stricken with unhappiness.

One morning, three weeks later, I was visiting from London, having taken a weekend break from my studies. There was a shout from Crawfy that brought both myself and my father running to her in alarm. She was standing in the middle of the entrance hall and was clutching a letter that she had just opened. The envelope lay discarded on the floor before her.

It was immediately clear to us that the letter must contain some news of Mariana and I feared the worst. We stood, motionless, waiting for whatever Crawfy might say.

She read aloud the letter. It is one that we have always kept and is still now in my possession. This is it, exactly.

My dear Jane,

I send you this letter, knowing that you can pass on to James and Edward as much of the content as you wish.

I have only just discovered that I am a "missing person"! Well, I have been found, and now know that you will have suffered great anxiety about my welfare, even my survival. I am so sorry, Jane, but I did not know that you would be returning to my little home, the morning after our "party." Indeed, I thought that you would already be on your way with James back to your lovely home in England.

All did seem so well at the party, did it not? Such splendid emotions from my sister, and such a wish that all be repaired between us. I was ready to let you all benefit from that. Even Don Angel was convinced, and I do believe that he has decided to let this particular twin go, though I suspect Jane, that you may have some influence in that.

However, I know my sister, and all that she is capable of. Just for a moment I believed her, but there were three things that changed that.

As you were all leaving, she and I were still embraced and she whispered in my ear, "My darling sister, we cannot leave things as they are. We will let these others go, but tomorrow I will return. It will be just you and I on our birthday."

And all I could feel in response to this was dread. To me her whisper was like poison breathed into my ear. And then she left and went to the carriage and you, Jane, came in and we had just a few moments together. How much I wish they could have been longer and that their content could have been different. You were not convinced by Marguerite's professed love for me and still you feared for me. You had to tell me that.

You also had to know whether the Comte de St Germain had abused us as children, as this, Marguerite had told you. But it was her lie and in this lie she was trying to turn you against the man who was my protector. It convinced me that my fear of her deadly wishes was real.

And there was something else you said. I believe that you almost forgot to tell me, as it was like an afterthought, just before you left. You told me that there was a Carmelite nun, a Mother Superior in the Almeria monastery, who knew me from the Aphrodite temple in Alexandria—and that she wished me to know this.

As soon as you all left, I gathered together the main things I would need and put them in a bag and went outside. Up on a hill, in his cart, was my dear guardian Carlos. James will remember him as he brought him to me—I believe he was quite scared of him. And there he was, gazing down with his one watchful eye. He had been troubled by my visitors. Actually, he may have felt rather jealous, as he has become quite possessive. Never mind, it had kept him there watching out for any danger to me. A wave from me was enough to bring him down to the cabaña, and I knew exactly where I needed to go. He took me straight to the Carmelite monastery.

And here I am, safe. Not even the Marques could trouble me here. And I do believe that my new guardian, the Reverend Mother would be his match in any contest. But, always, it would be Marguerite that is my concern. But she can never penetrate these walls. Not that I am a prisoner! I do, no doubt, have special treatment. It is only I that the Reverend Mother can speak to about Alexandria! And she does seem to have a very special affection for her time serving Aphrodite. I have a little cabin in the grounds where I am allowed to live. There is no need for me to take any vows. I do help the nuns out with some of their chores, but I have much time to contemplate and above all, to write.

And Jane, I think you will know, and James will know this too, that my loss of the Alexandria temple, left me with such a longing; a desperate one, really. The desert helped me in that, as I felt at one with it, but even that is no match for the union that I feel now, with the nuns and the truly Reverend Mother— who loves me. You might say that a Christian monastery of nuns is hardly the same as a temple of Aphrodite with its priestesses, but have a think about that. I certainly feel that I no longer have to yearn for Alexandria.

And Jane, you held me close when I was lost. We lay on the grass, and the night sky above us was so full of stars that they seemed to be tussling with each other for room, and here, at night, in the monastery garden, I look up at the sky and always I think of that, and of you.

You know that the Carmelites are very reclusive, but you can visit me here. Just write first and we can arrange it. I do, so much, want to see you.

And give my love to James and tell him that he was such a help to me when we were together in Almeria. And also, to your Edward. I know that he is a valiant man and cares for me greatly.

With much love and gratitude,

Mariana

CHAPTER THIRTY THREE

A view of time

It is now 40 years on. My own life has progressed, through other relationships, and through my career as a neurologist and my involvement with the new science of psychoanalysis. I needed something more, though, to fully realise those events in the years 1864 to 1869. So, I decided to record with the written word everything that I could. And now I have completed the task; much helped by dear Crawfy, who lent me her diaries and also shared thoughts, feelings, and recollections that she had not written down. Every week, I see her in the little apartment where she now lives, close to my own, and now, in her mid-70s, she is as clear thinking and as delightful to be with as ever.

Of course, we have shared so much that we can hardly share with others. There are truths, unworldly happenings, that can only be told to those who are receptive, and they are few. Still, occasionally, we would have evenings in which we would invite those to join us whom we knew would be open to our memories, and who would respond with some of their own. It was a relief to find that we were not the only ones in the world to have had such strange encounters! There was an especially fine evening when the theosophist Annie Besant joined us with two of her colleagues, as she told us of her own encounter with the Comte de St Germain.

And so, what of the Count?

When we arrived back at Whitby, we felt sure he would visit. But we heard not a word and as the years passed, so did our expectations of seeing him. Our need for him was greatly lessened by our knowledge that Mariana was well and content in her new home. That was always bolstered by the latest reports from Crawfy, who would visit Mariana at least twice a year and stay with her for several weeks before returning with the latest news.

My father was gallant enough to allow Crawfy to visit Mariana without too much show of jealousy. And his own life had continued in success. Despite the considerable upheaval brought by the twins, their advent added something special to his work. There was a greater edge to his formal portraits and he indulged much more in the occasional imaginative scene, usually sketched in watercolour. And his career was rewarded by a knighthood which put him on a good level with his friends and contemporaries. His close friend Leighton was already a Lord and Tennyson had been created a Baron. My father died five years ago, having recovered much of his "joie de vivre."

My account of our time with the twins has been written and may one day be read by others. My initial scrawl is carefully scribed in three nice, leather-bound, note books.

I had placed them in a draw and made ready to focus more on the matters of every-day existence. But then, I received a surprise visit and it has required this addition to the story, and one with which I will now end it.

I had finished my consultations for the day and was preparing to leave for home, when my secretary advised me that a gentleman had arrived and was asking to see me. I, of course, asked her to offer him an appointment for later in the week.

She returned to say that he apologised profusely for having arrived unannounced, but that I would understand that this was his normal way and that as we had not met for 40 years, could I please grant him the boon of seeing me. Not only that, but he was due very soon to leave for China!

My secretary looked concerned that perhaps we had a madman at the doorstep, but I had heard enough to know that I should allow this meeting.

He wore a formal, grey suit in the current style. His dark hair was brushed back from his forehead and was secured behind his neck with a small black ribbon. Apart from this, there was nothing exceptional about his appearance except for the rings that seemed to cover every finger. He, of course, looked no older than he had 40 years before.

I was surprised at the lack of respect with which I greeted him. "Monsieur le Comte. At last, you appear!"

He was unperturbed by my boldness. "Monsieur James—though I should say doctor now! It is a pleasure to see you."

"Monsieur—it is 40 years!"

"Well, yes, I know that forty years can seem like a long time."

"Forgive me Monsieur le Comte—your visit is so unexpected, yet you bring with you so much of the past."

"Indeed, and, of course, it is the past that brings me here, since we have no future business. I understand that your life is on a firm footing and you will need no meddling from me."

My secretary had not yet left, though she was donning her hat and coat. I asked her if she could make us tea and she readily agreed, as much as anything, I believe, to have another look at this man who had arrived in such an unusual way. I returned to the Count.

I said, "Jane Crawford is well."

"Ah yes, I know. I do stay aware of Madame Crawford. She is special you know. I expect she has told you."

"She was always special to us, Monsieur, but yes, she has told me of these other qualities that you have predicted.

"Monsieur le Comte. Though I feel increasingly pleased to see you, I feel compelled to ask you the reason for your visit. You will understand that you have not always been the bringer of good news."

"I asked much of your family, James, and expected you to act with little knowledge of the foe that you would need to confront. My current business brings me to London, so I take the opportunity to see you now."

"After 40 years, Monsieur, it is surely time!"

"Quite so. You must forgive me. My concept of time can sometimes stray away from the norm. I appreciate that you may view my relative dismissal of what for some is a lifetime, as flippant and even an expression of arrogance, but our experience of time is relative to how much of it we have, and of this I do have what can truly be described as 'an expanse.'

"I know that there will be unanswered questions for you and that these can remain as a terrible irritant, especially when they pertain to such powerful events.

"I admit that I was ready to leave you with enigmas, but I now think better of it. I realise that it is the peculiar nature of my own existence on this earth, and also of the Spaniard, the Marques de Mansura, that can be so unfathomable. You will understand, that if I were to explain the existence of creatures such as us to all that I have dealings with, I would be endlessly repeating myself and would, therefore, suffer great boredom. Many, of course, would not be able to believe a word of it anyway. Which I think introduces perhaps the main reason—that we generally consider that there are only a few whose spiritual level entitles them to share some knowledge of the majestic forces that we serve. As you see, James, I am including you amongst those few!

"So—there are those of us who are tasked to embody and to impart those truths that are essential for the development of mankind— dreadfully slow though the process should be. It is the case, however, that, very rarely, one of us will become errant and through their excessive pride, will enact all that we serve to resist and to counter.

"Such is the way, and this leads us to the Marques de Mansura. He likes to think of himself as my 'twin.' This I absolutely refute. It is part of his mischief and malevolent humour. He is, though, thinking back to the very ancient times in which he began his existence and the philosophy and religion that spawned him.

"I should tell you that however old I am, and you will know that I speak of centuries, he is far older. He has presented himself in recent times as a Spanish gentleman. This is purely his current whim. He is, in fact, Persian, though we will allow him to be Spanish as this is how you have known him. I will now give you some details of his origin, from which you will also see the relevance of his obsession with twins.

"Identical twins have always fascinated mankind. They have been revered and also dreaded and persecuted. I do not find this strange. They are such a rare occurrence, and they impinge so much on the individual's wish to be the only one of himself that exists. Except that, deep down in the human psyche, there can be a wish that is the very opposite: the longing for there to be another who is just the same—to offer the ultimate intimacy and the relief from the utter aloneness of being oneself.

"And in ancient religions, twins have been viewed as the personification of duality, the embodiment of feelings that are in conflict. I believe that it is too great a simplification to assign this purely to the opposition of good and evil. Though Don Angel, the Marques de

Mansura is certainly one of 'evil's' ambassadors in this world and leaves a trail of destruction, there are those who remember their time under his spell as gifting an intensity of pleasure that they forever wish to regain. There have been those that look to him as a god of freedom. Yet his principle is one of destruction and his drive will always be towards that end. Take that away and he would have no reason to exist—he exists to embody it—so he will hardly give it up!

"And I must counter his efforts as well as I can.

"So, here is a piece of history for you that may offer some further understanding.

"We must think of a time three and a half thousand years ago. It is the beginning of the bronze age with mankind just beginning to forgo stone for metal. The place is, well we cannot be precise, but let us say the Steppes of Asia. A priest is about to conduct a ceremony of the Spring. He is of Iranian heritage. It is a beautiful clear morning and he walks to the river to collect water. And water in its purity is a revered element and will be part of the ceremony. He wades into the river to where the water is deeper and free from the mud and gravel of the banks and dips his vessels and lets the current fill them to the brim. He turns to head back to the land. The cold water is around his thighs and a light breeze brushes his forehead and cheeks. Though it is early, there is already warmth from the sun. The sun is low in the sky and it shines brightly into his eyes, so that for a moment, he cannot see. But then its light grows stronger still and is no longer just sunlight, but a white light which is so intense, so dazzling, that it is all there is. Just light. He stumbles onto the river bank and falls upon his knees. He fears to look up, but there is a voice that calls him, and so raising his head, he begins to see in the midst of the light, the shape of a figure, and the figure speaks and tells him that he must follow. The priest tries to stand, but all the strength has left his limbs and he falls to the ground. The figure then raises him up and they journey, but not in physical space but within the light, until he is set down and again, falls to his knees. There is another voice and this has great command, so that the priest is compelled to look up into the brightness of the white light that he fears will destroy his eyes. There he sees a magnificent figure and there are five others who stand with him and the one who has raised him up joins them, so that they become seven. And then the priest, who was Zarathustra, received his instructions from the God who was Ahura Mazda.

"Zarathustra, whom we should now call Zoroaster, because he was so named by the Greeks, became a great prophet. He believed utterly in the good in mankind and in nature and the world, and that all the finest qualities of mankind would eventually triumph. But his visions were not only of Ahura Mazda, the God of virtue. It was Zoroaster's vision that all that was good would always be prey to the terrible attacks of another elemental creature, Angra Mainyu. He had no doubt at all of this. Everything had to be invested in protecting and preserving the virtues of Ahura Mazda, who had created mankind and who had invested it with the potential for holiness. But Zoroaster was sure that, until the day of judgement, the great fight in the minds and the spirits of both men and women must be against the evil of Angra Mainyu. And he declared that these two primal spirits, one magnificent and the other malign and terrible, were twins, and that one represented life and the other not-life.

"And we might say that the vision of Zoroaster was true. The power of evil was enough to seduce one of his most favoured and accomplished followers, the creature that you know as, Don Angel, the Marques. By then, this religion had taken hold amongst the Persians and he was amongst its most senior priests. He had built within himself the most considerable mental and occult powers, but turned his allegiance away from the true God and instead, gave it, with utter completeness, to Angra Mainyu. A pact with the devil for a return of even greater powers. Oh, how those powers can seduce! Their acquisition is the gain of the advanced soul, but also his greatest danger. This errant priest took his place amongst the closest followers of the evil one and the reward for the terrible heresy was to be granted a place amongst the spirits who were the cohorts of the evil twin. He joined the daevas. These days, we call them demons.

"For those of us, both just and unjust, who exist in these realms, time ceases its normal confines. We live less in the realities that are bordered by the 'finite.' And so, our Marques de Mansura, has existed for aeons. Perhaps, in some strange way, he missed being a priest of Zoroaster. He could never again belong to any group or to anyone except to his patron Angra Mainyu. But, over centuries, even Angra Mainyu faded into being just a concept, a concept that became embodied in this world by such as the Marques.

"He spent at least a century in Alexandria. It became such a thriving part of the ancient world and the Macedonian, warrior king, Alexander the Great, had, by then, conquered his native Persia. He found there a small temple, on the banks of the great lake Mareotis, dedicated to the cult of Aphrodite. And the priestesses worshipped Aphrodite as not only the goddess of love, but also as her opposite, a powerful and war-like deity. The Marques knew well the history of Aphrodite: that she had once been the Innana of the Sumerians and the Ishtar of Babylon, both loving and benevolent, but capable of the greatest strife and cruelty. And the duality pleased and suited him as he saw not one goddess, but Aphrodite twins.

"So, James, when he discovered those human twins that came to stay with your family, two beautiful and identical girls, he saw such potential for play and for a pleasure that could entertain him for half a century. They were, of course, by no means his first twin subjects.

"I really do not know where the Marques de Mansura is now, though, no doubt, I will again be required to resist him. Although decreasing, his powers are considerable and still greater than mine, so I always have to hope for a little human help to assist me. Which your family did their best to offer me. And of course, he will have your Crawfy to contend with in the future.

"James, this cannot explain everything, I know, but I trust that it will give, at least, some grounding within the context of the miraculous!

"And as to Marguerite Mercier: a woman with no ambivalence and no guilt and a remarkable certitude that some might admire. It can give the bearer immense power, though, usually, only for destruction. Her debauched life eventually caught up with her, though not before she had married a Count and become one of the richest women in France. She had a daughter, you know, in secret. The daughter, Geneviève became a nun, a Mother Superior in fact. But that is another story. Marguerite did not die a happy woman.

"I wished to share these things with you James. It might add some reasoning to the history. But I have taken up your time at the end of a busy day. You will want to return to the comfort of your home. And I envy you this. One, such as I, has many places to dwell, yet none that he can often call home."

My mood had changed considerably and I thanked the Count warmly for his visit. I walked with him through the reception room, where my secretary was once again attempting to don her hat and coat and making sure that it seemed she had not had her ear to the door. I could hardly blame her for her interest.

As he approached the main door, I thought to say, "I will, of course let Crawfy know of your visit."

"But James, you have no need. I am on my way to her now. There are a few things that she will need to know and that will be a help to her."

And his visit to me was not quite over. "You know James, people depart from us: Your father, your father's friend Tennyson—such a fine poet—I met him once and shared some verses and he was so fond of Mariana. They all descend into the great pool from which more life will spring. Nothing really ends, it just changes. Your Crawfy nears the end of her life, but I think she will remain a very long time in the next one. And I believe it will be for the good of the world."

He stood very still, just looking at me and I could do nothing but gaze back at him. And as I did so, his appearance changed. Before my eyes, he became incredibly old. Older than a person could ever be. An age that belonged to human history rather than to any individual. And then, very gradually, as if to nurse me through the experience, he changed back. He smiled as he left and I realised that it was an expression that I had rarely seen upon his face.

I do not believe that my secretary had viewed what I had, but she had heard enough to leave her standing quite motionless, with only one arm successfully embedded in her coat. I knew I would have to offer some explanation, but it would not be that evening. So, for then, it was a shrug and a smile that said, "How strange life can be."

I will not meet whatever, or whoever, Crawfy will become. She may be re-born before I die and be a child, somewhere in the world, but this will be unknown to me.

And what will become of me? Well, it would seem that I am not to join the immortals. But I have a home and a contented life and fond memories that contain and give life to all whom I have loved and that include my time with Mariana, when we were in the South.

AUTHOR'S NOTE

In this tale, historical figures mingle with the purely fictional, with whom they do battle, share escapades, make love, and converse.

Of the historical characters, I am grateful to the memory of the artists Gustave Moreau, Gustave Doré, Félicien Rops and the poet Alfred, Lord Tennyson. Much information can, of course, be easily found on these. The references to a particular liking of the less formal, watercolour works by Gustave Moreau are influenced by my own affection for them.

Félicien Rops has claimed a space in all three of my novels, with a medium role in this, a brief and elderly appearance in 'Camille and the Raising of Eros', and a major role in 'The Strange Case of Madeleine Seguin' in which he is in his ostentatious prime. In all three he is known as the lover/adversary of the fictional Marguerite Mercier (later the Countess of Bolvoir).

Gustave Doré did indeed have a close friendship with the courtesan Cora Pearl, and according to some accounts, they considered marriage, which would presumably have brought about an unlikely change to her career.

And so, to Cora herself, who, remarkably, did exist and whose reputation and status in her profession is faithfully reported in the narrative with no exaggeration. And this, from her origins in a lower middleclass family in Plymouth. There are some biographies and 'The Pearl from Plymouth' by W.H. Holden and 'Cora Pearl' by Polly Binder have been particularly helpful.

And the Comte de St Germain? He must be included as a historical figure, but was he merely a fiction whom for some became a reality? If real, he would belong, and the present tense must be used, with those who are sometimes called the 'Masters': beings of great spiritual advancement whose life spans are immeasurable. The present author was certainly intrigued and moved to write about this character who so aptly inhabits a space which allows the imagination to range far and wide and in which the passions of the ordinary world can mix with visions of the fantastical.

ACKNOWLEDGEMENTS

I have once again been helped by the participation of Mary Hughes and Paula Charles. They were there for each chapter as the story developed, and in their interest and enthusiasm, they became fellow travellers along the way. I am most grateful to them.

Paula Charles is also the artist Lynn Paula Russell. She made the design for my previous novel 'Camille and the Raising of Eros' and she delighted me by offering to do the same for this current work. The splendid idea for the cover image is hers, as well as its execution.

My thanks, as well, to the publishers Sphinx Books. I have benefited greatly from their calm, friendly and supportive approach.

William Rose

CPSIA information can be obtained
at www.ICGtesting.com
Printed in the USA
JSHW050829061122
32688JS00004B/6

9 781912 573820